Cathy Williams can remember reading Mills & Boon books as a teenager, and now that she is writing them she remains an avid fan. For her, there is nothing like creating romantic stories and engaging plots, and each and every book is a new adventure. Cathy lives in London. Her three daughters—Charlotte, Olivia and Emma—have always been, and continue to be, the greatest inspirations in her life

New York Times and *USA TODAY* bestselling author **Jane Porter** has written forty romances and eleven women's fiction novels since her first sale to Mills & Boon Modern Romance in 2000. A five-time RITA® finalist, Jane is known for her passionate, emotional and sensual novels, and she loves nothing more than alpha heroes, exotic locations and happy-ever-afters. Today Jane lives in sunny San Clemente, California, with her surfer husband and three sons. Visit www.janeporter.com.

Award-winning author **Jules Bennett** is no stranger to romance—she met her husband when she was only fourteen. After dating through high school, the two married. He encouraged her to chase her dream of becoming an author. Jules has now published nearly thirty novels. She and her husband are living their own happily-ever-after while raising two girls. Jules loves to hear from readers through her website, julesbennett.com, her Facebook fan page or on Twitter.

About the Authors

The Love Islands

COLLECTION

March 2019

April 2019

May 2019

June 2019

July 2019

August 2019

Love Islands:
Red-Hot
Sunsets

CATHY WILLIAMS

JANE PORTER

JULES BENNETT

MILLS & BOON

First published in Great Britain 2019
by Mills & Boon, an imprint of HarperCollins*Publishers*
1 London Bridge Street, London, SE1 9GF

Love Islands: Red-Hot Sunsets © 2019 Harlequin Books S.A.

Cipriani's Innocent Captive © 2017 Cathy Williams
Bought to Carry His Heir © 2017 Jane Porter
A Royal Amnesia Scandal © 2015 Jules Bennett

ISBN: 978-0-263-27552-0

MIX
Paper from
responsible sources
FSC™ C007454

This book is produced from independently certified FSC™ paper to ensure responsible forest management.

For more information visit: www.harpercollins.co.uk/green

Printed and bound in Spain
by CPI, Barcelona

CIPRIANI'S INNOCENT CAPTIVE

CATHY WILLIAMS

CHAPTER ONE

'MR CIPRIANI IS ready for you now.'

Katy Brennan looked up at the middle-aged, angular woman who had earlier met her in the foyer of Cipriani Head Office and ushered her to the directors' floor, where she had now been waiting for over twenty minutes.

She didn't want to feel nervous but she did. She had been summoned from her office in Shoreditch, where she worked as an IT specialist in a small team of four, and informed that Lucas Cipriani, the ultimate god to whom everyone answered, requested her presence.

She had no idea why he might want to talk to her, but she suspected that it concerned the complex job she was currently working on and, whilst she told herself that he probably only wanted to go through some of the finer details with her, she was still…*nervous.*

Katy stood up, wishing that she had had some kind of advance warning of this meeting, because if she had she would have dressed in something more in keeping with the über-plush surroundings in which she now found herself.

As it was, she was in her usual casual uniform of jeans and a tee-shirt, with her backpack and a lightweight bomber jacket, perfect for the cool spring weather, but utterly inappropriate for this high-tech, eight-storey glasshouse.

She took a deep breath and looked neither left nor right as she followed his PA along the carpeted corridor, past the hushed offices of executives and the many boardrooms where deals worth millions were closed, until the corridor ballooned out into a seating area. At the back of this was a closed eight-foot wooden door which was enough to send a chill through any person who had been arbitrarily summoned by the head of her company—a man whose ability to make deals and turn straw into gold was legendary.

Katy took a deep breath and stood back as his PA pushed open the door.

Staring absently through the floor-to-ceiling pane of reinforced glass that separated him from the streets below, Lucas Cipriani thought that this meeting was the last thing he needed to kick off the day.

But it could not be avoided. Security had been breached on the deal he had been working on for the past eight months, and this woman was going to have to take the consequences—pure and simple.

This was the deal of a lifetime and there was no way he was going to allow it to be jeopardised.

As his PA knocked and entered his office, Lucas slowly turned round, hand in trouser pocket, and looked at the woman whose job was a thing of the past, if only she knew it.

Eyes narrowed, it hit him that he really should catch up on the people who actually worked for him, because he hadn't expected this. He'd expected a nerd with heavy spectacles and an earnest manner, whilst the girl in front of him looked less like a computer whizz-kid and more like a hippy. Her clothes were generic: faded jeans and a tee-shirt with the name of a band he had never heard of. Her shoes were masculine black boots, suitable for heavy-duty construction work. She had a backpack slung over her shoulder, and stuffed into the top of it was some kind of jacket, which she had clearly just removed. Her entire dress code contradicted every single thing he associated with a woman, but she had the sort of multi-coloured coppery hair that would have had artists queuing up to commit it to canvas, and an elfin face with enormous bright-green eyes that held his gaze for reasons he couldn't begin to fathom.

'Miss Brennan.' He strolled towards his desk as Vicky, his secretary, clicked the heavy door to his office shut behind her. 'Sit, please.'

At the sound of that deep, dark, velvety voice, Katy started and realised that she had been holding her breath. When she had entered the office she'd thought that she more or less knew what to expect. She vaguely knew what her boss looked like because she had seen pictures of him in the company magazines that occasionally landed on her desk in Shoreditch, far away from the cutting-edge glass building that housed the great and the good in the company: from Lucas Cipriani, who sat at the very top like a god atop Mount Olympus, to his team of powerful executives who made sure that his empire ran without a hitch.

Those were people whose names appeared on letterheads and whose voices were occasionally heard down the end of phone lines, but who were never, ever seen. At least, not in Shoreditch, which was reserved for the small cogs in the machine.

But she still hadn't expected *this*. Lucas Cipriani was, simply put, beautiful. There was no other word to describe him. It wasn't just the arrangement of perfect features, or the burnished bronze of his skin, or even the dramatic masculinity of his physique: Lucas Cipriani's good looks went far beyond the physical. He exuded a certain power and charisma that made the breath catch in your throat and scrambled your ability to think in straight lines.

Which was why Katy was here now, in his office, drawing a blank where her thoughts should be and with her mouth so dry that she wouldn't have been able to say a word if she'd wanted to.

She vaguely recalled him saying something about sitting down, which she badly wanted to do, and she shuffled her way to the enormous leather chair that faced his desk and sank into it with some relief.

'You've been working on the Chinese deal,' Lucas stated without preamble.

'Yes.' She could talk about work, she could answer any question he might have, but she was unsettled by a dark, brooding, in-your-face sensuality she hadn't expected, and when she spoke her voice was jerky and nervous. 'I've been working on the legal side of the deal, dedicating all the details to a programme that will enable instant access to whatever is required, without having to sift through reams of documentation. I hope there isn't a problem. I'm running ahead of schedule, in actual fact. I'll be honest with you,

Mr Cipriani, it's one of the most exciting projects I've ever worked on. Complex, but really challenging.'

She cleared her throat and hazarded a smile, which was met with stony silence, and her already frayed nerves took a further battering. Stunning dark eyes, fringed with inky black, luxuriant lashes, pierced through the thin veneer of her self-confidence, leaving her breathless and red-faced.

Lucas positioned himself at his desk, an enormous chrome-and-glass affair that housed a computer with an over-sized screen, a metallic lamp and a small, very artfully designed bank of clocks that made sure he knew, at any given moment, what time it was in all the major cities in which his companies were located.

He lowered his eyes now and, saying nothing, swivelled his computer so that it was facing her.

'Recognise that man?'

Katy blanched. Her mouth fell open as she found herself staring at Duncan Powell, the guy she had fallen for three years previously. Floppy blond hair, blue eyes that crinkled when he grinned and boyish charm had combined to hook an innocent young girl barely out of her teens.

She had not expected this. Not in a million years. Confused, flustered and with a thousand alarm bells suddenly ringing in her head, Katy fixed bewildered green eyes on Lucas.

'I don't understand…'

'I'm not asking you to understand. I'm asking you whether you know this man.'

'Y-yes,' she stammered. 'I… Well, I knew him a few years ago…'

'And it would seem that you bypassed certain security systems and discovered that he is, these days, employed by the Chinese company I am in the process of finalising a deal with. Correct? No, don't bother answering that. I have a series of alerts on my computer and what I'm saying does not require verification.'

She felt dazed. Katy's thoughts had zoomed back in time to her disastrous relationship with Duncan.

She'd met him shortly after she had returned home to her parents' house in Yorkshire. Torn between staying where she was and facing the big, brave world of London, where the lights were bright and the job prospects were decidedly better, she had taken up a temporary post as an assistant teacher at one of the local schools to give herself some thinking time and to plan a strategy.

Duncan had worked at the bank on the high street, a stone's throw from the primary school.

In fairness, it had not been love at first sight. She had always liked a quirky guy; Duncan had been just the opposite. A snappy dresser, he had homed in on her with the single-minded focus of a heat-seeking missile with a pre-set target. Before she'd even decided whether she liked him or not, they had had coffee, then a meal, and then they were going out.

He'd been persistent and funny, and she'd started rethinking her London agenda when the whole thing had fallen apart because she'd discovered that the man who had stolen her heart wasn't the honest, sincere, single guy he had made himself out to be.

Nor had he even been a permanent resident in the little village where her parents lived. He'd been there on a one-year secondment, which was a minor detail he had cleverly kept under wraps. He had a wife and twin daughters keeping the fires warm in the house in Milton Keynes he shared with them.

She had been a diversion and, once she had discovered the truth about him, he had shrugged and held his hands up in rueful surrender and she had known, in a flash of pure gut instinct, that he had done that because she had refused to sleep with him. Duncan Powell had planned to have fun on his year out and, whilst he had been content to chase her for a few months, he hadn't been prepared to take the chase to a church and up an aisle, because he had been a fully committed family man.

'I don't understand.' Katy looked away from the reminder of her steep learning curve staring out at her from Lucas's computer screen. 'So Duncan works for their company. I honestly didn't go hunting for that information.' Although, she *had* done some basic background checks, just out of sheer curiosity, to see whether it was the same creep once she'd stumbled upon him. A couple of clicks of a button was all it had taken to confirm her suspicion.

Lucas leaned forward, his body language darkly, dangerously menacing. 'That's as may be,' he told her, 'but it does present certain problems.'

With cool, clear precision he presented those *certain problems* to her and she listened to him in ever-increasing alarm. A deal done in complete secrecy…a family company rooted in strong values of tradition… a variable stock market that hinged on nothing being leaked and the threat her connection to Duncan posed at a delicate time in the negotiations.

Katy was brilliant with computers, but the mysteries of high finance were lost on her. The race for money had never interested her. From an early age, her parents had impressed upon her the importance of recognising value in the things that money couldn't buy. Her father was a parish priest and both her parents lived a life that was rooted in the fundamental importance of putting the needs of other people first. Katy didn't care who earned what or how much money anyone had. She had been brought up with a different set of values. For better or for worse, she occasionally thought.

'I don't care about any of that,' she said unevenly, when there was a brief lull in his cold tabulation of her transgressions. It seemed a good moment to set him straight because she was beginning to have a nasty feeling that he was circling her like a predator, preparing to attack.

Was he going to sack her? She would survive. The bottom line was that that was the very worst he could do. He wasn't some kind of mediaeval war lord who could have her hung, drawn and quartered because she'd disobeyed him.

'Whether you care about a deal that isn't going to impact on you or not is immaterial. Either by design or incompetence, you're now in possession of information that could unravel nearly a year and a half of intense negotiation.'

'To start with, I'm obviously very sorry about what happened. It's been a very complex job and, if I accidentally happened upon information I shouldn't have, then I apologise. I didn't mean to. In fact, I'm not at all interested in your deal, Mr Cipriani. You gave me a job to do and I was doing it to the best of my ability.'

'Which clearly wasn't up to the promised standard, because an error of the magnitude of the one you made is inexcusable.'

'But that's not fair!'

'Remind me to give you a life lesson about what's fair and what isn't. I'm not interested in your excuses, Miss Brennan. I'm interested in working out a solution to bypass the headache you created.'

Katy's mind had stung at his criticism of her ability. She was good at what she did. Brilliant, even. To have her competence called into question attacked the very heart of her.

'If you look at the quality of what I've done, sir, you'll find that I've done an excellent job. I realise that I may have stumbled upon information that should have not been available to me, but you have my word that anything I've uncovered stays right here with me.'

'And I'm to believe you because…?'

'Because I'm telling you the truth!'

'I'm sorry to drag you into the world of reality, Miss Brennan, but taking things at face value, including other people's *sincerely meant promises*, is something I don't do.' He leaned back into his chair and looked at her.

Without trying, Lucas was capable of exuding the sort of lethal cool that made grown men quake in their shoes. A chit of a girl who was destined for the scrapheap should have been a breeze but for some reason he was finding some of his formidable focus diluted by her arresting good looks.

He went for tall, career-driven brunettes who were rarely seen without their armour of high-end designer suits and killer heels. He enjoyed the back and forth of intellectual repartee and had oftentimes found himself embroiled in heated debates about work-related issues.

His women knew the difference between a bear market and a bull market and would have sneered at anyone who didn't.

They were alpha females and that was the way he liked it.

He had seen the damage caused to rich men by airheads and bimbos. His fun-loving, amiable father had had ten good years of marriage to Lucas's mother and then, when Annabel Cipriani had died, he had promptly lost himself in a succession of stunningly sexy blondes, intelligence not a prerequisite.

He had been taken to the cleaners three times and it was a miracle that any family money, of which there had been a considerable sum at the starting block, had been left in the coffers.

But far worse than the nuisance of having his bank accounts bled by rapacious gold-diggers was the *hope* his father stupidly had always invested in the women he ended up marrying. Hope that they would be there for him, would somehow give him the emotional support he had had with his first wife. He had been looking for love and that weakness had opened him up to being used over and over again.

Lucas had absorbed all this from the side lines and had learned the necessary lessons: avoid emotional investment and you'd never end up getting hurt. Indeed, bimbos he could handle, though they repulsed him. At least they were a known quantity. What he really didn't do were women who demanded anything from him he knew he was incapable of giving, which was why he always went for women as emotionally and financially independent as him. They obeyed the same rules that he did and were as dismissive of emotional, overblown scenes as he was.

The fact was that, if you didn't let anyone in, then you were protected from disappointment, and not just the superficial disappointment of discovering that some replaceable woman was more interested in your bank account than she was in *you*.

He had learned more valuable lessons about the sort of weaknesses that could permanently scar and so he had locked his heart away and thrown away the key and, in truth, he had never had a moment's doubt that he had done the right thing.

'Are you still in contact with the man?' he murmured, watching her like a hawk.

'No! I am *not*!' Heated colour made her face burn. She found that she was gripping the arms of the chair for dear life, her whole body rigid with affront that he would even ask her such a personal question. 'Are you going to sack me, Mr Cipriani? Because, if you are, then perhaps you could just get on with it.'

Her temples were beginning to throb painfully. Of course she was going to be sacked. This wasn't going to be a ticking off before being dismissed back to Shoreditch to resume her duties as normal, nor was she simply going to be removed from the task at which inadvertently she had blundered.

She had been hauled in here like a common criminal so that she could be fired. No one-month's notice, no final warning, and there was no way that she could even consider a plea of unfair dismissal. She would be left without her main source of income and that was something she would just have to deal with.

And the guy sitting in front of her having fun being judge, jury and executioner didn't give a hoot as to whether she was telling the truth or not, or whether her life would be affected by an abrupt sacking or not.

'Regrettably, it's not quite so straightforward—'

'Why not?' Katy interrupted feverishly. 'You obviously don't believe a word I've told you and I know I certainly wouldn't be allowed anywhere near the project again. If you just wanted me off it, you would have probably told Tim, my manager, and let him pass the message on to me. The fact that I've been summoned here tells me that you're going to give me the boot, but not before you make sure I know why. Will you at the very least give me a reference, Mr Cipriani? I've worked extremely hard for your company for the past year and a half and I've had nothing but glowing reports on the work I've done. I think I deserve some credit for that.'

Lucas marvelled that she could think, for a minute, that he had so much time on his hands that he would personally call her in just to sack her. She was looking at him with an urgent expression, her green eyes defiant.

Again distracted, he found himself saying, 'I noticed on your file that you only work two days a week for my company. Why is that?'

'Sorry?' Katy's eyes narrowed suspiciously.

'It's unusual for someone of your age to be a part-time employee. That's generally the domain of women with children of school age who want to earn a little money but can't afford the demands of a full-time job.'

'I… I have another job,' she admitted, wondering where this was heading and whether she needed to be on her guard. 'I work as an IT teacher at one of the secondary schools near where I live.'

Lucas was reluctantly fascinated by the ebb and flow of colour that stained her cheeks. Her face was as transparent as glass and that in itself was an unusual enough quality to hold his attention. The tough career women he dated knew how to school their expressions because, the higher up the ladder they climbed, the faster they learned that blushing like virginal maidens did nothing when it came to career advancement.

'Can't pay well,' he murmured.

'That's not the point!'

Lucas had turned his attention to his computer and was very quickly pulling up the file he had on her, which he had only briefly scanned before he had scheduled his meeting with her. The list of favourable references was impressively long.

'So,' he mused, sitting back and giving her his undivided attention. 'You work for me for the pay and you work as a teacher for the enjoyment.'

'That's right.' She was disconcerted at how quickly he had reached the right conclusions.

'So the loss of your job at my company would presumably have a serious impact on your finances.'

'I would find another job to take its place.'

'Look around the market, Miss Brennan. Well paid part-time work is thin on the ground. I make it my duty to pay my employees over the odds. I find that tends to engender commitment and loyalty to the company. You'd be hard pressed to find the equivalent anywhere in London.'

Lucas had planned on a simple solution to this unexpected problem. Now, he was pressed to find out a bit more about her. As a part-time worker, it seemed she contributed beyond the call of duty, and both the people she answered to within the company and external clients couldn't praise her enough. She'd pleaded her innocence, and he wasn't gullible enough to wipe the slate clean, but a more detailed hearing might be in order. His initial impressions weren't of a thief who might be attracted to the lure of insider trading but, on the other hand, someone with a part-time job might find it irresistible to take advantage of an unexpected opportunity, and Duncan Powell represented that unexpected opportunity.

'Money doesn't mean that much to me, Mr Cipriani.' Katy was confused as to how a man whose values were so different from hers could make her go hot and cold and draw her attention in a way that left her feeling helpless and exposed. She was finding it hard to string simple sentences together. 'I have a place to myself but, if I had to share with other people, then it wouldn't be the end of the world.'

The thought of sharing space with a bunch of strangers was only slightly less appalling to Lucas than incarceration with the key thrown away.

Besides, how much did she mean that? he wondered with grim practicality, dark eyes drifting over her full, stubborn mouth and challenging angle of her head. What had been behind that situation with Powell, a married man? It wasn't often that Lucas found himself questioning his own judgements but in this instance he did wonder whether it was just a simple tale of a woman who had been prepared to overlook the fact that her lover was a married man because of the financial benefits he could bring to the table. Although, he'd seen enough of that to know that it was the oldest story in the world.

Maybe he would test the waters and see what came out in the wash. If this had been a case of hire and fire, then she would have been clearing out her desk eighteen hours ago, but it wasn't, because he couldn't sack her just yet, and it paid to know your quarry. He would not allow any misjudgements to wreck his deal.

'You never thought about packing in the teaching and taking up the job at my company full time?'

'No.' The silence stretched between them while Katy frantically tried to work out where this sudden interest was leading. 'Some people aren't motivated by money.' She finally broke the silence because she was beginning to perspire with discomfort. 'I wasn't raised to put any value on material things.'

'Interesting. Unique.'

'Maybe in *your* world, Mr Cipriani.'

'Money, Miss Brennan, is the engine that makes everything go, and not just in my world. In everyone's world. The best things in life are not, as rumour would have it, free.'

'Maybe not for you,' Katy said with frank disapproval. She knew that she was treading on thin ice. She sensed that Lucas Cipriani was not a man who enjoyed other people airing too many contradictory opinions. He'd hauled her in to sack her and was now subjecting her to the Spanish Inquisition because he was cold, arrogant and because *he could.*

But what was the point of tiptoeing around him when she was on her way out for a crime she hadn't committed?

'That's why you don't believe what I'm saying,'

she expanded. 'That's why you don't trust me. You probably don't trust anyone, which is sad, when you think about it. I'd hate to go through life never knowing my friends from my enemies. When your whole world is about money, then you lose sight of the things that really matter.'

Lucas's lips thinned disapprovingly at her directness. She was right when she said that he didn't trust anyone but that was exactly the way he liked it.

'Let me be perfectly clear with you, Miss Brennan.' He leaned forward and looked at her coolly. 'You haven't been brought here for a candid exchange of views. I appreciate you are probably tense and nervous, which is doubtless why you're cavalier about overstepping the mark, but I suggest it's time to get down from your moral high ground and take a long, hard look at the choices you have made that have landed you in my office.'

Katy flushed. 'I made a mistake with Duncan,' she muttered. 'We all make mistakes.'

'You slept with a married man,' Lucas corrected her bluntly, startling her with the revelation that he'd discovered what he clearly thought was the whole, shameful truth. 'So, while you're waxing lyrical about my tragic, money-orientated life, you might want to consider that, whatever the extent of my greed and arrogance, I would no more sleep with a married woman than I would jump into the ocean with anchors secured to my feet.'

'I...'

Lucas held up one hand. 'No one speaks to me the way you do.' He felt a twinge of discomfort because that one sentence seemed to prove the arrogance of which he had been accused. Since when had he become so *pompous*? He scowled. 'I've done the maths, Miss Brennan and, however much you look at me with those big, green eyes, I should tell you that taking the word of an adulterer is something of a tall order.'

Buffeted by Lucas's freezing contempt and outrageous accusations, Katy rose on shaky legs to direct the full force of her anger at him.

'How *dare you*?' But even in the midst of her anger she was swamped by the oddest sensation of vulnerability as his dark eyes swept coolly over her, electrifying every inch of her heated body.

'With remarkable ease.' Lucas didn't bat an eyelid. 'I'm staring the facts in the face and the facts are telling me a very clear story. You want me to believe that you have nothing to do with the man. Unfortunately, your lack of principles in having anything to do with him in the first place tells a tale of its own.'

The colour had drained away from her face. She hated this man. She didn't think it would be possible to hate anyone more.

'I don't have to stay here and listen to this.' But uneasily she was aware that, without her laying bare her sex life, understandably he would have jumped to the wrong conclusions. Without her confession that she had never slept with Duncan, he would have assumed the obvious. Girls her age had flings and slept with men. Maybe he would be persuaded into believing her if she told him the truth, which was that she had ended their brief relationship as soon as she had found out about his wife and kids. But even if he believed that he certainly wouldn't believe that she hadn't *slept* with the man.

Which would lead to a whole other conversation and it was one she had no intention of having. How would a man like Lucas Cipriani believe that the hussy who slept with married guys was in fact a virgin?

Even Katy didn't like thinking about that. She had never had the urge to rush into sex. Her parents hadn't stamped their values on her but the drip, drip, drip of their gentle advice, and the example she had seen on the doorstep of the vicarage of broken-hearted, often pregnant young girls abandoned by men they had fallen for, had made her realise that when it came to love it paid to be careful.

In fairness, had temptation knocked on the door, then perhaps she might have questioned her old-fashioned take on sex but, whilst she had always got along just fine with the opposite sex, no one had ever grabbed her attention until Duncan had come along with his charm, his overblown flattery and his *persistence*. She had been unsure of where her future lay, and in that brief window of uncertainty and apprehension he had burrowed in and stolen her heart. She had been ripe for the picking and his betrayal had been devastating.

Her virginity was a millstone now, a reminder of the biggest mistake she had ever made. Whilst she hoped that one day she would find the guy for her, she was resigned to the possibility that she might never do so, because somehow she was just out of sync with men and what they wanted.

They wanted sex, first and foremost. To get to the prince, you seemed to have to sleep with hundreds of frogs, and there was no way she would do that. The thought that she might have slept with *one* frog was bad enough.

So what would Lucas Cipriani make of her story?

She pictured the sneer on his face and shuddered.

Disturbed at the direction of her thoughts, she tilted her chin and looked at him with equal cool. 'I expect, after all this, I'm being given the sack and that Personnel will be in touch—so there can't be any reason for me to still be here. And you can't stop me leaving. You'll just have to trust me that I won't be saying anything to anyone about your deal.'

CHAPTER TWO

SHE DIDN'T GET FAR.

'You leave this office, Miss Brennan, and regrettably I will have to commence legal proceedings against you on the assumption that you have used insider information to adversely influence the outcome of my company's business dealings.'

Katy stopped and slowly turned to look at him.

His dark eyes were flat, hard and expressionless and he was looking right back at her with just the mildest of interest. His absolute calm was what informed her that he wasn't cracking some kind of sick joke at her expense.

Katy knew a lot about the workings of computers. She could create programs that no one else could and was downright gifted when it came to sorting out the nuts and bolts of intricate problems when those programs began to get a little temperamental. It was why she had been carefully headhunted by Lucas's company and why they'd so willingly accommodated her request for a part-time job only.

In the field of advanced technology, she was reasonably well-known.

She didn't, however, know a thing about law. What

was he going on about? She didn't really understand what he was saying but she understood enough to know that it was a threat.

Lucas watched the colour flood her face. Her skin was satiny smooth and flawless. She had the burnished copper-coloured hair of a redhead, yet her creamy complexion was free of any corresponding freckles. The net result was an unusual, absurdly striking prettiness that was all the more dramatic because she seemed so unaware of it.

But then, his cynical brain told him, she was hardly a shrinking violet with no clue of her pulling power, because she *had* had an affair with a married guy with kids.

He wondered whether she thought that she could turn those wide, emerald-green eyes on him and get away scot-free.

If she did, then she had no idea with whom she was dealing. He'd had a lifetime's worth of training when it came to spotting women who felt that their looks were a passport to getting whatever they wanted. He'd spent his formative years watching them do their numbers on his father. This woman might not be an airhead like them, but she was still driven by the sort of emotionalism he steered well clear of.

'Of course—' he shrugged '—my deal would be blown sky-high out of the water, but have you any idea how much damage you would do to yourself in the process? Litigation is something that takes its time. Naturally, your services would be no longer required at my company and your pay would cease immediately. And then there would be the small question of your legal costs. Considerable.'

Her expression was easy to read and Lucas found that he was enjoying the show.

'That's—that's ridiculous,' Katy stuttered. 'You'd find out that I haven't been in touch with…with Duncan for years. In fact, since we broke up. Plus, you'd *also* find out that I haven't breathed a word about the Chinese deal to…well, to anybody.'

'I only have your word for it. Like I said, discovering whether you're telling the truth or not would take time, and all the while you would naturally be without a penny to your name, defending your reputation against the juggernaut of my company's legal department.'

'I have another job.'

'And we've already established that teaching won't pay the rent. And who knows how willing a school would be to employ someone with a potential criminal record?'

Katy flushed. Bit by bit, he was trapping her in a corner and, with a feeling of surrendering to the inexorable advance of a steamroller, she finally said, 'What do you want me to do?'

Lucas stood up and strolled towards the wall of glass that separated him from the city below, before turning to look at her thoughtfully.

'I told you that this was not a straightforward situation, Miss Brennan. I meant it. It isn't a simple case of throwing you out of my company when you can hurt me with privileged information.' He paced the enormous office, obliging her to follow his progress, and all the time she found herself thinking, *he's almost too beautiful to bear looking at.* He was very tall and very lean, and somehow the finely cut, expensive suit did little to conceal something raw and elemental in his physique.

She had to keep dragging her brain back to what he was telling her. She had to keep frowning so that she could give the appearance of not looking like a complete nitwit. She didn't like the man, but did he have this effect on *all* the women he met?

She wondered what sort of women he met anyway, and then chastised herself for losing the thread when her future was at stake.

'The deal is near completion and a fortnight at most should see a satisfactory conclusion. Now, let's just say that I believe you when you tell me that you haven't been gossiping with your boyfriend...'

'I told you that Duncan and I haven't spoken for years! And, for your information, we broke up because *I found out that he was married.* I'm not the sort of person who would ever dream of going out with a married guy—!'

Lucas stopped her in mid-speech. 'Not interested. All I'm interested in is how this situation is dealt with satisfactorily for me. As far as I am concerned, you could spend all your free time hopping in and out of beds with married men.'

Katy opened her mouth and then thought better of defending herself, because it wasn't going to get her anywhere. He seemed ready to hand down her sentence.

'It is imperative that any sensitive information you may have acquired is not shared, and the only way that that can be achieved is if you are incommunicado to the outside world. Ergo that is how it is going to be for the next fortnight, until my deal is concluded.'

'Sorry, Mr Cipriani, but I'm not following you.'

'Which bit, exactly, Miss Brennan, are you not following?'

'The *fortnight* bit. What are you talking about?'

'It's crystal clear, Miss Brennan. You're not going to be talking to anyone, and I mean *anyone,* for the next two weeks until I have all the signatures right where I want them, at which point you may or may not return to your desk in Shoreditch and we can both forget that this unfortunate business ever happened. Can I get any clearer than that? And by "incommunicado", I mean no mobile phone and no computer. To be blunt, you will be under watch until you can no longer be a danger to me.'

'But you can't be serious!'

'Do I look as though I'm doing a stand-up routine?'

No, he didn't. In fact, without her even realising it, he had been pacing the office in ever decreasing circles and he was now towering right in front of her; the last thing he resembled was a man doing a stand-up routine.

Indeed, he looked about as humorous as an executioner; she quailed inside.

Mentally, she added 'bully' to the growing list of things she loathed about him.

'Under watch? What does that even mean? You can't just…just *kidnap* me for weeks on end because you have a deal to complete! That's a crime!'

'Incendiary words, Miss Brennan.' He leaned over and placed both hands on either side of her chair, caging her in so that she automatically cringed back. The power of his personality was so suffocating that she had to make an effort to remember how to breathe. 'I won't be kidnapping you. Far from it. You can walk out of here, but you know the consequences of that if you do. The simple process of consulting a lawyer would start racking up bills you could ill afford, I'm sure. Not to mention the whiff of unemployability that would be attached to you at the end of the long-winded and costly business. I am an extremely powerful man, for my sins. Please do us both a favour by not crossing me.'

'Arrogant.' Katy's green eyes narrowed in a display of bravado she was inwardly far from feeling. 'That's what you are, Mr Cipriani! You're an arrogant, domineering bully!' She collided with eyes that burned with the heat of molten lava, and for a terrifying moment her anger was eclipsed by a dragging sensation that made her breathing sluggish and laborious.

Lucas's eyes drifted to her full lips and for a second he was overwhelmed by a powerful, crazy urge to crush them under his mouth. He drew back, straightened and resumed his seat behind his desk.

'I'm guessing that you're beginning to see sense,' he commented drily.

'It's not ethical,' Katy muttered under her breath. She eyed him with mutinous hostility.

'It's perfectly ethical, if a little unusual, but then again I've never been in the position of harbouring suspicions about the loyalties of any of my employees before. I pay them way above market price and that usually works. This is a first for me, Miss Brennan.'

'I can't just be *kept under watch* for *two weeks*. I'm not a specimen in a jam jar! Plus, I have responsibilities at the school!'

'And a simple phone call should sort that out. If

you want, I can handle the call myself. You just need to inform them that personal circumstances will prevent you from attending for the next fortnight. Same goes for any relatives, boyfriends and random pets that might need sorting out.'

'I can't believe this is happening. How is it going to work?'

'It's simple.' He leaned forward, the very essence of practicality. 'You will be accommodated without benefit of your phone or personal computer for a fortnight. You can consider it a pleasant holiday without the nuisance of having your time interrupted by gadgets.'

'A *pleasant holiday*?' Her breathing was ragged and her imagination, released to run wild, was coming up with all sorts of giddying scenarios.

Lucas had the grace to flush before shrugging. 'I assure you that your accommodation will be of the highest quality. All you need bring with you are your clothes. You will be permitted to return to your house or flat, or wherever it is you live, so that you can pack what you need.'

'Where on earth will I be going? This is mad.'

'I've put the alternative on the table.' Lucas shrugged elegantly.

'But where will I be *put*?'

'To be decided. There are a number of options. Suffice to say that you won't need to bring winter gear.' In truth, he hadn't given this a great deal of thought. His plan had been to delegate to someone else the responsibility of babysitting the headache that had arisen.

Now, however, babysitting her himself was looking good.

Why send a boy to do a man's job? She was lippy, argumentative, stubborn, in short as unpredictable as a keg of dynamite, and he couldn't trust any of his guys to know how to handle her.

She was also dangerously pretty and had no qualms when it came to having fun with a married guy. She said otherwise, but the jury was out on that one.

Dangerously pretty, rebellious and lacking in a moral compass was a recipe for disaster. Lucas looked at her with veiled, brooding speculation. He frankly couldn't think of anyone who would be able to handle this. He had planned to disappear for a week or so to consolidate the finer details of the deal, without fear of constant interruption, and this had become even more pressing since the breach in security. He could easily kill two birds with one stone, rather than delegating the job and then wasting his time wondering whether the task would go belly up.

'So, to cut to the chase, Miss Brennan...' He buzzed and was connected through to his PA. In a fog of sick confusion, and with the distinct feeling of being chucked into a tumble drier with the cycle turned to maximum spin, Katy was aware of him instructing the woman who had escorted her to his office to join them in fifteen minutes.

'Yes?' she said weakly.

'Vicky, my secretary, is going to accompany you back to...wherever you live...and she will supervise your immediate packing of clothes to take with you. Likewise, she will oversee whatever phone calls you feel you have to make to your friends. Needless to say, these will have to be cleared with her.'

'This is ridiculous. I feel as though I'm starring in a low-grade spy movie.'

'Don't be dramatic, Miss Brennan. I'm taking some simple precautions to safeguard my business interests. Carrying on; once you have your bags packed and you've made a couple of calls, you will be chauffeured back here.'

'Can I ask you something?'

'Feel free.'

'Are you always this...*cold*?'

'Are you always this outspoken?' Eyes as black as night clashed with emerald-green. Katy felt something shiver inside her and suddenly, inexplicably, she was aware of her body in a way she had never been in her life before. It felt heavy yet acutely sensitive, tingly and hot, aching as though her limbs had turned to lead.

Her mouth went dry and for a few seconds her mind actually went completely blank. 'I think that, if I have something to say, then why shouldn't I? As long as I'm not being offensive to anyone, we're all entitled to our opinions.' She paused and tilted her chin at a challenging angle. 'To answer your question.'

Lucas grunted. Not even the high-powered women who entered and exited his life made a habit of disagreeing with him, and they certainly never criticised. No one did.

'And to answer yours,' he said coolly, 'I'm cold when the occasion demands. You're not here on a social visit. You're here because a situation has arisen that requires to be dealt with and you're the root cause of the situation. Trust me, Miss Brennan, I'm the opposite of cold, given the right circumstances.'

And then he smiled, a long, slow, lazy smile and her senses shot into frantic overdrive. She licked her lips and her body stiffened as she leant forward in the chair, clutching the sides like a drowning person clutches a lifebelt.

That smile.

It seemed to insinuate into parts of her that she hadn't known existed, and it took a lot of effort actually to remember that the man was frankly insulting her and that sexy smile was not directed at her. Whoever he was thinking of—his current girlfriend, no doubt—had instigated that smile.

Were he to direct a smile at her, it would probably turn her to stone.

'So you stuff me away somewhere...' She finally found her voice and thankfully sounded as composed as he did. 'On a two week *holiday*, probably with those bodyguards of yours who brought me from the office, where I won't be allowed to do anything at all because I'll be minus my mobile phone and minus my computer. And, when you're done with your deal, you might just pop back and collect me, provided I've survived the experience.'

Lucas clicked his tongue impatiently. 'There's no need to be so dramatic.' He raked his fingers through his hair and debated whether he should have taken a slightly different approach.

Nope. He had taken the only possible approach. It just so happened that he was dealing with someone whose feet were not planted on the ground the way his were.

'The bodyguards won't be there.'

'No, I suppose it would be a little *chancy* to stuff

me away with men I don't know. Not that it'll make a scrap of difference whether your henchmen are male or female. I'll still be locked away like a prisoner in a cell with the key thrown away.'

Lucas inhaled deeply and slowly, and hung on to a temper that was never, ever lost. 'No henchmen,' he intoned through gritted teeth. 'You're going to be with me. I wouldn't trust anyone else to keep an eye on you.'

Not without being mauled to death in the process.

'With *you*?' Shot through with an electrifying awareness of him, her heart sped up, sending the blood pulsing hotly through her veins and making it difficult to catch her breath. *Trapped somewhere with him?* And yet the thought, which should have filled her with unremitting horror, kick-started a dark, insurgent curiosity that frankly terrified her.

'I have no intention of having any interaction with you at all. You will simply be my responsibility for a fortnight and I will make sure that no contact is made with any outside parties until the deal is signed, sealed and delivered. And please don't tell me the prospect of being without a mobile phone or computer for a handful of days amounts to nothing short of torture, an experience which you may or may not survive! It *is* possible to live without gadgets for a fortnight.'

'Could *you*?' But her rebellious mind was somewhere else, somewhere she felt it shouldn't be.

'This isn't about me. Bring whatever books you want, or embroidery, or whatever you might enjoy doing, and think about it positively as an unexpected time out for which you will continue to be paid. If you're finding it difficult to kick back and enjoy the experience, then you can always consider the alternative: litigation, legal bills and no job.'

Katy clenched her fists and wanted to say something back in retaliation, even though she was dimly aware of the fact that this was the last person on the planet she wanted to have a scrap with, and not just because he was a man who would have no trouble in making good on his threats. However, the door was opening and through the haze of her anger she heard herself being discussed in a low voice, as if she wasn't in the room at all.

'Right.'

She blinked and Lucas was staring down at her, hands shoved in his trouser pockets. Awkwardly she stood up and instinctively smiled politely at his secretary, who smiled back.

He'd rattled off a chain of events, but she'd only been half listening, and now she didn't honestly know what would happen next.

'I'll have to phone my mum and dad,' she said a little numbly and Lucas inclined his head to one side with a frown.

'Of course.'

'I talk with them every evening.'

His frown deepened, because that seemed a little excessive for someone in her twenties. It didn't tally with the image of a raunchy young woman indulging in a steamy affair with a married man, not that the details of that were his business, unless the steamy affair was ongoing.

'And I don't have any pets.' She gathered her backpack from the ground and headed towards the door in the same daze that had begun settling over her the second his secretary had walked into the room.

'Miss Brennan...'

'Huh?' She blinked and looked up at him.

She was only five-three and wearing flats, so she had to crane her neck up. Her hair tumbled down her back in a riot of colour. Lucas was a big man and he felt as though he could fit her into his pocket. She was delicate, her features fine, her body slender under the oversized white shirt. Was that why he suddenly felt himself soften after the gruelling experience he had put her through? He had never in his life done anything that disturbed his conscience, had always acted fairly and decently towards other people. Yes, undeniably he could be ruthless, but never unjustly so. He felt a little guilty now.

'Don't get worked up about this.' His voice was clipped because this was as close as he was going to get to putting her mind at ease. By nature, he was distrustful, and certainly the situation in which he had encountered her showed all the hallmarks of being dangerous, as she only had to advertise what she knew to her ex. Yet something about her fuelled an unexpected response in him.

Her eyes, he noted as he stared down into them, were a beguiling mix of green and turquoise. 'This isn't a trial by torture. It's just the only way I can deal with a potential problem. You won't spend the fortnight suffering, nor is there any need to fear that I'm going to be following you around every waking moment like a bad conscience. Indeed, you will hardly notice my presence. I will be working all day and you'll be free to do as you like. Without the tools for communicating with the outside world, you can't get up to any mischief.'

'But I don't even know where I'm going!' Katy cried, latching on to that window of empathy before it vanished out of sight.

Lucas raised his eyebrows, and there was that smile again, although the empathy was still there and it was tinged with a certain amount of cool amusement. 'Consider it a surprise,' he murmured. 'A bit like winning the lottery which, incidentally, pretty much sums it up when you think about the alternative.' He nodded to his secretary and glanced at his watch. 'Two hours, Vicky. Think that will do it?'

'I think so.'

'In that case, I will see you both shortly. And, Miss Brennan…don't even think about doing a runner.'

Over the next hour and a half Katy experienced what it felt like to be kidnapped. Oh, he could call it what he liked, but she was going to be held prisoner. She was relieved of her mobile phone by Lucas's secretary, who was brisk but warm, and seemed to see nothing amiss in following her boss's high-handed instructions. It would be delivered to Lucas and held in safekeeping for her.

She packed a bunch of clothes, not knowing where she going. Outside, it was still, but spring was making way for summer, so the clothes she crammed into her duffel bag were light, with one cardigan in case she ended up somewhere cold.

Although how would she know what the weather was up to when she would probably be locked in a room somewhere with views of the outside world through bars?

And yet, for all her frustration and downright *anger,* she could sort of see why he had reacted the way he had. Obviously the only thing that mattered to Lucas Cipriani was making money and closing deals. If this was to be the biggest deal of his career—and dipping his corporate toes into the Far East would be—then he would be more than happy to do what it took to safeguard his interest.

She was a dispensable little fish in the very big pond in which he was the marauding king of the water.

And the fact that she knew someone at the company he was about to take over, someone who was so far ignorant of what was going on, meant she had the power to pass on highly sensitive and potentially explosive information.

Lucas Cipriani, being the sort of man he was, would never believe that she had no ongoing situation with Duncan Powell because he was suspicious, distrustful, power hungry, arrogant, and would happily feed her to the sharks if it suited him, because he was also ice-cold and utterly emotionless.

'Where am I being taken?' she asked Vicky as they stepped back into the chauffeur-driven car that had delivered her to her flat. 'Or am I going to find myself blindfolded before we get there?'

'To a field on the outskirts of London.' She smiled. 'Mr Cipriani has his own private mode of transport there. And, no, you won't be blindfolded for any of the journey.'

Katy subsided into silence and stared at the scenery

passing by as the silent car left London and expertly took a route with which she was unfamiliar. She seldom left the capital unless it was to take the train up to Yorkshire to see her parents and her friends who still lived in the area. She didn't own a car, so escaping London was rarely an option, although, on a couple of occasions, she *had* gone with Tim and some of the others to Brighton for a holiday, five of them crammed like sardines into his second-hand car.

She hadn't thought about the dynamics of being trapped in a room with just Lucas acting as gaoler outside, but now she did, and she felt that frightening, forbidding tingle again.

Would other people be around? Or would there just be the two of them?

She hated him. She loathed his arrogance and the way he had of assuming that the world should fall in line with whatever he wanted. He was the boss who never made an effort to interact with those employees he felt were beneath him. He paid well not because he was a considerate and fair-minded guy who believed in rewarding hard work, but because he knew that money bought loyalty, and a loyal employee was more likely to do exactly what he demanded without asking questions. Pay an employee enough, and they lost the right to vote.

She hoped that he'd been telling the truth when he'd said that there would be no interaction between them because she couldn't think that they would have anything to talk about.

Then Katy thought about seeing him away from the confines of office walls. Something inside trembled and she had that whooshing feeling again, as if she

had been sitting quietly on a chair, only to find that
the chair was attached to a rollercoaster and the switch
had suddenly been turned on. Her tummy flipped
over; she didn't get it, because she really and truly
didn't like the guy.

She surfaced from her thoughts to find that they
had left the main roads behind and were pulling into
a huge parking lot where a long, covered building
opened onto an air field.

'I give you Lucas's transport…' Vicky murmured.
'If you look to the right, you'll see his private jet. It's
the black one. But today you'll be taking the helicopter.'

Jet? Helicopter?

Katy did a double-take. Her eyes swivelled from
private jet to helicopter and, sure enough, there he
was, leaning indolently against a black and silver helicopter, dark shades shielding his eyes from the early-
afternoon glare.

Her mouth ran dry. He was watching her from behind those shades. Her breathing picked up and her
heart began to beat fast as she wondered what the heck
she had got herself into, and all because she had stumbled across information she didn't even care about.

She didn't have time to dwell on the quicksand
gathering at her feet, however, because with the sort
of efficiency that spoke of experience the driver was
pulling the car to a stop and she was being offloaded,
the driver hurrying towards the helicopter with her
bag just as the rotary blades of the aircraft began to
whop, whop, whop in preparation for taking off, sending a whirlwind of flying dust beneath it.

Lucas had vanished into the helicopter.

Katy wished that she could vanish to the other side of the world.

She was harried, panic-stricken and grubby, because she hadn't had a chance to shower, and her jeans and shirt were sticking to her like glue. When she'd spoken to her mother on the phone, under the eagle eye of Vicky, she had waffled on with some lame excuse about being whipped off to a country house to do an important job, where the reception might be a bit dodgy, so they weren't to worry if contact was sporadic. She had made it sound like an exciting adventure because her parents were prone to worrying about her.

She hadn't thought that she really *would* end up being whipped off to anywhere.

She had envisaged a laborious drive to a poky holding pen in the middle of nowhere, with Internet access cruelly denied her. She hadn't believed him when he had told her to the contrary, and she certainly had not been able to get her head around any concept of an unplanned holiday unless you could call *incarceration* a holiday.

She was floored by what seemed to be a far bigger than average helicopter, but she was still scowling as she battled against the downdraft from the blades to climb aboard.

Lucas had to shout to be heard. As the small craft spun up, up and away, he called out, 'Small bag, Miss Brennan. Where have you stashed the books, the sketch pads and the tin of paints?'

Katy gritted her pearly teeth together but didn't say anything, and he laughed, eyebrows raised.

'Or did you decide to go down the route of being

a good little martyr while being held in captivity against your will? No books…no sketch pads…no tin of paints…and just the slightest temptation to stage a hunger strike to prove a point?'

Clenched fists joined gritted teeth and she glared at him, but he had already looked away and was flicking through the papers on his lap. He only glanced up when, leaning forward and voice raised to be heard above the din, she said, 'Where are you taking me?'

Aggravatingly seeming to read her mind, privy to every dark leap of imagination that had whirled through her head in a series of colourful images, Lucas replied, 'I'm sure that you've already conjured up dire destinations. So, instead of telling you, I'll leave you to carry on with your fictitious scenarios because I suspect that where you subsequently end up can only be better than what you've wasted your time imagining. But to set your mind at rest…'

He patted the pocket of the linen jacket which was dumped on the seat next to him. 'Your mobile phone is safe and sound right there. As soon as we land, you can tell me your password so that I can check every so often: make sure there are no urgent messages from the parents you're in the habit of calling on a daily basis…'

'Or from a married ex-boyfriend?' She couldn't resist prodding the sleeping tiger and he gave her a long, cool look from under the dark fringe of his lashes.

'Or from a married ex-boyfriend,' he drawled. 'Always pays to be careful, in my opinion. Now why don't you let me work and why don't you…enjoy the ride?'

CHAPTER THREE

THE RIDE PROBABLY TOOK HOURS, and felt even longer, with Katy doing her best to pretend that Lucas wasn't sitting within touching distance. When the helicopter began descending, swinging in a loop as it got lower, all she could see was the broad expanse of blue ocean.

Panicked and bewildered, she gazed at Lucas, who hadn't looked up from his papers and, when eventually he did, he certainly didn't glance in her direction.

After a brief hovering, the helicopter delicately landed and then she could see what she had earlier missed.

This wasn't a shabby holding pen.

Lucas was unclicking himself from his seat belt and then he patiently waited for her to do the same. This was all in a day's work for him. He turned to talk to the pilot, a low, clipped, polite exchange of words, then he stood back to allow her through the door and onto the super-yacht on which the helicopter had landed.

It was much, much warmer here and the dying rays of the sun revealed that the yacht was anchored at some distance from land. No intrusive boats huddled anywhere near it. She was standing on a yacht that was almost big enough to be classified as a small liner—sleek, sharp and so impressive that every single left wing thought about money not mattering was temporarily wiped away under a tidal wave of shameless awe.

The dark bank of land rose in the distance, revealing just some pinpricks of light peeping out between the trees and dense foliage that climbed up the side of the island's incline.

She found herself following Lucas as behind them the helicopter swung away and the deafening roar of the rotary blades faded into an ever-diminishing wasp-like whine. And then she couldn't hear it at all because they had left the helipad on the upper deck of the yacht and were moving inside.

'How does it feel to be a prisoner held against your will in a shabby cell?' Lucas drawled, not looking at her at all but heading straight through a vast expanse of polished wood and expensive cream leather furniture. A short, plump lady was hurrying to meet them, her face wreathed in smiles, and they spoke in rapid Italian.

Katy was dimly aware of being introduced to the woman, who was Signora Maria, the resident chef when on board.

Frankly, all she could take in was the breath-taking, obscene splendour of her surroundings. She was on board a billionaire's toy and, in a way, it made her feel more nervous and jumpy than if she had been dumped in that holding pen she had created in her fevered, over-imaginative head.

She'd known the guy was rich but when you were

as rich as this, rich enough to own a yacht of this calibre, then you could do whatever you wanted.

When he'd threatened her with legal proceedings, it hadn't been an empty threat.

Katy decided that she wasn't going to let herself be cowed by this display. She wasn't guilty of anything and she wasn't going to be treated like a criminal because Lucas Cipriani was suspicious by nature.

She had always been encouraged by her parents to speak her mind and she wasn't going to be turned into a rag doll because she was overwhelmed by her surroundings.

'Maria will show you to your suite.' He turned to her, his dark eyes roving up and down her body without expression. 'In it you will find everything you need, including an *en suite* bathroom. You'll be pleased to hear that there is no lock on the outside of your room, so you're free to come and go at will.'

'There's no need to be sarcastic,' Katy told him, mouth set in a sullen line. Her eyes flicked to him and skittered away just as fast before they could dwell for too long on the dark, dramatic beauty of his lean face because, once there, it was stupidly hard to tear her gaze away.

'Correction—there's *every* need to be sarcastic after you've bandied around terms such as *kidnapped*. I told you that you should look on the bright side and see this as a fully paid two-week vacation.' He dismissed Maria with a brief nod, because this looked as though it was shaping up to be another one of *those* conversations, then he shoved his hands in his pockets and stared down at her. She looked irritatingly unrepentant. 'In the absence of your books, you'll find that there is a private home cinema space with a comprehensive selection of movies. There are also two swimming pools—one indoor, one on the upper deck. And of course a library, should you decide that reading is a worthwhile option in the absence of your computer.'

'You're not very nice, are you?'

'Nice people finish last so, yes, that's an accolade I've been more than happy to pass up, which is something you'd do well to remember.'

Katy's eyes narrowed at the bitterness in his voice. Was he speaking from experience? What experience? She didn't want to be curious about him, but she suddenly was. Just for a moment, she realised that underneath the ruthless, cool veneer there would be all sorts of reasons for him being the man he was.

'Nice people don't always finish last,' she murmured sincerely.

'Oh, but they do.' Lucas's voice was cool and he was staring at her, his head at an angle, as if examining something weird he wasn't quite sure about. 'They get wrapped up in pointless sentimentality and emotion and open themselves up to getting exploited, so please don't think I'll be falling victim to that trait while we're out here.'

'Get exploited?' Katy found that she was holding her breath as she waited for his answer.

'Is that the sound of a woman trying to find out what makes me tick?' Lucas raised his eyebrows with wry amusement and began walking. 'Many have tried and failed in that venture, so I shouldn't bother if I were you.'

'It's very arrogant of you to assume that I want

to find out about you,' Katy huffed. 'But, as you've reminded me, we're going to be stuck here together for the next two weeks. I was just trying to have a conversation.'

'Like I said, I don't intend to be around much. When we do converse, we can keep it light.'

'I'm sorry.' She sighed, reaching to loop her long hair over one shoulder. 'Believe it or not, I can almost understand why you dragged me out here.'

'Well, at least *drag* is an improvement on *kidnap*,' Lucas conceded.

'I'm hot, tired and sticky, and sitting quietly at my desk working on my computer feels like a lifetime ago. I'm not in the best of moods.'

'I can't picture you sitting quietly anywhere. Maybe I've been remiss in not getting out and seeing what my employees are doing. What do you think? Should I have left my ivory tower and had a look at which of my employees were sitting and meekly doing their jobs and which ones were pushing the envelope?'

Katy reddened. His voice was suddenly lazy and teasing and her pulses quickened in response. How could he be so ruthless and arrogant one minute and then, in a heartbeat, make the blood rush to her head because of the way he was able to laugh at himself unexpectedly?

She didn't know whether it was because she had been yanked out of her comfort zone, but he was turning her off and on like a tap, and it unsettled her.

After Duncan, she had got her act together; she had looked for the silver lining and realised that he had pointed her in the right direction of what to look for in a man: someone down-to-earth, good-natured, genuine. Someone *normal.* When she found that man, everything else would fall into place, and she was horrified that a guy like Lucas Cipriani could have the sort of effect on her that he did. It didn't make sense and she didn't like it.

'I think my opinion doesn't count one way or another,' she said lightly. 'I can't speak for other people, but no one in my office actually expects you to swoop down and pay a visit.'

'You certainly know how to hit below the belt,' Lucas imparted drily. 'This your normal style when you're with a man?'

'You're not a man.'

Lucas laughed, a rich, throaty laugh that set her senses alight and had her pulses racing. 'Oh, no,' he murmured seriously. 'And here I was thinking that I was…'

'You know what I mean.' Rattled, Katy's gaze slid sideways and skittered away in confusion.

'Do I? Explain.' This wasn't the light conversation he had had in mind, but that wasn't to say that he wasn't enjoying himself, because he was. 'If I'm not a man, then what am I?'

'You're…you're my *captor.*'

Lucas grinned. 'That's a non-answer if ever there was one, but I'll let it go. Besides, I thought we'd got past the kidnap analogy.'

Katy didn't answer. He was being nice to her, teasing her. She knew that he still probably didn't trust her as far as he could throw her, but he was worldly wise and sophisticated, and knew the benefits of smoothing tensions and getting her onside. Constant sniping would bore him. He had been forced into a situation he hadn't banked on, just as she had, but he wasn't throwing temper tantrums. He wasn't interested in having meaningful conversations, because he wasn't interested in her and had no desire to find out anything about her, except what might impact on his business deal; but he would be civil now that he had told her in no uncertain terms what the lay of the land was. He had laughed about being called her captor, but he was, and he called the shots.

Instead of getting hot and bothered around him, she would have to step up to the plate and respond in kind.

They had reached the kitchen and she turned her attention away from him and looked around her. 'This is wonderful.' She ran her fingers over the counter. 'Where is Maria, your…chef?' She remained where she was, watching as he strolled to an over-sized fridge, one of two, and extracted a bottle of wine.

He poured them both a glass and nodded to one of the grey upholstered chairs tucked neatly under the metal kitchen table. Katy sat and sipped the wine very slowly, because she wasn't accustomed to drinking.

'Has her own quarters on the lower deck. I dismissed her rather than let her hang around listening to…a conversation she would have found puzzling. She might not have understood the meaning but she would have got the gist without too much trouble.'

Lucas sat opposite her. 'It is rare for me to be on this yacht with just one other person. It's generally used for client entertaining and occasionally for social gatherings. Under normal circumstances, there would be more than just one member of staff present, but there seemed little need to have an abundance of crew for two people. So, while we're here, Maria will clean and prepare meals.'

'Does she know why I'm here?'

'Why would she?' Lucas sounded genuinely surprised. 'It's none of her business. She's paid handsomely to do a job, no questions asked.'

'But wouldn't she be curious?' Katy couldn't help asking.

Lucas shrugged. 'Do I care?'

'*You* might not care,' she said tartly. 'But maybe *I* do. I don't want her thinking that I'm… I'm…'

'What?'

'I wouldn't want her thinking that I'm one of your women you've brought here to have a bit of fun with.'

Lucas burst out laughing. When he'd sobered up, he stared at her coolly.

'Why does it matter to you what my chef thinks of you? You'll never lay eyes on her again once this two-week stint is over. Besides…' he sipped his wine and looked at her over the rim of his glass '…I often fly Maria over to my place in London and occasionally to New York. She has seen enough of my women over the years to know that you don't fit the mould.'

Katy stared at him, mortified and embarrassed, because somehow she had ended up giving him the impression that…*what*? That she thought he might fancy her? That she thought her precious virtue might be *compromised* by being alone with him on this yacht, when she was only here because of circumstances? The surroundings were luxurious but this wasn't a five-star hotel with the man of her dreams. This was a prison in all but name and he was her gaoler…and since when did gaolers fancy their captives?

'Don't fit the mould?' she heard herself parrot in a jerky voice, and Lucas appeared to give that some consideration before nodding.

'Maria has been with me for a very long time,' he said without a shade of discomfort. 'She's met many of my women over the years. I won't deny that you have a certain appeal, but you're not my type, and she's savvy enough to know that. Whatever she thinks, it won't be that you're here for any reasons other than work. Indeed, I have occasionally used this as a work space with colleagues when I've needed extreme privacy in my transactions, so I wouldn't be a bit surprised if she puts that spin on your presence here.' He tried and failed to think of the woman sitting opposite him in the capacity of *work colleague*.

You have a certain appeal. Katy's brain had clunked to a stop at that throwaway remark and was refusing to budge. Why did it make her feel so flustered; hadn't she, two seconds ago, resolved not to let him get to her? She wanted to be as composed and collected as he was but she was all over the place.

Why was that? Was it the unsettling circumstances that had thrown them together? Lucas was sexy and powerful, but he was still just a man, and male attention, in the wake of Duncan, left her cold. So why did half a sentence from a man who wasn't interested in her make her skin prickle and tingle?

She forced her brain to take a few steps forward and said faintly, 'I didn't realise men had a type.' Which wasn't what she had really wanted to say. What she had *really* wanted to say was '*what's your type?*'

Rich men were always in the tabloids with women dripping from their arms and clinging to them like limpets. Rich men led lives that were always under the microscope, because the public loved reading about the lifestyles of the rich and famous, but she couldn't recall ever having seen Lucas Cipriani in any scandal sheets.

'All men have a *type*,' Lucas informed her. He had a type and he was clever enough to know *why* he had that particular type. As far as he was concerned, knowledge in that particular area was power. He would never fall victim to the type of manipulative women that his father had. He would always be in control of his emotional destiny. He had never had this sort of conversation with a woman in his life before, but then again his association with women ran along two tracks and only two. Either there was a sexual connection or else they were work associates.

Katy was neither. Yes, she worked for him, but she was not his equal in any way, shape or form.

And there was certainly no sexual connection there.

On cue, he gazed away from her face to the small jut of her breasts and the slender fragility of her arms. She really was tiny. A strong wind would knock her off her feet. She was the sort of woman that men instinctively felt the need to protect.

It seemed as good a time as any to remember just the sort of women he went for and, he told himself, keeping in the practical vein, to tell *her,* because, work or no work, aside from his chef there were only the two of them on board his yacht and he didn't want her to start getting any ideas.

She was a nobody suddenly plunged into a world of extreme luxury. He'd had sufficient experience over the years with women whose brains became scrambled in the presence of wealth.

'Here's *my* type,' he murmured, refilling both their glasses and leaning towards her, noting the way she reflexively edged back, amused by it. 'I don't do clingy. I don't do gold-diggers, airheads or any women who think that they can simper and preen their way to my bank balance—but, more than that, I don't care for women who demand more than I am capable of giving them. I lead an extremely pressurised working life. When it comes to my private life, I like women to be soothing and compliant. I enjoy the company of high fliers, career women whose independence matches my own. They know the rules of my game and there are never any unpleasant misunderstandings.'

He thought of the last woman in his life, a raven-haired beauty who was a leading light in the field of international law. In the end their mutually busy schedules had put paid to anything more than a six-month dalliance although, in fairness, he hadn't wanted more. Even the most highly intelligent and ferociously independent woman had a sell-by date in his life.

Katy was trying to imagine these high-flying, saintly paragons who didn't demand and who were also soothing and compliant. 'What would constitute them demanding more than you're capable of giving them?' she asked impulsively and Lucas frowned.

'Come again?'

'You said that you didn't like women who demanded more than you were capable of giving them. Do you mean *love and commitment*?'

'Nicely put,' Lucas drawled. 'Those two things are

off the agenda. An intellectually challenging relation-ship—with, of course, ample doses of fun—is what I look for and, fortunately, the women I go out with are happy with the arrangement.'

'How do you know?'

'How do I know what?'

'That they're happy. Maybe they really want more but they're too scared to say that because you tell them that you don't want a committed relationship.'

'Maybe. Who knows? We're getting into another one of those deep and meaningful conversations again.' He stood up and stretched, flexing muscles that rippled under his hand-tailored clothes. 'I've told you this,' he said, leaning down, hands planted squarely on the table, 'Because we're here and I wouldn't want any *wow* moments to go to your head.'

'I beg your pardon?'

'You're here because I need to keep an eye on you and make sure you don't do anything that could jeop-ardise a deal I've been working on for the past year and a half,' he said bluntly, although his voice wasn't unkind. He was unwillingly fascinated by the way her face could transmit what she was thinking, like a shining beacon advertising the lay of the land. 'I know you're out of your comfort zone but I wouldn't want you to get any ideas.'

Comprehension came in an angry rush...although, a little voice whispered treacherously in her head, *hadn't* she been looking at him? Had he spotted that and decided to nip any awkwardness in the bud by putting down 'no trespass' signs? She wasn't his type and he was gently but firmly telling her not to start thinking that she might be. 'You're right.' Katy sat back and folded her arms. 'I *am* out of my comfort zone and I *am* impressed. Who wouldn't be? But it takes more than a big boat with lots of fancy gadgets to suddenly turn its owner into someone I could *ever* be attracted to.'

'Is that a fact?'

'Yes, it is. I know my place and I'm perfectly happy there. You asked me why do I continue to work in a school? Because I enjoy giving back. I only work for your company, Mr Cipriani, because the pay enables me to afford my rent. If I could somehow be paid more as a teacher, then I would ditch your job in a heartbeat.' Katy thought that, at the rate she was going, she wouldn't have to ditch his job because *it* would be ditching *her*. 'You don't have to warn me off you and you don't have to be afraid that I'm going to start suddenly wanting to have a big boat like this of my own...'

'For goodness' sake, it's a *yacht*, not a *boat*.' And the guy who had overseen its unique construction and charged mightily for the privilege would be incandescent at her condescending referral to it as a boat. Although, Lucas thought, his lips twitching as he fought off a grin, it would certainly be worth seeing. The man, if memory served him right, had embodied all the worst traits of someone happy to suck up to the rich while stamping down hard on the poor.

Katy shrugged. 'You know what I mean. At any rate, Mr Cipriani, you don't want to be stuck here with me and I don't want to be stuck here with you either.'

'Lucas.'

'Sorry?'

'I think it's appropriate that we move onto first names. The name is Lucas.'

Flustered, Katy stared at him. 'I wouldn't feel right calling you by your first name,' she muttered, bright red. 'You're my boss.'

'I'll break the ice. Are you hungry, Katy? Maria will have prepared food and she will be unreasonably insulted if we don't eat what she has cooked. I'll call her up to serve us, after which she'll show you to your quarters.'

'Call her up?'

'The food won't magically appear on our plates.'

'I don't feel comfortable being waited on as though I'm royalty,' Katy told him honestly. 'If you direct me, I'm sure I can do whatever needs doing.'

'You're not the hired help, Katy.'

Katy shivered at the use of her name. It felt...*intimate.* She resolved to avoid calling him by his name unless absolutely necessary: perhaps if she fell overboard and was in the process of drowning. Even then she knew she would be tempted to stick to Mr Cipriani.

'That's not the point.' She stood up and looked at him, waiting to be directed, then she realised that he genuinely had no idea in which direction he should point her. She clicked her tongue and began rustling through the drawers, being nosy in the fridge before finding casserole dishes in the oven.

She could feel his dark, watchful eyes following her every movement, but she was relieved that he hadn't decided to fetch Maria, because this was taking away some of her jitters. Instead of sitting in front of him, perspiring with nerves and with nowhere to

rest her eyes except on *him,* which was the least restful place they could ever land, busying herself like
this at least occupied her, and it gave her time to get
her thoughts together and forgive herself for behaving out of character.

It was understandable. Twenty-four hours ago,
she'd been doing her job and going through all the
usual daily routines. Suddenly she'd been thrown
blindfolded into the deep end of a swimming pool
and it was only natural for her to flounder before she
found her footing.

She could learn something from this because,
after Duncan, being kind to herself had come hard.
She had blamed herself for her misjudgements. How
could she have gone so wrong when she had spent a
lifetime being so careful and knowing just what she
wanted? She had spent months beating herself up for
her mistake in not spotting the kind of man he had
been. She had been raised by two loving parents who
had instilled the right values in her, so how had she
been sucked into a relationship with a man who had
no values at all?

So here she was, acting out of character and going
all hot and cold in the company of a man she had just
met five seconds ago. It didn't mean anything and
she wasn't going to beat herself up over it. There was
nothing wrong with her. It was all a very natural reaction to unforeseen circumstances.

Watching her, Lucas thought that this was just the
sort of domestic scene he had spent a lifetime avoiding. He also thought that, despite what he had said
about his high-flying career women wanting no more
than he was willing to give them, many of them had

tentatively broached the subject of a relationship that would be more than simply a series of fun one-night stands. He had always shot those makings of uncomfortable conversations down in flames. But looking at the way Katy was pottering in this kitchen, making herself at home, he fancied that many an ex would have been thrilled to do the same.

'I like cooking,' she told him, bringing the food to the table and guilt-tripping him into giving her a hand because, as he had pointed out with spot-on accuracy, she *wasn't* the hired help. 'It's not just because it feels wrong to summon Maria here to do what I could easily do, but I honestly enjoy playing around with food. This smells wonderful. Is she a qualified chef?'

'She's an experienced one,' Lucas murmured.

'Tell me where we're anchored,' Katy encouraged. 'I noticed an island. How big is it? Do you have a house there?'

'The island is big enough for essentials and, although there is some tourism, it's very exclusive, which is the beauty of the place. And, yes, I have a villa there. In fact, I had planned on spending a little time there on my own, working flat-out on finalising my deal without interruptions, but plans changed.'

He didn't dwell on that. He talked, instead, about the island and then, as soon as he was finished eating, he stood up and took his plate to the sink. Katy followed his lead, noticing that his little foray into domesticity didn't last long, because he remained by the sink, leaning against it with his arms folded. She couldn't help but be amused. Just like the perplexed frown when he had first entered the kitchen, his obvious lack of interest in anything domestic was something that came across as ridiculously macho yet curiously endearing. If a man like Lucas Cipriani could ever be *endearing,* she thought drily.

'You can leave that,' was his contribution. 'Maria will take care of it in the morning.'

Katy paused and looked up at him with a half-smile. Looking down at her, he had an insane urge to...to *what?*

She had a mouth that was lush, soft and ripe for kissing. Full, pink lips that settled into a natural, sexy pout. He wondered whether they were the same colour as her nipples, and he inhaled sharply because bringing her here was one thing, but getting ideas into his head about what she might feel like was another.

'I'll show you to your cabin,' he said abruptly, heading off without waiting while she hurriedly stacked the plates into the sink before tripping along behind him.

Let this be a lesson in not overstepping the mark, she thought firmly. They'd had some light conversation, as per his ground rules, but it would help to remember that they weren't pals and his tolerance levels when it came to polite chit chat would only go so far. Right now, he'd used up his day's quota, judging from the sprint in his step as he headed away from the kitchen.

'Have you brought swimsuits?' he threw over his shoulder.

'No.' She didn't even know what had happened to her bag.

Maria, as it turned out, had taken it and delivered it to the cabin she had been assigned. Lucas pushed open the door and Katy stood for a few seconds, looking at the luxurious bedroom suite, complete with a proper king-sized bed and a view of the blue ocean, visible through trendy oversized port holes. Lucas showed her a door that opened out onto a balcony and she followed him and stood outside in a setting that was impossibly romantic. Balmy air blew gently through her hair and, looking down, she saw dark waves slapping lazily against the side of the yacht. She was so conscious of him leaning against the railing next to her that she could scarcely breathe.

'In that case, there's an ample supply of laundered swimsuits and other items of clothing in the walk-in wardrobe in the cabin alongside yours. Feel free to help yourself.'

'Why would that be?'

'People forget things. Maria digs her heels in at throwing them out. I've stopped trying to convince her.' He raked his fingers through his hair and watched as she half-opened her mouth, and that intensely physical charge rushed through him again.

'Okay.'

'You have the freedom of my yacht. I'll work while I'm here and the time will fly past, just as long as we don't get in one another's way...'

CHAPTER FOUR

LUCAS LOOKED AT the document he had been editing for half an hour, only to realise that he had hardly moved past the first two lines.

At this point in time, and after three days of enforced isolation on his yacht, he should have been powering through the intense backlog of work he had brought with him. Instead, he had been wasting time thinking about the woman sharing his space on his yacht.

Frustrated, he stood up, strolled towards the window and stared out, frowning, at a panoramic view of open sea. Every shade of blue and turquoise combined, in the distance, into a dark-blue line where the sea met the skyline. At a little after three, it was still very hot and very still, with almost no breeze at all rippling the glassy surface of the water.

He'd looked at this very skyline a hundred times in the past, stared through this very window of his office on the lower deck, and had never been tempted to leave it for the paradise beckoning outside. He'd never been good at relaxing, and indeed had often found himself succumbing to it more through necessity than anything else. Sitting around in the sun doing nothing was a waste of valuable time, as far as he was concerned; and on the few occasions he had been on weekend breaks with a woman he had found himself enduring the time spent playing tourist with a certain amount of barely concealed impatience.

He was a workaholic and the joys of doing nothing held zero appeal for him.

Yet, he was finding it difficult to concentrate. If he had noticed Katy's delicate, ridiculous prettiness on day one, and thought he could studiously file it away as something he wasn't going to allow to distract him, then he'd made a big mistake because the effect she was having on him was increasing with every second spent in her company.

He'd done his best to limit the time they were together. He'd reminded himself that, were it not for an unfortunate series of events, the woman wouldn't even be on his yacht now, but for all his well-constructed, logical reasons for avoiding her his body remained stubbornly recalcitrant.

Perversely, the more uptight he felt in her company, the more relaxed she seemed to be in his.

Since when had the natural order of things been rearranged? For the first time in his life, he wasn't calling the shots, and *that* was what was responsible for his lack of focus.

Being stuck on the yacht with Katy had made him realise that the sassy, independent career women he dated had not been as challenging as he had always liked to think they were. They'd all been as subservient and eager to please as any vacuous airhead keen to burn a hole in his bank account. In contrast, Katy didn't seem to have a single filter when it came to telling him what she thought about…anything and everything.

So far, he had been regaled with her opinions on money, including his own. She had scoffed at the foolishness of racing towards power and status, without bothering to hide the fact that he was top of her list as a shining example of someone leading the race. She had quizzed him on what he did in his spare time, and demanded to know whether he ever did anything that was actually *ordinary*. She seemed to think that his lack of knowledge of the layout of his own private yacht's kitchen was a shocking crime against humanity, and had then opined that there was such a thing as more money than sense.

In short, she had managed to be as offensive as any human being was capable of being and, to his astonishment, he had done nothing to redress the balance by exerting the sort of authority that would have stalled her mid-sentence.

He had the power in his hands to ruin her career but the thought had not crossed his mind.

She might have been in his company for all the wrong reasons, but he was no longer suspicious of her motives, especially when she had no ability to contact anyone at all, and her openness was strangely engaging.

It was also an uncomfortable reminder as to how far he normally went when it came to getting exactly what he wanted, and that he had surrounded himself with people who had forgotten how to contradict him.

Without giving himself a chance to back out, he headed to his quarters and did the unthinkable: he swapped his khakis for a pair of swimming trunks that hadn't seen the light of day in months, if not years, and a tee-shirt.

Barefoot, grabbing a towel on the way, he headed up to the pool area where he knew Katy was going to be.

She had been oddly reticent about using the swimming pool and, chin tilted at the mutinous angle he was fast becoming accustomed to, she had finally confessed that she didn't like using stuff that didn't belong to her.

'Would you rather the swimsuits all sit unused in cupboards until it's time for the lot to be thrown away?'

'Would you throw away perfectly good clothes?'

'I would if it was cluttering up my space. You wouldn't have to borrow them if you'd thought ahead and brought a few of your own.'

'I had no idea I would be anywhere near a pool,' she had been quick to point out, and he had dealt her a slashing grin, enjoying the way the colour had rushed into her cheeks.

'And now you are. Roll with the punches, would be my advice.'

His cabin was air-conditioned, and as he headed up towards the pool on the upper deck he was assailed by heat. It occurred to him that she might not be there, that she might have gone against her original plan of reading in the afternoon and working on ideas for an app to help the kids in her class with their homework, something he had discovered after some probing. If she wasn't there, he'd be bloody disappointed, and that nearly stopped him in his tracks because disappointment wasn't something he associated with the opposite sex.

He enjoyed the company of women. He wasn't promiscuous but the truth was that no woman had ever had the power to hold his attention for any sustained length of time, so he had always been the first to do the dispatching. By which point, he was always guiltily relieved to put the relationship behind him. In that scenario, disappointment wasn't something that had ever featured.

Katy, with her quirky ways and forthright manner, was yanking him along by some sort of invisible chain and he was uneasily aware that it was something he should really put a stop to.

Indeed, he paused, considering that option. It would take him less than a minute to make it back down to his office where he could resume work.

Except…would he be able to? Or would he sit at his desk allowing his mind idly to drift off to the taboo subject of his sexy captive?

Lucas had no idea what he hoped to gain by hitting the upper deck and joining her by the pool. So what if she was attractive? The world was full of attractive women and he knew, without a shred of vanity, that he could have pretty much any of them he wanted.

Playing with his reluctant prisoner wasn't on the cards. He'd warned her off getting any ideas into her head so there was no way he was going to try to get her into his bed now.

Just thinking about that, even as he was fast shoving it out of his head, conjured up a series of images that sent his pulses racing and fired up his libido as though reacting to a gun at the starting post.

He reached out one hand and supported himself heavily against the wall, allowing his breathing to settle. His common sense was fighting a losing battle with temptation, telling him to hot foot it back to the office and slam the metaphorical door on the siren lure of a woman who most definitely wasn't his sort.

He continued on, passing Maria in the kitchen preparing supper, and giving a brief nod before heading up. Then the sun was beating down on him as he took a few seconds to appreciate the sight of the woman reclining on a deck chair, eyes closed, arms hanging loosely over the sides of the chair, one leg bent at the knee, the other outstretched.

She had tied her long, vibrant hair into some kind of rough bun and a book lay open on the ground next to her.

Lucas walked softly towards her. He hadn't seen her like this, only just about decently clothed, and his breathing became sluggish as he took in the slender daintiness of her body: flat stomach, long, smooth legs, small breasts.

He cleared his throat and wondered whether he would be able to get his vocal cords to operate. 'Good job I decided to come up here…' He was inordinately thankful for the dark sunglasses that shielded his expression. 'You're going pink. Where's your sunblock? With your skin colouring, too much sun and you'll end up resembling a lobster—and your two-week prison sentence might well end up being longer than you'd bargained for. Sun burn can be a serious condition.'

'What are you *doing* here?' Katy jack-knifed into a sitting position and drew her knees up to her chest, hugging herself and glowering from a position of disadvantage as he towered over her, all six-foot-something of bronzed, rippling muscle.

Her eyes darted down to his legs and darted away again just as fast. Something about the dark, silky hair shadowing his calves and thighs brought her out in a sweat.

She licked her lips and steadied her racing pulse. She'd kept up a barrage of easy chatter for the past few days, had striven to project the careless, outspoken insouciance that she hoped would indicate to him that she wasn't affected by him, *not at all,* and she wasn't going to ruin the impression now.

He'd warned her not to go getting any ideas and that had been the trigger for her to stop gaping and allowing him to get under her skin. She was sure that the only reason he had issued that warning was because he had noticed her reaction to him and, from that moment onwards, she had striven to subdue any wayward reactions under a never-ending stream of small talk.

To start with, she'd aimed to keep the small talk *very* small, anything to break the silence as they had shared meals. In the evenings, before he left to return to the bowels of the yacht, they'd found themselves continuing to talk over coffee and wine.

Her aim had been harder to stick to than she'd thought because something about him fired her up. Whilst she managed to contain her body's natural impulse to be disobedient—by making sure she was physically as far away from him as possible without being too obvious—she'd been seduced into provoking him, enjoying the way he looked at her when she said something incendiary, head to one side, his dark eyes veiled and assessing.

It was a subtle form of intellectual arousal that

kept her on a permanent high and it was as addictive as a drug.

In Lucas's presence, Duncan no longer existed.

In fact, thanks to Lucas's all-consuming and wholly irrational ability to rivet her attention, Katy had reluctantly become aware of just how affected she had been by Duncan's betrayal. Even when she had thought she'd moved on, he had still been there in the background, a troubling spectre that had moulded her relationships with the opposite sex.

'I own the yacht,' Lucas reminded her lazily. He began stripping off the tee-shirt and tossed it onto a deckchair, which he pulled over with his foot so that it was right next to her. 'Do you think I should have asked your permission before I decided to come up here and use the pool?'

'No, of course not,' Katy replied, flustered. 'I just thought that you had your afternoon routine and you worked until seven in the evening...'

'Routines are made to be broken.' He settled down onto the deck chair and turned so that he was looking at her, still from behind the dark shades that gave him a distinct advantage. 'Haven't you been lecturing me daily on my evil workaholic ways?'

'I never said that they were *evil*.'

'But you were so persuasive in convincing me that I was destined for an early grave that I decided to follow your advice and take some time out.' He grinned and tilted his shades up to look at her. 'You're not reacting with the sort of smug satisfaction I might have expected.'

'I didn't think that you would actually listen to

what I said,' Katy muttered, her whole body as rigid as a plank of wood.

She wanted to look away but her greedy eyes kept skittering back to him. He was just so unbelievably perfect. More perfect than anything she had conjured up in her fevered imaginings. His chest was broad and muscular, with just the right dusting of dark hair that made her draw her breath in sharply, and the line of dark hair running down from his belly button electrified her senses like a live wire. How was it possible for a man to be so sexy? So sinfully, darkly and *dangerously* sexy?

Every inch of him eclipsed her painful memories of Duncan and she was shocked that those memories had lingered for as long as they had.

Watching him, her imagination took flight. She thought of those long, clever fingers stroking her, touching her breasts, lingering to circle her nipples. She felt faint. Her nipples were tight and pinched, and between her legs liquid heat was pooling and dampening her bikini bottoms.

She realised that she had been fantasising about this man since they had stepped foot on the yacht, but those fantasies had been vague and hazy compared to the force of the graphic images filling her head as she looked away with a tight, determined expression.

It was his body, she thought. Seeing him like that, in nothing but a pair of black trunks, was like fodder for her already fevered imagination.

Under normal circumstances, she might have looked at him and appreciated him for the drop-dead, gorgeous guy that he was, but actually she wouldn't have turned that very natural appreciation into a full-on mental sexual striptease that had him parading naked in her head.

But these weren't normal circumstances and *that* was why her pragmatic, easy-going and level-headed approach to the opposite sex had suddenly deserted her.

'Tell me about the deal.' She launched weakly into the first topic of conversation that came into her head, and Lucas flung himself back into the deck chair and stared up at a faultlessly blue, cloudless sky.

He was usually more than happy to discuss work-related issues, except right now and right here that was the last thing he wanted to do. 'Persuade me that you give a damn about it.' He slanted a sideways look at her and then kept looking as delicate colour tinged her cheeks.

'Of course I do.' Katy cleared her throat. 'I'm here *because* of it, aren't I?'

'Are you enjoying yourself?' He folded his arms behind his head and stared at her. 'You're only here because of the deal but, now that you *are* here, are you having a good time?'

Katy opened her mouth to ask him what kind of question that was, because how on earth could she be having a good time when life as she knew it had been turned upside down? Except she blinked and thought that she *was* having a good time. 'I've never been anywhere like this before,' she told him. 'When I was a kid, holidays were a week in a freezing-cold British seaside town. Don't get me wrong, I adored my holidays, but this is…out of this world.'

She looked around her and breathed in the warm breeze, rich with the salty smell of the sea. 'It's a different kind of life having a father who's the local parish priest,' she confided honestly. 'On the one hand, it was brilliant, because I never lacked love and support from both my parents, especially as I was an only child. They wanted more but couldn't have them. My mum once told me that she had to restrain herself from lavishing gifts on me, but of course there was always a limit to what they could afford. And besides, as I've told you, they always made sure to tell me that money wasn't the be-all and end-all.' She looked at Lucas and smiled, somewhat surprised that she was telling him all this, not that any of it was a secret.

Never one to encourage confidences from women, Lucas was oddly touched by her confession because she was usually so outspoken in a tomboyish, challenging way.

'Hence your entrenched disregard for money,' he suggested drily. 'Tell me about the down sides of life in a vicarage. I'll be honest with you, you're the first daughter of a man of the cloth I've ever met.'

The image of the happy family stuck in his mind and, in a rare bout of introspection, he thought back to his own troubled youth after his mother had died. His father had had the love, but he had just not quite known how to deliver it and, caught up in his own grief and his never-ending quest to find a substitute for the loss of his wife, he had left a young Lucas to find his own way. The independence Lucas was now so proud of, the mastery over his own emotions and his talent for self-control, suddenly seemed a little tarnished at the edges, too hard-won to be of any real value.

He dismissed the worrying train of thought and

encouraged her to keep talking. She had a very melodic voice and he enjoyed the sound of it as much as he enjoyed the animation that lit up her ravishingly pretty, heart-shaped face.

'Down sides… Well, now, let me have a think…!' She smiled and lay down on the deck chair so that they were now both side by side, faces upturned to the brilliant blue sky above. She glanced across at him, expecting to see amusement and polite interest, just a couple of people chatting about nothing in particular. Certainly nothing that would hold the interest of a man like Lucas Cipriani. But his dark, fathomless eyes were strangely serious as he caught her gaze and held it for a few seconds, and she shivered, mouth going dry, ensnared by the gravity of his expression.

'So?' Lucas murmured, closing his eyes and enjoying the warmth and the rarity of not doing anything.

'So…you end up always knowing that you have to set a good example because your parents are pillars of the community. I could never afford to be a rebel.'

Even when she had gone to university her background had followed her. She'd been able to have a good time, and stay out late and drink with the best of them, but she had never slept around or even come close to it. Maybe if she hadn't had so many morals drilled into her from an early age she would have just got sex out of the way and then would have been relaxed when it came to finding relationships. Maybe she would have accepted that not all relationships were serious, that some were destined to fall by the wayside, but that didn't mean they weren't worthwhile.

It was a new way of thinking for Katy and she gave

it some thought because she had always assumed, post-Duncan, that she would hang on to her virginity, would have learned her lesson, would be better equipped to make the right judgement calls.

Thinking that she could deviate from that path gave her a little frisson of excitement.

'Not that I was ever tempted,' she hurriedly expanded. 'I had too much experience of seeing where drugs and drink and casual sex could lead a person. My dad is very active in the community and does a lot outside the village for down-and-outs. A lot of them ended up where they did because of poor choices along the way.'

'I feel like I'm talking to someone from another planet.'

'Why?'

'Because your life is so vastly different from anything I've come across.'

Katy laughed. Lying side by side made it easier to talk to him. If they'd been sitting opposite one another at the table in the kitchen, with the yacht rocking softly as they ate, she wasn't sure she would have been able to open up like this. She could spar with him and provoke him until she could see him gritting his teeth in frustration—in fact, she got a kick out of that—but this was different.

She couldn't even remember having a conversation like this with Duncan, who had split his time talking about himself and flirting relentlessly with her.

'What do you come across?' she asked lightly, dropping her hands to either side of the deck chair and tracing little circles on the wooden decking.

'Tough career women who don't make a habit of

getting too close to down-and-outs,' Lucas told her wryly. 'Unless, in the case of at least a couple of them who were top barristers, a crime had been committed and they happened to be confronted with one of those down-and-outs in a court of law.'

'I remember you telling me,' Katy murmured, 'About those tough career women who never wanted more than you were prepared to give them and were always soothing and agreeable.'

Lucas laughed. That had been when he'd been warning her off him, just in case she got ideas into her head. On cue, he inclined his head slightly and looked at her. She was staring up at the sky, eyes closed. Her long, dark lashes cast shadows on her cheeks and her mouth, in repose, was a full, pink pout. The sun had turned her a pale biscuit-gold colour and brought out shades of strawberry blonde amidst the deep russets and copper of her hair. Eyes drifting down, he followed the line of her shoulders and the swell of her breasts under the bikini, which he had not really been able to appreciate when she had been hugging her knees to herself, making sure that as little of her body was on show as humanly possible.

The bikini was black and modest by any modern standard but nothing could conceal the tempting swell of her pert, small breasts, the barely there cleavage, the jut of her hip bones and the silky smoothness of her thighs.

Lucas didn't bother to give in to consternation at the hot, pulsing swell of his arousal which, had she only opened her big green eyes and cast a sideways glance at him, she'd have noticed was distorting his swimming trunks.

He'd acknowledged her appeal from day one, from the very second she had walked into his office. No red-blooded male could have failed to. He'd also noted her belligerence and lack of filter when it came to speaking her mind, which was why he had decided to take on babysitting duties personally until his deal was safely in the bag. When you took into account that she had shimmered into his line of vision as a woman not averse to sleeping with married men, one who could not be trusted, it had seemed the obvious course of action.

But he knew, deep down, that even though he had dismissed any notion of going anywhere near Katy the prospect of being holed up with her for a fortnight had not exactly filled him with distaste.

He wondered whether he had even played with the forbidden thought of doing what his body wanted against the wishes of his brain. Or maybe he had been invigorated just by the novelty of having that mental tussle at all. In his well-ordered life, getting what he wanted had never posed a challenge, and internal debates about what he should or shouldn't do rarely featured, especially when it came to women.

He thought that if she had lived down to expectations and proved herself to be the sort of girl who had no morals, and really *might* have tried her luck with him, he would have had no trouble in eating, breathing and sleeping work. However, she hadn't, and the more his curiosity about her had been piqued the more he had been drawn to her like a wanderer hearing the call of a siren.

Which was so not him *at all* that he almost didn't know how to deal with it.

Except, his body was dealing with it in the time-honoured way, he thought, and then hard on the heels of that thought he wondered what she would do if she looked and saw the kind of response she'd awakened in him.

Katy wasn't sure whether it was the sudden silence, or just something thick and electric in the air, but she opened her eyes and turned her head, her mouth already opening to say something bland and chirpy to dispel the sudden tension.

His eyes caught hers and she stopped breathing. She had a drowning sensation as she was swallowed up in the deep, dark, quiet depths of his eyes. Those eyes were telegraphing a message to her, or they seemed to be. Was she imagining it? She had no experience of a man like him. That cool, brooding, speculative expression seemed to be inviting a response, but was it? Flustered and confused, her eyes dipped...

And then there was no doubt exactly what message was being telegraphed.

For a few seconds, Katy froze while her mind went into free fall. He was *turned on*. Did he think that he could try it on and she would fall in line because she was easy? Who knew, he probably still believed that she was the sort who had affairs with married men, even though he surely should know better, because she had shared stuff with him, told him about her childhood and her parents and the morals they had instilled in her. Maybe he hadn't believed her. Maybe he had taken it all with a pinch of salt because he was suspicious and mistrustful.

She *wasn't* easy. And yet, unleashed desire flooded through her in an unwanted torrent, crashing through common sense and good intentions. *She wanted this man, this unsuitable man, and she wanted him with a craving that was as powerful as a depth charge.*

The shocking intensity of a physical response she had never, *ever* felt towards any man, including Duncan, scared the living daylights out of her. Mumbling something under her breath, she leapt to her feet, the glittering blue of the infinity pool beckoning like an oasis of safety away from the onslaught of confusion overwhelming her.

Heart hammering in her chest, she scrambled forward, missed the step that gave down to the smooth wood around the pool and found herself flying forward.

She landed with a painful thump, her knees stinging where she had grazed them after her airborne flight.

Clutching her leg, she watched in fascinated slow motion as Lucas strode towards her, every lean muscle of his body intent.

'What were you thinking?' he asked urgently, scooping her up and ignoring her protests that he put her down because she was *absolutely fine*. 'You took off like a bat out of hell. Something I said?'

He was striding away from the pool area, carrying her as easily as he would carry a couple of cushions. Katy clutched his broad shoulders, horribly aware that in this semi-folded position there were bits of her on view that made her want to die an early death from embarrassment.

One glance down and he would practically be able to see the shadow of one of her nipples.

'Where are you taking me?' she croaked. 'This is ridiculous. I tripped and fell!'

'You could have broken something.'

'I haven't broken *anything*!' Katy practically sobbed.

'How do you know?'

'Because if I had I wouldn't be able to walk!'

'You're not walking. I'm carrying you. How much do you weigh, by the way? You're as light as a feather. If I didn't see how much food you're capable of putting away, I'd be worried.'

'I've always been thin,' Katy said faintly, barely noticing where they were going because she was concentrating very hard on making sure no more of her bikini-clad body went on show. She felt she might be on the verge of passing out. 'Please just take me to my cabin. That would be fine. I can clean my knee up and I'll be as right as rain.'

'Nonsense. How could I live with myself if I didn't do the gentlemanly thing and make sure you're all right? I wasn't brought up to ignore damsels in distress.'

'I'm not one of those!'

'Here we are,' Lucas intoned with satisfaction. He kicked open the door and, when Katy tore her focus away from her excruciating attempts to keep her body safely tucked away in the swimsuit, she realised where he had taken her.

Away from the safety of the pool and straight into the hellfire of his private quarters.

CHAPTER FIVE

LUCAS'S CABIN WAS different from hers insofar as it was twice the size and unnervingly masculine: dark-grey silky throw on the bed, dark-grey pillows, built-in furniture in rich walnut that matched the wooden flooring. He laid her on the bed and she immediately wriggled into a sitting position, wishing that she had something to tug down to cover herself, but instead having to make do with arranging herself into the most modest position possible, back upright, legs rammed close together and hands primly folded on her lap.

Sick with tension, she watched him disappear into an adjoining bathroom, that made hers look like a shower cubicle, to return a minute later with a first-aid kit.

'This really isn't necessary…er… Lucas.'

'You managed the first name. Congratulations. I wondered whether you would.'

'I have a few grazes, that's all.'

He was kneeling in front of her and he began to feel her ankle with surprisingly gently fingers. 'Tell me if anything hurts.'

'Nothing,' Katy stated firmly. She gave a trial tug

of her leg so that Lucas could get the hint that this was all pretty ridiculous and overblown but he wasn't having it.

Relax, she told herself sternly; *relax and it'll be over and done with in a second and you can bolt back to your cabin.* But how could she even begin to relax when those fingers were doing all sorts of things to her body?

The feathery delicacy of his touch was stirring her up, making her breathing quicken and sending tingling, delicious sensations racing through her body like little lightning sparks. She looked at his down-bent head, the raven-black hair, and had to stop herself from reaching out and touching it just to see what it felt like between her fingers.

Then she thought of the bulge of his arousal and felt faint all over again.

'I'm surprised you have a first-aid kit to hand,' she said breathlessly, tearing her fascinated gaze away from him and focusing hard on trying to normalise the situation with pointless conversation.

'Why?' Lucas glanced up briefly before continuing with his exceedingly slow exploration of her foot.

'Because you don't seem to be the type to do this sort of thing,' Katy said honestly.

'It's essential to have a first-aid kit on board a sailing vessel. In fact, this is just one of many. There's a comprehensive supply of medical equipment in a store room on the middle deck. You would be surprised at the sort of unexpected accidents that can happen when you're out at sea, and there's no ambulance available to make a five-minute dash to collect and take you to the nearest hospital.' He was working his way gently up her calf, which was smooth, slender and sprinkled with golden hair. Her skin was like satin and still warm from the sun.

'And you know how to deal with all those unexpected accidents?' Lucas's long, clever fingers were getting higher and, with each encroaching inch, her body lit up like a Christmas tree just a tiny bit more. Any higher and she would go up in flames.

'You'd be surprised,' Lucas drawled. 'Your knees are in a pretty terrible state, but after I've cleaned them up you should be fine. You'll be pleased to know that nothing's been broken.'

'I told you that,' Katy reminded him. 'Why would I be surprised?'

He was now gently swabbing her raw, torn skin and she winced as he patted the area with some oversized alcohol wipes, making sure to get rid of every last bit of dirt.

'Because,' Lucas said wryly, not looking at her, 'I get the feeling you've pigeonholed me as the sort of money-hungry, ambitious businessman who hasn't got time for anything other than getting richer and richer and richer, probably at the expense of everyone around him. Am I right?'

'I never said that,' Katy told him faintly.

'It's hard not to join the dots when your opening words to me were to accuse me of being capable of kidnapping you.'

'You *were* kidnapping me, in a manner of speaking!'

'Tell me how it feels to be a kidnap victim.' His voice was light and teasing as he continued to tend to her knee, now applying some kind of transparent ointment, before laboriously bandaging it and then turning his attention to foot number two. 'I always wanted to be a doctor,' he surprised her and himself by saying.

'What happened?' For the first time since she had been deposited on his bed, Katy felt herself begin to relax, the nervous tension temporarily driven away by a piercing curiosity. Lucas could be many things, as she had discovered over the past few days. He could be witty, amusing, arrogant and always, always wildly, extravagantly intelligent. But confiding? No.

'My father's various wives happened,' Lucas said drily. 'One after each other. They looked alike and they certainly were all cut from the same cloth. They had their eyes on the main prize and, when their tenure ran out, my father's fortune was vastly diminished. By the time I hit sixteen, I realised that, left to his own devices, he would end up with nothing to live on. It would have killed my father to have seen the empire his grandfather had built dwindle away in a series of lawsuits and maintenance payments to greedy ex-wives.

'I knew my father had planned on my inheriting the business and taking over, and I had always thought that I'd talk to him about that change of plan when the time was right; but, as it turned out, the time never became right because without me the company would have ended up subdivided amongst a string of gold-diggers and that would have been that.'

'So you gave up your hopes and dreams?'

'Don't get too heavy on the pity card.' Lucas laughed, sitting back on his heels to inspect his work, head tilted to one side. He looked at her and her mouth went dry as their eyes tangled. 'I enjoy my life.'

'But it's a far cry from being a doctor.' She had never imagined him having anything to do with the caring profession and something else was added to the swirling mix of complex responses she was stockpiling towards him. She thought that the medical profession had lost something pretty big when he had decided to pursue a career in finance because, knowing the determination and drive he brought to his chosen field of work, he surely would have brought tenfold to the field of medicine.

'So it is,' Lucas concurred. 'Hence the fact that I actually enjoy being hands-on when it comes to dealing with situations like this.'

'And have you had to deal with many of them?' She thought of him touching another woman, one of the skinny, leggy ones to whom those thong swimsuits forgotten on the yacht belonged, carefully stored just in case someone like her might come along and need to borrow one of them.

'No.' He stood up. 'Like I said, my time on this yacht is limited, and no one to date has obliged me by requiring mouth-to-mouth resuscitation whilst out to sea.' He disappeared back into the bathroom with the kit and, instead of taking the opportunity to stand up and prepare herself for a speedy exit, Katy remained on the bed, gently flexing both her legs and getting accustomed to the stiffness where the bandages had been applied expertly over her wounds.

'So I'm your first patient?'

Lucas remained by the door to the bathroom, lounging against the doorframe.

Katy was riveted at the sight. He was still wearing his bathing trunks although, without her even noticing when he had done it, he had slung on his tee-shirt. He was barefoot and he exuded a raw, animal sexiness that took her breath away.

'Cuts and grazes don't honestly count.' Lucas grinned and strolled towards her, holding her spellbound with his easy, graceful strides across the room. He moved to stand by the window which, as did hers, looked out on the blue of an ocean that was as placid as the deepest of lakes. His quarters were air-conditioned, as were hers, but you could almost feel the heat outside because the sun was so bright and the sky was so blue and cloudless.

'I'm sorry if I ruined your down time.'

'You never told me why you leapt off your deck-chair and raced for the pool as though the hounds of hell were after you,' Lucas murmured.

She was in his bedroom and touching her had ignited a fire inside him, the same fire that had been burning steadily ever since they had been on his yacht. He knew why she had leapt off that deck chair. He had enough experience of the opposite sex to register when a woman wanted him, and it tickled him to think that she wasn't doing what every other woman would have done and flirting with him. Was that because she worked for him? Was that holding her back? Maybe she thought that he would sack her if she was too obvious. Or maybe she had paid attention to the speech he had given her at the start when he had told her not to get any crazy ideas about a relationship developing between them.

He almost wished that he hadn't bothered with that

speech because it turned him on to imagine her making a pass at him.

Lucas enjoyed a couple of seconds wondering what it would feel like to have her begin to touch him, blushing and awkward, but then his innate pragmatism kicked in and he knew that she was probably playing hard to get, which was the oldest game in the world when it came to women. She had revealed all sorts of sides to her that he hadn't expected, but the reality was that she *had* had an affair with a married man. She'd denied that she'd known about the wife and kiddies, and maybe she hadn't. Certainly there was an honesty about her that he found quite charming but, even so, he wasn't going to be putting any money on her so-called innocence any time soon.

'It was very hot out there,' Katy muttered awkwardly, heating up as she recalled the pivotal moment when raging, uncontrolled desire had taken her over like a fast-moving virus and she had just *had to escape*. 'I just fancied a dip in the pool and unfortunately I didn't really look where I was going. I should head back to my room now. I think I'll give my legs a rest just while I have these bandages on—and, by the way, thank you very much for sorting it out. There was no need, but thanks anyway.'

'How long do you think we should carry on pretending that there's nothing happening between us?' Which, frankly, was a question Lucas had never had to address to any other women because other women had never needed persuading into his bed. Actually, it was a question he had not envisaged having to ask *her,* considering the circumstances that had brought them together. But he wanted her and there was no

point having a mental tussle over the whys and where-
fores or asking himself whether it made sense or not.

On this occasion, self-denial probably made sense,
but Lucas knew himself and he knew that, given the
option of going down the route of what made sense
or the less sensible route of scratching an itch, then
the less sensible route was going to win the day hands
down every time.

He also knew that he wasn't a man who was into
breaking down barriers and jumping obstacles in
order to get any woman between the sheets—and
why would he do that anyway? This wasn't a game
of courtship that was going anywhere. It was a case
of two adults who fancied one another marooned on
a yacht for a couple of weeks..

In receipt of this blunt question, presented to her
without the benefit of any pretty packaging, Katy's
eyes opened wide and her mouth fell open.

'I beg your pardon?'

'I've seen the way you look at me,' Lucas murmured, moving to sit on the bed right next to her, and
depressing the mattress with his weight so that Katy
had to shift to adjust her body and stop herself from
sliding against him.

She should have bolted. His lazy, dark eyes on her
were like lasers burning a hole right through the good,
old-fashioned, grounded common sense that had dic-
tated her behaviour all through her life—with the exception of those few disastrous months when she had
fallen for Duncan.

The slow burning heat that had been coursing
through her, the exciting tingle between her legs and
the tender pinching of her sensitive nipples—all re-

sponses activated by being in his presence and feeling his cool fingers on her—were fast disappearing under a tidal wave of building anger.

'The way I *look at you*?'

'Don't be embarrassed. Believe me, it isn't usually my style to force anyone's hand, but we're here and there's a sexual chemistry between us. Are you going to dispute that? It's in the air like an invisible electric charge.' He laughed with some incredulity. 'You're not going to believe this, but it's something I can't remember feeling in a very long time, if ever.'

'And you think I should be *flattered*?'

Lucas frowned because this wasn't the reaction he had been expecting. 'Frankly, yes,' he told her with complete honesty.

Katy gaped, even though she knew very well why a woman would be flattered to be the object of attention from Lucas Cipriani. He was drop-dead gorgeous and a billionaire to boot. If he made a pass at a woman, then what woman was going to stalk off in the opposite direction and slam the door in his face? He probably had a queue of them waiting to be picked.

Her lips tightened because what he saw as a flattering, complimentary approach was, to her, downright insulting.

At least the creep Duncan had had the wit to approach her a little less like a bull stampeding through a china shop.

But then, Katy concluded sourly, time wasn't on Lucas's side. They were here for a limited duration, so why waste any precious time trying to seduce her into bed the old-fashioned way?

'That's the most egotistical, arrogant thing I have ever heard *in my entire life*!'

'Because I've been honest?' But Lucas flushed darkly. 'I thought you were all in favour of the honest approach?'

'Who do you think I am?'

'I have no idea where you're going with this.'

'You think that you just have to snap your fingers and someone like me will dump all her principles and come running, don't you?'

'Someone like you?' But she had scored a direct hit, and he was guiltily aware that he *had* indeed compartmentalised her, however much he had seen evidence to the contrary.

'The sort of person,' Katy informed him with scathing distaste, 'Who needs a good, long lecture on making sure her little head doesn't get turned by being on a big, expensive boat—oh, sorry, *super-yacht*—with the great Lucas Cipriani! The sort of person,' she added for good measure, 'Who comes with a dubious reputation as someone who thinks it's okay to hop into bed with a married guy!' It made her even madder to think that she had fallen into the trap of forgetting who he really was, won over by his charm and the random confidences he had thrown her way which she had sucked up with lamentable enthusiasm.

And what made her even madder *still* was the fact that he had managed to read her so correctly! She thought she'd been the model of politeness, but he'd seen right through that and homed in laser-like on the fevered core of her that was attracted to him.

'You're over-analysing.' Lucas raked his fingers

through his hair and sprang to his feet to pace the cabin before standing by the window to look at her.

'I am *not* over-analysing,' Katy told him fiercely. 'I know what you think of me.'

'You don't.' Unaccustomed to apologising for anything he said or did, Lucas now felt…like a cad. He couldn't credit how she had taken his interest in her and transformed it into an insult, yet he had to admit to himself that his approach had hardly been handled with finesse. He'd been clumsy, and in no one's wildest imagination could it have passed for *honesty*.

'I know exactly what you think of me! And you've got a damned cheek to imagine that I would be so easy that I'd just fall into bed with you because you happened to extend the invite.'

'I… I apologise,' Lucas said heavily, and that apology was so unexpected that Katy could only stare at him with her mouth open. He looked at her with a roughened sincerity and she fought against relenting.

Glaring, she stood up. Her good intentions of sweeping out of his cabin with her head held high, now that she had roundly given him a piece of her mind, were undermined by the fact that she was wearing next to nothing and had to hobble a bit because the grazes on her knees were killing her.

'Katy,' he murmured huskily, stopping her in her tracks. He reached out to stay her and the pressure on her arm where his fingers circled her skin was as powerful as a branding iron. She had to try not to flinch. Awareness shot through her, rooting her to the spot. 'I don't, actually, think that you're easy and I certainly don't take it for granted that you're going to fall into bed with me because that's the kind of person you are. And,' he continued with grudging sincerity, 'If there's a part of me that is still wary, it's because it's my nature to be suspicious. The bottom line is that I want you, and I might be wrong but I think it's mutual. So tell me…is it?'

He took half a step closer to her, looked down and suppressed a groan at the delicious sight of her delicate breasts encased in stretchy fabric. 'If I've misread the signals,' he told her, 'Then tell me now and I'll back off. You have my word. Nor will I let it affect whatever lies down the line in terms of your position in my company. Say no, and this is never mentioned again. It will never have happened.'

Katy hesitated. She so badly wanted to tell him that, no, she most certainly was *not* interested in him *that* way, but then she thought of him backing away and leaving her alone and she realised with a jolt how much she enjoyed spending time in his company when they were tossing ideas around and sparring with one another. She also now realised that underneath that sparring had been the very thread of sexual attraction which he had picked up with his highly developed antennae.

'That's not the point,' she dodged feebly.

'What do you mean?'

'I mean…' Katy muttered *sotto voce*, red-faced and uncomfortable, 'It doesn't matter whether we're attracted to one another or not. It would be mad for us to do anything about it. Not that I would,' she continued at speed, face as red as a beetroot. 'After Duncan, I swore to myself that I would never make the mistake of throwing myself into anything with someone unless I really felt that they were perfect for me.'

'I've never heard such nonsense in my entire life,' Lucas said bluntly, and, feathers ruffled, Katy tensed and bristled.

'What's wrong with wanting the best?' she demanded, folding her arms, neither leaving the room nor returning to the bed, instead just standing in the middle as awkward as anything. He, on the other hand, looked totally at ease even though he was as scantily clad as she was. But then, he obviously wasn't the sort who gave a jot if his body was on display.

'Nothing's wrong with wanting the best,' Lucas concurred. 'But tell me, how do you intend to find it? Are you going to present each and every candidate with a questionnaire which they will be obliged to fill out before proceeding? I'm going to take a leap of faith here and assume that you didn't know about Powell's marital status. You went out with the man and presumably you believed that he was the right one for you.'

'I made a mistake,' Katy said defensively.

'And mistakes happen. Even if you're not being deliberately misled by a guy, you could both go out in good faith, thinking that it will go somewhere, only to discover that you hit obstacles along the way that make it impossible for you both to consider a life together.'

'And you're an expert because…?' Katy asked sarcastically.

'People are fond of self-deception,' Lucas delivered with all-knowing cool. 'I should know because I witnessed it first-hand with my father. You want something badly enough and you try and make it work and, if it all makes sense on paper, then you try all the harder to make it work. In a worst case scenario, you might actually walk up the aisle and then into a maternity ward, still kidding yourself that you've got the real deal, only to be forced to concede defeat, then cutting the ties is a thousand times more complicated.'

'You're so cynical...about *everything*.' She harked back to the lack of trust that had made him think that the only solution to saving his deal was to isolate her just in case.

'There's no such thing as the perfect man, Katy. With Powell, you got someone who deliberately set out to deceive you.' He shrugged. 'You might think I'm cynical but I'm also honest. I have never in my life set out to deceive anyone. I've never promised a bed of roses or a walk up the aisle.' He looked at her thoughtfully. 'You had a crap time with some guy who strung you along...'

'Which is why you should have believed me when I told you that I'd rather have walked on a bed of hot coals than have anything to do with him in my life again.'

'That's beside the point. At the time, I looked at the facts and evaluated them accordingly. What I'm trying to tell you is this: the world is full of men who will do whatever it takes to get a woman into bed, and that includes making promises they have no intention of keeping. With me, what you see is what you get. We're here, we're attracted to one another and that's all there is to it.'

'Sex for the sake of sex.' That was something she had never considered and surely *would* never consider. It contravened pretty much everything she had been taught to believe in. Didn't it? It was what Duncan had been after and that had repulsed her. Sex and love were entwined and to disentangle them was to reduce the value of both.

Lucas laughed at the disapproving, tight-lipped expression on her face. 'It could be worse,' he drawled. 'It could be sex for the sake of a happy-ever-after that is never going to be delivered.'

The air sizzled between them. Katy was mesmerised by the dark glitter in his eyes and could feel herself being seduced by opinions that were so far removed from her own. Yet he made them sound so plausible. Instead of giving her the freedom to enjoy a healthy and varied sex life, to take her time finding the right man for her, her experience with Duncan had propelled her ever further into a mind-set that rigidly refused to countenance anything but the guy who ticked all the boxes.

Wasn't Lucas right in many ways? How could you ever be sure of finding Mr Right unless you were prepared to bravely face down the probability that you might have to risk some Mr Wrongs first?

And who was to say that all Mr Wrongs were going to be creeps like Duncan? Some Mr Wrongs might actually be *fun*. Not marriage material, but *fun*.

Like Lucas Cipriani. He had Mr Wrong stamped all over him and yet...wouldn't he be fun?

For the first time in her life, Katy wondered when and how she had become so protective of her emotions and so incapable of enjoying herself in the way all other girls of her age would. Her parents had never laid down any hard and fast rules but she suspected now, looking back down the years, that she had picked things up in overheard conversations about some of

the young women in distress they had helped. She had
seen how unwanted pregnancies and careless emotional choices could destroy lives and she had con-
signed those lessons to the back of her mind, little
knowing how much they would influence her later
decisions.

Lucas could see the range of conflicting emotions
shadowing her expression.

The man had really done a number on her, he
thought, and along with that thought came another,
which was that the first thing he would do, provided
the deal went through, was to sling Powell out on his
backside.

Whatever experiences she had had before the guy,
he had clearly been the one she had set her sights on
for a permanent relationship, and throwing herself
into something only to find it was built on lies and
deceit would have hit her hard.

For all her feisty, strong-willed, argumentative personality, she was a romantic at heart and that probably
stemmed from her background. Sure she would have
enjoyed herself as a girl, would have had the usual
sexual experiences, but she would have kept her heart
intact for the man she hoped to spend the rest of her
life with, and it was unfortunate that that man happened to have been a married guy with a penchant
for playing away.

'You may think that I don't have the sort of high
moral code that you look for,' Lucas told her seriously.
'But I have my own code. It's based on honesty. I'm
not in search of involvement and I don't pretend to be.
You were hurt by Powell but you could never be hurt
by me because emotions wouldn't enter the equation.'

Katy looked at him dubiously. She was surprised that she was even bothering to listen but a Pandora's box had been opened and all sorts of doubts and misgivings about that high moral code he had mentioned were flying around like angry, buzzing wasps.

'I'm not the type you would ever go for.' Lucas had never thought he'd see the day he actually uttered those words to a woman. 'And quite honestly, I second that, because I would be no good for you. This isn't a relationship where two people are exploring one another in the hope of taking things to the next level. This is about sex.'

'You're confusing me.'

'I'm taking you out of your comfort zone,' Lucas murmured, yearning to touch her, only just managing to keep his hands under lock and key. 'I'm giving you food for thought. That can't be a bad thing.'

Katy looked at him and collided with eyes the colour of the deepest, darkest night. Her heart did a series of somersaults inside her chest. He was temptation in a form she was finding irresistible. Every word he had said and every argument he had proffered combined to produce a battering ram that rendered her defenceless.

'You're just bored,' she ventured feebly, a last-ditch attempt to stave off the crashing ache to grab hold of what he was offering and hold on tight. 'Stuck here without a playmate.'

'How shallow do you think I am?' Lucas grinned, his expression lightening, his eyes rich with open amusement. 'Do you think I need to satisfy my raging libido every other hour or risk exploding? I'm tired of talking. I don't think I've ever spent this much time trying to persuade a woman into bed with me.'

'Should I be flattered?'

'Most definitely,' Lucas returned, without the slightest hesitation.

Then he reached out, trailed a long finger against her cheek and tucked some strands of coppery hair behind one ear. When he should have stopped and given her time to gather herself, because she was all over the place, he devastated her instead by feathering his touch along her collarbone then dipping it down to her cleavage.

Gaze welded to his darkly handsome face, Katy remained rooted to the spot. Her nipples were pinched buds straining against the bikini top. If she looked down she knew that she would see their roused imprint against the fabric. Her eyelids fluttered and then she breathed in sharply as he stepped closer to her and placed both of his big hands on her rib cage.

He had been backing her towards the bed without her even noticing and suddenly she tumbled back against the mattress and lay there, staring up at him.

She was about to break all her rules for a one-night stand and she wasn't going to waste any more time trying to tell herself not to.

CHAPTER SIX

EXCEPT KATY WASN'T entirely sure how she was going to initiate breaking all those rules. She'd never done so before and she was dealing with a man who had probably cut his teeth breaking rules. He'd made no bones about being experienced. Was he expecting a similar level of experience? Of course he was!

She quailed. Mouth dry, she stared at him in silence as he whipped off his shirt in one fluid movement and then stood there, a bronzed god, staring down at her. She greedily ate him up with her eyes, from his broad shoulders to his six-pack and the dark line of hair that disappeared under the low-slung swimming trunks.

Lucas hooked his fingers under the waistband of the trunks and Katy shot up onto her elbows, fired with a heady mixture of thrilling excitement and crippling apprehension.

What would he do if she were to tell him that she was a virgin? *Run a mile*, was the first thought that sprang to mind. Katy didn't want him to run a mile. She wanted him near her and against her and inside her. It made her feel giddy just thinking about it.

In the spirit of trying to be someone who might actually know what to do in a situation like this, she reached behind her to fumble unsuccessfully with the almost non-existent spaghetti strings that kept the bikini top in position.

Lucas couldn't have been more turned on. He liked that shyness. It wasn't something with which he was familiar. He leant over her, caging her in.

'You smell of the sun,' he murmured. 'And I don't think I've ever wanted any woman as much as I want you right now.'

'I want you too,' Katy replied huskily. She tentatively traced the column of his neck then, emboldened, his firm jawline and then the bunched muscles of his shoulder blades. Her heart was thumping hard and every jerky breath she took threatened to turn into a groan.

He eased her lips apart and flicked his tongue inside her mouth, exploring and tasting her, and setting off a dizzying series of reactions that galvanised every part of her body into furious response. Her small hands tightened on his shoulders and she rubbed her thighs together, frantic to ease the tingling between them.

Lucas nudged her with his bulging erection, gently prising her legs apart and settling himself between them, then moving slowly as he continued to kiss her.

He tugged at her lower lip with his teeth, teasing her until she was holding her breath, closing her eyes and trembling like a leaf.

Katy didn't think that anything in the world could have tasted as good as his mouth on her and she pulled him against her with urgent hands.

She wished she'd rid herself of her bikini because now it was an encumbrance, separating their bodies.

She wriggled under him, reaching behind herself and, knowing what she wanted to do, Lucas obliged, urging her up so that he could tug free the ties. Then he rose up to straddle her and looked down, his dark eyes slumberous with desire.

Katy had never thought about sex without thinking about love and she had never thought about love without painting a tableau of the whole big deal, from marriage to babies in a thirty-second fast-forward film reel in her head.

Big mistake. In all those imaginings, her body had just been something all tied up with the bigger picture and not something needing fulfilment in its own right. The fact she had never been tempted had only consolidated in her head that sex was not at all what everyone shouted about.

Even the momentous decision that desire had propelled her into making, to ditch her hard and fast principles and sleep with him, had been made with no real prior knowledge of just how wonderfully liberating it would feel for her.

Yes, she had imagined it.

In practice, it was all oh, so wildly different. She felt joyously free and absolutely certain that what she was doing was the right thing for her to do.

Burning up, she watched Lucas as he looked at her. He was so big, so dangerously, *sinfully* handsome, and he was gazing at her as though she was something priceless. The open hunger in his eyes drove away all her inhibitions and she closed her eyes on a whimper as he leaned back down to trail his tongue against her collarbone.

Then he pinned her hands to her sides, turning her

into a willing captive so that he could fasten his mouth on one nipple. He suckled, pulling it into his mouth while grazing the stiffened bud with his tongue.

This was sex as Katy had never imagined it. Wild, raw and basic, carrying her away on a tide of passion that was as forceful as a tsunami. This wasn't the physical connection from a kind, considerate and thoughtful guy who had wooed her with flowers and talked about a happy-ever-after future. This was the physical connection from a guy who had promised nothing but sex and would walk away from her the minute their stay on his yacht had come to an end.

His mouth and tongue against her nipple were sending piercing arrows of sensation through her body. She was on fire when he drew back to rid himself of his swimming trunks. The bulge she had felt pressing against her was impressively big, big enough for her to feel a moment of sheer panic, because how on earth could something so big fit inside her and actually feel good?

But that fear wasn't allowed to take root because desire was smothering it. He settled back on the bed and then tugged down the bikini bottoms.

Katy closed her eyes and heard him laugh softly.

'Don't you like what you see?' Lucas teased and she cautiously looked at him. 'Because I very much like what *I* see.'

'Do you?' Katy whispered, very much out of her depth and feverishly making all sorts of comparisons in her head between her boyish figure and the women he probably took to his bed. She wasn't going to dwell on it, but she wasn't an idiot. Lucas Cipriani could have any woman he wanted and, whilst she was con-

fident enough about her looks, that confidence took a
very understandable beating when she considered that
the man in bed with her was every woman's dream
guy. 'Sexy' didn't get more outrageous.

Lucas felt a spurt of pure rage against Powell, a
man whose existence he had known nothing about a
week ago. Not only had he destroyed Katy's faith in
the opposite sex, but he had also pummelled her self-
esteem. Any human being with functioning eyesight
could have told her that she was a show-stopper.

He bent over to taste her pouting mouth whilst at
the same time gently inserting his hand between her
thighs.

She wasn't clean-shaven down there and he liked
that; he enjoyed the feel of her soft, downy fluff
against his fingers. He liked playing with it before
inserting one long finger into her.

It was electrifying. He slid his finger lazily in long
strokes, finding the core of her and the tight little bud
that throbbed as he zeroed in on it. In the grip of sensations she had never known before, Katy whimpered
and clutched him, all frantic need and craving. She
was desperate to ride the crest of a building wave and
her whimpers turned into soft, hitched moans as she
began to arch her spine, pushing her slight breasts up,
inviting him to tease a nipple with his tongue.

He released her briefly to fetch a condom from his
wallet then he was over her, nudging her legs apart
with his thigh and settling between them. Nerves
firmly back in place, Katy smoothed exploratory
hands along his back, tracing the hardness of muscle
and sinew.

Her coppery hair was in tangles over her shoulders,

spread like flames across the pillows. Lucas stroked some of the tangles back and kissed her.

'I want you,' Katy muttered into his mouth, and she felt him smile. Desire was a raging force inside her, ripping all control out of her grasp and stripping her of her ability to think straight, or even to think at all.

She felt his impatience and his need matching hers as he pushed into her, a deep, long thrust that made her cry out. He stilled and frowned.

'Don't stop,' she begged him, rising up so that he could sink deeper into her. She was so wet for him and so ready for this.

'You're so tight,' Lucas murmured huskily in a driven undertone. 'I can't describe the sensation, *mia bella*.'

'Don't talk!' Katy gasped, urging him on until he was thrusting hard, and the tight pain gave way to a soaring sense of pleasure as he carried her higher and higher until, at last, she came…and it was the most out-of-body experience she could ever have imagined. Wracked with shudders, she let herself fly until she weakly descended back down to planet Earth. Then, all she wanted to do was wrap her arms around him and hold him tightly against her.

Lucas was amused when she hugged him. He wasn't one for hugs, but there was something extraordinarily disingenuous about her and he found that appealing.

He gently moved off her and then looked down and frowned, his brain only slowly making connections that began to form into a complete picture, one that he could scarcely credit.

There wasn't much blood, just a few drops, enough

for him to work out that none of that shyness and hesitancy had been put on. She'd blushed like a virgin because that was exactly what she was. He looked at her as the colour drained from her face.

'This is your first time, isn't it?'

For Katy, that was the equivalent of a bucket of cold water being poured over her. She hadn't thought that he would find out. She had vaguely assumed that if she didn't say anything then Lucas would never know that she had lost her virginity to him. She hadn't wanted him to know because she had sensed, with every pore of her being, that he wouldn't be thrilled.

For a man who didn't do commitment, and who gave warnings about the perils of involvement, a virgin would represent the last word in unacceptable.

She quailed and clenched her fists because making love to Lucas had been the most wonderful thing in her life, just the most beautiful, *right* thing she had ever done, and now it was going to be spoiled because, quite rightly, he was going to hit the roof.

She wriggled and tried to yank some of the covers up because there was no way she was going to have an argument with him in the nude.

'So what?' She eyed him mutinously under the thick fringe of her lashes and glowered. 'It's really no big deal.'

'No big deal?' Lucas parroted incredulously. 'Why didn't you tell me?'

'Because I know how you would have reacted,' Katy muttered, hugging her knees to her chest and refusing to meet his eyes for fear of the message she would read there.

'You know, do you?'

Katy sneaked a glance at him, and just as fast her eyes skittered away. He was sprawled indolently on the bed, an in-your-face reminder of the intimacy they had just shared. She was covering up for all she was worth but he was carelessly oblivious to his nakedness.

'I wanted to do it.' She stuck her chin up and challenged him to argue with that. 'And I knew that if I told you that I'd never slept with anyone before you'd have run a mile. Wouldn't you?'

Lucas grimaced. 'I probably would have been a little cautious,' he conceded.

'Run a mile.'

'But I would have been flattered,' he admitted with even more honesty. 'I would also have been more gentle and taken my time.' He raked his fingers through his hair and vaulted out of the bed to pace the floor, before snatching a towel which was slung over the back of a chair and loosely settling it around his waist. Then he circled to sit on the bed next to her. 'It *is* a big deal,' he said gently. He took her hands in his and stroked her wrists until her clenched fists relaxed. 'And if I was a little rough for you, then I apologise.'

'Please don't apologise.' She smiled cautiously and stroked his face, and it was such an intimate gesture that she almost yanked her hand back, but he didn't seem to mind; indeed he caught her hand and turned it over so that he could place a very tender kiss on the underside of her wrist.

'You're beautiful, *cara.* I don't understand how it is that you've remained a virgin. Surely there must have been other men before Powell?'

Katy winced at the reminder of the man who had

been responsible for landing them here together on this yacht. It was fair to say that, however hateful her memories of him were, they seemed a lot less hateful now. Maybe one day she might even mentally thank him because she couldn't see how she could ever regret having slept with Lucas.

'That was another of those down sides to having parents who were pillars of the community.' Katy let loose a laugh. 'There were always expectations. And especially in a tiny place, when you're growing up, everyone knows everyone else. Reputations are lost in the snap of a finger. I didn't really think about that, though,' she said thoughtfully. 'I just knew that I wanted the whole love and marriage thing, so my standards were maybe a bit on the high side.'

She sighed and smiled ruefully at Lucas, who was looking at her with such sizzling interest that every pulse in her body raced into overdrive.

'When Duncan came along, I'd just returned from university and I wasn't quite sure what direction my life was going to take. I remember my mother and I talking about the social scene at university, and my mum asking me about the boys, and something must have registered that I needed to take the next step, which was finding someone special.' She gazed at Lucas. 'I slept with you because I really wanted to. You said a lot of stuff…basically about seizing the day…'

'I had no idea I was addressing a girl who had no experience.'

'But, you see, that's not the point.' Katy was keen to impress this on him. 'The point is that you made me think about things differently. I know this isn't going anywhere but at least you were honest about that and you gave me a choice.' Duncan had denied her the truth about himself and, even if this was just a one night stand, which was something she had always promised herself she would never do, was it really worse to lose her virginity to Lucas than to a liar like Duncan?

She gazed up at him earnestly and Lucas lowered his head and very tenderly kissed her on the lips. He could have taken her again, right then, but she would be sore. Next time, he intended to make it up to her, to take his time. It blew his mind to think that she had come to him as a virgin. It was a precious gift and he knew that, even though he couldn't fully understand what had led her to give it to him.

'Yes, *cara,* there will be no "for ever after" with us but believe me when I tell you that, for the time we're together, I will take you to paradise and back. But before that…can I interest you in a shower?' He stood up and looked down at her slender perfection.

'With you?'

'Why not?' Lucas raised his eyebrows. 'You'd be surprised how different an experience it can be when you're in a shower with your lover.'

Katy shivered pleasurably at that word…*lover.* She shook her head and laughed. 'I think I'm going to relax here for a bit, then I'll go back to my cabin.'

Of course there would be no 'for ever after'…and she was tempted to tell him that she understood that well enough without having to be reminded of it.

'Why?' Lucas frowned and then heard himself inviting her to stay with him, which was astonishing, because he had always relished his privacy, even when

he was involved with someone. Sex was a great outlet, and his appetite for it was as healthy as the next
man's, but when the sex was over his craving for his
own space always took precedence over post-coital
closeness. He'd never spent the night with a woman.

'Because I need to be on my own for a bit.'

Right then, Lucas felt that by the time they were
ready to leave this yacht he would have introduced
her to the joys of sharing showers and shown her how
rewarding it could be to spend the night in his bed...

Katy had fallen into something of a sleep when she
heard the bang on the door to her cabin. For the first
time since she had arrived on Lucas's cruiser, she had
retired to bed without anything to eat, but then it had
been late by the time she had eventually left his cabin.

Having intended to sneak out while he was showering, she had remained where she was and they had
spent the next few hours in one another's arms. To his
credit, he had not tried to initiate sex again.

'I can show you a lot of other ways we can satisfy
one another,' he had murmured, and he had proceeded
to do just that.

In the end, *she* had been the one whose body had
demanded more than just the touch of his mouth and
the feel of his long, skilful fingers. *She* had been the
one to guide him into her and to demand that he come
inside her.

It had been a marathon session and she had made
her way back to her cabin exhaustedly, still determined not to stay the night in his room, because if
she slept in her own bed then she would somehow be
able to keep control of the situation.

'Katy! Open up!'

Katy jerked up with a start at the sound of Lucas's voice bellowing at her through the locked door. She leapt out of the bed, half-drugged with sleep, and yanked open the door, every fibre in her body responding with panic to the urgency in his voice.

She looked at him in consternation. He was in a pair of jeans and a black, figure-hugging tee-shirt. Not the sort of clothes anyone would consider wearing for a good night's sleep. Her already panicked antennae went into overdrive.

'Lucas! What time is it?'

'You need to get dressed immediately. It's a little after five in the morning.'

'But why?'

'Don't ask questions, Katy. Just do it.' He forged into the room and began opening drawers, yanking out a pair of jeans, quickly followed by the first tee-shirt that came to hand. Even at that hour in the morning, it would be balmy outside. 'Maria is sick.' He looked at his watch. 'Very sick. It has all the makings of acute appendicitis. Any delay and peritonitis will kick in, so you need to dress and you need to dress fast. I can't leave you on this yacht alone.'

Katy dashed into the bathroom and began stripping off the oversized tee-shirt she slept in, replacing it with the jeans and tee-shirt she had grabbed from his outstretched hand.

'Do you think I might get up to no good if you're not around to keep an eye on me?' she asked breathlessly, only half-joking because that deeply intimate step she had taken with him had clearly not been a deeply intimate step for him. He was a man who could detach, as he had made perfectly clear.

'Not now, Katy.'

'How will we get her to the hospital?' She flushed, ashamed that her thoughts had not been one hundred percent on the woman of whom she had grown fond during the short time she had been on the yacht.

'Not by helicopter,' Lucas told her, his every movement invested with speed as he took her arm and began leading her hurriedly out of the bedroom. 'Too long to get my pilot here and nowhere to land near the hospital.'

They were walking quickly to a part of the yacht Katy hadn't known existed, somewhere in the bowels of the massive cruiser.

'Fortunately, I am equipped to deal with any emergency. And to answer your earlier question…' He briefly glanced down at her, rosy, tousled and so utterly adorable that she literally took his breath away. 'I'm not taking you with me because I think you might get up to no good in my absence. I'm taking you with me because if something happened to you and I wasn't around I would never forgive myself.'

Something flared inside her and she felt a lump in her throat, then she quickly told herself not to be an idiot, because that wasn't a declaration of caring; it was a simple statement of fact. If she was left alone on the yacht and she needed help of any sort, she would be unable to swim to shore and unable to contact him. How would he, or anyone in his position, be able to live with that?

Things were happening at the speed of light now. In a move she thought was as impressive as a master magician's sleight of hand, the side of the yacht opened up to reveal a speedboat, an expensive toy within an expensive toy. Maria, clearly in a great deal of pain but smiling bravely, was waiting for them and was soon ensconced, to be taken to the island.

Dawn was breaking as they hit the island, a rosy, blushing dawn that revealed lush trees and flowers and narrow, winding roads disappearing up sloping hills.

A car was waiting for them, a four-wheel drive with an elderly man behind the wheel. They reached the town in under half an hour and then Maria was met in Accident and Emergency and whizzed through in a wheelchair, everything moving as though orchestrated.

Katy had barely had time to draw breath. Only when the older woman had been wheeled into the operating theatre, and they were sitting in the small hospital café with a cup of coffee in front of them, did she begin to pay attention to her surroundings… and then it registered.

'Your name is all over this hospital…'

Lucas shifted uncomfortably and glanced around him. 'So it would seem.'

'But why?'

'My money went towards building most of it.' He shrugged, as though that was the most natural response in the world. 'My father's family owned a villa here and he spent his holidays on the island with my mother and me when I was very young. It's about the only thing my father didn't end up giving away to one of the ex-wives who fleeced him in their divorce proceedings. I expect he had strong sentimental attachments to it. There was a prolonged period when the villa got very little use but, as soon as I was able, I began the process of renovation. I have the money, so when the head of the hospital came to me for help it was only natural for me to offer it.'

It felt odd to be offering her this slither of personal information and for a few seconds he was uncomfortable with what felt like a loss of his prized self-control.

What was it about this woman that made him behave out of character? Not in ways that should be disconcerting, because she neither said nor did anything that raised red flags, but still...

He was intensely private, not given to sharing. However, this was the first time he had been on the island with any woman. He rarely came here but, when he did, he came on his own, relishing the feeling of being swept back to happier times. Was Katy's necessary presence here the reason why he was opening up? And why was he making a big deal of it anyway? he thought with prosaic irony. She couldn't help but have noticed his name on some of the wards, just as she couldn't have failed to notice how eager the staff were to please.

'The old hospital, which was frankly far from perfect, was largely destroyed some time ago in a storm. I made sure that it was rebuilt to the highest specification. The infrastructure here is not complex but it is essential it all works. The locals depend on exporting produce, and naturally on some tourism. The tourists, in particular, are the wealthy sort who expect things to run like clockwork. Including the hospital, should one of them decide to take ill.' He grinned. 'There's nothing more obnoxious than a rich tourist who finds himself inconvenienced.'

'And I'm guessing you don't include yourself in that category?' Katy teased. Their eyes met; butterflies fluttered in her tummy and her heart lurched. They hadn't had a chance to talk about what had happened because she had disappeared off to her own quarters, and here they were now, caught up in unexpected circumstances.

She had no idea whether this was something that would be more than a one-night stand. She hoped it was. She had connected with him and she would feel lost if the connection were abruptly to be cut. It panicked her to think like that but she had to be honest with herself and admit that Lucas was not the man she had originally thought he was. He still remained the last person on earth she could ever contemplate having an emotional relationship with, but he had shown her the power of a sexual relationship and, like a starving person suddenly led to a banquet, she didn't want the experience to end. Just yet.

But nothing had been said and she wasn't going to engineer round to the conversation.

'Do *you* think I'm obnoxious?' Lucas questioned softly and she blushed and squirmed, so very aware of those dark eyes fastened to her face.

'My opinion of you *has* changed,' Katy admitted, thinking back to the ice-cold man who had forced her hand for the sake of a deal. She thought that her opinion also *kept* changing. She didn't want to dwell on that, so instead she changed the subject. 'What about Maria? When will we find out what the outcome is?'

'There's every chance it will be a positive one.'

Lucas glanced at his watch. 'I personally know the surgeon and there's no one better. I've contacted her family, who will be in the waiting area, and as soon as the operation is over I've asked to be called. I don't anticipate any problems at all. However...'

'However?'

'It does mean that there will be a small change of plan.'

'How do you mean?'

'We will no longer be based on the yacht. For a start, without Maria around, there will be no one to attend to the cooking and all the other little things she takes care of, and it's too late to find a replacement who can stay on board. So we'll have to relocate to my villa. I can get someone to come in on a daily basis and, furthermore, I will be on hand in case there are any complications following surgery.'

He paused. 'Maria worked for my father before he...began steadily going off the rails. My mother was very fond of her, so I've made sure to look out for her and her family, and also made sure to carry on employing her in some capacity when my father's various wives decided that they would rather have somewhat smarter people holding the fort in the various properties.'

His mobile phone buzzed and he held up one hand as he spoke in rapid Italian to the consultant, the concerned lines on his face quickly smoothing over in reaction to whatever was being said on the other end.

'All's gone according to plan,' he said. 'But, had she not reached the hospital when she did, then it would have been quite a different story. Now, why don't you wait here while I have a word with some of her family? I won't be long. I'll also arrange for your clothes and possessions to be transported to the villa.' He looked at her, head tilted to one side, then he patted his pocket. 'You can call your parents, if you like,' he said gruffly. 'I've been checking your phone, and I see that they've taken you at your word and not texted, but I expect they'd like to hear from you.'

He handed over the phone and her eyes shone, because more than anything else this demonstrated that he finally trusted her, and she found that that meant a great deal to her.

'What can I say to them?' she asked, riding high on the fact that she was no longer under suspicion. A barrier between them had been crossed and that felt good in the wake of what they had shared.

'Use your discretion,' Lucas told her drily. 'But it might be as well not to mention too many names, not that I think anything can go wrong with the deal at this stage. It's a hair's breadth away from being signed.' He stood up, leaving her with her mobile phone, and it felt like the greatest honour bestowed on her possible. 'I'll see you shortly and then we'll be on our way.'

CHAPTER SEVEN

LYING ON THE wooden deckchair by the side of the infinity pool that graced the lush grounds of his villa and overlooked the distant turquoise of the ocean, Lucas looked at Katy as she scythed through the water with the gracefulness of a fish.

The finalising of the deal had taken slightly longer than Lucas had anticipated, but he wasn't complaining. Indeed, he had encouraged his Chinese counterparts to take their time in sorting out all the essential details on which the takeover pivoted. In the meantime...

Katy swam to the side of the pool and gazed at him with a smile.

Up above, the sun had burnt through the early-morning clouds to leave a perfectly clear, milky, blue sky. Around them, the villa afforded absolute isolation. It was ringed with trees and perched atop a hill commanding views of the sea. Lucas had always valued his privacy and never more so than now, when he didn't want a single second of his time with her interrupted by so much as a passing tradesman. Not that any passing tradesman would be able to make it past the imposing wrought-iron gates that guarded the property.

He had dismissed all help, ensuring that the villa was stocked with sufficient food for their stay.

Just him…and her…

Right now, she was naked. He had half-expected, after that tentative surrender four days ago when she had placed her small hand on his thigh and sent his blood pressure through the roof, that a three-steps-forward, one-step-back game might ensue. He had predicted a tussle with her virtuous conscience, with lust holding the trump card, but in fact she had given herself to him without a trace of doubt or hesitation. He had admired her for that. Whatever inner battles she had fought, she had put them behind her and given generously.

'It's beautiful in here.' She grinned. 'Stop being so lazy and come and swim.'

'I hope that's not the sound of a challenge,' Lucas drawled, standing up, as naked as she was. He couldn't see her without his libido reacting like a lit rocket and now was no exception.

'Is sex *all* you ever think about, Lucas?' But she was laughing as she stepped out of the pool, the water streaming off her slick body.

'Are you complaining?' His eyes darkened and he balled his hands into fists. The urge to take her was so powerful it made him feel faint. He wanted to settle her on a towel on the ground and have her hard and fast, like a teenager in the grip of too much testosterone. Around her he lost his cool.

'Not at the moment,' Katy said breathlessly, walking straight into his arms. They had a lot of sex but, in fact, they also talked as well, and laughed, and enjoyed a level of compatibility she would never have thought possible when she had first met him.

He was still the most arrogant man she had ever met but there was so much more to him as well. She had no idea what was going to happen when they returned to London and she didn't think about it. Maybe they would carry on seeing one another...although how that would work out when she was his employee she couldn't quite fathom. The gossip would be out of control and he would loathe that.

For the first time in her life, Katy was living in the moment, and she wasn't going to let fear of what might or might not lie round the corner destroy her happiness.

Lucas cupped her pert bottom, which was wet from swimming, and kneaded it between his hands, driving her closer to him so that his rock-hard erection pushed against her belly.

She held him, played with him, felt the way his breathing changed and his body stiffened. She couldn't stop loving the way he reacted to her. It made her feel powerful and sexy and very, very feminine.

'I'm too big for deck-chair sex,' Lucas murmured.

'Who said anything about sex?' Katy breathed. 'We could just...you know...'

'I think I'm getting the picture.' He emitted a low, husky laugh and settled her on the cushioned deck chair, arranging her as carefully as an artist arranging a model he was about to paint, lying her in just the right place with her legs parted, hanging over either side of the chair, leaving her open for his attentive ministrations.

Then, sitting at the foot of the chair on his over-sized beach towel, he tugged her gently down towards his mouth and began tasting her. He slid his tongue into her, found the bud of her clitoris and licked it delicately, feathering little explosions of sensation through her, and he continued licking and teasing, knowing at which point she would begin to buck against his mouth as those little explosions became more and more impossible to control.

When he glanced up, he could see her small breasts, pointed and crowned with the dusky pink of her nipples, which were pinched from the water cooling on them. Her lips were parted, her nostrils flared as she breathed laboriously and her eyes were closed.

A thought flashed through his head. His condoms were nowhere to hand. What would happen if he were to sweep her up right now, hoist her onto him and let her ride them both to one of the body-shattering orgasms that they seemed strangely adept at giving one another? What if he were to feel himself in her without the barrier of a condom? Would it be such a bad thing? It wasn't as if pregnancy would be a certainty.

Shock at even thinking such a thing stilled him for a second. He'd never had thoughts like that in his life before and it implied a lack of self-control he found disturbing.

He killed the wayward thought that had sprung from nowhere and drove a finger into her, rousing her deep inside, and feeling her begin to spasm as she began to soar towards a climax.

She came against his mouth, arching up with an

abandoned cry of intense satisfaction, and then and only then did he allow her to touch him, with her mouth and with her hands.

The errant desire to take her without protection had been ruthlessly banished from his head but it left a lingering taste of unease in his mouth as they both subsided and flopped back into the pool to cool off.

Katy swam to Lucas but he stiffened and turned away, striking out into the water and rapidly swimming four lengths, barely surfacing for air as she watched from the side. He'd rejected her just then. Or maybe she'd been imagining it. Had she? He certainly hadn't done the usual and held her against him, coming down from a high with his body still pressed up against hers.

Sensitive to the fact that this was not a normal situation, that it was the equivalent of a one-night stand stretched out for slightly longer than the one night, Katy got out of the pool and walked over to her towel, anchoring it firmly around her so that she was covered up. Then she watched him as he continued swimming, his strong, brown body slicing through the water with speed and efficiency.

He didn't spare her a glance and after five minutes she retired to the villa and to the *en suite* bathroom which had been designated for her but rarely used, now she and Lucas were lovers.

The villa was magnificent, interestingly laid out with lots of nooks and crannies in which to relax, and huge, open windows through which breezes could circulate freely through the house. It lacked the slick sophistication of his yacht and was rather colonial in style with a stunning mixture of wood,

billowing muslin at the windows, shutters and overhead fans. Katy loved it. She settled with her book
into a rocking chair on the wide veranda that fronted
the villa.

She kept waiting for Lucas to show up but eventually she gave up and nodded off. It was a little after
four but still baking hot and, as always, cloudless.

Allowing her mind to drift, yanking it back every
time it tried to break the leash and worry away at
Lucas's reaction earlier on, she was scarcely aware of
time going by, and it was only when she noticed the
tell-tale signs of the sun beginning to dip that she realised that several hours must have passed.

In a panic, she scrambled to her feet and turned
round, to find the object of her feverish imaginings
standing framed in the doorway...and he wasn't smiling. Indeed, the humorous, sexy guy she had spent
the past week with was noticeably absent.

'Lucas!' She plastered a smile on her face. 'How
long have you been standing there? I was reading...
er... I must have nodded off...'

Lucas saw the hurt beneath the bright smile and he
knew that he had put it there. He had turned his back
on her and swam off, and he had carried on swimming because he had needed to clear his head. When
he'd finally stopped, she was gone and he had fought
against the desire to seek her out because he was not
going to allow a simple sexual liaison to get out of
control. When they returned to London, this would
finish and his life would return to normal, which was
exactly as it should be. So he'd kept his distance and
that would have upset her. He clenched his jaw and fo-

cused on what really mattered now, which was a turn of events that neither of them could have predicted.

'You've been talking to your parents. What, exactly, have you told them?'

'Lucas, I have no idea what you're talking about.'

'Just try and think.' He moved to stand in front of her, the beautiful lines of his handsome face taut and forbidding. 'Did you tell either of them where you were? What you were doing here? Who you were with?'

'I...you're making me nervous, Lucas. Let me think...no; *no*. I just told Mum that I was in Italy and that it was lovely and warm and that I was fine and having a good time...'

'I have just spent the past hour on the phone with the Chinese company. It seems that they were told by Powell that I was the wrong kind of person to be doing business with—that I was the sort of guy who seduces innocent girls and shouldn't be trusted as far as I can be thrown. It would seem that news travelled and connections were made. Someone, somewhere, figured out that we're here together and social media has taken the information right into Powell's hands and given the man ammunition to blow my deal sky-high at the last minute.'

The colour drained from Katy's face. When he said that 'connections were made', it was easy to see how. They had been into the little town several times over the past few days, checking on Maria and doing all sorts of touristy things. He could have been recognised and, whilst *she* wouldn't have been, someone could have sneakily taken a picture of them together and tagged them in something they posted online. The mind boggled.

'This is *not* my fault, Lucas. You know how pervasive social media is.' But it *was* her fault. She was the one with the connection to Duncan and, if gossip had been spread, then who knew what her mum might have mentioned to anyone in the village? Someone might be friends with Duncan on Facebook or whatever. Guilt pinked her cheeks, but before she could go on the defensive he held up one imperious hand to close down her protest.

'I'm not going to waste time going back and forth with this.' He frowned down at her and sighed. 'I'm not playing blame games here, Katy, and you're right: there's no privacy left anywhere. If anyone is to blame, then it's me, because I should have been more circumspect in my movements here. The place is small, I'm a well-known face, it's close to the busiest time of year for tourists and they have smart phones. But the fact remains that I have now been left with a considerable problem.

'No, perhaps I should amend that: when I say that *I* have a considerable problem, it might be fairer to say that we *both* have a considerable problem. Your ex approached Ken Huang and told him a story, and there's an underlying threat to go to the press and take public this sordid tale of a young, innocent girl being taken advantage of by an unscrupulous billionaire womaniser.'

Katy paled. 'Duncan wouldn't…'

But he would.

'He's played up your innocence to the hilt.'

'He knew…' Katy swallowed painfully. 'He knew

that I was inexperienced. I never thought that he would use the information against me. I trusted him when I confided in him.'

In the midst of an unfolding nightmare, Lucas discovered that the deal which should have been uppermost in his mind was overshadowed by a gut-wrenching sympathy for her vulnerability, which Powell had thoroughly taken advantage of.

Lucas dragged over a chair to join hers and sat heavily, closing his eyes for a few seconds while he sifted through the possibilities for damage limitation. Then he looked at her.

'The man has an axe to grind,' Lucas stated flatly. 'Tell me why.'

'Does it matter?'

'In this instance, everything matters. If I need to use leverage, then I need to know where to apply it. I don't play dirty but I'm willing to make an exception in this case.'

'It ended really badly between me and Duncan.' She shot him a guilty, sidelong look before lowering her eyes. 'As you may have gathered. It wouldn't have been so bad if I'd found out about his wife and children *after* I'd slept with him, but I think he was doubly enraged that, not only did I find out that he was married, but he hadn't even succeeded in getting me into bed *before* I'd had a chance to find out.'

'Some men are bastards,' Lucas told her in a matter-of-fact voice. 'It has to be said that some women leave a lot to be desired as well. It's life.'

'You mean those women your father married,' Katy murmured, distracted, thinking that on some level their approaches to life had been similarly tarnished by unfortunate experiences with the opposite sex. It was easy to think that, because you came from a wildly different background from someone, the things that affected the decisions you made had to be different, but that wasn't always the case. Money and privilege had been no more guarantee of a smooth ride in his case than a stable family background had been in hers.

Lucas shrugged. 'I have no more time for the gold-diggers,' he gritted. 'At least a guy with his head screwed on has a fighting chance of recognising them for what they are and can take the necessary precautions. You, I'm guessing, had no chance against a skilled predator. Continue.'

'I'd confided in my best friend,' Katy said, with a grimace. 'I felt such a fool. Claire was far more experienced than me, and she was livid when I told her about the messages I'd accidentally seen on his phone from his wife. He'd made a mistake in leaving it on the table while he vanished off to the toilet when we'd been having a meal out. Up popped a reminder to phone the kids to say good night and to remember some party they were going to on the weekend. He'd told me he was going to be away on business. Weekends, he'd always said, were tricky for him because he was trying to kick-start a photography business and they were the only times he could do whatever he had to do—networking and the like—because he was at the bank during the week.'

'A skilled excuse,' Lucas said drily. 'The man obviously came with form.'

'That was what Claire said. She told me that I was

probably not the first, which needless to say didn't make me feel at all better.'

It was as though she was looking at a very young, very naïve stranger from the advantageous position of someone who was much older and wiser. And she had Lucas to thank for that.

'Anyway, she started doing a little digging around. The world's a small place these days.' Katy grimaced. 'She found that he was a serial womaniser and she went to see his wife.'

'Ah.'

'I had no idea at the time that that was her plan, and afterwards she confessed that she didn't quite know what had prompted her to take such drastic action. But she was upset on my behalf and, in a weird way, upset on behalf of all the other girls he had conned into sleeping with him. His marriage fell apart on the back of that, so…'

'I'm getting the picture loud and clear. The ex who hates you and holds you responsible for the breakdown of his marriage now has the perfect vehicle for revenge put into his hands.'

'If I had told you the whole story in the first place, you would have realised that there was no chance I could have been any kind of mole. Then we wouldn't have ended up here and none of this would be happening now.'

Lucas smiled wryly. 'Really think that would have been how it would have worked?'

'No,' Katy answered honestly. 'You wouldn't have believed me. I would have been guilty until proven innocent.' At that point in time, he'd been a one-dimensional autocrat—ruthless, suspicious, arrogant. At this point in time…

She didn't know what he was and she didn't want to think too hard about it. They had a situation and she began to see all the nooks and crannies of it. If Duncan decided to take his revenge by publicising a tale of some sordid love tryst between Lucas and herself, not only would Lucas's deal be ruined but he would have to face the horror of the world gossiping about him behind his back. His reputation would be in tatters because, however much a lie could be disproved, mud inevitably stuck. He was the sort of guy who would claim to shrug off the opinions of other people, but that would be a heck of a lot to shrug off.

And it would all have been *her* fault.

Could she allow that to happen?

And then, aside from Lucas, there was the matter of her and her parents. They would never live it down. She felt sick thinking about their disappointment and the whispers that would circulate around the village like a raging forest fire blazing out of control. When she returned to see them, people would stare at her. Her parents would shy away from discussing it but she would see the sadness in their eyes.

She would be at the heart of a tabloid scandal: 'desperate virgin in sordid tryst with billionaire happy to use her for a few days before discarding her'. 'Sad and gullible innocent lured to a villa for sex, too stupid to appreciate her own idiocy'.

'Marry me!' she blurted out and then looked at him with wide-eyed dismay.

She jumped to her feet and began pacing the ve-

randa, before curling onto the three-seater wicker sofa
and drawing her knees up.

'Forget I said that.'

'Forget that I've received a marriage proposal?'
Lucas drawled, strolling over to the sofa and sitting
down, body angled towards her. 'It's the first I ever
have...'

'It wasn't a marriage proposal,' Katy muttered,
eyeing him with a glower, her cheeks tinged with
heated colour.

'Sure about that? Because I distinctly heard the
words "marry me".'

'It wasn't a *real* marriage proposal,' Katy clarified,
hot all over. 'It just seemed that...if Duncan does what
he's threatening to do—and I guess he will, if he's already started dropping hints to your client—then it's
not just that your deal will be jeopardised—'

'Ruined,' Lucas elaborated for good measure.
'Shot down in flames...dead in the water and beyond salvation...'

'All those things,' Katy mumbled, guilt washing
over her with tidal force. She breathed in deeply and
looked him directly in the eyes. 'It's not even a marriage proposal,' she qualified. 'It's an *engagement*
proposal. If we're engaged then Duncan can't spread
any rumours about sordid trysts and he can't take your
reputation away from you by implying that you're the
sort of womaniser who's happy to take advantage of...
of...an inexperienced young girl...'

He wasn't saying anything and she wished he
would. In fact, she couldn't even read what he was
thinking because his expression was so shuttered.

'Your deal can go ahead,' she plunged on. 'And you

won't have to worry about people gossiping about you behind your back.'

'That sort of thing has never bothered me.'

Katy almost smiled, because that was just *such* a predictable response, then she thought about people gossiping about him and her heart clenched.

'What's in it for you?' Lucas asked softly.

'Firstly,' Katy told him with absolute honesty, 'You're here because of me, so this is pretty much my fault. Secondly, I know how much this deal means to you. Thirdly, it's not just about you. It's also about me. My parents would be devastated and I can't bear the thought of that. And *you* might not care about what other people think of you, but *I* care what other people think of me. I wouldn't be able to stay on at either of my jobs because of the shame, and I would find it really hard to face people at home who have known me all my life.'

It was slowly dawning on her that there had been something in his softly spoken words when he had asked her what would be in it for her, something she hadn't registered immediately but which she was registering fast enough now.

'It would work.' She tilted her chin at a defiant angle to rebut the hidden insinuation she had read behind his words. She might have been wrong in her interpretation but she didn't think so. 'And it would work brilliantly because there's no emotional bond between us. I mean, there's no danger that I would get it into my head that I was doing anything but role-playing. You could get your deal done, we could defuse a potential disaster and I would be able to live with myself.'

'You're presenting me with a business proposition, Katy?' He dealt her a slashing smile that threatened to knock her sideways. 'You, the ultimate romantic, are presenting me with a business proposition that involves a phoney engagement?'

'It makes sense,' she defended.

'So it does,' Lucas murmured. 'And tell me, how long is this phoney engagement supposed to last?' He couldn't help but be amused by this from the girl who typified everything that smacked of flowers, chocolates, soul mates and walks up the aisle in a frothy, meringue wedding dress. Then he sobered up as he was struck by another, less amusing thought.

Had he changed her into something she was never meant to be? He had shown Katy the marvels of sex without strings because it was something that worked for him, but had he, in the process, somehow *changed* her? For reasons he couldn't explain, he didn't like the thought of that, but he pushed those uneasy reservations to one side, choosing instead to go for the straightforward explanation she had given, which was that it was a solution that would work for her as well as it would work for him.

Katy shrugged. 'You still haven't said whether you think it's a good idea or not.'

'I couldn't have come up with something better myself.' Lucas grinned, then looked at her seriously. 'But you should know that I wouldn't ask you to do anything you feel uncomfortable about.'

Katy's heart did that weird, clenching thing again. 'I feel very comfortable about this and, as for how long it would last, I haven't given much thought to that side of things.'

'You'd be deceiving your parents,' Lucas pointed out bluntly.

'I realise that.' She sighed and fiddled with the ends of her long hair, frowning slightly. 'I never thought that the ends justified the means, and I hate the thought of deception, but, between the devil and the deep blue sea, this seems the less hurtful option.'

Lucas looked at her long and hard. 'So we're a loved-up couple,' he murmured, his dark eyes veiled. 'And in fact, so irresistibly in love with one another that we escaped for some heady time to my yacht where we could be together free from interruption from the outside world. Your colleagues at work might find it a little hard to swallow.'

'You'd be shocked at how many people believe in love at first sight.' Katy smiled. 'You know, just because *you're* such a miserable cynic when it comes to love, doesn't mean that the rest of us are as well…'

'So now I'm a miserable cynic,' Lucas drawled, reaching out to tug her towards him. 'Tell me how likely it is that you would fall head over heels for a miserable cynic?'

'Not likely at all!' Katy laughed, looking up at him, and her heart did that funny thing again, skipping a beat, which made her feel as though she'd been cruising along quite nicely only to hit a sudden patch of violent turbulence. 'I'm afraid what you have is a girl who could only fall head over heels for someone as romantic as she is!' She frowned and tried to visualise this special person but the only face to fill her head was Lucas's dark and devastatingly handsome one.

'If we're going to be engaged, then we need to get

to know one another a whole lot better,' Lucas told her, still admiring the very practical streak which had led her to propose this very practical solution. Although, why should he be that surprised? She was a whizz at IT and that, surely, indicated a practical side to her that she herself was probably not even aware of.

He stood up, his fingers still linked with hers, and led her back through the villa and in the direction of his bedroom.

'What are you going to do with me once the engagement is over?' he murmured, toeing open his bedroom door, and then propelling her backwards to his bed while she tried to contain her laughter. 'I mean...' he lowered his head and kissed her, flicking his tongue into her mouth and igniting a series of fireworks inside her '... I'm assuming that, since you are the one with the clever plan to stage a fake engagement, you'll likewise be the one with the clever plan when it comes to wriggling out of it. So how will you dispose of me?'

He slid his hand under her tee-shirt and the warmth of her skin sent his body immediately into outer orbit. She wasn't wearing a bra, and he curved his big hand over her breast and gently teased her nipple until it was ripe and throbbing between his skilful fingers. They tumbled onto the bed, he settled her under him and straddled her so that he could see her face as he continued to tease her.

As usual, Katy's brain was losing the ability to fire on all cylinders, especially when he pushed up the tee-shirt and lowered himself to suckle her nipple. He looked up and caught her eyes, then flicked his tongue over the stiffened bud before devoting his attention to her pouting lips, kissing her again until she felt as though she was coming apart at the seams.

'Well?' He nuzzled the side of her neck and she wriggled and squirmed underneath him, hands on his waist, pushing into the waistband of his trousers and feeling his buttocks.

'Oh, I think we'll just drift apart,' Katy murmured. 'You know the sort of thing. You'll be working far too hard and you'll be spending most of your time in the Far East because of the deal you've managed to secure. I'll grow lonely and…who knows?…maybe I'll find some hunky guy to help me deal with my loneliness…'

'Not if I have any say in the matter,' Lucas growled, cupping her between her legs and rubbing until the pressure of his hand did all sorts of things through the barrier of her clothes.

'No,' Katy panted, bucking against his hand as she felt the stirrings of an orgasm building. 'I have to admit,' she gasped, her fingers digging into his shoulders, 'That finding another man wouldn't work, so perhaps you'll have to tire of me not being around and find someone else instead…'

And how she hated the thought of that although, she laughed shakily to herself, in the game of make-believe, what was the big deal? 'Let's not talk about this.' She tugged apart the button on his trousers and awkwardly tried to pull down the zipper. She looked at him and met his eyes. 'We can be engaged…for two months. Long enough to find out that we're not really compatible and short enough for no lasting damage.'

'You're the one calling the shots.' Lucas nipped her

neck, reared up and yanked off his shirt, before proceeding to undress her very, very slowly and, when she was completely naked, pushing apart her thighs and gazing down for a few charged seconds at her stupendous nudity. 'And I like it… Now, stop talking. It's time for action, my wife-to-be…'

CHAPTER EIGHT

KATY HAD A week to think about what would happen when they arrived back in London. The surprise announcement of their engagement had hit the headlines with the fanfare of a royal proclamation. Sitting in the little square in the island's town, whilst they sipped coffees in the sunshine, she had scrolled through the newspapers on her phone and read out loud some of the more outrageous descriptions of the 'love at first sight' scenario which Lucas had vaguely hinted at when he had called, firstly, the anxious Ken Huang and then his personal assistant, who had been instructed to inform various elements of the press.

Lucas had been amused at her reaction to what, for him, was not entirely surprising, considering the extent of his wealth and eligibility.

Now, finally on the way back to London, with the helicopter that had delivered them to his super-yacht due to land in under half an hour, the events of the past few days no longer felt like a surreal dream that wasn't quite happening.

It was one thing to read the centre pages of the tabloids and marvel that she was actually reading about herself. It was quite another to be heading straight into the eye of the hurricane where, she had been warned by Lucas, there might still be some lingering press attention.

'At least there's been some time for the story to calm down a bit,' he had told her. 'Although there's nothing the public loves more than a good, old-fashioned tale of romance.'

'Except,' Katy had quipped, 'A good, old-fashioned tale of a break-up.'

Lucas had laughed but, now that the story was out in the open, now that her parents had been told and had doubtless told every single person in the village and beyond, Katy was beginning to visualise the fallout when the phoney engagement came to an end. In short, her theory about the end justifying the means was beginning to look a little frayed at the edges.

She had spoken to her parents every single day since the announcement and had played fast and loose with fairy stories about the way her heart had whooshed the minute she had clapped eyes on Lucas, the second she had *known* that it was the real thing. They had wanted details and she had given them details.

Katy knew that she would have to face all sorts of awkward questions when this charade was over. No doubt, she would be an object of pity. Her parents would be mortified that yet again she had been short-sighted enough to go for the wrong guy. If they ever happened to meet Lucas in the flesh, then they would probably suss that he was the wrong guy before the fairy tale even had time to come crashing down.

The world would feel sorry for her. Her friends would shake their heads and wonder if there was something wrong with her. And, inevitably, there would be malicious swipes at her stupidity in thinking that she could ever have thought that a relationship with someone like Lucas Cipriani could ever last the distance.

Who did she think she was?

And yet she was happy to close the door on reality because the thrill of living for the moment was so intense. It ate everything up. All her incipient doubts, and all her darkest imaginings about what lay beyond that two-month time line they had agreed upon, were swept aside and devoured by the intensity of appreciating every single second she had with him.

The timer had been set and every feeling, every sensation and every response was heightened to an excruciating pitch.

'I have something to tell you.' Lucas pulled her towards him. It still surprised him the way he couldn't get enough of her. 'Tonight we will be the main event at a black-tie ball.'

Katy stared at him in consternation. 'Tonight?'

'The Chinese company's throwing it. It seems that Ken Huang is keen to meet you, as are all the members of his family—and, in all events, with signatures now being put to paper, it's a fitting chance to celebrate our engagement publicly as well as the closing of the deal. Your parents, naturally have been invited to attend, as have your friends and other family members. Have you got any other family, as a matter of interest?'

Katy laughed. 'Shouldn't you know that?'

'I should,' Lucas said gravely, 'But these things sometimes get overlooked in a hectic whirlwind romance.' She was wearing a little blue top and some faded cut-off jeans and, if they had been anywhere remotely private, he would have enjoyed nothing better than getting her out of both items of clothing.

'I've never been to a ball in my life before,' Katy confided, brushing aside her unease because not only would she have to mix with people she had no experience of mixing with but she would also be *on show*. 'It would be nice if Mum and Dad came, but honestly, I doubt they will. It wouldn't be their thing at all, and my dad's calendar is so packed with community stuff that he will struggle to free up the time without more advance warning.' She sighed and looked at him a little worriedly.

Lucas was overwhelmed by a sudden surge of protectiveness that came from nowhere and left him winded. He drew back slightly, confused by an emotion that had no place within his vocabulary. 'It's no big deal.'

'It's no big deal *for you*,' Katy told him gently. 'It's a huge deal *for me.*'

Lucas frowned. 'I thought everyone liked that sort of thing,' he admitted. 'There'll be a host of well-known faces there.'

Katy laughed because his self-assurance was so deeply ingrained that it beggared belief. 'Part of me didn't really think about how this would play out when we returned to London,' she admitted. 'It felt very… unreal when we were in Italy.'

'Yes it did,' Lucas agreed. 'Yet surely you would have expected a certain amount of outside attention focused on us…?'

He knew that this very naivety was something he

found intensely attractive about her. Having experienced all the trappings of extreme wealth for the past fortnight, she still hadn't joined the dots to work out what came as part and parcel of that extreme wealth, and intrusive media coverage at a time like this was one of those things. Not to mention a very necessary and unfortunately inevitable black-tie event. He decided that it would be unwise to mention just how much attention would be focused on her, and not just from reporters waiting outside the venue.

'You're going to tell me I'm an idiot.'

'I've discovered I quite like idiots.' He touched her thigh with his finger and Katy shivered and came close to forgetting all her apprehensions and doubts. They might be acting out a charade when it came to an emotional involvement with one another, or at least the sort of emotional involvement that came under the heading of 'love', but when it came to physical involvement there was no reporter who wouldn't be convinced that what they had was the real deal.

'When we get to the airfield, don't be surprised if there are one or two reporters waiting and just follow my lead. Don't say anything. I've given them enough fodder to be getting on with. They can take a couple of pictures and that'll have to do. In a week, we'll be yesterday's salacious gossip. And don't worry—you'll be fine. You never run yourself down, and you're the only woman I've ever met who gets a kick out of telling me exactly what she thinks of me. Don't be intimidated by the occasion.' He laughed and said, only partly in jest, 'If you're not intimidated by me, then you can handle anything.'

Buoyed up by Lucas's vote of confidence, Katy

watched as the door of the helicopter was pushed open to blue sky, a cooler temperature than they had left behind and a fleet of reporters who flocked towards them like a pack of wolves scenting a fresh kill.

Katy automatically cringed back and felt his arm loop through hers, gently squeezing her reassuringly as he batted aside questions and guided her towards the black car waiting for them.

A reporter yelled out asking to see the engagement ring. Katy gazed in alarm at her ring-free finger and began stumbling out something vague when Lucas cut into her stammering non-answer, drawing briefly to a halt and smoothly explaining that the jeweller's was going to be their first stop as soon as they were back in the city.

'But it won't be, will it?' she asked as soon as they were settled into the back of the car with the glass partition firmly shut between the driver and them.

'Do you think you're going to be able to get away without a ring on your finger at the ball?' Lucas said wryly. 'Brace yourself for a lot more attention than you got from those reporters back there at the air field.' He settled against the door, inclining his big body towards her.

She was waking up to life in *his world*. Not the bubble they had shared in the villa, and even more so on his yacht, where they'd been secluded and tucked away from prying eyes, but the real world in which he moved. She was going to be thrown into the deep end and it couldn't be helped. Would she be able to swim or would she flounder?

He had told her that she would be fine and again he felt it—that strong streak of protectiveness when he thought about her lost and trying to find her way in a world that was probably alien to her. He knew from experience that the people who occupied his world could be harsh and critical. He disliked the thought of seeing her hurt, even though the practical side of him knew that the disingenuousness that he found so intensely appealing would be a possible weakness under the harsh glare of real life, away from the pleasant bubble in which they had been cocooned.

'We can stop for a bite to eat, get freshened up at my place and then head out to the jeweller's, or else we can go directly there. And, on the subject of things to be bought, there'll be a small matter of something for you to wear this evening.'

'Something to wear...'

'Fancy. Long.' He shrugged. 'Naturally you won't be expected to foot the bill for whatever you get, Katy.' He wondered whether he should go with her, hold her hand.

Katy stilled and wondered how the insertion of money into the conversation could make the hairs on the back of her neck stand on end. It felt as though something was shifting between them, although she couldn't quite put her finger on what that *something* was.

'Of course.' Politeness had crept into her voice where before there had only been teasing warmth, and she didn't like it. But how could she pretend that things hadn't changed between them? They had embarked on a course of action that wasn't *real* and perhaps that was shaping her reactions towards him, making her prickly and on edge.

Yes, she was free to touch, but there were now in-built constraints to their relationship. They were supposed to project a certain image, and that image would require her to step out of her comfort zone and do things she wasn't accustomed to doing. She was going to be on show and Lucas was right—she wasn't in the habit of running herself down and she wasn't going to start now. If she was hesitant and apprehensive, then that was understandable, but she wasn't going to let sudden insecurities dictate how she behaved.

'I think I'd rather get the ring and the outfit out of the way, then at least I can spend the afternoon relaxing, although I don't suppose I'll have much time to put my feet up.' She sighed and said with heartfelt honesty, 'I never thought I'd be getting an engagement ring under these circumstances.' She looked at her finger and tried to think back to those days when she had stupidly believed that Duncan was the man for her. Then she glanced across at Lucas and shivered. He was so ridiculously handsome, so madly self-assured. He oozed sex appeal and her body wasn't her own when she was around him. When she was around him, her body wanted to be his and only his.

What if this were a real engagement, not some crazy charade to appease other people?

She was suddenly filled with a deep, shattering yearning for a real relationship and for everything that came with it. This time it wasn't just for a relationship to rescue her from making decisions about her future, which had been the reason she'd allowed herself to be swept away by fantasies about tying the knot with Duncan.

Time slowed. It felt so right with Lucas and yet he was so wrong. How was that possible? She had proposed a course of action that had made sense, and she had imagined she could handle it with cool and aplomb because what she felt for Lucas was lust and lust was a passing fever. But looking at him now, feeling his living, breathing warmth next to her... The time they had spent together flickered like a slow-motion movie in her head: the laughter they had shared; the conversations they had had; their lazy love-making and the soaring happiness that had engulfed her when she had lain, warm and sated, in his arms.

Katy was overcome with *wanting more*. She transferred her gaze blindly down to her finger and pictured that ring on it, and then her imagination took flight and she thought of so much more. She imagined him on bended knee...smiling up at her...wanting her to be his wife *for real* and not a pretend fiancée for two months...

She loved him. She loved him and he certainly didn't love her. Sick panic filled her at the horror that she might have opened the door for hurt, and on a far bigger scale than Duncan had delivered. Indeed, next to Lucas, Duncan was a pale, ineffectual ghost and obviously one who had not taught her any lessons at all.

Lucas noted the emotions flickering across her face and instantly barriers that had been carefully crafted over many years fell back into place. He didn't do emotion. Emotions made you lose focus, sapped your strength, made you vulnerable in ways that were destructive. Gold-diggers had come close to destroying his business, but it had been his father's own emotions that had finally let him down. Lucas could feel himself mentally stepping back and he had the oddest

feeling that just for a while there he had been standing too close to an inferno, the existence of which he
had been unaware.

He leaned forward, slid the glass partition to one
side and instructed the driver to deliver them to a jeweller Katy had never heard of but which, she guessed,
would be the sort of place to deal with very, very exclusive clients.

'Where are we?' she asked forty-five minutes later,
during which time Lucas had worked on his computer,
catching up on transactions he had largely ignored
while they had been in Italy, he'd told her without
glancing at her.

'Jeweller's,' he said. 'Stop number one.'

'It doesn't look like a jeweller's...'

'We wealthy folk like to think that we don't fre-
quent the sort of obvious places every other normal
person does,' Lucas said, back in his comfort zone,
back in control.

'Interesting story here,' he expanded as the car
drew to a smooth halt and the driver stepped out to
open the door for her. 'The woman who owns the
place, Vanessa Bart, inherited it from her father and
employed a young girl to work here—Abigail Chris-
tie. Long story but, to summarise, it turned out that
she had a child from my friend Leandro, unbeknown
to him, and like star-crossed lovers they ended up
meeting again quite by chance, falling in love and
getting married a while back.'

'The fairy tale,' Katy said wistfully as they were
allowed into a shop that was as wonderful as Alad-
din's cave. 'It's nice that it happens now and again.'
She smiled and whispered, 'There's hope for me yet.'

'Wrong sentiment for a woman on the verge of wearing an engagement ring from the man of her dreams.' Lucas's voice was less amused than he would have liked. He laughed shortly and then they were being ushered into the wonderful den of exquisite gems and jewels, tray after tray of diamond rings being brought out for her to inspect, none of them bearing anything so trashy as a price tag.

Lucas watched her down-bent head as she looked at the offerings. He was a man on the verge of an engagement and, whether it was phoney or not, he suddenly had that dangerous, destabilising feeling again…the sensation of getting close to a raging inferno, an inferno he couldn't see and therefore could not protect himself against. He shifted uneasily and was relieved when she finally chose the smallest, yet as it turned out one of the dearest, of the rings.

'Rest assured,' Katy said quietly as they were once again passengers in the back seat of the car, 'That I won't be taking the ring with me when this is all over.'

'Let's just live a day at a time.' Lucas was still unsettled and frankly eager now to get to his office where he wouldn't be inconvenienced by feelings he couldn't explain. 'Before we start deciding who gets what when we're dividing the spoils.'

'Where do we go for the dress?'

'Selfridges. I've already got my PA to arrange a personal shopper for you.'

'A personal shopper…'

'I have to get to my office, so will be unable to accompany you.'

As their eyes tangled, Katy felt the thrill of being

here next to him, even if that thrill was underlain with the presence of danger and the prospect of unhappiness ahead. 'I wouldn't expect you to come with me. I don't need you to hold my hand. If you let me have the name of the person I'm supposed to meet, then I can take it from there. And, after I've done all the other stuff I'm supposed to do, then I think I'm going to head back to my place and get changed there.'

Begin stepping away, she thought sadly. *Begin a process of detachment. Protect yourself.*

Lucas was already putting the romance of Italy behind him. There would be a ring on her finger, but he wasn't going to be hankering for all that undiluted time in each other's company they had had at his villa. He was slipping back to his reality and that involved distancing himself from her; Katy could sense that.

'Why?' Lucas realised that he didn't want her not to be around when he returned to his apartment. He wanted her to be there for him and he was irritated with himself for the ridiculous gap in his self-control.

'Because I want to check on my place, make sure everything's in order. So I'll meet you at the venue. You can text me the details.' She sounded a lot brisker than she felt inside. Inside, she wanted so much more, wanted to take without consequence, just as she wanted to give without thought. She wanted him to love her back and she wanted to shove that feeling into a box and lock it away to protect her fragile heart.

'You'll be nervous.' Lucas raked his fingers through his hair, for once on the back foot with his legendary self-control. 'There'll be reporters there.

You won't know what to do. You'll need me to be there with you, by your side.'

Where had that come from?

'But…' His voice as smooth as silk, he regained his footing. 'I see that you might want to check your place and check your mail.' He was back on familiar ground and he relaxed. 'We've got our lives to be getting on with.' He smiled wryly. 'Why kid ourselves otherwise? Don't worry. In a few weeks' time, this will be little more than something you will one day laugh about with your kids.'

'Quite,' Katy responded faintly, sick with heartache, for which she knew that she had only herself to blame. 'I'll see you later.' She forced herself to smile and marvelled that he could be so beautiful, so cool, so composed when she was breaking up inside. But then, he hadn't crossed the lines that she had.

Katy had no idea where to start when it came to looking for something to wear to a black-tie event because she had never been to one in her life before, and certainly, in her wildest imagination, had never dreamt that she would be cast in the starring role at one. She had phoned her mother but, as predicted, it had been impossible at short notice, what with her father's community duties. She had promised that she would send lots of pictures. Now, suddenly, she felt quite alone as she waited for her personal shopper to arrive.

It took over two hours for a dress to be chosen and, no matter how much she told herself that this was all an act, she couldn't help wondering what it would feel like to be trying these clothes on for real, to parade for a man who returned her love, at an event that would celebrate a union that wasn't a charade.

The dress she chose was slim-fitting to the waist, with a back scooped so low that wearing a bra was out of the question, but with an alluringly modest top half that fell in graceful layers to the floor. When she moved, it swirled around her like a cloud, and, staring at the vision looking back in the mirror, she felt the way Cinderella might have felt when the wand had been waved and the rags had been replaced with the ball gown that would later knock Prince Charming off his feet.

Prince Charming, however, had left her thoroughly to her own devices. He was back in the real world and already distancing himself from her without even realising it.

The Fairy Godmother would have to come up with more from her little bag of tricks than ever to turn Lucas into anything more than a guy who had fancied her and had talked her into having sex with him. He would happily sleep with her until the designated time was over, and then he would shove her back into the nearest pumpkin and head straight back to the women he was accustomed to dating, the women who slotted into his lifestyle without causing too many ripples.

She had expected the car from earlier to collect her but when the driver called for her at home, punctual to the last second, and when she went outside, it was to find that a stretch limo was waiting for her.

She felt like a princess. It didn't matter what was real or what was fake, she was floating on a cloud. But that sensation lasted just until they arrived at the hotel and she spotted the hordes of reporters, the beautiful people stopping to smile and pose for photos and the crowds milling around and gaping, as though they were being treated to a live cabaret. The limo pulled to a slow stop and nerves kicked in like a rush of adrenaline injected straight into her blood system. She feared that she wouldn't be able to push her way through the throng of people.

Then, like magic, the crowd parted and she was looking at Lucas as she had never seen him before. Her eyes weren't the only ones on him. As one, everyone turned. He had emerged from the hotel and was impeccably dressed in his white dress shirt and black trousers, everything fitting like a dream. He was so breathtakingly beautiful that Katy could scarcely bring herself to move.

The scene was borderline chaos, with guests arriving, cameras snapping, reporters jostling for prime position, but all of that faded into the background for Lucas as his eyes zeroed in on the open door of the limo and the vision that was Katy stepping out, blinking but holding her own as cameras flashed all around her.

Lucas felt a surge of hot blood rush through him. Of course she was beautiful. He knew that. He had known it from the very first minute he had set eyes on her in his office, but this Katy was a feast for sore eyes, and she held him captive. Their eyes met and he was barely aware of walking towards her, hand outstretched, gently squeezing her small hand as she placed it in his.

'You look amazing, *cara*,' he murmured with gruff honesty.

Nerves threatening to spill over, and frantically aware of the popping of camera bulbs and the rapt attention of people who were so far removed from her world that they could have been from another planet, Katy serenely gazed up at him and smiled in her most confident manner.

'Thank you, and so do you. Shall we go in?'

CHAPTER NINE

KATY HAD TO call upon every ounce of showmanship and self-confidence acquired down the years to deal with the evening.

Blinded by the flash of cameras, which was only slightly more uncomfortable than the inquisitive eyes of the hundred or so people who had been selectively invited to celebrate the engagement of the year, she held on to Lucas's hand and her fixed, glassy smile didn't waver as she was led like a queen into the hotel.

Lucas had told her that she looked amazing, and that buoyed her up, but her heart was still hammering like a drum beating against her ribcage as she took in the flamboyant décor of the five-star hotel.

It was exquisite. She had no idea how something of this calibre could be rustled up at a moment's notice, but then money could move mountains, and Lucas had oodles of it.

In a daze, she took in the acres of pale marble, the impeccable line of waiting staff in attendance, the dazzling glitter of chandeliers and an informal bar area dominated by an impressive ice sculpture, around which was an even more impressive array of canapés for those who couldn't wait for the waitresses to swing by. There was a buzz of interest and curiosity all around them.

'You'll be fine,' Lucas bent to murmur into her ear. 'After an hour, you'll probably be bored stiff and we'll make our departure.'

'How can we?' Katy queried, genuinely bewildered. 'Aren't *we* the leading actors in the production?'

'I can do whatever I like.' Lucas didn't crack a smile but she could hear the rich amusement in his lowered voice. 'And, if you feel nervous, rest assured that you outshine every other woman here.'

'You're just saying that...they'll all be wondering how on earth you and I have ended up engaged.'

'Then we'd better provide them with an explanation, hadn't we?' He lowered his head and kissed her. His hand was placed protectively on the small of her back and his mouth on hers was warm, fleeting and, oh, so good. Everything and everyone disappeared and Katy surfaced, blinking, ensnared by his dark gaze, her body keening towards his.

She wanted to cling and carry on clinging. Instead, she stroked his cheek briefly with her fingers and then stepped back, recalling the way he had reminded her earlier that what was happening here was just a show.

'Perhaps you could introduce me to the man you're doing the deal with.' She smiled, looking around her and doing her best to blank out the sea of beautiful faces. 'And thanks,' she added in a low voice, while her body continued to sizzle in the aftermath of that kiss. 'That was an inspired way to provide an explanation. I think you're going to be far better at this than I could ever hope to be.'

'I'll take that as a compliment,' Lucas drawled, wanting nothing more than to escort her right back into his limo and take her to his bed. 'Although I'm not entirely sure whether it was meant to be. Now, shall we get this party started?'

Having been introduced to Ken Huang, who was there with his family and two men who looked very much like bodyguards, Katy gradually edged away from the protective zone around Lucas.

Curiosity warred with nerves and won. She was surrounded by the beautiful people you saw in the gossip magazines and, after a while, she found that she was actually enjoying the experience of talking to some of those famous faces, discovering that they were either more normal than she had thought or far less so.

Every so often she would find herself drifting back towards Lucas but, even when she wasn't by his side, she was very much aware of his dark gaze on her, following her movements, and that made her tingle all over. There was something wonderfully possessive about that gaze and she had to constantly stop herself from luxuriating in the fallacy that it was heartfelt rather than a deliberate show of what was expected from a man supposedly in love with the woman wearing his ring.

Katy longed to glue herself to his side but she knew that circulating would not only remind Lucas that she was independent and happy to get on with the business of putting on a good show for the assembled crowd, just as he was, but would also shore up the barriers she knew she should mentally be erecting between them.

Everything had been so straightforward when she had been living with the illusion that what she felt for him was desire and nothing more.

With that illusion stripped away, she felt achingly vulnerable, and more than once she wondered how she was going to hold on to this so-called relationship for the period of time they had allotted to it.

In theory, she would have her window, during which she could allow herself to really enjoy him, even if she knew that her enjoyment was going to be short-lived.

In practice, she was already quailing at the prospect of walking away from him. He would probably pat her on the back and tell her that they could remain good friends. The truth was that she wasn't built to live in the moment, to heck with what happened next. Investing in a future was a by-product of her upbringing and, even though she could admit to the down side of that approach, she still feverishly wondered whether she would be able to adopt the right attitude, an attitude that would allow her to live from one moment to the next.

Thoughts buzzing in her head like a horde of hornets released from their nest, she swirled the champagne in her glass and stared down at the golden liquid while she pictured that last conversation between them. She dearly wished that she had the experience and the temperament to enjoy what she had now, instead of succumbing to dark thoughts about a future that was never going to be.

From across the crowded room, Lucas found his fiancée with the unerring accuracy of a heat-seeking missile. No matter where she was, he seemed to possess the uncanny ability to locate her. She wasn't taller than everyone else, and her outfit didn't stand out as being materially different from every other fancy long, designer dress, but somehow she emanated a light that beckoned to him from wherever she was. It was as if he was tuned into her on a wave length that was inaudible to everyone except him.

Right now, and for the first time that evening, she was on her own, thoughtfully staring down into a flute of champagne as though looking for answers to something in the liquid.

Abruptly bringing his conversation with two top financiers to an end, Lucas weaved his way towards her, approaching her from behind.

'You're thinking,' he murmured, leaning down so that he could whisper into her ear.

Katy started and spun round, and her heart began to beat faster. *Thud, thud, thud.*

She had shyly told the three colleagues who'd been invited to the ball about Lucas, glossing over how they had met and focusing instead on how they had been irresistibly drawn towards one another.

'You know how it is,' she had laughed coquettishly, knowing that she was telling nothing but the absolute truth, 'Sometimes you get hit by something and, before you know it, you're going along for the ride and nothing else matters.'

Lucas's stunning eyes on her now really did make her feel as though she had been hit head-on by a speeding train and she had to look down just in case he caught the ghost of an expression that might alert him to the way she really felt about him.

'Tired?' Lucas asked, drawing her towards the dance floor.

A jazz band had been playing for the past forty-five minutes, the music forming a perfect backdrop to the sound of voices and laughter. The musicians were on a podium, in classic coat and tails, and they very much looked as though they had stepped straight out of a twenties movie set.

'A little,' Katy admitted. His fingers were linked through hers and his thumb was absently stroking the side of hers. It made her whole body feel hot and she was conscious of her bare nipples rubbing against the silky fabric of her dress. The tips were stiff and sensitive and, the more his thumb idly stroked hers, the more her body went into melt down.

This was what he did to her and she knew that if she had any sense at all she would enjoy it while she had it. Instead of tormenting herself with thoughts of what life would be like when he disappeared from it, she should be relishing the prospect of climbing into bed with him later and making love until she was too exhausted to move a muscle.

'It's really tiring talking to loads of people you don't know,' she added breathlessly as he drew her to the side of the dance floor and turned her to face him.

The lighting had been dimmed and his gorgeous face was all shadows and angles.

'But you've been doing a pretty good job of it,' Lucas assured her with a wry smile. 'And here I was imagining that you would be a little out of your depth.'

Katy laughed, eyes dancing as she looked up at him. 'That must have been a blessed relief for you.'

'What makes you say that?' After spending the

past hour or so doing the rounds, Lucas felt relaxed for the first time that evening. No one had dared ask him any direct questions about the engagement that had sprung from nowhere, and he had not enlightened anyone, aside from offering a measured explanation to Ken Huang and his wife, both of whom, he had been amused to note, were full of praise for the romance of the situation. He had thought them far too contained for flowery congratulations but he'd been wrong on that point.

Under normal circumstances, he would have used the time to talk business. There were a number of influential financiers there, as well as several political figures with whom interesting conversations could have been initiated. However, his attention had been far too taken up with Katy and following her progress through the room.

People were keen to talk to her; he had no idea what she'd told them, but whatever it was, she had obviously struck the right note.

With women and men alike. Indeed, he hadn't failed to notice that some of the men had seemed a lot busier sizing her up than listening to whatever she had had to say. From a distance, Lucas had had to swallow down the urge to muscle in on the scene and claim his property—because she wasn't his and that was exactly how it ought to be. Possessiveness was a trait he had no time for and he refused to allow it to enter into the arrangement they had between them.

But several times he had felt his jaw tighten at the way her personal space had been invaded by men who probably had wives or girlfriends somewhere in the room, creeps with fancy jobs and flash cars who figured that they could do what they wanted with whomever they chose. Arrangement or no arrangement, Lucas had been quite prepared to land a punch if need be, but he knew that not a single man in the room would dare cross him by overstepping the mark.

Still.

Had she even noticed the over-familiarity of some of those guys? Should he have warned her that she might encounter the sort of men who made her odious ex pale in comparison?

'I can't imagine you would have wanted to spend the evening holding my hand,' she teased with a catch in her voice. 'That kiss of yours did the trick, and I have to say no one expressed any doubt about the fact that the most unlikely two people in the world decided to get engaged.'

'Even the men who had their eyes on stalks when they were talking to you?'

Katy looked at him, startled. 'What on earth are you talking about?'

'Forget it,' Lucas muttered gruffly, flushing.

'Are you *jealous*?'

'I'm not the jealous type.' He downed his whisky in one long swallow and dumped the empty glass, along with her champagne flute, on a tray carried by one of the glamorous waitresses who seemed to know just where to be at the right time to relieve important guests of their empty glasses.

'No.' Katy was forced to agree because he really wasn't, and anyway, jealousy was the domain of the person who actually *felt* something. She smiled but it was strained. 'No need to point out the obvious!'

Lucas frowned even though she was actually saying all the right things. 'That kiss, by the way,' he murmured, shifting his hand to cup the nape of her neck, keen to get off a subject that was going nowhere, 'Wasn't just about making the right impression.'

'It wasn't?'

'Have you stopped to consider that I might actually have wanted to kiss you?'

Katy blushed and said with genuine honesty, 'I thought it was more of a tactical gesture.'

'Then you obviously underestimated the impact of your dress,' Lucas delivered huskily. 'When I saw you get out of the back of my limo, my basic instinct was to get in with you, slam the door and get my driver to take us back to my apartment.'

'I don't think your guests would have been too impressed.' But every word sent a powerful charge of awareness racing through her already heated body. He was just talking about sex, she told herself weakly. Okay, so he was looking at her as though she was a feast for the eyes, but that had nothing to do with anything other than desire.

Lucas was excellent when it came to sex. He was just lousy when it came to emotion. Not only was he uninterested in exploring anything at all beyond the physical, but he was proud of his control in that arena. If he had foresworn involvement on an emotional level because of one bad experience with a woman, then Katy knew that somehow she would have tried to find a way of making herself indispensable to him. A bad experience left scars, just as Duncan had left her with scars, but scars healed over, because time moved on and one poor experience would always end up buried under layers of day-to-day life.

But Lucas wasn't like that. He wasn't a guy who had had one bad experience but was essentially still interested in having a meaningful relationship with a woman. He wasn't a guy who, even deep down, had faith in the power of love.

Lucas's cynicism stemmed from a darker place and it had been formed at so young an age that it was now an embedded part of his personality.

'Do I look like the kind of man who lives his life to impress other people?' he asked, libido kicking fast into gear as his eyes drifted down to her breasts. Knowing what those breasts looked like and tasted like added to the pulsing ache in his groin. 'Quite honestly, I can't think of anything I'd rather do than leave this room right now and head back to my apartment. Failing that, rent a bloody room in the hotel and use it for an hour.'

'That would be rude.' But her eyes were slumberous as she looked at him from under her lashes. 'We should dance instead.'

'You think that dancing is a good substitute for having mind-blowing sex?'

'Stop that!' She pulled him onto the dance floor. The music's tempo had slowed and the couples who were dancing in the half-light were entwined with one another.

It was almost midnight. Where on earth had the time gone? Lucas pulled Katy onto the dance floor and then held her so close to him that she could feel the steady beat of his heart and the pressure of his body, warm and so, so tempting.

She rested her head on his chest and he curled his fingers into her hair and leant into her.

This was heaven. For the duration of this dance, with his arms around her, she could forget that she wasn't living the dream.

Lucas looked down and saw the glitter of the diamond on her finger. The ring had fitted her perfectly, no need to be altered. He had slipped it onto her finger and it had belonged there.

Except, it didn't. Did it?

They had started something in full knowledge of how and when it would end. Katy had proposed a course of action that had been beneficial to them both and at the time, which was only a matter of days ago, Lucas had admired the utter practicality of the proposal.

She had assured him that involvement was not an issue for either of them because they were little more than two people from different planets who had collided because of the peculiar circumstances that had hurled them into the same orbit.

They had an arrangement and it was an arrangement that both of them had under control.

Except, was it?

Lucas didn't want to give house room to doubt, but that ring quietly glittering on her finger was posing questions that left him feeling uneasy and a little panicked, if truth be known.

The song came to an end and he drew away from her.

'We should go and say goodbye to Huang and his family. I've spotted them out of the corner of my eye and they've gathered by the exit. Mission accomplished, I think.'

Katy blinked, abruptly yanked out of the pleasant little cloud in which she had been nestled.

For all that common sense was telling her to be wary of this beautiful man who had stolen her heart like a thief in the night, her heart was rebelling at every practical step forward she tried to take.

She should pull back, yet here she was, wanting nothing more than to linger in his arms and for the music to never end.

She should remember Duncan and the hurt he had caused because, however upset she had been—and she now realised it had been on the mild end of the scale—whatever she had thought at the time, it would be nothing compared to what she would suffer when Lucas walked away from her. But nothing could have been less important in that moment than her cheating ex. In fact, she could barely remember what he looked like, and it had been that way for ages.

She had weeks of this farce to go through! She should steel herself against her own cowardly emotions and do what her head was telling her made sense—which was appreciate him while she could; which was gorge herself on everything he had to offer and look for no more than that.

But her own silly romanticism undermined her at every turn.

She gazed up at him helplessly. 'Mission accomplished?'

'We did what we set out to do,' Lucas said flatly. 'You only spent a short while with Ken Huang and his family, but let me tell you that he was charmed by our tale of love at first sight.'

'Oh, good.' He had already turned away and she

followed him, hearing herself say all the right things to the businessman while sifting through her conflicting emotions to try and find a path she could follow. In a show of unity, Lucas had his arm around her waist lovingly, and she could see how thrilled Ken Huang and his wife were by the romance.

Mission accomplished, indeed.

'Time to go, I think.' Lucas turned to her the second Huang had departed.

'Where?'

'Where do you think? We're engaged, Katy. Getting my driver to deliver you back to your flat is a sure-fire way of getting loose tongues wagging.'

'We're going back to your place?'

'Unless you have a better idea?' He shot her a wolfish smile but this time her blood didn't sizzle as it would have normally. This time she didn't give that soft, yielding sigh as her body took over and her ability to think disappeared like water down a plughole.

Mission accomplished. It was back to business for Lucas, and for that read 'sex'. They would go to his apartment, like the madly in love couple they weren't, and he would take her to his bed and do what he did so very, very well. He would send her pliant body into the stratosphere but would leave her heart untouched.

'We need to talk.' Nerves poured through her. She couldn't do this. She'd admitted how she felt about Lucas to herself and now she couldn't see a way of continuing what they had, pretending that nothing had changed.

'What about?'

'Us,' Katy told him quietly, and Lucas stilled.

'Follow me.'

'Where are we going? I mean, I'd rather not have this conversation in your apartment.'

'I'm on nodding acquaintance with the manager of this hotel. I will ensure we have privacy for whatever it is you feel you need to talk about.'

The shutters had dropped. Katy could feel it in his body language. Gone was the easy warmth and the sexy teasing. She followed him away from the ball room, leaving behind the remaining guests. He had said his goodbyes to the people who mattered and, where she would have at least tried to circulate and make some polite noises before leaving, Lucas had no such concerns.

She hung back as he had a word with the manager, who appeared from nowhere, as though his entire evening had been spent waiting to see if there was anything he could do for Lucas. There was and he did it, leading them to a quiet seating area and assuring them that they would have perfect privacy.

'Will I need something stiff for this *talk*?' Lucas asked once the door was closed quietly behind them. On the antique desk by the open fireplace, there was an assortment of drinks, along with glasses and an ice bucket. Without waiting for an answer, he helped himself to a whisky and then remained where he was, perched against the desk, his dark eyes resting on her without any expression at all.

Katy gazed helplessly at him for a few seconds then took a deep, steadying breath.

'I can't do this.' She hadn't thought out what she was going to say but, now the words had left her mouth, she felt very calm.

'You can't do what?'

'This. *Us.*' She spread her arms wide in a gesture of frustration. His lack of expression was like an invisible force field between them and it added strength to the decision she had taken impulsively to tell him how she felt.

'This is as far as I can go,' she told him quietly. 'I've done the public appearance thing and I've had the photos taken and I... I can't continue this charade for any longer. I can't pretend that...that...'

Lucas wasn't going to help her out. He knew what she was saying, he knew why she was saying it and he also knew that it was something he had recognised over time but had chosen to ignore because it suited him.

'You love me.'

Those three words dropped like stones into still water, sending out ripples that grew bigger and bigger until they filled the space between them.

Stressed out, stricken and totally unable to tell an outright lie, Katy stared at him, her face white, her arms folded.

'I wish I could tell you that that wasn't true, but I can't. I'm sorry.'

'You knew how I felt about commitment...'

'Yes, I knew! But sometimes the heart doesn't manage to listen to the head!'

'I told you I wasn't in the market for love and commitment.' He recalled what he had felt when he had seen other men looking at her and then later, when his gaze had dropped to that perfect diamond on her finger, and something close to fear gripped him. 'I will *never* love you the way you want to be loved and the way you deserve to be loved, *cara.* I can desire you but I am incapable of anything more.'

'Surely you can't say that?' she heard herself plead in a low, driven voice, hating herself, because she should have had a bit more pride.

Lucas's mouth twisted. In the midst of heightened emotions, he could still grudgingly appreciate her bravery in having a conversation that was only ever going to go in a pre-ordained direction. But then she *was* brave, wasn't she? In the way she always spoke her mind, the way she would dig her heels in and defend what she believed in even if he was giving her a hard time. In the way she acted, as she had at an event which would have stretched her to the limits and taken her far out of her comfort zone.

'I can't feel the way you do,' Lucas said, turning away from her wide, green, honest eyes and feeling a cad. But it wasn't his fault that he just couldn't give her what she wanted, and it was better for him to be upfront about that right now!

And maybe this was a positive outcome. What would the alternative have been—that a charade born of necessity dragged on and on until he was forced to prise her away from him? She had taken the bull by the horns and was doing the walking away herself. She was rescuing him from an awkward situation and he wondered why he wasn't feeling better about that.

He hated 'clingy' and he didn't do 'needy' and a woman who was bold enough to declare her love was both. He should be feeling relieved!

'I've seen how destructive love can be,' he told her harshly. 'And I've sworn to myself that I would never allow it to enter my life, never allow it to destroy me.' He held up one hand, as though she had interrupted him in mid-flow when in fact she hadn't said a word.

'You're going to tell me that you can change me. I can't change. This is who I am—a man with far too many limitations for someone as romantic and idealistic as you.'

'I realise that,' Katy told him simply. 'I'm not asking you to change.'

Suddenly restless, Lucas pushed himself away from the desk to pace the room. He felt caged and trapped—two very good indications that this was a situation that should be ended without delay because, for a man who valued the freedom of having complete control over his life, *caged and trapped* didn't work.

'You'll meet someone…who can give you what you want and need,' he rasped, his normally graceful movements jerky as he continued to pace the room, only stopping now and again to look at her where she had remained standing as still as a statue. 'And of course, you'll be compensated,' he told her gruffly.

'I'm not following you.'

'Compensated. For what you've done. I'll make sure that you have enough money so that you can build your life wherever you see fit. Rest assured that you will never want for anything. You will be able to buy any house you want in any part of London, and naturally I will ensure that you have enough of a comfort blanket financially so that you need not rush to find another job. In fact, you will be able to teach full-time, and you won't have to worry about finding something alongside the teaching because you won't have to pay rent.'

'You're offering me money,' Katy said numbly, frozen to the spot and stripped bare of all her defences. Had he any idea how humiliating this was for her—

to be told that she would be *paid off* for services rendered? She wanted the ground to open up and swallow her. She was still wearing the princess dress but she could have been clothed in rags because she certainly didn't feel like Cinderella at the ball.

'I want to make sure that you're all right at the end of this,' Lucas murmured huskily, dimly unsettled by her lack of expression and the fact that she didn't seem to hear what he was saying. The colour had drained from her face. Her hair, in contrast, was shockingly vibrant, hanging over her shoulders in a torrent of silken copper.

'And of course, you can keep the ring,' he continued in the lengthening silence. 'In fact, I insist you do.'

'As a reminder?' Katy asked quietly. 'Of the good old days?'

The muscles in her legs finally remembered how to function and she walked towards him stiffly.

For one crazy, wild moment, Lucas envisaged her arms around him, but the moment didn't last long, because she paused to meet his eyes squarely and directly.

'Oh, Lucas. I don't want your money.' She felt the engagement ring with her finger, enjoying the forbidden thought of what it would feel like for the ring to be hers for real, and then she gently pulled it off her finger and held it out towards him. 'And I don't want your ring either.'

Then she turned and left the room, noiselessly shutting the door behind her.

CHAPTER TEN

BEHIND THE WHEEL of his black sports car, Lucas was forced to cut his speed and to slow down to accommodate the network of winding roads that circled the village where Katy's parents lived like a complex spider's web.

Since leaving the motorway, where he had rediscovered the freedom of not being driven by someone else, he had found himself surrounded on all sides by the alien landscape of rural Britain.

He should be somewhere else. In fact, he should be on the other side of the world. Instead, however, he had sent his next in command to do the honours and finalise work on the deal that had been a game changer.

Lucas didn't know when or how the thing he had spent the better part of a year and a half consolidating had faded into insignificance. He just knew that two days ago Katy had walked out of his life and, from that moment on, the deal that had once upon a long time ago commandeered all his attention no longer mattered.

The only thing that had mattered was the driving need to get her back and, for two days, he had fought that need with every tool at his disposal. For two days, Lucas had told himself that Katy was the very epitome of what he had spent a lifetime avoiding. She lived and breathed a belief in a romantic ideal that he had always scorned. Despite her poor experience, she nurtured a faith in love that should have been buried under the weight of disappointment. She was the sort of woman who terrified men like him.

And, more than all of that put together, she had come right out and spoken words that she surely must have known would be taboo for him.

After everything he had told her.

She had fallen in love with him. She had blatantly ignored all the 'do not trespass' signs he had erected around himself and fallen in love with him. He should have been thankful that she had not wept and begged him to return her love. He should have been grateful that, as soon as she had made that announcement, she had removed the engagement ring and handed it back to him.

He should have thanked his lucky stars that she had then proceeded to exit his life without any fuss or fanfare.

There would be a little untidiness when it came to the engagement that had lasted five seconds before imploding, and the press would have a field day for a week or so, but that hadn't bothered him. Ken Huang would doubtless be disappointed, but he would already be moving on to enjoy his family life without the stress of a company he had been keen to sell to the right bidder, and would not lose sleep over it because it was a done deal.

Life as Lucas knew it could be returned to its state of normality.

Everything was positive, but Katy had left him and, stubborn, blind idiot that he was, it was only when that door had shut behind her that he had realised how much of his heart she was taking with her.

He had spent two days trying to convince himself that he shouldn't follow her, before caving in, because he just hadn't been able to envisage life without her in it, at which point he had abandoned all hope of being able to control his destiny. Along with his heart, that was something else she had taken with her.

And now here he was, desperately hoping that he hadn't left everything too late.

His satnav was telling him to veer off onto a country lane that promised a dead end, but he obeyed the instructions and, five minutes later, with the sun fading fast, the vicarage she had told him about came into view, as picturesque as something lifted from the lid of a box of chocolates.

Wisteria clambered over faded yellow stone. The vicarage was a solid, substantial building behind which stretched endless acres of fields, on which grazing sheep were blobs of white, barely moving against the backdrop of a pink-and-orange twilit sky. The drive leading to the vicarage was long, straight and bordered by neat lawns and flower beds that had obviously taken thought in the planting stage.

For the first time in his life, Lucas was in a position of not knowing what would happen next. He'd never had to beg for anyone before and he felt that he might have to beg now. He wondered whether she had decided that replacing him immediately would be a cure for the pain of confessing her love to a guy who had sent her on her way with the very considerate offer of financial compensation for any inconvenience. When Lucas thought about the way he had responded to her, he shuddered in horror.

He honestly wouldn't blame her if she refused to set eyes on him.

He drove slowly up the drive and curled his car to the side of the vicarage, then killed the engine, quietly opened the door and got out.

'Darling, will you get that?'

Propped in front of the newspaper where she had been scouring ads for local jobs for the past hour and a half, Katy looked up. Sarah Brennan was at the range stirring something. Conversation was thin on the ground because her parents were both so busy tiptoeing around her, making sure they didn't say the wrong thing.

Her father was sitting opposite her with a glass of wine in his hand, and every so often Katy would purposefully ignore the look of concern he gave her, because he was worried about her.

She had shown up, burst into tears and confessed everything. She had wanted lots of tea and sympathy, and she had got it from her parents, who had put on a brave face and said all the right things about time being a great healer, rainbows round corners and silver linings on clouds, but they had been distraught on her behalf. She had seen it in the worried looks they gave one another when they didn't think she was looking, and it was there in the silences, where before there would have been lots and lots of chat and laughter.

'I should have known better,' Katy had conceded the evening before when she had finally stopped crying. 'He was very honest. He wasn't into marriage, and the engagement was just something that served a purpose.'

'To spare us thinking you were…were…' Her mother had stumbled as she had tried to find a polite way of saying *easy*. 'Do you honestly think we would have thought that, when we know you so very well, my darling?'

Katy could have told them that sparing them had only been part of the story. The other part had been her concern for Lucas's reputation. Even then, she must have been madly in love with him, because she had cared more about his reputation than he had.

She also didn't mention the money he had offered her. She felt cheapened just thinking about that and her parents would have been horrified. Even with Lucas firmly behind her, she still loved him so much that she couldn't bear to have her parents drill that final nail in his coffin.

The doorbell rang again and Katy blinked, focused and realised that her mother was looking at her oddly, waiting for her actually to do something about getting the door.

Her father was already rising to his feet and Katy waved him down with an apologetic smile. She wondered who would be calling at this time but then, for a small place it was remarkably full of people who urgently needed to talk to her parents about something or other. Just as soon as the cat was out of the bag, the hot topic of conversation would actually be *her*, and she grimaced when she thought about that.

She was distracted as she opened the door. The biggest bunch of red roses was staring her in the face. Someone would have to have wreaked havoc in a rose garden to have gathered so many. Katy stared down, mind blank, her thoughts only beginning to sift through possibilities and come up with the right answer when she noted the expensive leather shoes.

Face drained of colour, she raised her eyes slowly, and there he was, the man whose image had not been out of her head for the past two agonising days since they had gone their separate ways.

'Can I come in?' Unfamiliar nerves turned the question into an aggressive statement of fact. Lucas wasn't sure whether flowers were the right gesture. Should he have gone for something more substantial? But then, Katy hated ostentatious displays of wealth. Uncertainty gripped him, and he was so unfamiliar with the sensation that he barely recognised it for what it was.

'What are you doing here?' Katy was too shocked to expand on that but she folded her arms, stiffened her spine and recollected what it had felt like when he had offered to pay her off. That was enough to ignite her anger, and she planted herself squarely in front of him, because there was no way she was going to let him into the house.

'I've come to see you.'

'What for?' she asked coldly.

'Please let me in, Katy. I don't want to have this conversation with you on your doorstep.'

'My parents are inside.'

'Yes, I thought they might be here.'

'Why have you come here, Lucas? We have nothing to say to one another. I don't want your flowers. I don't want you coming into this house and I don't want you meeting my parents. I've told them everything, and now I just want to get on with my life and pretend that I never met you.'

'You don't mean that.'

'Yes. I do.'

Her voice was cold and composed but she was a mess inside. She badly wanted her body to do what her brain was urgently telling it to do, but like a runaway train it was veering out of control, responding to him with frightening ferocity. More than anything in the world, she wanted to creep into his arms, rest her head against his chest and pretend that her life wasn't cracking up underneath her; she hated herself for that weakness and hated him for showing up and exposing her to it.

She glanced anxiously over her shoulder. In a minute, she knew her father would probably appear behind her, curious as to who had rung the doorbell. Lucas followed her gaze and knew exactly what she was thinking. He was here and he was going to say what he had come to say and, if forcing his way in and flagrantly taking advantage of the fact that she wouldn't be able to do a thing about it because it would create a scene in front of her parents was what it took, then so be it.

What was the point of an opportunity presenting itself if you didn't take advantage of it?

So he did just that. Hand flat against the door, he stepped forward and pushed it open and, caught unawares, Katy fell back with a look that was part surprise, part horror and part incandescent rage.

'I need to talk to you, Katy. I need you to listen to me.'

'And you think that gives you the right to barge into my house?'

'If it's the only way of getting you to listen to me...'

'I told you, I'm not interested in anything you have to say, and if you think that you can sweet talk your way back into my bed then you can forget it!' Her voice was a low, angry hiss and her colour was high.

His body was so familiar to her that she was responding to him like an engine that had been turned on and was idling, ready to accelerate.

From behind, Katy heard her mother calling out to her and she furiously stepped aside as Lucas entered the house, *her sanctuary,* with his blasted red roses, on a mission to wreck her life all over again. No way was she going to allow her parents to think that a bunch of flowers meant anything, and she took them from him and unceremoniously dumped them in an umbrella stand that was empty of umbrellas.

'I should have bought you the sports car,' Lucas murmured and Katy glared at him. 'That wouldn't have fitted into an umbrella stand.'

'You wouldn't have dared.'

'When it comes to getting what I want, there's nothing I won't do.'

Katy didn't have the opportunity to rebut that contentious statement because her mother appeared, and then shortly after her father, and there they stood in the doorway of the kitchen, mouths round with surprise, eyes like saucers and brains conjuring up heaven only knew what. Katy shuddered to think.

And, if she had anticipated Lucas being on the back foot, the wretched man managed, in the space of forty-five minutes, to achieve the impossible.

After *everything* she had told her parents—after she had filled them in on her hopeless situation, told them that she was in love with a man who could never return her love, a man whose only loyal companion would ever be his work—she seethed and fumed from the sidelines as her parents were won over by a display of charm worthy of an acting award.

Why had Lucas come? Shouldn't he have been in China working on the deal that had ended up changing *her* life more than it had changed his?

He didn't love her and, by a process of common sense and elimination, she worked out the only thing that could possibly have brought him to her parents' house would be an offer to continue their fling. Lucas was motivated by sex, so sex had to be the reason he was here.

The more Katy thought about that, the angrier she became, and by the time her parents began making noises about going out for supper so that she and Lucas could talk she was fit to explode.

'How *dare* you?' That was the first thing she said as soon as they were on their own in the comfortable sitting room, with its worn flowered sofas, framed family photos on the mantelpiece and low coffee table groaning under the weight of the magazines her mother was addicted to. 'How *dare you* waltz into my life here and try and *take over*? Do you think for a moment that if you manage to get to my parents that you'll get to me as well?'

She was standing on the opposite side of the room to him, her arms folded, the blood running hot in her veins as she tried her hardest not to be moved by the dark, sinful beauty that could get to her every time.

It infuriated her that he could just *stand there,* watching her with eyes that cloaked his thoughts, leaning indolently against the wall and not saying anything, which had the effect of propelling her into hysterical, attacking speech. She was being precisely the sort of person she didn't want to be. If she wasn't careful, she would start throwing things in a minute, and she definitely wasn't going to sink to that level.

Lucas watched her and genuinely wasn't sure how to proceed. Where did you start when it came to talking about feelings? He didn't know because he'd never been there before. But she was furious, and he didn't blame her, and standing in silence wasn't going to progress anything.

'I really like your parents,' Lucas said, a propos of nothing, and she glared at him as though he had taken leave of his senses.

'You've wasted your time,' she told him flatly. 'I'm not interested in having another fling with you, Lucas. I don't care whether my parents fell in love with you. I want you to leave and I don't want to see you ever again. I just want to be left in peace to get on with my life.'

'How can you get on with your life when you're in love with me?'

Mortification and anger coursed through her, because just like that he had cut her down at the knees. He had taken her confession and used it against her.

'How can *I* get on with my life when I'm in love with *you*?' Lucas realised that he was perspiring. Sealing multi-million-pound deals were a walk in the park compared to this.

Thrown into instant confusion, Katy gaped, unwilling to believe him. If he'd loved her, he wouldn't have let her go, she thought painfully. He would have tried to stop her. He wouldn't have offered her money to compensate for all the other things he couldn't provide.

Lucas noted the rampant disbelief on her face, and again he couldn't blame her.

'You don't believe me and I understand that.' His voice was unsteady and he raked his fingers through his hair in an unusually clumsy gesture. 'I'd made it clear that I could never be interested in having the sort of relationship I knew you wanted. You were so...so *different* that I couldn't get my head around ever falling for you. I'll be honest—I could never get my head around falling for *anyone*. I'd always equated love with vulnerability, and vulnerability with being hurt.'

'Why are you telling me this?' Katy cried jerkily. 'Don't you think I don't know all that?' But the uncertainty on his face was throwing her off-balance, and hope was unfurling and blossoming fast, yanking the ground from under her feet and setting up a drumbeat inside her that was stronger than all the caution she was desperate to impose on herself.

'What you *don't* know is that you came along and everything changed for me. You made me feel...different. When I was around you, life was in Technicolor. I put it down to the incredible sex. I put it down to the fact that I was in a state of suspended animation, far from the daily demands of my office. I never put it down to the truth, which was that I was falling for you. I was blind, but then I'd never expected to fall in love. Not with you, not with any woman.'

'You mean it? Please don't say anything you don't mean. I couldn't bear it.' Was this some ploy to try and talk her into bed? He was right, the sex *had* been incredible. Was he working up to an encore by flattering her? But, when she looked at him, the discomfort on his face was palpable and it made her breathing shallow and laborious.

'You confused me. There were times when I felt disorientated, as though the world had suddenly been turned upside down, and when that happened I just told myself that it was because you were a novelty, nothing like what I was used to. But I behaved differently when I was around you. You made me say things I've never said to anyone else and I felt comfortable doing it.'

'But you didn't try and stop me,' Katy whispered. 'I told you how I felt and you…you let me walk away. No, worse than that, you offered me money.'

'Please don't remind me,' Lucas said quietly. Somehow, he had closed the gap between them, but he was still hesitant to reach out and touch her even though he badly wanted to do just that.

'You have to understand that money is the currency I'm familiar with, not love. My father was derailed after my mother's death. I grew up watching him get carried along on emotional riptides that stripped him of his ability to function, and that taught me about the importance of self-control and the need to focus on things that were constant. Relationships, in my head, were associated with frightening inconsistency and I wanted no part of that. The only relationship I would ever consider would be one that didn't impact on the quality of my life. A relationship with a woman who wanted the same sort of thing that I did.' He smiled wryly. 'Not an emotional, outspoken and utterly adorable firebrand like you.'

Katy liked all of those descriptions. She liked the expression on his face even more, and just like that her caution faded away and her heart leapt and danced and made her want to grin stupidly at him.

'Keep talking,' she whispered, and he raised his eyebrows and smiled at her.

'So here I am,' Lucas said simply. 'I'd worked like the devil for a deal that, in the end, won't mean anything if you aren't by my side. I think that was when I was forced to accept that the only thing that mattered to me was *you*. I should have guessed when I realised how protective you made me feel and how possessive. You make me the best person I could be, and that means someone who can be hurt, who has feelings, who's willing to wear his heart on his sleeve.' He pulled her towards him and Katy sighed as she was enveloped in a hug that was so fierce that she could feel the beating of his heart. He curled his fingers into her hair and tilted her face to deliver a gentle kiss on her lips.

'I never expected to fall in love with you either,' she admitted softly. 'I was so certain that I knew the sort of guy I should end up with, and it wasn't a guy like you. But it's like you fill in the missing pieces of me and make me complete. It's weird, but when I met Duncan I was looking for love, looking for that *something else*, but I wasn't looking for anything at all when I met you—yet love found me.'

'I know what you mean. I was comfortable *wanting* you because I understood the dynamics of desire. Strangely, loving you has made me understand how my father ended up becoming entangled in a series of inappropriate relationships. He was deeply in love with my mother and he wanted to replicate that. Before I met you, I just didn't get it, but then I never understood how powerful love could be and how it can turn a black-and-white life into something filled with colour and light.'

'And when I returned home,' Katy admitted, 'And I saw the interaction between my parents, I knew that I could never settle for anything less than what they have. I was so upset when you showed up because I thought you'd come to try and persuade me into carrying on with what we had. Maybe because of the deal, or maybe because you still fancied me, even though you didn't love me.'

'Now you know the real reason I turned up with those flowers that you dumped out of sight—you want the fairy-tale romance and I want to be the lucky person who gives it to you. Will you do me the honour of marrying me, my darling? For real and for ever?'

'Just try and stop me...'

EPILOGUE

KATY PAUSED AND looked at Lucas, who was standing staring out to the sea, half-naked because he enjoyed swimming at night, something he had yet to convince her to try.

There was a full moon and the light threw his magnificent body into shadow. To think that a little over a year ago she had come aboard this very yacht, kicking and screaming and accusing him of kidnapping her.

She smiled because that felt like a lifetime ago and so much had happened since then. The engagement that wasn't an engagement had turned into the real thing and they had been married, not once, but *twice.* There was a lavish affair, held a week after the actual wedding, where reporters had jostled for prime position and celebrities had emerged from limos dressed to kill for the event of the century. But first had come something altogether smaller, in her home village, where they had married at a ceremony officiated by her father at the picturesque local church. The reception there had been warm, small and cosy.

Lavish or cosy, Katy just knew that she was the happiest person in the world.

They had had their honeymoon in Italy, where they

had stayed with Lucas's father for a few days. Katy knew that she would be seeing a great deal more of Marco Cipriani, because he had got along with her parents like a house on fire, and plans were already afoot for him to discover the joys of the northern countryside at its finest at Christmas.

And she knew that during the festive season there would certainly be reason for a great deal of celebration.

'Lucas…'

Lucas turned, and his heart stopped just for a second as he watched the woman who had so taken over his life that contemplating an existence without her was unthinkable. He smiled, held his hand out and watched her walk towards him, glorious in a casual, long dress which he knew he would be removing later.

Katy walked straight into his open arms and then looked up at him with a smile. 'I have something to say… We both have eight months to start thinking of some names…'

'Names?'

'For our baby, my darling. I'm pregnant.' She tiptoed to plant a kiss on his very sexy mouth.

'My darling, perfect wife.' Lucas closed his eyes and allowed himself to be swept away in the moment before looking down at her with love. 'I never thought that life could get any better, but I do believe it has…'

* * * * *

BOUGHT TO CARRY
HIS HEIR

JANE PORTER

For Megan, Maisey and Carol—
three gorgeous girls I adore.

Thank you for the love and encouragement
when I needed it!

CHAPTER ONE

IT WAS A cold February afternoon in Atlanta, but the law office of Lyles, Laurent & Abraham at One Atlantic Center on West Peachtree Street was even more frigid.

The prominent Atlanta attorney James Laurent fiddled with his glasses, his expression withering. "You signed the contracts, Miss Nielsen. They are absolutely binding in every country—"

"I have no problem with the contract," Georgia interrupted, more annoyed than cowed by the attorney's icy contempt, because she was absolutely committed to carrying the baby only to relinquish him. That was the job of a surrogate, and she took the job seriously. "The baby is his. But there is nothing in the contract that stipulates where I am to give birth, nor was anything ever communicated to me in advance about giving birth overseas. I wouldn't have agreed to serve as Mr. Panos's surrogate if that had been the case."

"Miss Nielsen, Greece is not a third world country. You will receive excellent medical care in Athens before, during and after delivery."

She gave him a long look, hands relaxed on the arms of the leather chair, fighting to keep her temper in check. "I'm a med student at Emory. I'm not worried about my medical care. But I am disturbed by your condescension. If a mistake was made, it was your client's...or yours. You were, after all, the one who drew up the papers for the surrogacy. You know what the agreement covered. And it didn't cover me getting on a plane and flying five thousand six hundred and sixty-six miles to give birth."

"It's a citizenship issue, Miss Nielsen. The baby must be born in Greece."

Georgia Nielsen glanced past the attorney to the huge map that had been framed and hung on the wall of Mr. Laurent's office. It was an old map, a collector's item, and from the boundaries and labels, she'd guess it was from the late nineteenth century, the 1880s or maybe 1890s, with Africa divided by European colonial claims. But even old and yellowed, Greece was identifiable…right where it had been for thousands of years, giving birth to Western civilization.

And right where she was expected to give birth.

If Georgia were in a better mood, she might find it ironic. She might even be amused. But she wasn't in a good mood. She was furious and frustrated. From the start, she'd taken care of herself, paid close attention to proper health and the well-being of the baby. Her job as a surrogate was to bear a healthy baby, and she was doing her part. Eating right, sleeping as much as possible, getting lots of exercise and keeping stress to a minimum—not always easy when in medical school, but she had her priorities right. But going to Greece? And going soon? That was *not* on her agenda.

"The travel arrangements are being finalized as we speak," Mr. Laurent added. "Mr. Panos will send his personal jet for you. As you can imagine, the jet is state-of-the-art and quite luxurious. You'll have staff and a good rest, and before you know it, you'll be there—"

"I haven't even reached the third trimester. Seems to me that making travel plans now is incredibly premature."

"Mr. Panos would prefer not to place undue stress on you or the baby. Specialists do not recommend international travel in the third trimester."

"Yes, for high-risk pregnancies, but this isn't one."

"It is IVF."

"There have been no complications."

"And my client prefers to keep it that way."

Georgia bit her tongue to keep from saying something she might regret. She understood that Nikos Panos's concern was for the baby, his son. She understood, too, that her wants and needs did not factor in. She was a vessel…a womb…nothing more. As it should be until the very end, when she delivered a healthy baby and saw him placed in the arms of his protective father. That was when her job would be done. Then, and only then.

But that didn't mean she wanted to leave Atlanta or the world she knew. Going halfway around the world would be stressful. Leaving her support systems would be challenging, especially as she neared the end of the pregnancy. This was a job, a way to provide for her sister, but she wasn't totally naive. It was hard not to have any feelings for the life inside her, and those emotions were becoming stronger. Hormones were already shifting. She could only imagine how ambivalent she'd feel in another three and a half months.

But motherhood wasn't her future. Her future was medicine, and her course was set.

For a long moment there was just silence in the office.

Mr. Laurent pressed his fingers together, creating a tense steeple. "What will it take to get you on that plane this Friday?"

Ridiculous. There was no way she could go so soon. "I have school. I have studies."

"You have just finished the preclinical block. You are studying for the medical licensing exam, and you can study just as well in Greece as in Georgia."

"I'm not going to leave my sister for three and a half months."

"She's twenty-one and lives in North Carolina."

"Yes, she's a senior at Duke University, but she's financially and emotionally dependent on me. I am her only living relative." Georgia met his gaze and held it. "I am all she has left."

"And the child you carry?"

"Isn't mine." Her lips firmed. "Your client paid for the egg and the surrogacy, so if Mr. Panos wants to be present for the birth of his son, he can come to Atlanta. Otherwise, the baby's nurse will take the infant to him. As agreed."

"Mr. Panos is not able to fly."

Georgia lifted her chin, air bottled inside her lungs. She was not going to engage. She refused to be drawn into this. A contract was a contract. "That is not my concern. Your client is not my concern. Once I give birth, the infant is not my concern. I have been paid not to care, and, Mr. Laurent, I intend to keep my end of the bargain."

The attorney closed his eyes and rubbed at an invisible spot between his bushy gray eyebrows, bumping his glasses from his nose. For a moment the only sound in the room was the antique grandfather clock tick-ticking against the wall.

Mr. Laurent opened his eyes, fixed his gaze on her. "How much will it cost to get you on the plane on Friday? And before you say I'm not listening, I know everyone has a price. You do, too. It's why you agreed to donate the egg and carry the fertilized embryo. You were satisfied with the compensation. So, let's not bicker over the terms. Tell me what you need to get on that plane, and I will see that the money is wired into your account first thing in the morning."

Georgia stared at the older man, her serene expression hiding her anxiety, as well as her frustration. Yes, money was tight, but she didn't want more money. She just wanted to finish what she'd started. It had been a mistake to do this. She thought she'd manage as a surrogate, but lately she was finding it increasingly difficult to keep her emotions in check. But it was too late to back out now. There was no changing her mind, either. The contracts were binding. The child wasn't hers. And, yes, she carried him, and each little flutter kick made her heart ache, but the baby was Nikos Panos's, and she couldn't forget it.

Which meant she had to move forward. It was her only option. And the moment she delivered, the moment the baby was whisked away, she'd black this year from her memory. Georgia never wanted to think about any of this again. It was the only way to survive something so challenging. Fortunately, she had practice in surviving challenging situations. Grief was a good teacher.

"Name it," Mr. Laurent said quietly.

"It's not about the money—"

"But it will pay bills, so pay your bills. Provide for your sister. I understand she, too, wants to attend medical school. Take advantage of the offer so you never have to do something like this again."

That last bit hit home. Her gaze locked with his, and her short, filed nails curled into her palms.

Mr. Laurent was right. She could never do something like this again. It was breaking her heart. But she'd survived worse. And it wasn't as if she was abandoning a child to a monster. Nikos Panos wanted this baby desperately.

Drawing a short, sharp breath, Georgia named an outrageous figure, a sum that would cover Savannah's medical school and living expenses, plus some. Georgia made the sum deliberately high, intending to shock the old lawyer.

But Mr. Laurent didn't blink. Instead he scribbled something down on a printed sheet of paper. "The addendum," he said, pushing the paper across the desk toward her. "Sign here, and date there."

She swallowed, shocked he'd so readily agreed to her "outrageous" demand. He must have been prepared for her to ask for even more. She probably could have asked for millions and he would have said yes. Stupid pride. Why couldn't she be a proper mercenary?

"You're agreeing to leave Friday," Mr. Laurent said as she reached for the page. "You will spend the last trimester of your pregnancy in Greece, at Nikos Panos's villa on Kamari, which is a short flight from Athens. After delivery, once you have been cleared to travel, my client will send you back to Atlanta, either on his private jet or first class on the airline of your choice. Any questions?"

"The money? It will be wired into my account first thing tomorrow?"

He handed her a pen. "It will be there by nine a.m." He smiled as she signed.

"I'm so glad we were able to come to terms."

Georgia stood, heartsick but too far in to see a way out. "As you said, everyone has a price. Goodbye, Mr. Laurent."

"Enjoy your time in Greece, Miss Nielsen."

CHAPTER TWO

IT WAS A long trip from Atlanta. Nearly thirteen hours, which meant that Georgia had plenty of time to sleep, study and even watch a movie or two when she was too tired to read one more sample question from the test.

The movies helped occupy her mind. She didn't want to think. If she wasn't going to sleep, she needed entertainment and diversion to keep from replaying her goodbye with Savannah, who'd driven down from Duke to see her off.

Or more accurately, who'd driven down to beg Georgia not to go.

Savannah had been beside herself, alternating between tears and anger, asking repeatedly what Georgia knew about this Greek tycoon in the first place.

What do you even know about him? And who cares if he's a billionaire? He could be dangerous, seriously deranged, and who will be able to help you when you're on his island in the middle of nowhere?

Savannah had never been the practical one, but in this instance, she was right.

Georgia had researched Nikos Panos—and, yes, he was a Greek billionaire, and he'd turned his family's struggling company around with shrewd investments, and he'd done it at a young age, taking over the helm of the company while in his midtwenties—but she didn't have any references on him. Nothing on his morals or his character. She just had the attorney and the payments for services rendered.

She started to rub her tummy. Her bump was becoming increasingly pronounced. Her skin was sensitive, and warm, and even when she didn't want to think about the pregnancy, or the surrogacy, she was aware of the life inside her.

And not just a life, but a boy. There were no boys in her family. Just girls. Three sisters. Georgia couldn't even imagine what it'd be like to raise a little boy.

But she wouldn't go there. She never let herself go there. She wasn't going to let herself become invested.

But as the jet made its final descent into what looked like an endless sea of blue, the baby did a flutter kick as if recognizing that he was almost home. Georgia held her breath, fighting panic.

She could do this. She would do this.

The baby wasn't hers.

She wasn't attached.

She'd been paid not to care.

She wouldn't care.

But those fierce admonishments did little to ease the wave of grief and regret washing through her heart.

"Just three and a half months," she whispered. Three and a half months and she'd be free of this horrific thing she'd agreed to do.

Three and a half months, Nikos Panos told himself, standing at the far end of the landing strip, narrowed gaze fixed on the white Dassault Falcon jet. It had been a rough landing owing to the windy day, which wasn't unusual for this time of year in the Cyclades. But the jet was safely parked and the door was open, revealing twenty-four-year-old Georgia Nielsen.

From where he stood, she appeared very slender and very blonde in a soft-knit apricot tunic, dark gray tights and high-heel boots that covered her knees. He frowned at the height of the heels on her boots, baffled as to why a pregnant woman would wear boots with heels four inches high. Her boots were a problem, and so was her dress.

Her tunic's knit hem hit just above midthigh, revealing a lot of leg.

Nikos knew from her profile that Georgia Nielsen would be pretty, but he hadn't expected *this*.

Standing at the top of the stairs with the blustery wind grabbing at her hair and the sun haloing the bright golden mass, she looked so much like Elsa that it made his chest tighten and ache.

He'd wanted a surrogate that looked like Elsa.

But he didn't want Elsa.

In that moment, he wondered if he'd made a terrible mistake. He had to be more than a little bit mad to search the world for a woman that looked like his late wife, and certifiably insane to bring that doppelgänger here, to Kamari.

The American surrogate must have spotted him because she suddenly straightened and, lifting a hand to her hair, held the billowing golden mane back from her face as she came down the jet's stairs quickly. It wasn't quite a run, but definitely with speed, and purpose.

Not Elsa, he grimly corrected, moving forward to meet her.

His Elsa had been quiet and gentle, even a bit timid, while this leggy blonde crossed the tarmac as if she owned it. He met her halfway, determined to slow her down. "Careful," he ground out.

Georgia lifted her head and looked at him, brows pulling. "Of what?" she countered, a hint of irritation in her voice.

From afar she was striking. Close, she was astonishingly pretty. Even prettier than Elsa, maybe, if such a thing was possible.

And for the second time he thought this was a critical error, bringing her here, now, when there was so much time left before the baby's birth. Not because he was in danger of falling in love with his late wife's ghost, but because his relationship with Elsa had never been easy, and her sense-less death had filled him with guilt. He hoped the baby would ease some of the guilt. He hoped that becoming a father would force him to move forward and live. And feel.

Elsa wasn't the only ghost in his life. He'd become one, too.

"You could trip and fall," he said shortly, his deep voice rough even to his own ears. He didn't speak much on Kamari. Not even to his staff. They knew their duties, and they did them without unnecessary conversation.

One of her winged eyebrows arched higher. She gave him a long, assessing look, sizing him up—inspecting, cataloging, making a dozen mental notes. "I wouldn't do that," she said after a moment. "I have excellent balance. I would have loved to be a gymnast, but I grew too tall." She extended her hand to him. "But I appreciate your con-cern, Mr. Panos."

He looked down at her hand for what would probably be considered too long to be polite. He'd never been overly concerned about manners and niceties before the fire, and now he simply didn't care at all. He didn't care about any-thing. That was the problem. But the Panoses couldn't die out with him. Not just because the company needed an heir; he was the last Panos. It wasn't right that he al-lowed his mistakes to end hundreds of years of a family lineage. Surely his family shouldn't pay for who he was… what he'd done…

The baby would hopefully change that. The child would be the future. God knew he needed a future.

Taking her hand, his fingers engulfed hers, his grip firm, her skin warm against his. "Nikos," he corrected.

Then he lifted his head and turned his jaw from her to give her a good look at the right side of his face, letting her see who he was now. What he was now.

A monster.

The Beast of Kamari.

He turned his head back the other way and met her gaze.

She looked straight back at him without a flicker of horror or fear. Nor did she reveal surprise. Instead her blue eyes, with their specks of gray and bits of silver, were wide and clear. He found it intriguing that she didn't appear discomfited by the burns on his temple and cheek.

"Georgia," she replied, giving his hand an equally firm shake.

Like the proverbial Georgia peach, he thought, releasing her hand. Her name suited her. Too well.

Despite the long hours flying, despite the pregnancy—or maybe because of it—she looked fresh, ripe, glowing with health and vitality.

Nikos, who hadn't wanted anything or anyone for nearly five years, felt the stirring of curiosity, and the dull ache of desire. He hadn't felt anything in so long that the stirring of his body was as surprising as the questions forming in his mind.

Was the attraction because she resembled Elsa, or was he intrigued because she seemed fearless when confronted by his scars?

Touching her hand, feeling her warmth, made something within him uncoil and reach out to her, wondering just who she was, wondering what she looked like naked, wondering what she would taste like if he put his mouth to her skin—

And just like that, after years of feeling nothing, and being nothing, and living as if numb or dead, he hardened, his body responding to her despite whatever else was happening in his head.

And yet this was what couldn't happen. And this was why he lived on Kamari, away from people. It wasn't to protect himself, but to protect others.

Nikos ruthlessly clamped down on the surge of desire, smashing it by reminding himself of what he'd done to Elsa, and what Elsa's death had done to him.

But she wasn't Elsa, wasn't his wife. And even though she wasn't a wife, he still wouldn't take chances. She carried his son. Her health and well-being were essential for his son's health and well-being. And so he'd take excellent care of the surrogate, but only because she was the surrogate. She was nothing to him beyond that. Just help…a hired womb…that was all.

All, he repeated, looking past her to his flight crew. He gestured, indicating that her luggage should be placed in the back of the restored 1961 military Land Rover. It was the best vehicle for Kamari's rugged terrain, handling the steep twisting roads with ease. It was also his preferred vehicle since he could drive in summer without the soft top. In winter he kept the soft top up, but there were no windows. No glass to trap him.

He started for the vehicle, and then remembered the American's ridiculous footwear. "Those shoes are not appropriate for Kamari," he said curtly.

She gave him another long look and then shrugged. "I'll keep that in mind," she said before setting off, heading toward the passenger side of his green Land Rover with her careless, leggy, athletic grace, the wind catching at her bright hair, making it shimmer and dance.

Definitely not Elsa, he thought.

Nothing about Elsa shimmered and danced. But she had once, hadn't she? She'd been happy once…before she'd married him. Before she'd come to regret everything about her life with him…

Nikos smashed his hand into a tight fist, squeezing hard, fighting the past that haunted him always. He prayed the baby would mean new life…not just for the child but for him, too. He prayed that if he were a good father, he'd find peace. Redemption.

Or was it too late for that?

He forced his attention to Georgia. A footstool had been placed on the ground for her, making it easier for her to enter the lifted four-wheel drive vehicle, but she seemed amused by the stool, her full lips quirking as she stepped onto it and swung easily into the passenger seat.

He didn't understand her smile. He didn't understand such brazen confidence, either. She seemed to be throwing down the gauntlet. Challenging him.

He wasn't sure he liked it. She'd only just arrived.

Fortunately he had his temper well in check. His pulse had quickened, but he was still in control. Once upon a time his temper had been legendary. But it was better now that he was older. He'd matured, thank God. He'd never really lost his temper with Elsa, but she'd been nervous around him. Skittish.

He shook his head, chasing away the memories. He didn't want to think of Elsa now. Didn't want to be haunted by the past any longer. It was why he'd hired the donor and surrogate. He was trying to move forward, trying to create a future where there hadn't been one in far too long.

Climbing behind the steering wheel, he glanced at Georgia. She was fastening her seat belt and pale, gleaming hair spilled over her shoulders and down her back like a golden waterfall. Beautiful hair. Longer than Elsa's had ever been.

Nikos felt a lance of appreciation, and then clamped down on the sensation, more than a little bit baffled by his attraction. He didn't want to find Georgia Nielsen attractive. Didn't want to find anything about her attractive. She was here as a surrogate…

A vessel.

A womb.

But his body had a mind of its own, and the heavy ache

in his groin grew, his body tight with a testosterone-fueled tension that made him ruthless and restless. A tiger on the prowl. A beast out of the cage.

He didn't like feeling this way. He didn't like anything—or anyone—that tested him, challenging him, reminding him of his dark edges. He hadn't known until he married Elsa that he had such a frightening personality. He hadn't known until Elsa began hiding from him that he was such a beast…a monster…

Thirio.

Teras.

If he'd known who he was before he married, he wouldn't have married. If he'd known he would destroy his beautiful wife with his temper, he would have remained a bachelor.

And yet he'd wanted children. He'd very much wanted to create a family. To have people of his own…

From the corner of his eye he saw Georgia cross one leg over the other, drawing his attention to her legs. The tunic hit high on her thigh and the boots stopped at her knee and her legs, in the gray tights, were slim and shapely.

"We're about fifteen minutes from the house," he said roughly, starting the engine, battling his thoughts, battling the desire that made him feel as if he had gasoline in his veins instead of blood.

"And town?" she asked, adjusting the belt across her lap.

His gaze followed, focusing on her waist. For the first time, he could see the gentle swell of her belly. She was most definitely pregnant. The cut of the cashmere tunic had just hidden the bump earlier.

The bump jolted him. *His* child. *His* son.

For a split second he couldn't breathe. It was suddenly real. The life he'd made…his seed…her egg…

"Do you want to touch him?" she asked quietly.

He looked up into her face. Her cheeks were pale, and

yet her gaze was direct, steady. "He's moving around," she added, lips curving faintly. "I think he's saying hello."

Nikos dropped his gaze to her hands resting at her side, and then back to the gentle curve of her belly.

"Isn't it too soon for me to feel him moving?" he asked.

"It might have been a week or two ago, but not anymore."

He stared at her bump for another moment, conflicted. He wanted to feel his son kick, but he couldn't bring himself to touch her, not wanting to feel the tautness of her belly or the warmth of her skin. She wasn't supposed to matter in any way, and yet suddenly she wasn't this vessel, this hired womb, but a stunning young woman carrying his son.

"Not right now," he said, fingers curling around the stick shift, changing gears, driving forward. His gut was hard, tight. Air ached in his lungs. What had he done bringing this woman to him? How could he have thought this would be a good idea? "But it is good to know that he's moving and seems healthy."

"He's very healthy. I trust you've been getting the reports and sonograms from my checkups?"

"Yes." But he didn't want to talk about the baby. He didn't want to talk at all. She was here now so she didn't have to fly late in the third trimester, but he hadn't brought her to Kamari to create a friendship. There would be no relationship between them. He needed her to be safe, but beyond that he wanted nothing more to do with her, and the sooner she understood that, the better.

"And town?" she repeated, catching a fistful of billowing golden hair.

He shifted gears as he accelerated. "There's no town. It's a private island."

She was looking at him now. "Yours?"

"Mine," he agreed.

"And the house? What's that like?"

"It's close to the water, which is nice in summer."

"But not as nice in winter?"

He shot her a swift glance. "It's an old house. Simple. But it suits me."

Her hand shifted on her mass of hair. "Mr. Laurent referred to it as a villa." She shot him another curious look. "Was he wrong?"

"In Greece, a villa is usually one's country house. So, no, he wasn't wrong, but I myself do not use that word. This is where I live now. It's my home."

She opened her mouth to ask another question but he cut her short, his tone flat and flinty even to his own ears. "I am not much of a conversationalist, Georgia."

If Georgia hadn't been quite so queasy, she might have laughed. Was that his way of telling her to stop asking questions?

She shot him a swift glance, taking in his hard carved features and the black slash of eyebrows above dark eyes.

Just looking at him made her feel jittery, putting an odd whoosh in her middle, almost as if she were back on the plane and coming in for that rocky landing all over again.

He wasn't what she'd expected. She'd imagined a solid, comfortably built tycoon in his early to midthirties, but there was nothing comfortable about Nikos Panos. He was tall with broad shoulders and long limbs. He had thick, glossy black hair, piercing eyes and beautiful features... at least on one half of his face. The other side was scarred around the temple and cheekbone. The scars were significant but not grotesque, but then she understood what they were—burns—and she could only imagine how painful the healing process must have been.

If one could look past the scars, he was the stuff of little girls' fairy tales and teenage fantasies.

Correction, if you could look past the scars and brusque manner.

I am not much of a conversationalist, Georgia.

What did that even mean? Was there no one she would be able to talk to during her stay here?

Mr. Laurent had told her there was no Mrs. Panos. Mr. Laurent had said his client would be raising the child as a single father. Was this where the child would be raised?

On this arid volcanic island, in the middle of this sea?

"Where will you live?" she asked abruptly. "Once the baby is born?"

His black eyebrows flattened. "Here. This is my home."

Georgia held her breath and stared out at the narrow road that clung to the side of the mountain. The road was single lane, barely paved, and it snaked down and around the hillside. She wished there was a guardrail.

She wished she was back in Atlanta.

She wished she'd never agreed to any of this.

Georgia fought her anxiety and practiced breathing—a slow, measured inhale, followed by an even slower exhale.

Why was she doing this? Why was she here?

The money.

Her chest ached with bottled air. She was doing it for the money.

Sometimes focusing on the two huge sums that had been wired to her bank account gave her perspective when her hormones and emotions threatened to overwhelm her, but it wasn't working now.

Maybe it was the long flight or jet lag or just the relentless nausea, but Georgia's stomach heaved once, and then again. "Please pull over," she begged, grabbing the car's door handle. "I'm going to be sick."

CHAPTER THREE

IN HER ROOM at the villa, Georgia slept for hours, sleeping away the remainder of the day.

She dreamed of Savannah, of her goodbye with Savannah yesterday, her younger sister's emotional cry playing out in her dream.

What do you even know about him?

He could be dangerous...seriously deranged...

Who will be able to help you when you're on his island in the middle of nowhere?

The dream was broken by the dull, but insistent, pounding on her bedroom door.

Georgia heard it but didn't want to wake, and for a moment she lay in the strange bed, heart racing, pulse pounding, late-afternoon sunlight slanting through wooden blinds, as she tried to cling to the last of the dream, missing Savannah already.

But the knocking on her door wouldn't stop.

Georgia dragged herself into a sitting position and was just about to rise when her door crashed open and Nikos came charging into her room.

"What on earth are you doing?" she cried, rising.

"Why didn't you answer the damn door?"

"I was asleep!"

"We've been trying to rouse you for the past hour." He stalked toward the bed, his dark eyes glittering. "I thought you were dead."

She pulled on the hem of her cotton pajama top, trying to hide the skin gaping beneath. She was just starting to need maternity clothes. She hadn't bought any maternity wear until recently, not wanting to spend money until absolutely necessary. "Not dead, as you can see."

"You gave me quite a scare," he gritted out.

She was still trembling with shock. She lifted a hand to show him how badly her hand shook. "How do you think I feel? You broke my door—"

"It can be fixed."

"But who does that? I thought that was just cops in movies."

"I'll have someone repair it when you come upstairs for lunch."

She wanted an apology, but it seemed she wasn't going to get it. He really didn't think he'd done anything wrong. Georgia glanced to the shuttered window with the late-afternoon sunlight stabbing through the gaps and cracks in the wood, trying to calm down and regain her composure. "I would think it's dinnertime, not lunch."

"We don't eat dinner until ten or later, so we're having a late lunch for you now. Dress and come upstairs—"

"Can you not send something to the room?" she interrupted, irritated all over again by his curtness. He lacked manners and the basic social graces. "After the long flight I would prefer to stay in my pajamas and just read a bit—"

"Head straight up the stairs to the third floor, we're on the second floor now, and then through the living room to the doors to the terrace," he concluded as if she'd never spoken.

She frowned, increasingly annoyed. "Mr. Laurent led me to believe that I would be able to have my own space and as much privacy as I desired."

"You have your own space. Three rooms, all for you. But once a day we will meet and visit and have a meal together, and we might as well begin tonight as it will help establish a routine."

"I don't see why we need to meet daily. We have nothing to say to each other."

"That is correct, and I am in complete agreement. You and I have nothing to say to each other, but I have plenty to say to my son, and since he is inside of you, you are required to be present, as well."

She clamped her jaw tight to hold back the caustic comment that was tingling on the tip of her tongue, and then she couldn't. "I am sorry you have to endure my dreadful company for the next three months, then."

"We both are making sacrifices," he answered. "Fortunately, you are being compensated for yours." He nodded at her and turned to leave.

"I would like to shower first."

"Fine."

She had to hold back another caustic comment. "And you'll have someone repair the door while I'm upstairs?"

"I already said that."

Leaving Georgia's room, Nikos summoned Adras, the older man who oversaw the running of the villa, and told him that his guest's bedroom door needed to be repaired. And then Nikos went up to the shaded, whitewashed terrace to wait for Georgia.

The sun had shifted, deepening the colors of the sky and sea. The terrace was protected from the worst of the wind, with the most protection closest to the house. Nikos stood at the wall, looking out over the sea, and the wind caught at his shirt and hair. His hair was perhaps too long, but it helped hide the scars on his temple and cheekbone.

It was easy to ignore the breeze as he was anticipating Georgia's appearance. It was strange to have her in the house. He wasn't used to having visitors. Kamari was his own rock, 323 acres in the northwestern Cyclades in the Aegean Sea. Amorgós was the closest island to Kamari, with a hospital, ferry, shops and monastery, but Nikos hadn't been to Amorgós in years. There was no point. There was nothing good on Amorgós...not for him.

Instead everything he needed was flown in from the mainland, and if he wanted company, he'd fly to Athens. Not that he ever wanted company. It'd been months and months since he'd left his rock. He had a home in Athens, along with his corporate headquarters. He had another place on Santorini, but that was the old family estate, a former winery that had once been his favorite place in the world and now the source of his nightmares.

Nikos had lived alone so long that he couldn't imagine being part of the outside world. His son would not need the outside world, either. He would teach his son to live simply, to love nature, to be independent. He'd make sure his son knew what was good and true...not money, not accolades, praise, success. But this island, this sky, this sea.

But perhaps the years of living so isolated had made him rough and impatient. He felt so very impatient now, waiting for her. She wasn't rushing her shower. She wasn't hurrying up to meet him. She was taking her time. Making him wait.

Finally the sound of the wooden door scraping the tumbled marble floor made him turn.

Georgia stepped outside, onto the terrace, her expression wary. She was dressed in black tights, a long black-and-white knit jumper, high-heeled ankle boots, and her shimmering blond hair was drawn back in a high ponytail. Even though she was wearing no makeup, she looked far more rested than she had earlier, but her guarded expression bothered him.

He didn't want to be a monster. He didn't enjoy scaring women. "You found it," he said gruffly.

"I did."

"Something to drink?" he asked, gesturing to the tray

with pitchers of water and juice that had been brought up earlier.

"Just water. Please."

He filled a tall glass and brought it to her. She was standing now where he'd been just seconds ago, looking out over the Aegean Sea. He wasn't surprised. The view was spectacular from the terrace, and the setting sun had gilded the horizon, turning everything purple and bronze.

"How are you feeling?" he asked.

"Fine," she said crisply, keeping her distance.

He should apologize. He wasn't sure where to begin, though. The words stuck in his throat. He wasn't very good at this sort of thing, and he was certain that the apology would be rebuffed.

"Do you get carsick easily?" he asked, trying to find a topic that would help them move forward.

"Not usually. Everything is different when you're pregnant, though."

"My pilots did say it was a turbulent landing. We get very strong winds this time of year." He hesitated. "I apologize."

She arched an elegant eyebrow, her expression cool. "You can't control the wind," she said, taking a sip of the water before adding, "But you can control yourself. Don't break down my door again. Please."

Nikos wasn't used to apologies, but he also wasn't accustomed to criticism. His temper flared. He battled it back down. "I've assured you that the door will be fixed."

"That's not the point. Your use of force was excessive. I'm sure there must be an intercom or house phone you could use next time you wish to check on me."

"Maybe you don't lock the door next time."

Her brows pulled. "I always lock my bedroom door."

"Even in your own home?"

"I live alone. I lock doors."

"Is Atlanta so very dangerous?"

"The world is dangerous." Her voice was cool, almost clinical. "If I don't lock my door, I can't sleep."

"You're safe here."

Her chin lifted, her smooth jaw firming as her gaze met his. "I'm not sure what that means."

He was baffled by her response. "You can relax here. Nothing will hurt you here."

"Does that include you?"

Nikos stiffened. He took a step away, glancing past her to the water, and yet all he could see was Elsa. Elsa, who had been afraid of everything he was.

"I wouldn't hurt you," he ground out, forcing his gaze back to Georgia. "The reason you are here now is that I want to ensure your safety. Your well-being is imperative to my son's well-being. You will have only the best of care on Kamari."

She stared back at him, blue eyes bright and clear, as well as thoughtful. She was weighing his words, assessing them for herself. "I don't need *care*. I need space and respect."

"Which you will have, along with proper *care*."

She continued to hold his gaze. "I am not sure your idea of proper care and mine are the same thing. In fact, I'm sure it's not. For me, proper care would have been remaining at home, close to my sister and obstetrician. I would have felt healthier and safer with my doctor and family nearby."

"I have hired the best obstetrician and pediatrician in Greece. Both will attend the delivery, and the obstetrician will see you once a month until you are close to delivery."

"I would have been happier at home, though."

"Once the newness wears off, I think you will find it quite restful here."

A spark flickered in her eyes. Her lips compressed. "I

don't think you're understanding what I'm saying. When I agreed to the surrogacy I never expected spending time here, with you. That wasn't part of the initial agreement. Indeed, I wouldn't have agreed to the surrogacy if I'd known that I had to spend the final trimester here. I'm not happy being here. This isn't good for me."

"You've been compensated for coming to Kamari, generously compensated."

"But money isn't everything." Her chin notched up. "And I am not going to have you throwing money in my face. It's rude and demeaning."

"But you chose to be a donor and surrogate for the money."

"I needed to pay for medical school for my sister and me, but I also wanted to do something good. And I have. I've created life. You can't put a price on that." Her voice suddenly cracked, and she looked away, her lower lip caught between her teeth.

He studied her beautiful profile, saw a hint of moisture in her eyes and wondered if they were real tears or if this was perhaps part of a game. He didn't trust tears, and it crossed his mind that she could be trying to manipulate him. It was possible. Elsa had taught him that.

"And you have no qualms about giving this precious life up?" he asked, unable to mask the ruthless edge in his voice. He was not the same man he'd been before Elsa. He doubted he'd ever be that man again.

Georgia made a soft, rough sound, and when she spoke again, her voice was husky. "It's your son, not mine."

"Your egg. Your womb."

Her lips curved faintly, but the smile didn't reach her eyes. "I am little more than a fertile garden. The soil doesn't weep when you sow or reap."

An interesting answer, he thought. She was an interesting woman. "The soil isn't a young female, either. Nurturing...maternal—"

"I'm not maternal," she said, cutting him off, her tone almost icy.

"And yet you're doing this to help provide for your sister."

"That's different. She is my family. She is already my responsibility. But I have no desire to ever have children of my own. No desire to add to that family, or assume more responsibilities."

"You may feel differently later."

She leaned forward, her expression intent. "Do you want me to feel differently later?"

He was shocked, not just by her words but by the way she moved in toward him. No one invaded his space. No one wanted to be near him. He intimidated women. He made people uncomfortable. And yet she leaned in, she challenged him, and after the shock faded, he understood why.

She wasn't timid. She wasn't weak. She was strong, and she was going to give him as good as he gave her.

He admired her boldness and her confidence. He admired strength and courage, but what she didn't realize was that her challenge just whetted his appetite.

He wasn't about to move back and give her distance and breathing room. He was going to move in. Get closer. Crowd her.

Not because he wanted to scare her, but her energy and resistance were waking him up, making him feel things he hadn't felt in forever. And yet what was good for him wouldn't necessarily be good for her.

He was troubled by his response to her. She fascinated him. And, yes, she looked like Elsa, but her personality was nothing like Elsa's. While Elsa had needed to be shielded, protected, Georgia charged at him, refusing to shy away from conflict.

He found her stimulating.

Refreshing.

But he should warn her. He ought to tell her that she was stirring the beast, rattling his cage. He should let her know that she wouldn't like it when he woke…that it was better, safer, smarter to keep him leashed, caged, dormant.

"Of course I don't want you to feel differently later," Nikos said now. "He is my son."

"Good. I am glad we are in complete agreement on that." She walked away from him then, heading to the sitting area under the thatched roof and taking a seat on the white slipcovered bench against the house.

He watched her cross her legs and sit back, the picture of calm and cool, but her air of calm, that cloak of control, jolted him. A shot of adrenaline. Another shot of hunger. But he needed to smash the desire, not encourage the response. Hungry wasn't good. Hungry would hurt her.

He walked slowly toward her, studying her expression. From across the terrace she exuded serenity, and yet as he neared he saw a flicker in her eyes. She wasn't sleepy or lazy. She was alert and very much on guard.

He dropped into a chair across from her, his long legs extending, taking some of her space. "In the car you asked me where I was going to raise my son." Nikos paused a moment, his gaze skimming her stunning features, dropping from her full pink lips down the elegant throat to the pulse he could see beating at the base of her neck. She was not as calm as she pretended to be. Not by a long shot. "Why did you ask?" he added.

Her shoulders twisted. "Curious."

"Curious about the life he'll live, or curious about me?"

She shrugged again, even more carelessly than before. "I was just making conversation. I'm sorry if I made you uncomfortable."

"I wasn't at all uncomfortable. I love Kamari, so it was

easy to answer. I will raise my son here. We will live here, and I will teach him about his family, his lineage, and make sure he is prepared to inherit the Panos business and fortune. He is my legacy. He is the future."

For a moment after he'd finished speaking there was just silence. It wasn't an easy silence. She was very much processing every word he was saying. Georgia Nielsen was no intellectual lightweight.

He gestured to her already nearly empty glass. "More water, Georgia?"

"I'm fine."

Yes, she was. She was actually more than fine, and it would be a problem if he didn't check his interest immediately. What they needed were boring topics. Safe subjects. And distance. "We Greeks like our water. We serve water with coffee, water with dessert. It's often the beverage of choice—" His voice was drowned out by the roar of an engine.

He fell silent as the white Falcon that had brought Georgia to the island flew directly overhead. Georgia's head tipped, and she watched the plane take off, soaring up into the sky.

"Your plane doesn't stay here?"

"No. The hangar's in Athens."

She was still watching the jet. He watched her, appreciating the elegant lines and delicate angles of her face. The gold of her hair. The cool blue-gray of her eyes. Her complexion wasn't pink but palest cream with just a hint of gold.

Elsa's complexion hadn't been honey, but pink and cream. Roses and porcelain. The blue of her eyes had been more violet. Her lips were smaller, her eyes set a little wider. Doll-like.

Georgia was nothing like a doll.

She turned her attention from the sky back to him. "Why Athens?"

"It's where I keep all of my planes."

"You have more?"

"Yes. Helicopters, too."

"Any boats?"

"Of course. I live on a remote island."

She pushed a blond tendril back from her brow. "Is it too late to tour the island now?"

"The sun will be setting in the next hour. It's better to wait for the morning. I'll show you the gardens, the walking paths and the pool. I imagine you'll want to get your exercise in." He rose and went to get the water pitcher and refill her glass. "Mr. Laurent said you exercise regularly. Is that still the case?"

"I walk, swim and cycle and lift weights—"

"No more weights."

She laughed, amused, the sound soft and husky. "We're not talking Olympic moves here."

"No weights," he repeated. "I don't think it's necessary to stress you, or the baby, that much."

She opened her mouth to protest but closed it, shrugged.

"The pool is heated," he added. "I think you'll find it quite pleasant."

She leaned all the way back against the cushion and extended her long legs. "Will it be this way for the next three and a half months?"

"What does that mean?"

"Will you be supervising my nutrition along with my exercise?"

He heard the mockery in her voice, and it didn't anger him as much as stir his senses. She had no idea how appealing he found her. He should warn her. If not for her sake then his. "Yes," he answered smoothly. "It will be this way." There was no point denying it. She was here so he could monitor the pregnancy and make sure the third trimester went well.

Her lips curved faintly. Amusement lurked in her eyes. "Then we have a problem."

"Not if you're compliant."

She gave him another long look, one perfect brow lifting. "And is that how Mr. Laurent described me? Docile... sweet...compliant?"

The air was suddenly charged, crackling with tension and resistance.

No, he couldn't imagine her ever being described as any of those, and he hadn't been throwing down a challenge, either, just setting forth his expectations. But she was turning his expectations into something more.

Heat rushed through him, hot and heavy in his veins. His body ached. His blood hummed. He was waking up. It felt far too good.

"I don't believe that was ever Mr. Laurent's description," Nikos replied gently, aware of the dance they were being drawn into. "I think my attorney used words like *intelligent, gifted, successful, ambitious*."

Her blue gaze held his. She was looking so deeply, so directly, that he wondered what she was thinking...seeing. She didn't appear threatened. Didn't seem the least bit uneasy. If anything she radiated confidence. Control.

For being just twenty-four, Georgia Nielsen struck him as a powerful woman in her element.

Not the surrogate he'd expected. Not the surrogate he wanted.

But just possibly a woman he wanted.

Careful, he told himself. *Do not be stupid...do not complicate things...*

"I'm not accustomed to being told what to do," she said, her voice pitched low and firm. "And I might be your guest here for the next few months, but I am my own person."

And he wasn't accustomed to negotiating with anyone,

certainly not a woman. But he found it exciting. She was exciting. "Can you not think of it as care and concern for the well-being of my son?"

A light flickered in her eyes. "I have taken excellent care of him so far."

"I appreciate that. But as his father, I expect you to respect my wishes."

She stared back at him, unrepentant.

There was definitely a power struggle taking place. He hadn't anticipated that, either. She was carrying his son. She was hired to carry his son. All she had to do was heed his wishes. But it appeared that Georgia either couldn't, or wouldn't, and her resistance was like gasoline to a flame.

He wasn't angry. Not in the least. But his heart was thudding, and blood was drumming in his veins.

Nikos placed her glass on the corner table and sat back down across from her. "I think we have a misunderstanding." His tone was pleasant. There was no need to snarl. He knew just how dangerous he was…just how dangerous he could be. "Maybe it's a language barrier. Maybe it's cultural—you are American, I am Greek—but business is business. You entered into an arrangement with me, and I have met my end of the agreement. I have paid you, handsomely, for your service—"

"We are discussing my body. I am not a shipping container or a maritime vessel. I am not your employee, either. I am a woman who is giving you a gift—"

"Providing a service," he interrupted. "We have to call it what it is."

"Yes, the *gift* of life," she shot back, tone defiant, blue eyes blazing. "But I'm not just any woman. I'm the one you wanted to be both egg donor and surrogate. There was a reason you picked me. You could have picked any woman, but you selected me, which means you have me, and I am not going to be pushed around. I don't respect men who throw their weight around, either. You can have a conversation with me, but don't dictate to me."

For a long moment there was just silence.

Georgia felt the weight of Nikos's inspection. He wasn't happy. At all. She wasn't afraid, just alert. Aware. Aware of his intensity, and how energy seemed to crackle around him. He wasn't moving, and yet she could feel the air hum.

She'd never met anyone like him before. And if she weren't here, trapped on an isolated island with him, she'd be intrigued. She'd be tempted to test the fire and energy, but she was trapped here, and the survivalist in her told her she needed to be careful, and she needed to get off the island. Soon.

"Does no one else live on Kamari?" she asked, filling the taut silence.

"Just my staff."

"Are there many?"

"A half dozen or so, depending on the day and occasion."

"And do you ever leave here? Will we ever go anywhere?"

His mouth quirked, his dark eyes narrowing. "You've only been here a few hours. Are you already so anxious to leave?"

"I've never been to Greece."

"And here you are."

She smiled and glanced past him, her attention drawn to the blue horizon. "But I see other islands. They cannot be that far."

"The closest is Amorgós. It is twenty-six kilometers away."

"How do you get there?"

"I don't."

She allowed her smile to grow, stretch. "What if I wanted to visit?" she asked lightly.

"And why would you want to do that?"

"I might want to shop—"

"You want to buy olives…bread…soap? Because that is all the shops have there this time of year. It's not high season. In winter, Amorgós is not for tourists. It has a few small shops with meat and produce, but that is all."

"Surely there is more to the island than that."

His broad shoulders shifted. "There is a ferry, a hospital and a monastery—plus churches. Many churches. But no museums, no café culture, nothing that would appeal to you."

"You don't know me. How do you know what would appeal to me?"

"You are young and beautiful. Young, beautiful women like to have a good time."

She laughed, entertained. Or at least, it was what she'd have him think. The quickest way to lose control was to get emotional. "That is so incredibly sexist."

"Not sexist. I'm just honest. And before you think I am being unfair to the female gender, let me add that young, beautiful men like to have a good time, too."

"But not you."

"I am neither young nor beautiful."

"Are you fishing for compliments?"

He leaned forward so that they were just inches apart and stared deeply into her eyes. "Look at me."

Oh, she was, and this close his eyes weren't just dark brown, but rich chocolate ringed with a line of espresso. His lashes were black, thick, long, perfectly framing the rich brown irises. His black brows were strong slashes. "I'm looking," she said calmly, her cool voice belying the change in her pulse, her heart beginning to race. She didn't know what was happening, but it was hard to breathe. She was growing warm, too warm. It was no longer easy to concentrate. "And you are still young, and despite the scars, you are still beautiful."

The space between them, those precious inches, shimmered with heat and tension. Even the air felt charged. Georgia dragged in a breath, feeling feverish.

"Is this a game to you?" he growled.

"No."

"Then look again."

"I am. So tell me, what am I supposed to be seeing?"

He reached up, and shoved his dark hair back from his temple, revealing the swath of mottled skin. "*Now* look at them."

"I am. They are burns," she said, struggling to sound clinical and detached as she reached out and lightly traced the thickened scar tissue. "They extend three inches above your brow, into your hairline, and then follow your temple down to your ear and out to the top of your cheekbone." Her fingers shook as she drew her hand back. She curled her hand in her lap. "How long ago did it happen?"

"Five years."

"They've healed well."

"There were a number of reconstructive surgeries."

His words told her one thing, but his espresso eyes said something else. She was far too warm and unsettled to want to analyze what was happening.

Too much was happening, and much too fast.

She hadn't come to Kamari prepared for any of this...
For him.

He was so overwhelming in every way. The sheer physicality of him—his height, his size, the width of his shoulders, the thick angle of his jaw—coupled with his electric energy was knocking her sideways, making it difficult to think.

The next three and a half months would be impossible if she didn't throw up some boundaries, get some control. Normally she wasn't easily intimidated, but Nikos Panos was getting under her skin. She needed space and distance, fast.

"I'm exhausted," she said, rising. "I think I should return to my room."

"You need to eat."

"Then perhaps you'd be so kind as to send something to my room for me? I'm dying to eat and crawl back into bed." She managed a small, tight smile. Seeing that he was about to protest, she added quickly, "I might as well sleep now, while I can. I understand it won't be easy towards the end of this next trimester."

His brow furrowed. He didn't seem happy with her decision, but after a moment he rose. "I'll walk you back."

"No need."

"You are a guest here, and you've only just arrived. I'll see you to your room. It'll give me a chance to check your door, make sure it has been repaired."

She couldn't argue with his logic, and if she was going to survive here, she'd need to acquiesce now and then. She might as well allow him to win small victories.

They went down a flight of stairs, passing through the gleaming white living room and then out into a whitewashed hall that reflected gold-and-red light from the row of windows overlooking the sea.

Rays of burnished gold fell on Nikos, highlighting the width of his shoulders and haloing his dark head with light. With the sunset illuminating his strong profile he looked like an oil painting come to life, or perhaps a page lifted from a book on the Greek gods. One of Zeus's immortal sons here on earth...

"My room is just down there," he said, nodding to a corridor. "Should you need anything later."

"I won't need anything," she said.

"But if there's an emergency."

"There won't be."

He stopped outside her room. Her door was closed. He gave a twist to the door handle. It opened soundlessly. He closed it again. It closed smoothly. "It seems to be working properly."

She stepped past him and checked the door herself. It opened and shut, but the paint was scraped clean in a spot. A bit of hardware was missing.

The lock had been removed.

Georgia turned to face him. "This is not all right."

"The door shuts."

"You had the lock taken off. I told you—"

"And I told you that I need to be able to reach you should there be an emergency," he ground out, silencing her. "If you cannot sleep without a locked door due to anxiety or fear of being attacked, then I will sleep in your room with you—"

"No. That will not happen."

"Then deal with an unlocked door, because those are your options." He towered over her, features hard. "I will have a tray sent to you now, and I will see you in the morning for the tour of the house and gardens."

CHAPTER FOUR

IT TOOK FOREVER for Georgia to fall asleep.

She'd only been in Greece a few hours and yet she was already wishing she'd never agreed to travel to Kamari. The money wasn't worth it—

She stopped herself there.

The money would be worth it, if she calmed down and focused. Getting upset wasn't going to help. She'd been through many difficult experiences in her life and she could handle this one.

With that said, it would have been better to have known more about Nikos Panos than she did. Mr. Laurent had told her a little bit about the Panos family when she'd been selected for the surrogacy. He'd explained that the Panos family's fortune was fairly recent, only since the end of World War II, and that they'd made their money rebuilding war-torn Europe, then branched from construction into shipping and from shipping into retail.

She did a little more research on her own at that point. The Panos story wasn't all sunshine and roses. The company had floundered during the past decade, poor investments and too much expansion in the wrong direction. Teetering on the brink of bankruptcy, son and heir Nikos Panos took the helm and turned the floundering company around.

Nikos's success had reassured her. She'd assumed he was successful and stable. She needed to learn not to make assumptions.

Or perhaps she needed to stop thinking about Nikos. Maybe she needed to practice detachment. And not just about Nikos, but the pregnancy, too.

She'd lost so much when her parents and sister and grandparents died. And now she had to be careful she didn't get her heart broken again. He wasn't her baby. He wasn't her son. Nor would he ever be.

Georgia finally fell asleep, but the morning came far too quickly. Waking, she frowned at the bright sunshine. She was not ready for the tour or more time with him.

Boundaries and distance, she told herself, showering and then dressing, choosing skinny jeans and an oversize gray cashmere sweater and gray ankle boots. The sky was clear, but her room was cold and outside the wind howled, buffeting the stone villa.

Boundaries and distance, she repeated when Nikos knocked at her bedroom door a few minutes later, coming to collect her personally for the morning tour.

It was a shock seeing him in the windowless hall, cloaked in shadows. He was wearing black trousers and a black shirt, and although she was tall, he towered over her, his broad shoulders filling the doorway, consuming space.

His dark gaze swept over her before focusing on her feet. "Please change the boots to something more practical."

She choked on an uncomfortable laugh, thinking he was joking, but he didn't laugh or smile. Her brows lifted, unable to believe they were starting a new day this way. "You're serious?"

"That's the third pair of boots. Heeled boots—"

"These are practically flats. The heel is maybe an inch tall."

"They are two inches or more, and you're not going to wear them and risk twisting an ankle or breaking your neck."

"I don't know what clumsy women you dated in the past—"

"We are not on a date. You are a surrogate. Change your shoes."

She laughed. She couldn't help it.

From the darkening of his expression, he hadn't expected that response, which made another bubble of laughter rise. She struggled to smash this one, too, but the sound escaped, and she bit the inside of her lip, trying to muffle her amusement and failing miserably.

Did he really expect her to jump to his bidding? Was he accustomed to women bowing and scraping?

Clearly he had no idea who *he* was dealing with. The Nielsen sisters were not pushovers. Neither Savannah nor Georgia were known to be quiet, timid, pliable women. The daughters of Norwegian American missionaries, they'd grown up overseas, moving with their parents from mission to mission, before losing their family in a horrific assault four years ago. Georgia and her sister had battled through the grief together and had emerged stronger than ever.

And Nikos should know that.

He'd selected *her* from thousands of egg donors and potential surrogates. Mr. Laurent told her that Nikos had examined her profile in great depth as he was very specific about what he wanted—age, birth date, height, weight, blood type, eye color, natural hair color, education, IQ.

"You laugh," Nikos said grimly.

"Yes, I did, and I will again if you continue to act as if you're a barbarian. I might be your *paid* surrogate, but I've a good brain, and I don't need you telling me what to do every time I turn around."

"Then your *good* brain and your *common* sense should tell you that wearing impractical shoes is asking for trouble."

"They are ankle boots, with a tiny stacked heel." She held up her fingers, showing him a sliver of space between her thumb and pointer finger. *"Tiny."*

His sigh was heavy and loud. "You are as exasperating as a child."

"I don't know how much experience you've had with children, but you do seem to be an expert in belittling women—"

"I'm not belittling women in general. We're discussing you."

"You might be surprised to discover that I don't want your attention. I don't want your company, either. You are insufferably arrogant. I completely understand why you live on a rock in the middle of the sea. Nobody wants to be your neighbor!"

"And I think you enjoy fighting."

"I don't enjoy fighting, but I'm not about to bow and scrape. I don't like conflict, but I won't let you, or anyone, bulldoze over me." She was breathing fast, and her hands knotted at her sides. "You started this, you know. You talk to me as if I'm feebleminded—"

"I'm helping you."

"You'd help me more by staying out of my business. I don't tell you how to eat or exercise. I don't tell you how to dress or what shoes to wear—"

"I'm not pregnant."

"No, I am—that's correct. And when I'm upset my blood pressure goes up and my hormones change and the baby feels all of it. Do you think it's good for your child when you get me all worked up? Or maybe since he is your son he enjoys a good fight."

Nikos scowled at her. "I don't enjoy a fight, and nor does he."

"Then if you don't enjoy a fight, don't provoke one."

"Maybe you are the one that needs to compromise."

"I am. I have. I'm here!" Georgia gestured to the room, the window, the view beyond. "I left my home to be your guest for three and a half months, and I've given up everything to make you happy. You can try to make me happy, Nikos."

He stretched out his arms, putting an elbow on either side of the plastered doorway, his shoulders forming a thick, muscular wall. He drew a slow, deep breath, his dark eyes burning, revealing his chaotic emotions. "We are not going to do this for the next three-plus months," he growled as a lock of his thick black hair fell forward, half hiding one dark eye, concealing the scars at his temple. "This is my home, my sanctuary. It's where I live to be calm and in control—"

"And would it hurt you so much to give up a little control?" she interrupted furiously. "Is it impossible for you to back off and just give me breathing room?"

"You only just arrived."

"Exactly. And yet you've already broken down my door—"

"Which I apologized for."

She snorted. "You didn't apologize. You just fixed it. But that's not an apology. And now you're hanging from my door, your giant body blocking my room, as you lecture me about calm and control while you act like a crazed werewolf—" She broke off, gulped air. "Mr. Laurent should have told me the whole story. He shouldn't have sold me on how smart and successful you were. He shouldn't have portrayed you to be this brilliant Greek tycoon. He should have told me the truth. You're a *nightmare*!"

Georgia knew immediately by the flare of hot white light in his eyes that she'd gone too far, said too much. But she was also in too deep, her emotions too stirred up to do anything but end the conversation as fast as she could.

"You're right," she added breathlessly. "This isn't working. Let's forget the tour. I'll find my way around. I think it's best if you just do your thing and let me do mine." And then she slammed the door shut, praying that as the door scraped shut, it didn't take off his face.

For a split second after Georgia closed the door, she felt wildly victorious. The rush of adrenaline was pure and strong, and she praised herself for handling the situation—and him—without revealing cowardice or weakness.

Perhaps he'd learn from this, she mentally added, heading toward the sitting area, where she'd piled her books. Perhaps he'd realize that his controlling boorish behavior was detrimental to the well-being of them all—

And then her door flew open, and he stormed across the threshold. Georgia's heart tumbled to her feet. All self-congratulating ended when she saw his livid expression.

She backed up a step, and then another as he continued to charge across the room. "What are you doing?" she cried, praying he didn't hear the wobble in her voice. "Get out! This is my room—"

"No, *gynaika mou*, it seems you are in need of a little lesson. This isn't your room. It's a room in my house that I am allowing you to use," he gritted out, marching toward her. "So to repeat, so we can be absolutely clear, this is my house. My room. You are *my* surrogate carrying *my* son."

Her heart drummed double time as he bore down on her but she wasn't about to retreat. "It might be your house, and the baby might be your son, but I am not *your* surrogate. I do not belong to you, and I will never be any man's possession."

"You took my money—"

"Not that again!"

"So until you give birth, you are mine."

"Wrong." She threw her shoulders back. "Not yours. I will never be yours. In fact, I'd like to call Mr. Laurent right now. I think it's time he and I had a little conversation and sorted things out."

"You don't need to call anyone."

"Oh, but I do. I've had enough of your hospitality and think I'd be more comfortable in a hotel somewhere in Athens—"

"That's not going to happen."

"You can't keep me here."

"But I can. You're my responsibility. You're in my care."

"Are you telling me that I can't leave?"

For a moment there was just silence. His jaw tightened. His dark eyes glowed, and then his lashes dropped, concealing his expression. "You are safe here," he said quietly. "Safer here than anywhere else in Greece."

"But I don't feel safe. You don't respect me, nor do you respect my need for distance and boundaries."

He frowned. "How am I not respecting your boundaries? I haven't touched you, haven't threatened you in any way."

"If you don't know what respect is, I am certainly not going to try to explain it to you. But it does renew my concern about staying here, living in such close proximity to you. Safety isn't just physical. It's psychological—"

"Renew your concern? What does that mean? You were not comfortable coming here?"

"Of course I wasn't comfortable. I didn't know you. I still don't. But what I've learned since arriving isn't flattering." She held his gaze. "I feel as if you and Mr. Laurent deliberately deceived me—"

"Deceived you how? Were you not paid? Were you not given an incredibly generous bonus for traveling here?"

"Now that I know you, it wasn't enough. In fact, I don't think you could have ever paid me enough to put up with your nonsense."

He threw his head back. "Nonsense?"

"Yes. You're behaving like a thug, a bully—"

"That's enough, *gynaika*."

She had no idea what he'd called her in Greek, but she

didn't particularly care, not when his tone and words were so insufferably patronizing. "I'd like to use your phone. I want to call Mr. Laurent."

"And what do you think Mr. Laurent is going to do?"

"Get me a plane ticket out of here."

"Mr. Laurent works for me. He is *my* attorney."

"He promised me…" Her voice faded, and she swallowed hard as she struggled to remember just what Mr. Laurent had promised. She drew a blank. Surely Mr. Laurent had promised her something…?

"And what did my attorney promise you, Georgia?" Nikos drawled, seeing her uncertainty.

She held her breath, fighting her nerves. Her heart hammered hard. "He said you were a good person. He said you could be trusted." She stared him in the eye. "And I believed him. And I believed in you. So, either you respect my wishes, and leave my room now, or I will know everything he said, and everything you are, is a lie."

Thank God her voice was clear, strong, authoritative. It was the right voice for emergencies.

And Nikos Panos was most definitely an emergency, especially when he stood toe to toe with her, hands clenched, jaw tight. His dark eyes continued to bore into her, scorching her, demanding her to back down. Acquiesce.

Georgia didn't acquiesce. *Ever.*

"No one speaks to me with such impertinence," he ground out.

"Perhaps if they did, you'd have better manners."

"Enough," he snapped, silencing her. "Enough with your words. The sound of your voice exhausts me. I am quite certain my son is fed up, as well." And then he walked out.

Georgia dropped onto the couch in the living room and curled her legs up under her, stunned. She felt as if she'd been through a major battle and she was wiped out.

Nikos Panos was not like any man she'd ever met before, and she sincerely hoped she'd never meet anyone like him again.

Even after sitting for several minutes she continued to shake. She wasn't afraid, just shell-shocked.

She couldn't believe his behavior. She couldn't imagine anyone acting that way, much less to the woman hired to carry his child.

How did he think she'd react when he threw his weight around, told her how to dress, how to behave?

A rap sounded on her door. She knew from the firm knock who it was.

"Yes?" she called, too worn-out to get off the couch.

The door opened, and Nikos stood on the threshold, looking not much happier than he had ten minutes ago when he'd stormed out.

"May I come in?" he asked with terse civility.

"If we're done fighting," she answered.

He entered her suite of rooms, walking toward her. "I don't enjoy it, either."

She arched a brow but didn't contradict him.

He paced the living room floor, up and back, his jaw hard, his glossy black hair tousled but still framing his handsome features perfectly.

When he wasn't talking and enraging her, he was a beautiful man.

"I am not a barbarian," he said at length. "I'm not a caveman or a werewolf." He turned, faced her, arms folded over his powerful chest. "I am just a man. That is all."

There was something different in his voice and eyes. Something almost vulnerable. She felt a peculiar ache in her chest, and she swallowed around the lump forming in her throat.

When he wasn't growling at her and stalking her and making her heart beat too fast, he was quite handsome, and just possibly a tiny bit appealing. But he growled and muttered and intimidated far more than necessary.

"I am sorry if I hurt your feelings," she said carefully, "but your world here isn't my world. Your life here—it's what you know—but it's all new for me. And it's not normal for me."

"I have never intended to disrespect you. I have merely tried to help you."

She nearly smiled at his idea of being helpful, and then her smile faded as she remembered his last words before he marched out. "I can forgive nearly all of it, but you were deliberately cruel when you said that your son was fed up with the sound of my voice."

He said nothing. He just looked at her.

A lump filled her throat, making it hard to swallow. Her eyes burned, and her heart felt so sore. If she wasn't careful, she'd cry, and she never cried. At least, she rarely cried, and she never cried in front of strangers. Or Savannah. She never wanted to frighten Savannah. Georgia prided herself on her strength.

Now she knotted her hands in her lap and blinked hard to clear her eyes. "You do know that your son lives in my body." She was fighting the lump in her throat now. It had doubled in size and was making it difficult to speak. "Your son doesn't even know you yet, Nikos. The only thing he knows right now is *me*. My voice. My heartbeat. And for your information, he likes both, quite a bit."

Nikos's jaw flexed, a tiny muscle bunching in his jaw, near his ear. "I'm certain he does," he said quietly. "I'm sure he thinks you're his mother."

The words, gently spoken, cut her to the quick.

The tears she'd fought to hold back now flooded her eyes, and she looked away and bit down ruthlessly into her lower lip, forcing her teeth into the soft skin, drawing blood to distract her from the pain Nikos had just caused.

He was right, of course.

Absolutely right.

And yet she had never once let herself think those words, or feel the power of them.

The baby would lose his mother, just as she had lost her mother...

It wasn't fair, not for him. Maybe not for any of them. But it was the decision she had made to help provide for her sister. It was the only thing she could think to do given their circumstances.

She blinked hard, fiercely, trying to dry the tears, praying he didn't see them.

"Which is why you are here," he added flatly. "To allow my son to know me, to become familiar with my voice, to establish a bond so that when you leave the hospital after delivery, he won't be in distress as he will have me...his father."

Nikos wasn't making things better. He was making it worse. And his words felt like he'd poured salt all over an open wound.

So the baby won't be in distress...

So that when you leave, he won't suffer...

For a second she couldn't catch her breath. Pain splintered in her heart, radiating in every direction.

She'd never gone here...to this place...

She'd never really let herself think of him, though, cognizant of the fact that the child wasn't hers. It had been almost too easy these past six months to remind herself of that as she wasn't the maternal type, that she'd never played house or cuddled dolls as a little girl, not like Savannah or Charlie, her youngest sister, who wouldn't go anywhere without a doll in the crook of her arm.

She'd constantly reminded herself that she was the tomboy. That she didn't need touch, didn't need cuddles, didn't need tenderness. No, she was tough. A tomboy. She'd always preferred to run and jump and swim. Growing up, she'd been happiest challenging others to races. She loved competition. She was good at all subjects and brilliant at math. She loved doing complicated problems in her head, loved solving equations, and once she began studying chemistry, she found another favorite subject.

Life made sense in a lab. Math made sense.

Emotions and the heart…those didn't make sense. Those couldn't be managed and controlled.

So no, she'd told herself she didn't want children. She told herself throughout the hormone treatments and egg retrieval that she hadn't inherited a maternal gene. She'd repeated this during the IVF transfer, focusing on her lack of patience and her inability to compromise and yield as reasons why she shouldn't be a mother.

And then when she got the call that she was pregnant, that the embryo transfer had taken hold, her fierce, tough heart missed a beat.

She'd felt shock and joy, and then she'd suppressed the joy and focused on the future. Her future in medicine.

Conceiving the baby had been a scientific act, one with predictable steps and measurable progress. Of course there were uncertainties, just as there were with every pregnancy, but so far the pregnancy had been smooth.

At least, she'd been able to pretend it was smooth. But now Nikos had lifted the lid on Pandora's box. The baby had become real. And she could say she wasn't maternal, but she suddenly feared for the baby, feared for the life he might have to live…

Without her.

Georgia drew a panicked breath. Her fingers lightly grazed her bump, as if reassuring the baby that all would be well. But truthfully, now that she was here, now that she saw where the child would grow up, and how he'd grow up, and who would raise him, she wasn't at all sure he would be okay.

This wasn't the life she'd imagined for him...not that she'd spent that much time imagining a future she wouldn't be part of, but she'd smashed her worries with a blind confidence that the child was part of an immensely wealthy family and he'd lead a privileged life.

She'd told herself he'd have the best of everything: education, opportunity, protection.

Now she wondered if that would be enough.

Stop. Stop, Georgia, stop. She couldn't think like this, couldn't go there in her head, either. She'd known from the beginning she wouldn't keep the baby; she'd known she had no say in his future. She was a vessel. She was nothing more than a womb. She'd signed away every right to him.

Not her child.

His.

"Are you crying?" he asked, sitting next to her on the couch.

"No." She was not a crier. She couldn't remember when she'd last wept in public over anything.

"You are," he contradicted, taking her chin and lifting her face to his inspection, his dark gaze scrutinizing every inch of her face, making her cheeks flush and her eyes sting and burn. "What is happening? One moment you are laughing—the next you are crying. I don't understand."

That made two of them. She didn't understand, either. "Maybe it's the jet lag."

He gazed at her intently, staring into her eyes, as if able to see all the way through her. "Or pregnancy hormones?"

She could feel the heat of his fingers on her jaw, and a sensitive prickling in her skin. She couldn't remember the last time a man touched her. She'd dated plenty but medical school had been so consuming for the past few years that there was no time for serious relationships, and even if Georgia had time, she wasn't one to jump in and out of bed. It wasn't her upbringing—she wasn't pious in the least—but trust. Or lack of trust. She wasn't comfortable stripping bare, becoming vulnerable. She wasn't comfortable exposing her body or her heart.

"Emotions are definitely more volatile when pregnant," she conceded, trying to ignore the crazy pulse leaping in response, wondering if he could feel the rapid staccato in her jaw, hoping he couldn't, as the mad beating of her heart wasn't due to fear, but something else...something worse.

She was reacting to him. Responding to him.

"I am not usually emotional," she added.

"So you said on the application."

"I'm not," she insisted. "It's you. Your effect on me."

His brow furrowed. "Are you afraid of me?"

"No. Not afraid. But you are intense. I'm sure I'd be calm...or calmer...if you gave me a little bit more space." She'd tried to sound matter-of-fact, but the words came out breathless, her voice suddenly pitched low and husky.

He heard the husky note, and a light entered his dark eyes. His hand slipped from her jaw, sliding down over her neck, and her lips parted in a silent gasp.

She didn't like him, but clearly some part of her liked his touch. Pleasure rippled through her.

She didn't know if he'd heard her gasp, or felt her shiver, but his gaze focused on her mouth, and his fingertips lightly stroked her neck, as if intent on discovering just how she'd been wired.

The problem was, she'd been wired very well. She'd always been a little too physically sensitive. A little too aware of pleasure. And pleasure coursed through her. She gasped again, no longer connected by muscle and bone, but by nerves and sensation. Shocking to think that some twisted part of her enjoyed his touch.

"You are not the surrogate I believed I was getting,"

he said, drawing his hand back, but not before his fingertips grazed her collarbone, sending another little flurry of sparks shooting through her.

She longed to fall back, needing air and space and oxygen, but her feet felt leaden and her brain was fuzzy. "I will change those shoes," she said faintly. "Shall I meet you outside?"

"I'll wait by the door."

"Nikos, I'm not going to fall as I change my shoes."

"And I'm not taking chances."

The villa was a large, broad three-story square building that appeared to be attached to the mountain, as if it had grown from the volcanic rock jutting from the sea. The foundation of the villa went all the way down into the water, and each of the three floors above the foundation had access to a different outdoor terrace.

Georgia could tell that someone, at some point, had attempted to turn the collection of rooms into habitable space with a slap of plaster and a wash of white paint. The worn plaster might have had more charm if so many of the rooms weren't cold. There were moments during the tour that Georgia was certain that it was warmer outside than inside. Clearly, this was not the Greece of travel brochures. Or at least, not modern Greece.

"Originally this was a fortress and then a medieval merchant's warehouse and then, during the Renaissance, a monastery. Now it is just my home," Nikos told her as they left the formal dining room and entered what had to have been a chapel and was now a room lined with bookshelves. The soaring vaulted ceiling gave the room a spaciousness that was lacking elsewhere. "My library," he said. Then adding, "You're welcome to study here."

She appreciated the offer, thinking she would enjoy studying here, and not just for the room's beauty but for its comfort. The large ceramic-glazed heater in the corner was making the library toasty warm.

After leaving the house, Nikos showed her the gardens. There weren't many shrubs and plants in the ground, as there was little rainfall in this part of the Cyclades, just a half-dozen potted bougainvillea close to the house and a scattering of gnarled cypress trees farther away, dotting the numerous walking paths.

Nikos escorted her on the various paths, wanting her to be comfortable with each. Some of the paths were laid with stones, others were packed with crushed gravel. Nearly all had a bench somewhere, providing a place to sit and enjoy the stunning views of the sea, dotted with distant islands.

Georgia would never tell Nikos, but she was glad he'd had her change into proper walking shoes, and it felt good to walk and stretch her muscles and breathe in the fresh, brisk air.

Twenty minutes after setting off, they returned to the villa, passing through a different walled garden on the third level to reach the house. She'd expected more benches, or perhaps a table and chairs, but instead there was an enormous outdoor pool, the water a sparkling aquamarine, glinting beneath the sun. The pool had lane lines for lap swimming as well as broad steps in a corner of the shallow end. Padded lounge chairs flanked both ends and pots of lemon trees dotted the courtyard, while a burst of red bougainvillea clung to one dazzling white wall.

It was lovely and so inviting. It was the kind of pool one would see at a very exclusive resort and yet Nikos had it all to himself. "You said last night that you keep it heated," she said.

He nodded. "I love the water and like to swim year-round." He walked her to the little whitewashed, tiled-roof pool house at the far end. "Towels, robes, shower and a sauna," he said. "Although the sauna is off-limits for you."

She shot him a reproving glance. "You don't need to do that. I am very much aware of what I should and shouldn't do during a pregnancy."

"Because you're a med student?"

"Because I've been reading all the books and researching what I don't know, and listening to what my doctor tells me. Most of it is common sense anyway." She dug her hands into the back pocket of her jeans. "But speaking of medical school, I do need to get some studying done. I tried during the flight but wasn't very successful."

"Mr. Laurent said your exam was scheduled for late June. But isn't that pushing it a bit, considering you'll be delivering late May, or possibly early June?"

"I should be fine. Provided I study."

He took her back then, past the pool, into the house and then down the stairs to the second floor, where their bedrooms were. They were silent as they walked, their footsteps ringing on the hard tumbled marble floor, passing through whitewashed halls with brief glimpses out the windows at the startlingly blue sky and sea. She felt Nikos's mood change as they walked, and she darted a glance at him, wondering what had happened to make the silence feel dark and brooding.

She needed to understand him, or the next three and a half months would be beyond miserable.

"Why are you doing this?" she asked as they reached her bedroom door. "Surely there are better, easier, as well as cheaper, ways to become a father."

"I want a child, not a wife."

"Are wives such awful things?" She was trying to be light and funny but he didn't smile.

"I was married. Marriage isn't for me."

"Maybe a different wife—"

"No." His expression hardened. "I'm not marriage material. I do not make a good husband."

"Your edges can be rough, but you're not all bad. You're quite protective, maybe overly protective—"

"You haven't seen the real me."

"No?"

"No."

She should have felt trepidation then, but she didn't. Instead he'd simply made her curious. He reminded her of a puzzle or equation that wanted solving. "What is the real you like?"

He hesitated a long moment. "Aggressive." His dark eyes found hers and held. "Carnal."

His answer, in that deep, rough voice, sent a rush of heat through her. *Carnal.*

She couldn't remember the last time she'd heard anyone use that word. It was such a biblical word...

Her mind scrambled to think of something to say even as her mouth went dry and her body grew hot, skin prickling, every inch of her suddenly painfully sensitive.

Before she could think of an appropriate response, he nodded and was gone, heading back down the hall.

CHAPTER FIVE

NIKOS WALKED SWIFTLY down the hall, his right hand squeezed into a fist. He couldn't get away from Georgia's rooms fast enough.

He knew why he'd told her those things about himself. It had meant to be a warning, to ensure she kept her distance, but his words hadn't scared her.

If anything, the warning had the opposite effect. She'd looked at him with her wide, thoughtful eyes, her expression intrigued.

But she shouldn't be intrigued. She needed to know who she was dealing with...what she was dealing with...

He'd scarred Elsa—broken her—and he didn't want to ever hurt another woman in the same way. He'd sworn off women. Sworn off love and passion. But he was determined to be a father, determined to break the curse, if there really was a curse...

Maybe then the wounds would heal.

Maybe there would be more. A future. New life.

Three and a half months until his son was here. Three and a half months until he could close the door on the past. And Elsa.

Once the baby was here, there would be no Elsa and no grief. There would be hope. And yet it hadn't been easy getting to this point. There had been so many dark moments and endless nights.

He might be the devil incarnate, but apparently even the devil could be a father. And he'd wanted to be a father since he was a boy. He'd wanted a family, maybe because he'd been so lonely as a boy. He'd married Elsa certain there would be children, but it hadn't worked out that way.

* * *

Nikos kept his distance the next day, aware that she had her studies to occupy her attention and he had his business.

But late in the afternoon he sent word to her room that he'd see her at five on the terrace for drinks and a lite bite, and then dinner would be at ten.

She was already on the terrace when he arrived, dressed in peach-and-gray cashmere. Her long hair had been braided into a simple side plait, with a couple of long golden strands loose to frame her face. He glanced down at her feet. Gray ankle boots. Small one-inch heel.

If he'd told Elsa no heels, she would have never worn anything but flats for the rest of their marriage. Clearly Georgia was no Elsa.

He nearly smiled, not sure why he was amused. Maybe it was just the relief that Georgia wasn't Elsa.

But before he could greet Georgia or offer her a drink, she lifted her laptop from the couch and approached him with it. "I haven't been able to figure out how to get on the internet," she said. "I am hoping you know the trick, or maybe it's password-protected."

"There isn't a trick," he said. "I don't really have reliable internet. It's satellite based, so imagine old-fashioned dial-up speeds and endless dropped file downloads, coupled with information darkness that lasts for hours, or worse, days."

He saw her jaw drop and eyes widen. "How do you go online?"

"I don't."

"At all?"

"Rarely."

"How can that be? I live on the internet. I use it for everything."

He shrugged. "When you don't have access to it, you learn to live without it."

"But in Athens you must have it."

"Yes."

"But why not here?"

"Greece has over six thousand islands and islets, and only two hundred and twenty-seven are populated. And where we are, in the Cyclades, there are very few people living. The Greek government can't afford to put in the cables and fiber optics needed for reliable and fast internet, and I'm certainly not going to pay for it, either."

"So how do you manage your business from Kamari without the internet?"

"I have a phone for meetings and emergencies, and once a week mail arrives—more frequently if something is urgent—and I'm quite happy with that."

Clearly she wasn't happy with the news. Her brows flattened, and she pursed her lips and studied him as if he were a dinosaur...or worse.

"I thought Mr. Laurent warned you," he said. "I asked him to prepare you. You were to have brought textbooks and whatever you could download onto your computer's hard drive—"

"I did do that."

"So you can study."

"Yes, but so many resources are online."

He shrugged again. "I guess you will have to do it the old-school way."

Her blue eyes blazed. "This isn't a game. This is serious."

"I'm not mocking you. I'm stating a reality. There is no internet. You need to rely on hard copies of everything."

She turned away from him, eyes closing for a moment, and then she drew a slow breath, as if trying to compose herself. "I also noticed you don't have TV or radio," she said quietly. "Is that true, or did I just miss seeing where you'd stashed them?"

"You are correct. I do not have TV or radio here."

Georgia walked to the white slipcovered couch and sat down, cradling her laptop against her. "You have nothing here for diversion."

She looked so stricken that he almost felt sorry for her. "I don't need it," he answered. "I like my thoughts. I read. I work."

"You're a hermit."

"I like the quiet, yes."

Georgia hugged the laptop closer to her. "It's rather frightening how isolated you are."

"It's not frightening, and you know I have a satellite phone when I need it."

He went to the tray with the pitchers of water and juice. "Want something?"

"Yes. A ticket to Athens, please."

His brow quirked. "Is that a name of an American cocktail?"

She gave him a long look. "You know it's not."

"What can I pour for you?"

"I'm not thirsty."

"You'll feel better if you stay hydrated, and this one is really good." He filled a tall glass and carried it to her. "Pomegranate juice and something else."

She took the glass from him and set it on the table next to her without drinking. "And you really never leave here?"

"Haven't in a year."

"What about when you...did your part...to make the baby?"

"The medical team came here."

"And what about when I need a checkup? In Atlanta, I saw the obstetrician once a month, just to make sure the baby was doing well. Will I really have that here, or are you just placating me?"

"Not placating you. The doctor will come here every four weeks to check on you, and the baby."

"You can afford to fly your doctor in, but you can't afford internet?"

"Laying fiber optics can cost millions to billions of dollars. Having a doctor make a house call is a lot less." He studied her a long minute. "Is it really so tragic not having access to the internet? Does it feel like a punishment to be so far removed from society?"

She was silent even longer, and then she reached for her juice glass and took a sip, and then another. "This is good," she said. "And unlike most American girls, I grew up without internet and TV and radio. We were lucky just to have electricity sometimes. There aren't many bells and whistles when you're the daughter of missionaries."

"So you can survive here without."

"Of course I can. The lack of internet will not break me. It's more of an issue of do I want to be without the internet? And the answer is no."

"You'll get used to it."

"Just like people get used to jail."

It was his turn to look at her hard. She blinked at him, wide-eyed innocence, and then smiled.

And her smile was not at all innocent.

It had been quite the day. Georgia practically drooped as she ate dinner. She wasn't hungry. She was too exhausted and numb to be hungry. But she couldn't call it a night until she'd exacted a promise from Nikos.

She wanted the lock put back on her door.

Was she afraid that Nikos would attack her in the night? No.

But she wasn't yet comfortable in the old villa and she would feel better with a door that locked. It'd give her a sense of security here, as well as a feeling of control.

She'd given up her world to come to Greece. How could he not make this concession for her? And Georgia didn't know if it was a birth-order thing, or just a survivor thing, but control was important to her. It was why she'd agreed to be a donor... She felt as if she was the one with control.

The surrogacy was another matter.

In hindsight it was a terrible mistake, but she was too tired tonight to go there and think about that. The only way she'd get through this last trimester was by just living one day at a time.

Nikos watched Georgia from across the dinner table, taking in the way the flickering candlelight illuminated her face, creating arcs of gold light as well as mysterious shadows and hollows.

It had been a tense cocktail hour, but dinner ended up being surprisingly relaxed. There wasn't a great deal of conversation during the meal, but Nikos didn't think Georgia minded the quiet. She didn't strike him as a woman who needed to constantly be chattering. He wasn't sure if that was because of the way she was raised or her own personality, but either way, he was grateful. He wasn't one who needed endless talk and conversation.

Early in his marriage, Elsa had somehow interpreted his silence to mean he was angry or upset. It created tremendous friction between them, and he'd tried to explain that he'd been a loner since he was a young boy, an only child in a small, strict family.

Unlike traditional Greek families, with lots of cousins and aunts and uncles, it was just his parents and him, and a grandfather even less inclined to talk than his father, forcing him to learn how to entertain himself, teaching him how to be his own friend. By the time he was a teenager, he was comfortable with his thoughts. The quiet gave him a chance to sort out problems—like how to help save the family business. His father wasn't a born leader, nor a savvy businessman, and when Nikos was still young, his father took bad advice from the wrong people and made a series of horrible decisions.

Those horrible decisions resulted in Nikos's father over-extending the company, investing in the wrong things and threatening to bankrupt them all when the entire country's economy crumbled.

If it hadn't been for Nikos's aggressive plan, Panos Enterprise would have been carved up and sold off to the highest bidder, leaving the family embarrassed and broke.

Nikos was twenty-four when he took over at Panos. Twenty-six when he married Elsa, and a widower at twenty-eight.

After Elsa's death he'd retreated here to Kamari, and he'd been living in virtual isolation for the past five years. He hadn't attended a wedding or a social occasion since Elsa's death.

He'd stopped traveling, too, as his burns drew attention and he didn't want to be stared at, didn't want to hear the whispers that would accompany his appearance somewhere. Once a year he forced himself to show up at the Panos headquarters in Athens, but the rest of the time, he flew his management in for meetings on Kamari.

There were no women in the upper management of his company, and that was deliberate, too, as he never wanted to be accused of forcing himself on women, nor did he want women whispering about his face.

He knew he was scarred.

He knew what people said about him.

Beast. Monster. Animal.

Werewolf. *Lykánthropos.*

Georgia's words came back to haunt him. He swallowed quickly and glanced past her, looking to the dining room window with the view of the moonlight reflecting off the sea.

Lykánthropos. That was a new one. He'd have to remember it and one day share a good laugh with his son.

"Nikos."

Hearing his name, he turned his attention back to Georgia. She was leaning toward him, her silken hair spilling over her shoulders, gleaming in the candlelight.

"Yes?" he said, sensing that all the calm was about to change.

"I want a lock for my door, Nikos." Her voice was quiet and steady but at the same time determined. She wasn't asking a question. She wasn't pleading. She was making a statement. A demand.

He tensed, his ease vanishing. So there was going to be drama after all.

He groaned inwardly, wishing Mr. Laurent had been more honest with him. The Atlanta attorney had made Georgia out to be a paragon of female intelligence and beauty, a combination of Athena and Aphrodite. Mr. Laurent had it wrong. Maybe he didn't know his goddesses, because Georgia was more like Artemis than Athena or Aphrodite. Artemis was the most independent spirit, and was known as the goddess of the hunt, nature and birth.

"We discussed this yesterday," he said, rolling the heavy silver napkin ring between his palm and the table. "You know why I don't want you to have a locked door."

"And I need you to understand why I want a lock on my door. I know it doesn't make sense to you—most men don't understand—but I won't sleep if I don't feel safe. And I don't feel safe—"

"Even though there is nothing here that can hurt you?"

"Surely you have irrational fears. Surely you understand that it's not about reality but about perception. Having a lock on my door gives me a sense of control, and that sense of control allows me to feel safer."

"I am not belittling your fears. You know why I removed the lock. I must be able to reach you if there's an emergency."

"You managed to kick the door down last time." Her lips curved, but the smile didn't reach her eyes. "And I'm sure if there was a real emergency, you could do it again."

"I was lucky that first day."

She reached across the table and touched his hand. *"Please."*

He flinched at the shock of her skin against his. Sparks shot through him, and his groin tightened. His gaze dropped to her hand resting on his. Her hand was pale against his skin, her fingers slender and narrow. He pictured stripping her tunic off, pictured the pale honey of her skin as she lay stretched naked in his bed.

He ground his teeth together, his molars clamped tight.

Georgia made him want things...made him want to do things...fierce, hard, hot. All the things that Elsa hadn't wanted. All the things sweet, gentle Elsa had been afraid of. Sex. Passion. Skin.

Carefully he disengaged, drawing his hand free of Georgia's. He struggled to organize his thoughts. She'd caught him completely off guard. And it wasn't just the touch, but her fearlessness.

Artemis.

He ached from head to foot, throbbing with sensation, his body hot with desire, the desire so new after so many years of feeling nothing, feeling dead.

Maybe a locked door would be a good thing.

"You could have a key," she added quietly. "In case of an emergency."

He looked up at her, and she was watching him intently,

her blue gaze unblinking. "But only you," she added. "No one else. I trust no one else."

He almost laughed. "You trust me?"

"You're the father of my b—" She broke off, swallowed. "This baby. I have to trust you. Don't I?"

The lock was installed that very night.

It was past midnight when Georgia finally went to bed, but she slept well. There were no bad dreams. There were no dreams at all, thank God.

But Nikos couldn't sleep.

He spent hours castigating himself. He shouldn't have brought her here. He should have waited until the very end of the pregnancy, and then arranged for Georgia to give birth in Athens. That would have been the way to go. That might still be the way to go. Have his plane come pick her up and send her to live at his house in Athens. His staff would care for her, and she'd be comfortable there—probably far more comfortable than here. She could shop and relax, attend the theater and eat good meals out.

But he wouldn't be there, and he wouldn't be able to keep an eye on her.

He wouldn't be able to protect her if things went wrong.

Which was why he'd brought her to Kamari.

What he needed to do was smash the desire. He had to control the attraction, and he could, if he just kept Elsa in his mind.

He'd crushed Elsa. He couldn't do that to Georgia.

The next morning when Georgia woke, she was grateful she'd slept well, but she couldn't quite smash the little anxious voice inside her, the one that kept reminding her of what she'd almost said last night at dinner.

My baby.

She'd caught herself in time, and didn't think Nikos had

noticed the slip, or her swift substitution, but she had, and it was eating at her.

This was a problem.

Why had she even thought the words? *My baby...?*

Where had that possessive pronoun come from? It had never been her baby... It wasn't ever going to be her baby. She didn't even like referring to the child as a he, preferring the impersonal "it" as a way of keeping distance... remaining detached.

Now she worried she wasn't quite as detached as she'd imagined.

Determined to silence the nagging voice, Georgia pushed the button that alerted the staff that she was awake. When one of the housemaids appeared at her door, Georgia asked for a light breakfast so she could start studying.

A tray arrived fifteen minutes later filled with bowls and dishes—thick, creamy yogurt, sliced fruit, warm pastries and an impressive silver pot of coffee.

Georgia ate at the little table in her living room, and then she set the tray aside and grabbed her books. She studied at the table all morning, and then at noon took a break to go to the pool to swim. She had swum yesterday and had managed thirty laps. Today she wanted to see if she could do forty, hoping the extra exercise would quiet her anxiety. She was right to have been worried about being here on Kamari for the third trimester. It wasn't going to be easy. She didn't feel calm or secure.

Hoping it was just hormones, she retrieved her goggles and kickboard from the pool house and began her swim.

She was halfway through her laps and paused at the wall to catch her breath. As she lifted her swim goggles, she spotted Nikos diving in the other end of the pool.

She caught only a glimpse of his body before he disappeared into the water, but he was in amazing shape—well built and tan, with hard, cut muscles everywhere.

He swam underwater halfway down the pool to finally surface on his back. Nikos did a couple of easy strokes, showing impressive form, before flipping over onto his stomach to continue down the pool, toward her.

Georgia felt a flutter of nerves and quickly pulled her goggles into place and set off down her lane. It was a big pool, and the white lane line divided the length into sides. He wasn't in her side, he'd taken the empty lane, but that didn't calm her down. Even though there was plenty of room for both of them, she felt increasingly self-conscious, especially when she could see him pass on the other side, his big bronze body slicing through the water.

He was a very good swimmer, a very strong swimmer. Gradually Georgia found herself watching him instead of continuing with her own laps.

He'd only just gotten in but he'd already swum six laps, making quick progress with his dark head down, his stroke smooth and steady. He had that kind of kick that was powerful without creating lots of splashing.

Each time he reached the wall, he did a neat flip turn, pushing off the tiles to glide beneath the water, before surfacing midway down the pool to continue swimming to the end.

She was impressed. He had to have once been a competitive swimmer.

Intrigued, Georgia grabbed her kickboard and began kicking her way down the pool, keeping her chin tucked in the water to try to hide the fact that she was watching Nikos.

She liked that he wasn't paying her any attention. She enjoyed just looking at him, studying his muscles and the way they bunched and tightened as he sliced through the water. From his tanned skin it was obvious he swam often, and he kept swimming for the next thirty minutes.

Georgia gave up, though. She found it too distracting to

have him there. She was heading for the steps when Nikos suddenly appeared at her side.

"All done?" he asked.

She sat down quickly on the middle step, the warm water lapping at her shoulders, hiding her figure. She wasn't usually prudish, but she felt almost naked in the suit, which was difficult when your body no longer felt like your body. Her breasts were so much fuller. Her belly was rounded. Every inch of her skin prickled, sensitive. "Yes." She was nervous, and she didn't even know why. "Do you swim daily?" she added, trying to fill the silence.

"I try to. I like that it's something I can do year-round."

"You're good."

"I'm calmer after a swim. I find it's good to work off aggression and tension."

She studied his profile. She was beginning to realize that he was always careful to present her with the side of his face that wasn't scarred. That made her feel a pang of sorrow. He was so aware of how he looked to others, so aware that his scars must be unpleasant to others.

"Were you always…aggressive?" she asked, using his word, not sure if it was truly the right word for him. The more she got to know of him, the less aggressive she found him. He struck her as a man who was protective and prideful, but what man wasn't?

"No." He flashed white teeth. "I was quite shy as a boy. Painfully introverted."

"What changed you?"

He opened his mouth to answer and then changed his mind, giving her a shrug instead.

"Something must have happened," she persisted.

"I grew up. Became a man."

She wanted to reach out and turn his face. She wanted to see the pink scars, see where they disappeared into his hairline, and how they changed the hairline, and how they curved over his ear. She suspected he wore his hair loose and long to hide as much of the scars as he could.

"If your son inherits your good looks, he will be very lucky," she said with a smile.

Nikos frowned and looked at her quickly, his expression shuttered. "Is that a joke?"

She blinked in surprise. "No. You're very, very good-looking, Nikos—"

"You are pulling my leg."

"I'm not."

"I know what I am." His dark gaze met hers. "I know what you called me. *Lykánthropos.*" The edge of his mouth curled up. "That was a first, but it fits."

"I don't know what you just said."

"Werewolf." He was still smiling, but the smile hurt her. It was so hard and fierce and yet behind the smile she sensed a world of pain.

"I didn't mean it like that," she whispered, feeling a pang of guilt and shame. "It had nothing to do with your scars."

"It's okay. As I said, it fits."

"That's not why I said it."

"I've heard worse—"

"Nikos." She could barely say his name. Her heart hurt. "It wasn't your face. It's not the scars. It's the way you were hanging on my door, filling the space up. Your energy was just so big, so physical. You are so physical…" Her voice faded as she could see he wasn't even listening to her. "I'm sorry."

"Don't be. Now you know why I swim. I have a lot of energy. I've been told that I come across as very physical, and it's unpleasant for others. I don't want to be unpleasant for others. I wasn't raised to make women uncomfortable."

For a moment she couldn't speak or breathe. Her eyes stung, hot and gritty. Her heart felt impossibly tender.

Somehow everything had changed between them. Somehow she felt as though she were the aggressor and she was hunting him, chasing him with a pitchfork…

"I have a feeling you've been labeled unfairly," she said when she was sure she could speak. "I don't know that you are as aggressive as you think you are. In fact, I would say you are more protective than aggressive."

"That's because you don't know me well."

"What do you do that is so aggressive?"

"I have a forceful personality."

"This is true. But what specifically do you do that warrants the label? Do you yell…hit…punch…shake? Do you threaten women—"

"No! None of that. That is terrible."

"So what do you do? Are you hostile towards people? Antagonistic?"

"I try to avoid most people. That's why I live here. Works out better for everyone."

"And yet even here, you have to swim to manage your aggression and tension?"

"Maybe I should have said that swimming helps me burn off excess energy."

"That does sound better than aggressive." The wind blew across the pool and Georgia slid lower under the water to stay warm. "You and I have clashed, and I don't agree with some of your rules, including recommended footwear, but I wouldn't describe you as a hostile person. I'd say you're assertive."

"But in English, are they not the same things—aggressive and assertive?"

"For me, they are different. Assertive means being direct and strong, and, yes, forceful, but in a commanding sort of way, whereas I view aggressive to be far more negative. Aggressive can imply a lack of control, as well as unpleasantly hostile."

His mouth quirked. "Based on your definition, I would prefer to be assertive instead of aggressive."

She was thinking hard now on the word, and the various ways it could be used in the English language, and aggressive wasn't always negative. In fact, in medicine, an aggressive treatment was often the best treatment. "You know, aggressive can mean dynamic. In battle, you want to be aggressive. When dealing with cancer, you need an aggressive plan of attack."

"Sounds as if you are giving me permission to be aggressive."

She pushed at the water, creating small waves. "If it's for the right reason." She gave another push at the water, sending more ripples across the pool. "In business, I would think you'd have to be aggressive. Successful businesses are rarely complacent. I'm quite sure successful people are the same."

He ran a hand over his inky-black hair, muscles bunching and rippling in his bicep and shoulder. "You keep surprising me." His voice was rough, deep. "You're not what I expected. You are more." His head turned, and she glimpsed the scars he always tried so hard to hide. "My son is lucky to have had you as his...mother."

Georgia felt a lance of pain, her chest squeezing, air bottling. She struggled to smile, hiding the hurt as well as the wash of panic.

Mother...his mother...

Why did Nikos say that? Why would he say that? Something buried deep inside her wanted to scream, punch, lash out.

She wasn't this child's mother. She wasn't his mother. She wasn't. She'd signed those rights away forever, and it was the right thing to do. She wasn't prepared to be a mother, and certainly not a single mother who was only halfway through medical school.

Georgia rose and climbed from the pool. It was chilly out and shivering; she grabbed her towel and thick terry-cloth robe. The entire time she blotted herself dry she fought for calm and control.

She was someone who liked control, *needed* control, and yet she'd agreed to a contract that gave her no control…and was starting to turn her heart inside out.

Dropping the towel, Georgia quickly slid her arms into the robe, tying the sash around her waist, determined to get a grip. She couldn't panic. It wouldn't help to panic.

"I'll see you later tonight," she said to Nikos before rushing away. She dropped the damp towel in the laundry hamper at the pool house and then continued up to her room.

Her teeth chattered as she walked. She was scared. She didn't like this feeling. The pregnancy had changed everything, including her.

Her senses of taste and smell were different. Her emotions were more intense, and her moods were more volatile.

And now she was here, on a private island, in the middle of the Aegean Sea, with no phone and no internet and no way to distract herself from what was happening. And what was happening was beginning to rattle her.

She was having a baby, and then she was giving the baby away, before going away herself.

Good God. What had she done?

And why had she thought this was something she could actually do?

CHAPTER SIX

IT HAD BECOME custom to meet at sunset for drinks on the terrace. Quite often it was their first time seeing each other each day. Today had been different. They'd met at the pool during her swim and now they were together again, outside on the terrace on the third floor, taking in the sunset, making pleasant but inane conversation. She hoped the meaningless words would keep her from thinking, or feeling, because she was scared.

It was too late to have regrets. Too late to wish she'd never agreed to be a surrogate. An egg donor was one thing, but to carry the child, and then fly halfway across the world to deliver him in a foreign country?

And then leave him behind with a billionaire father who was both reclusive and eccentric?

It was a lot to digest, even for her.

Disruptive little thoughts had needled her all afternoon.

Her parents would be heartbroken if they knew what she was doing. And then there was Savannah, who'd been convinced from the outset that this would end badly. Savannah hadn't been as concerned about Georgia being an egg donor since a number of female medical students considered it an opportunity to do something good while improving their situation financially, but surrogacy was another matter.

And now Georgia was worried she'd completely lost sight of the big picture.

She'd agreed to this arrangement because it would provide a future for her and Savannah, but the future was becoming cloudy. Georgia felt emotional and confused. It wasn't a good combination. She had to get hold of her thoughts now. She needed to exert some control. It would be foolish, not to mention dangerous, to let the pregnancy hormones do her in. She had to remember her goals, focus on the objectives. There was a lot to come: the exam this summer, the rest of medical school, the right residency at the right hospital.

"More juice?" Nikos asked, interrupting her circular thoughts.

She lifted the special juice cocktail the cook had prepared for her—blood orange juice and sparkling water—and saw it was nearly gone. Beyond her glass, the sky burned, glowing with fiery orange and burnished gold.

"I'm fine, thank you," she said, gaze riveted now to the horizon, transfixed by the sun dropping into the sea. "What an incredible sunset. Every night it's different, too."

"That's why I come up here every night. It's why I live here. I'm surrounded by beauty without all the madness."

She turned to look at him, seeing already such a different man than the one she'd met four days ago. "What is the madness?"

"Cities. Noise. People." He hesitated. "Gossip."

Her brows pulled. "I don't understand."

Nikos's expression turned mocking. But she sensed he wasn't mocking her as much as himself. "You're better off not knowing," he said. "And there is no reason to know. You'll be leaving here in a couple months. It's not your problem."

Her frown deepened. Nikos was baffling. She was just beginning to realize he might be as scarred on the inside as he was on the outside, which raised the question—was he mentally and emotionally healthy enough to raise a child on his own?

Would he be a fit parent?

One more question she didn't have an answer for, but a question she knew she couldn't ignore. She did worry about him raising the child alone here. She worried that maybe he was a little too antisocial, worried that he was more isolated than was good for him.

She might not be able to change the terms of her agreement, but maybe she could change…him.

Or at the very least, help him prepare to become a father so that he'd be the best father possible. But to do that, it would mean spending more time with him, not less.

It would mean focusing on who he really was, and getting him to drop his guard…that rough mask…and seeing if he couldn't open up…become more emotionally available.

She had a little over three months until the baby was born. Couldn't she use this time to study and help him?

She just needed to formulate a treatment plan. She'd do the same thing here that she did in school: learn everything she could, soak up every bit of information, memorize every fact, every detail, and then review her case at the end of each day to monitor progress and make sure she hadn't overlooked anything.

Perhaps helping Nikos prepare for the birth would comfort her in June when it was time for her to go. Perhaps she'd feel more at ease with her decision.

Perhaps this was the missing piece.

Perhaps.

Georgia didn't sleep well. She woke when it was still dark, her room icy cold, but she was so hot she couldn't breathe. She kicked the covers back from her legs, her nightgown sticking to her damp skin. She shivered, chilled and pulled the covers back.

She'd had the old dream, although dream was an inaccurate description. It was more of a nightmare. Losing her family. Chasing through the trees for Savannah, trying to save her sister from the rebels, certain any minute she'd

be killed, too. She was crying as she ran and then someone was there with a huge machete and she was begging
for her life because she was pregnant…

That was when she woke up.

She was having the old dreams again, but this time she
was pregnant.

Maybe because she was pregnant.

Lying in bed, Georgia drew great gulps of air, feeling
overwhelmed and suffocated by grief and despair.

This was not going how it was supposed to go. She
was beginning to panic, and it was too late for that. She'd
signed contracts and agreements and beyond the contracts
and agreements, she was in med school, studying to become a doctor.

She didn't want to become a mother. She *couldn't* become a mother.

Georgia turned on her lamp and checked her watch.
Four thirty in the morning. She wasn't going to be able
to sleep again. She wondered if she could maybe go to
the kitchen and make a pot of tea. The activity would
be good. It'd distract her, help push the vividness of the
dream away.

She pulled a thin cashmere sweater over her nightgown
and then added a thicker button-down cardigan over that.
After stepping into slippers, she headed for the kitchen
on the ground floor.

She'd never been all the way inside the kitchen, and
there was no microwave, so it was a bit of a game trying
to find everything she needed. But at least the kettle was
on the stove and she had a box of loose tea, a teapot and
a tea strainer.

Georgia hovered over the stove as she waited for the
kettle to boil, and her thoughts returned to the bad dream.
And it was such a bad dream. But at least it was only a
dream. What happened to her family wasn't.

For the past six months she'd told herself that the pregnancy wasn't a bad thing, either, because she was bringing life and light into the world.

She'd convinced herself that she was doing something good; she was giving Nikos Panos a gift. And, no, her mother and father wouldn't have approved, but they were gone. Her baby sister Charlie was gone. Her grandparents, who'd been visiting in Africa at the time of the assault, were gone, too. Georgia and Savannah were the only ones left, and in view of such darkness and tragedy, wasn't creating life a good thing?

Wasn't a new baby a miracle?

And since she was not going to ever be a mother, wasn't this a chance to do something good while providing for Savannah?

"Everything all right?" A deep voice spoke from the kitchen doorway.

Georgia jumped and turned around just as the kettle whistled. She startled again. Swearing—or it sounded as if he swore, she didn't know as it was a stream of muttered Greek—Nikos crossed the kitchen, pushed her away from the stove and turned off the burner.

"Sit down," he said sharply. "You're about to get burned."

"You scared me," she said, but she was happy to sit in one of the blue-painted chairs with the woven straw seats. She watched him use a pot holder to lift the copper kettle and fill her mug. Steam swirled up, shrouding his hand. "I had a bad dream, so I came here for tea. But I was trying to be quiet. I'm sorry to wake you up."

"I'm a light sleeper."

"Then I'm definitely sorry to wake you."

He flashed her a rare smile, and her heart did a strange, funny beat.

He was devastatingly attractive when he smiled. And

right now, watching him make her tea, his black hair thick and tousled, his long black lashes shadowing his cheek-bones, his full lips slightly curved, she felt her pulse drum faster.

She shouldn't want to know him. She shouldn't care at all, but she found him fascinating, and his scars just made her want to know more. They added an air of mystery. How did he get them? And why had he exiled himself to this rock of an island?

He'd virtually cut himself off from the world, and now he planned on raising his son here. Why?

"How did you get burned?"

He shot her a swift glance over his big shoulder, black brows flattening. He didn't look angry as much as sur-prised. "It's an old story. Not very interesting."

She didn't believe it for a minute. "I have a feeling it's very interesting."

"Not to me," he answered flatly, bringing the pot and cup to the table. "Do you drink it with milk or sugar?"

"Honey?"

He went to one of the painted cabinets and dug through bottles and jars but came up empty.

"Don't worry," she told him as he went to look in a bas-ket of jars and bottles next to the stove.

"It's here," he said, bringing a small ceramic bowl with a lid to the table. "Why do you have nightmares?"

So that was what they were doing. Tit for tat. "I've told you about losing my family in Africa."

"Not really. You just say you lost them. I'm interested in the details." And then his piercing dark eyes met hers. "I'd find it interesting."

"So if I tell you about my nightmares, you'll tell me about how you were burned?"

"If you tell me about your nightmares, I'll tell you about the burns…sometime, soon. Just not now."

"Why?"

"You have to trust me on that."

An interesting choice of words, she thought, stirring in the honey. *You have to trust me...*

The word *trust* had come up several times now.

"Okay," she said, not sure she was entirely comfortable with their agreement but thinking they had to start somewhere, building this trust, and she did want to trust him. She needed to trust him, otherwise how could she live with herself after she'd delivered the baby and returned to Atlanta? "But maybe you could tell me something else—"

"You're the one with the nightmares, not me."

She drew a deep breath. "The nightmares started a little over four years ago, after the assault. It happened when I was twenty, and in my final year at university. My sister Savannah had come to visit me, and we were looking at colleges together, so she wasn't at the mission when the attack happened. Thank God. She escaped."

Georgia looked down into her steaming tea, and for a long moment she battled the awful pain and tightness in her chest. The emotion was so intense. It made thinking, much less speaking, nearly impossible.

"They all died," she whispered. "My parents, my grandparents, my baby sister—Charlie. They all perished on the church grounds."

It was awful saying the words out loud, and the silence afterward was painful and heavy.

"What are the nightmares?" he asked after a moment.

She blinked hard, determined to stay calm. "I'm there and I'm supposed to save them. And I can't." She looked up at him. He was leaning against one of the kitchen counters, his arms braced against the countertop, and he looked so big, so sure of himself, and she envied him then. Envied his size and strength. Envied his fierceness and vitality.

The nightmares always made her feel so small and help-less. Vulnerable. She hated it, and she worked hard to keep from ever feeling weak.

"Is that what you dreamed tonight?"

"More or less."

"Tell me about tonight's dream."

She made a soft, rough sound. "It's too sad."

"Maybe talking will help."

She lifted her head and gave him a hard look. "Does talking about the accident that burned you ever help?"

"No."

She lifted her cup and sipped the tea. It was hot and al-most burned her tongue. Again tears started to sting her eyes. She blinked hard, determined not to cry.

"What's wrong?" he asked.

"Tea is too hot."

"That's not why you're upset."

Nikos was far too perceptive. "I just wish I hadn't told you about the attack—"

"If it's any consolation, you didn't say much. You didn't say how it happened. You didn't tell me who did it, or if they were ever caught."

"I hate discussing it."

"Is that why the information wasn't part of your donor file?"

"There's no reason for people to know. Savannah tends to be a bit more open about it. I can't stand talking about it. I get too angry."

"Angry...why?"

"My parents knew their work was dangerous. They knew what they were doing was risky, and it's one thing to put their own lives in jeopardy, but to put my sisters in danger? Charlie was just twelve. She shouldn't have been there. She should have been protected."

"And you said you weren't maternal."

Georgia's eyes felt hot and gritty, and impatiently she shook her head, regretting sharing. "I think I'll take my tea back to my room. If I'm lucky, I'll be able to fall back asleep." She rose and gathered her things, china cup and pot clinking as she accidentally knocked them together.

Nikos crossed the floor. He took the dishes from her, placed them on the table and then took her hands. "You're shaking."

"I miss them." And just like that tears filled her eyes. She turned her face away, trying to hide the tears.

"You loved them."

"So much."

She didn't know how it happened, didn't know what happened, but suddenly her face was tipped up and his head dipped and his lips covered hers.

It was impossible to know what his intentions were, impossible to know if the kiss had meant to comfort, because the moment his mouth touched hers, Georgia jolted as if she'd stumbled into a live wire. Sensation rushed through her in electric waves, making her shudder.

Nikos deepened the kiss, his lips parting hers, and she shuddered again at the pleasure of his tongue stroking the inside of her sensitive lower lip and then finding her upper lip.

It'd been ages since she'd kissed anyone. She couldn't even remember her last kiss, and Nikos was in total control, drawing her close, his hard body pressed to the length of her as lips and tongue made her melt.

She felt hot and explosive, her blood humming in her veins. She shivered as his hand moved beneath her long hair to cup her nape and then down her neck, stirring every nerve ending in her skin.

She couldn't remember ever feeling so much. Hunger gnawed at her, and her nipples ached, pebbled tight and pressed to his chest.

His tongue swept the inside of her mouth, teasing her, making her grow warmer, making her feel wet.

She shouldn't want this or like it. She should push him back, break free, and yet a small, scientific part of her mind was amazed.

This was unlike any kiss she'd ever known.

This was shockingly electric.

Chemistry.

His hands were on her waist, and then sliding up to cup her breasts, and she whimpered against his mouth. She felt wild with need, starved for sensation. Georgia pressed her chest against him, trying to assuage the ache.

And then just as fast as the kiss happened, it was over, with Nikos breaking it off and stepping back, muttering in Greek.

She'd bet a thousand dollars he was cursing again.

She looked up at him, and he looked grim as anything. Clearly he was regretting the kiss.

She fled. It was that or collapse in a puddle on the kitchen floor.

In her room, she locked the door and leaned against it, legs still shaking.

What just happened?

She'd never felt anything so consuming…pleasure and hunger and something else, something so intense that it continued to ripple through her in hot, dizzying waves.

Desire. Lust. Need.

Georgia exhaled slowly, trying to get control, needing to clear her head, and yet all she could feel was the pressure of Nikos's body against hers and the feel of his mouth… as well as his taste.

He tasted like heat and honey and licorice.

She'd never tasted anything like it. And God help her, she wanted more.

* * *

Nikos headed out at dawn to run his mountain. It was what he did when he wasn't calm, and couldn't think.

He put on running shoes and forced himself to run up his mountain to the top, where he'd put in the landing strip for his planes, and then at the top, he did wind sprints across the tarmac, letting the Cyclades northwesterly wind buffet him.

By the time he was finished, he was exhausted. The beast had been subjugated. He could return to the house without fearing for Georgia's safety.

He couldn't hurt her. He couldn't scare her. He must not disgust her with his sexual appetite.

That didn't mean he didn't still want her—he did—but he wouldn't break her door down to put his mouth on her taut nipple or kiss behind her knee until she opened her thighs for him.

As a boy he'd been fascinated by sex. As a young man he discovered he was quite good at it…pleasing women, making them sigh, making them come. He'd never imagined that you could like sex too much. It hadn't crossed his mind that he liked it too much, at least, not until he married Elsa and everything he thought about the world was wrong.

Correction, everything he thought about himself was wrong.

He'd thought in the beginning she was just inexperienced. He imagined she'd just need time to get used to married life, but it only got worse with time. She'd close her eyes when he kissed her and then turn her head away when he entered her; she'd hold her breath, waiting for his "animal side" to end.

Nikos had fallen in love with a woman who didn't love him, or even like him. It was a disaster from the start, and by the time the marriage was over, he loathed everything about himself.

And now Elsa's doppelgänger was living in his house, her belly round with his son, and he'd kissed her, and the kiss had been potent.

He wanted…

He wanted her.

But he couldn't have her. He couldn't. Even a monster like him could see why she was off-limits.

CHAPTER SEVEN

THE KISS CHANGED EVERYTHING.

Georgia had thought they'd formed a tentative friendship, but that was gone. Nikos avoided her like the plague—including skipping drinks at sunset—and even dinner for two nights after the kiss.

After two more days of punishing silence, Georgia went in search of him, which wasn't easy. He wasn't in his bedroom or the library. She circled the house, visiting each of the patios and terraces, as well as the pool. She returned to the house and checked all public rooms before going back to his bedroom. The staff said he was here; he hadn't left Kamari, which meant he was somewhere else on Kamari.

Georgia went out for a walk, determined to track him down. She finally found him on one of the more rugged paths that circled the mountain.

He'd been running, and his gray shirt clung to his damp chest. He was breathing hard as he drew to a stop on the gravel path. "What are you doing out here?"

She shrugged, not about to tell him that she'd been looking for him for almost an hour. "Getting some air."

"This isn't one of the garden paths. You shouldn't be this far from the villa."

"I'm less than a fifteen-minute walk from the house."

"But no one could hear you if you needed help. You need to stay close—"

"Stop it. I'm not going to do this with you."

He shoved black hair back from his brow. A ruddy flush colored his cheekbones, and his dark eyes sparked. "I didn't know you had an option."

She was fed up with his behavior. "I'm beginning to

understand why you required a surrogate to provide you with an heir. No one else would have your baby."

He wagged his finger in front of her face, nearly tapping her lips. "Is your mouth good for nothing but insults?"

She would have bitten his finger if she could. "Who do you think you are?"

"Your host and home for the next trimester." He leaned toward her, and his head dropped, his voice a deep rumble in her ear. "So I would try a bit harder to be cordial."

Heat radiated off him and she could smell the salt of his skin, and somehow on him, it was a good smell, but she didn't like his attitude and wasn't about to be scolded by him when he'd all but abandoned her for the past four days.

She shoved her hand against his chest to back him off but only managed to gain a couple of inches. "Please tell me that not all Greek men are as barbaric as you."

The corner of his mouth lifted. His eyes, with that curious ring of espresso, glowed hot. She wasn't sure what she saw there—frustration, yes—but there was something else, something powerful and seductive.

"I'm not asking you to be a submissive." His deep voice rumbled from his chest. "Just work with me."

"I'm trying! Can you not see that? It's why I'm here now. Why I went looking for you—" She broke off, realizing what she'd said.

He'd heard it, too, and he said nothing, content to just look at her, study her. Georgia felt the energy spark and grow. His dark eyes said things she knew he wouldn't say aloud. There was a chemistry between them that always simmered but had been teased to a flame now.

He wanted her. He found her attractive. And the attraction wasn't one-sided. She found him physically desirable, but this wasn't about love or long term. It was lust, plain and simple.

His word came to her—*carnal*.

She thought she was beginning to understand. He wanted her, and he'd bed her, and it would probably fulfill every sensual, sexual need, but that was all it would be. He wasn't going to want a relationship with her after the baby was born. And for that matter, she didn't want one, either. There was no future.

This…attraction…was potent, but it was only a distraction. It was just something that would pass the time.

But maybe that was a good thing.

Maybe that was the right thing.

Maybe she didn't want anything from him but this… the sparks, the heat.

From the moment she'd arrived there had been something raw and physical between them. They'd clashed over rules and she'd struggled for control, but she understood now that her struggle was resisting him.

But the simmering chemistry was about to boil over. Everything was catapulting forward, hot, hot and explosive.

"Carnal," she murmured, her mouth so dry she had to dampen her upper lip with the tip of her tongue.

"You're playing with fire now," he answered, his voice just as husky as hers.

A shiver raced through her. Excitement…anticipation. But she was nervous, too. She didn't want to take him on, wasn't trying to provoke him or challenge him. She just wanted to be closer to his heat and energy. It was electric. It made her heart race and her blood warm, and it felt so good to feel something strong and powerful, but the desire was also treacherous. It masked their true selves. It confused reason.

It confused her.

She had to remember why she was here. She had to remember who they were and what was happening… There were consequences for everything.

"You're not sure, are you?" he said, reaching for her, taking her by the arm and pulling her against him, into the circle of his arms.

She didn't provide much resistance. Truthfully she wanted him to kiss her again. Wanted to see if he still tasted of licorice and honey and him. And standing so close, his body pressed to hers, she felt the hard, taut muscles of his body and his warmth penetrating her clothes and she ached for more skin, direct heat. She longed to lift her top and peel his shirt up and let them touch, skin to skin. But if that happened, there would be no stopping them. She knew that.

Not because he'd force her, but because she'd beg him to touch her and taste her and take her.

She'd never wanted a man the way she wanted Nikos. It didn't make sense... There was no reason she should want him as much as she did. Maybe it was the pregnancy hormones. Maybe—

And then there was no more thought as he tipped her head up and kissed the corner of her mouth so lightly that her skin prickled and tingled all over. "You haven't answered me," he said, kissing the other corner, and then the bow-shaped upper lip. "Which makes me think you aren't sure this is a good idea."

"No," she answered, struggling to speak as pleasure streaked through her. The light kisses were maddening and delicious. She didn't want him to stop, but she couldn't lie to him, either. "Not sure at all."

He stroked her hair back from her face, his thumb caressing the high sweep of her cheekbone. "That's smart. Glad someone is thinking."

"Not clearly, though."

His dark eyes bored into her, the deep cocoa mesmerizing. "Which makes me think we should not be doing this. I will never take advantage of you."

"You're not."

"I'm not convinced." He stepped away. "We should go back."

She didn't know how he did that. Turn the heat on and off. She was still turned on. She couldn't quite find her off.

It made her want to hate him. Instead she silently walked next to him as they returned to the house.

Nikos left her at her door without a word, and she went inside and locked the door, not to keep him out but to keep herself in.

She practically threw herself onto the bed and grabbed a pillow to pull over her face to muffle the sound of her crying. She didn't even know why she was crying, but something inside her was cracking, changing, trying to break free.

Emotion. Control. Fear. Grief.

She was losing her mind. He was making her crazy. She couldn't remember any other man ever getting under her skin this way, and she wanted to think it was because he was arrogant and insufferable, but it wasn't that at all.

It wasn't his looks.

It wasn't the chemistry.

It was him.

The tough, fierce alpha who'd been terribly wounded somewhere along the way and was determined to live alone…apart…

It wasn't right. Nikos deserved better. And the baby deserved better, too. The baby deserved a family…a mother…

The baby…

Her hand went to the bump, and she stroked the curve of her belly, soothing him. *Poor baby…*

Her eyes burned all over again, stinging with fresh hot tears. She blinked and blinked again, but the tears were spilling.

What had she done?

* * *

She didn't go upstairs for drinks or dinner. She couldn't. She was still so upset, so heartsick.

Everything was coming undone.

She was coming undone.

She'd started feeling, and now she couldn't stop thinking, and it was overwhelming her reality.

She'd signed dozens of agreements and contracts. Everything had been completely binding. And she'd said she understood, over and over. She said she was prepared, that she was comfortable signing away her rights, comfortable because she was doing something good, she was helping someone become a father.

But now she knew who that father was, and she knew he had struggles and pain and he suffered...

At ten thirty a tray arrived at her door, even though she hadn't asked for anything.

She left it outside her door, not hungry. But she did go to the bathroom and shower and rinse her face. The shower didn't hide the puffiness at her eyes or how red they were from crying.

Georgia put on pajamas and crawled into bed with her books. She had to divert her attention or she'd never be able to sleep.

Half an hour later there was a pounding on her door. Only one person would pound on her door. Aware that he could very well force his way in, she opened the door to save him the trouble.

But opening the door to him was just opening herself to more heartache. Her heart did a free fall as she opened the door.

Just looking at him and her heart did another dizzying nosedive, the emotion wild and overwhelming.

He lifted a brow. "You look terrible," he said, his gaze sweeping over her.

She hated that he filled the narrow hall so well. Hated that he looked intimidating and sexy all at the same time in his wardrobe of black and black. "Thank you."

"You've been crying."

"Buckets." She gave herself permission to examine him as thoroughly as he looked at her, and she allowed her gaze to sweep slowly, leisurely taking him in from head to toe. "And why is it you wear black all the time? Are you a rebel or an outlaw?"

He ignored her jab. "You haven't eaten your dinner."

"I'm not hungry."

"Maybe not, but the baby is."

"No. The baby is fine."

His jaw tightened. "Don't do this."

Her own chin lifted a fraction. "I'm not doing anything but trying to survive here, Nikos. It isn't easy. You're not easy—"

"Never said I was."

"Thanks. That is really helpful."

He lifted the tray, carried it into her room and put it on the table. "Eat," he said, pointing to the chair before the tray.

She remained at the door, heart thudding. "I don't want to eat. I won't be able to eat."

His mouth compressed. His chest seemed to widen. "I'm not asking you. I'm telling you, Georgia."

"That's not going to help!"

"Then what will?"

"I don't know, but you playing the heavy won't. It'll just make me angrier."

"Can't have that." He pulled her against him, his arm wrapping securely around her waist, locking her against him. She shivered at the hard press of his body, his chest crushing her sensitive breasts, his corded thighs moving between hers.

"Stop fighting me, *gynaika mou*," he rasped, his mouth covering hers in a searing kiss. It was a kiss to punish, to establish dominance, to remind her he was the boss, the man, and this was his house. And Georgia knew all this, and felt all this, but it did nothing but flame the fire.

She'd been through far too much in her life to ever be a doormat. He wasn't going to take anything from her. She would take from him. Use him. She'd turn his aggression into pleasure.

Standing on tiptoe, she wrapped her arms around his neck, fingers dragging through his thick, long hair, welcoming the kiss, opening her mouth beneath the pressure of his.

He widened his stance and drew her even closer so that she could feel the urgent press of his erection through his trousers. His hands were on her hips, and he rubbed her against his shaft, the thick tip stroking her right at her core, finding her where she was so very sensitive.

She groaned deep in her throat, feverish.

As his tongue played with hers, stabbing into her mouth and then sucking on the tip of her tongue, she squirmed and rubbed herself on him, wanting the contact, craving closeness.

To burn like this…

To need like this…

She'd peel her skin off if she could…

"This is insane," he muttered as one of his hands reached up to cup her breasts and then captured the tight, aching nipple.

The pleasure was so intense her legs trembled. He worked the nipple once more, and she saw stars. She'd never felt anything like this, had never felt any sensation so intense. Her body had taken on a life of its own and she was shuddering as he cupped both breasts, thumbs teasing the peaks. She wasn't going to be able to stand much longer, wasn't going to be able to take much more…

And then his hand was at her waist, fingers stroking down to her hip and then trailing over her outer thigh. Every place he touched felt hot and tingly. The kiss was consuming, and yet Georgia was constantly aware of the caressing fingers on her hip bone and thigh, and then the press of his palm against her mound.

He worked the heel of his palm against her, applying just enough pressure to the sensitive nub to draw a muffled groan from her.

It felt good to be touched, and he knew how to touch her. He was making her melt on the inside, and she wanted more…more skin, more sensation, more pleasure.

She arched as his hand moved to her waistband, playing with the elastic band before easing it open. She felt the whoosh of cool air on her stomach and then the warmth of his hand on her skin.

Georgia closed her eyes as he slid his hand down across her belly, fingers light on her tummy, caressing to her hip bone, stroking there and setting fire to all the nerves everywhere.

She hadn't known her hip bone was sensitive, but clearly he knew something about women's bodies that she didn't. He was stroking down her hip and then beneath the curve of her buttock, cupping the cheek, sending shivers of pleasure everywhere. His touch was maddening, the caress stimulating not soothing. She ached between her thighs, her core clenching, and she pressed her breasts to his chest, rubbing the peaked tips across his, craving friction.

She wasn't wearing anything under her pajama pants and all she could think about was how much she liked the feel of his skin on hers, and the pressure of his hand, and the way his fingertips sent rivulets of pleasure racing through her. And while it was good, she wasn't satisfied. She wanted more…his hand between her thighs, his fingers on the sensitive nub.

But Nikos wasn't in a hurry. He seemed to enjoy the slow exploration, discovering who she was, and how she responded. She tried to be patient, tried to savor the feel of his warm palm sliding across her hip and thigh, drawing circles of fire wherever he touched, but she was melting on the inside and aching for relief.

His hand now was there, between her legs, tracing the seam of her, and then parting the soft folds. She began to shake, and she leaned against him for support, her legs no longer steady. Her thoughts were becoming incoherent as her body took over, focused on friction, sensation, satisfaction.

He stroked her, and she could feel how slick his fingers were just from touching her. "You are so wet," he growled, biting at her neck and then kissing where he'd just bit.

She was, too. She could feel the slippery tip of his finger stroke where she was so sensitive, and she groaned against his mouth. He did it again, this time drinking the cry of pleasure from her.

He caressed her until she dug her nails into his chest, and then he slid a finger inside her, carefully, gently, finding that spot that made sensation even more intense. He worked his hand, in and out, stroking her there, and she trembled against him. He seemed to know what she wanted before she even wanted it, drawing her in, making her ache and arch, yearning for that release that was just beyond her.

"Nikos," she sighed huskily, clinging to him.

He buried his finger deep, and she rocked on it, but the release wouldn't come. Hot, frustrated tears burned the backs of her eyes. She ached and wanted and needed.

"Nikos," she repeated, pleading for what she knew he could give her.

"Agapiméni," he murmured.

She didn't know what he said, she didn't care just then what the word meant, either. She only knew she needed him. She kissed him desperately, hands clasping his face, lips and mouth drawing the very air from his lungs. She kissed him as if he were her last breath on earth, and maybe he was, because suddenly his thumb was there, at her nub, stroking her.

Georgia was already wound so tight, nerves stretched to breaking, that just those couple of flicks of his thumb across her clit made her shatter, climaxing violently. The orgasm ricocheted through her, and she clung helplessly to him, her body shuddering with pleasure.

For a long minute after, she just leaned against him, listening to his heart, feeling the firm, even thud beneath her ear, struggling to catch her breath.

She didn't know why everything between them was so explosive, but the chemistry was beyond anything she'd ever felt, and just when she thought it couldn't be hotter, or more electric, he proved her wrong.

She slowly peeled away to look at him. Her pulse still raced and her body felt deliciously weak as she gazed up at Nikos, unable to think of a single thing to say.

He stared back at her, his eyes dark and focused and mysterious in the soft lighting of her bedroom. "Say it," he ground out tautly, adjusting the waist on her pajama pants and tugging her pajama top down.

She frowned a little, trying to figure out what he wanted from her. His expression was hard. White lines formed at his mouth. He looked almost…heartsick.

"Say what?" she whispered.

"How I disgust you, and how I forced you—"

"But you didn't, and you don't disgust me." She reached out to touch his chest, but he put a hand up, blocking her.

He made a hoarse sound and walked out, the door slamming loudly behind him.

Nikos avoided her the next day, and the day after.

Georgia told herself that she shouldn't have been surprised that he'd pulled away. It was the pattern now. But that didn't make the rejection any easier.

And the closer she and Nikos became, the more the distance hurt.

What had happened in her bedroom was intense—physically, emotionally—and part of her felt raw and rejected, but another part of her told her that Nikos was struggling even more.

She didn't know why intimacy was so difficult for him, but there was obviously an issue. He lived alone in the middle of the ocean, refusing to even visit the Greek mainland for medical appointments, insisting everyone come to him.

So, yes, she felt rejected, abandoned, but he was also wrestling with demons, and after two days of silence and distance, Georgia had had enough.

She found him on the top of the mountain, running sprints. He didn't see her there, not at first, and she watched him for almost five minutes, seeing him tear across the tarmac at full speed, running as if the devil himself was at his back.

Her heart ached. He was so tortured. His suffering baffled her.

What had happened? And why?

Obviously he blamed himself.

But this kind of self-abasement wasn't healthy. The way he handled stress worried her. Was this how he'd raise the baby? Would he handle problems as a father with the same punitive attitude?

She walked onto the tarmac, crossing the broad warm asphalt until she stood right where he was running.

Nikos dragged himself to an abrupt stop. He pulled out his earbuds, let them fall onto his shoulders. She could hear loud, pulsating rock music. It was the percussion-heavy, guitar-blazing, head-banging kind.

He was sweating profusely. His olive cheeks had a dark, dusky glow.

He looked past her, and then returned his focus to her. "How did you get here?"

"I walked."

"It's a long, steep climb."

"I took my time." She folded her arms over her chest, chilled by the wind. It was a blustery day. She'd been fine while walking, but standing still, she was cold.

Nikos just looked at her, distant, detached. There was no light or warmth in his eyes. She was reminded of the day she'd arrived. He was that Nikos Panos. Icy. Authoritative. Slightly hostile.

Her upper lip curled. It was smile or she'd cry. When she realized he wasn't going to speak, she did. "I'm worried about you, Nikos."

"There is no need to worry about me. I am not your concern."

"The nightmares were worse last night."

His head jerked up, and he gave her a sharp look. "Am I part of the nightmares?"

"You were last night, yes."

"What did I do?"

Her chest tightened. It hurt to breathe. "Nothing." She saw he didn't understand. "You did nothing, and that was the problem. The baby cried and cried, and you wouldn't hold him or pick him up and I couldn't get there and I couldn't help him—"

"So this wasn't about your family or you. This was about me and my son?"

Her heart did a painful double beat. "I'm worried about you, and how it will be when I leave. You can't just run away from things, Nikos. You have to face them—"

"I don't need the lecture, *gynaika*."

She'd found out from the cook what that word, *gynaika*, meant. It was woman. *I don't need the lecture, woman.*

She exhaled in a little puff of sound. He was positively medieval, and when he glowered at her—as he was now—scary as hell, but she couldn't back down. She had to do this, if not for his sake, then for the child they'd created.

"I am concerned. And you need to know that I'm troubled by what I see. You have moments where you are present and attentive, but then there are times like now, where you're so detached it's frightening. Nikos, this isn't the life I imagined for the baby." She saw his expression darken, the set of his mouth becoming grim. "It is one thing for you to retreat and detach if you have a wife and family, but you don't. You will be a single father, and you are so isolated here. The baby will be so isolated here. It's worrying."

"Worrying?" he repeated.

She heard the edge in his voice. Her pulse quickened in response. She had to be careful; she was walking on dangerous ground. "You must admit that is not going to be a conventional upbringing, living here on Kamari with just the two of you."

"I have staff."

"That is fine, then, if you are comfortable with them becoming extended family…grandparents, uncles, aunts—"

"They are staff."

She swallowed around the lump in her throat. "Don't you want your son to have more? Don't you want him to be loved and have family?"

"I will love him."

"Love is being present and accessible. But when confronted by something difficult you retreat…withdrawing for days. The child will suffer."

"You can't project what is between you and me onto him."

"Why not?"

"Because it will be different."

"Maybe. But maybe not. And because I know what I've seen here, and felt personally, I worry that when you need time alone, the child won't have enough love. I worry that he'll be…lonely. He should have others, Nikos, others in his world, others who will love him, too."

"I wasn't raised in a big, traditional family. My son will not miss anything."

She didn't say anything. What could she say?

His black eyebrows flattened. "You don't believe me."

She shrugged, trying to contain her frustration. "Children need community. They need to feel secure and loved—"

"I will do that."

"But what if something happens to you? Who will be there for him?"

"Nothing will happen to me."

"You don't know that! You're not God. You're mortal—"

"I think it's time you took a step back, Georgia. I am not sure why you are making my business yours. The child is mine, not yours." He stared at her, expression brooding. "Are you having second thoughts?"

She almost laughed. *Second thoughts? Oh, yes, second and third and fourth…*

She was consumed with regret. The guilt ached inside her. How could she have imagined she would be able to do this…conceive and carry a child and then just give him away?

"I carry your son," she said icily, "and I protect him with every breath I take."

"But he is *my* son," he repeated, "not yours, and therefore, not your concern. You waived your rights when you accepted payment. You waived those rights when you signed the fifty-some-page agreement. You waived those rights months ago, and you will never get them back."

Her fingers itched to slap him. He was hard and hateful, and his arrogant tone matched his arrogant expression.

It was all she could do to stand there and hold his gaze without crying or yelling. She stared up at him, staring hard to show she wasn't afraid and wouldn't be cowed. He needed to know that he wasn't a god. He wasn't the sun and the moon, the stars and the universe. He was just a man. A flawed man that had been broken and scarred along the way and survived by throwing his weight at the universe, thinking that he could control everything by being tough, cold, mean.

And she wouldn't shed one tear for someone who was determined to be tough and cold and mean.

She wouldn't feel anything for a man who was more beast than man. But at the same time, how could she hand a helpless newborn—so tender, so innocent—over to such a man?

"You're angry," he said shortly.

"Furious," she agreed, voice pitched low, vibrating with emotion. "And offended."

"Because I remind you of the facts? I force you to recognize the truth?"

"Because that kiss in my room, it changed you, and you in turn took something that was lovely and wonderful and made it ugly and sordid. You made me feel so good when you kissed me, and touched me, and then you pulled away and you've become hateful. You've become a monster... like the Minotaur in the labyrinth. You want to crush me now, but I won't let you. I might be a woman, and I might not have your size or muscles, but I am stronger than you. I will not break. And I will not let you break our son."

She turned around and started walking back the way she'd come, moving quickly, almost jogging back to the road, and then once on the road, she kept jogging, running, as if she could escape him, her and the truth.

She loved the baby.

The baby was hers…

She was grateful Nikos didn't chase after her. She would have had to run faster, and she didn't want to fall. She just wanted to get back to her room, to lock her door and hide.

But the moment she reached her room, she felt ill, cold and shaky and nauseous. She dashed into the bathroom, leaning over the toilet, stomach rolling, churning.

Her heart would break if she gave the baby up. Her heart would never be the same. How could she do this?

How could she hand him over and never look back?

It wasn't just because Nikos was detached and cold and hard. It actually had nothing to do with him, and everything to do with her. She loved the baby. She loved him and talked to him at night, and in her heart she talked to him throughout the day…

Tears streamed as she emptied her stomach.

Afterward, she clung weakly to the toilet, trying to catch her breath, trying to get her stomach to settle.

But her stomach wouldn't settle. The tears wouldn't stop. She'd made a pact with the devil. She'd sold her soul to make sure her sister would be financially taken care of, but the cost was too high.

The cost was unbearable.

She'd spent all this time telling herself it wasn't her baby, wasn't her son, but it was a lie.

He was hers.

And she loved him.

And it would break what was left of her heart if she left this island without him.

"This isn't good," Nikos said from the bathroom doorway, his deep, rough voice echoing in the small space.

She used her sleeve to dry her damp eyes. "Did you break the door down?" she asked hoarsely.

"I used the key."

"Thank you."

He disappeared from the bathroom and returned a minute later with a glass of water. He handed her the glass. "Rinse, spit and come talk to me in the living room."

She did as he suggested, and when she emerged he pointed to the couch.

"Sit," he said.

She wanted to tell him not to be bossy, but she didn't have the energy. Instead she sank onto the cushion and curled her legs up under her.

Nikos faced her, hands on his hips. "I don't like to see you this way. It's not good for—"

"The baby. I know." Her chin lifted. "I'm aware of that, and I don't want to stress him in any way."

Nikos's jaw tightened. "I was going to say *you*. It's not good for *you*."

She didn't know how to answer. She just looked at him, her heart so raw, her emotions wild.

"What is happening here?" he ground out. "I don't understand it."

"Understand what? That you kiss me and then run away...or that I tell you I'm scared and then you tell me it's none of my business?"

He muttered something beneath his breath. She couldn't make out the words, wasn't even sure if he was speaking English.

"What did you say?" she demanded.

"It's not important."

"I think it is. I think it's time you talked to me, Nikos. Not yell, not shame, not intimidate, not berate. Talk to me. Have a conversation."

"I'm not good at this."

"You'll get better with practice, and even if you don't want to do it for me, do it for your son's sake. He will need you to talk and listen. He will need you to not close down the moment you feel threatened—"

"I don't feel threatened!"

"You're terrified of emotion."

"That's not true."

"You run from intimacy like a little, scared schoolboy."

"What?"

"It's true. Conflict isn't going to kill you, Nikos. Having an uncomfortable conversation is just that—uncomfortable—but it's not the end. It doesn't mean we hate each other or won't still be friends—"

"Are we friends?" he interrupted, standing over her, black eyebrows flattened over dark, piercing eyes.

She had to think about the definition of the word for a moment. "Yes. At least, I think we should be. It's the only way to get through this. It's the only way I can possibly manage this last part…getting through to the end."

"So you do have misgivings now?"

"I don't know what kind of woman I would be not to feel conflicted. I feel him moving. He'll give a kick when I talk. When I go to bed, he gets active. It's like a game we play." Her throat ached, and the lump she'd been fighting grew. She couldn't say more. It would be impossible to say more, especially when the emotion was right there on the surface.

He dropped into a chair next to the couch and leaned forward, looking at her intently. "I have been making it harder for you, haven't I?"

"The whole thing is hard." She struggled to smile. "I don't know how we're going to get out of this in one piece."

"You make me nervous when you say that."

"And you make me nervous when I imagine you isolating a child from the world. Promise me you'll take him on trips and adventures…promise me you'll expose him to a life outside Kamari."

He searched her eyes. "I promise."

She blinked back tears. "Good."

"I will be a good father to him, too, Georgia. I will love him, and I will protect him—"

"Protect him from what, Nikos? From the world, or from you?"

He shifted, uneasy.

"You are only really, truly dangerous when you detach and disappear," she said. "I don't like your rough edges or your coldness when you're angry, but the distance…that feels like rejection. Abandonment. No one wants that."

"I pull away to keep from hurting you."

"You only hurt me when you pull away."

"I hurt you on the tarmac. I made you run away in tears."

"Because you'd pulled away! You and I had this incredible moment in my room and then you disappeared completely for days. It hurt. So tell me now, why do you do that after we're close? Why do you punish me?"

"I'm not punishing you. I'm punishing me." There was an edge in his voice, and tension washed off him in waves. "I should have had more control. I should have not taken advantage of you."

"You didn't take advantage of me. I took advantage of you. I wanted everything you did, and more."

Heat flared in his eyes, and she nodded. "I loved being close to you. You are so good at what you do…you're wow. Seriously, wow. You make me feel so good, but then you leave and I feel ashamed because I think my pleasure disgusts you—"

"No."

She lifted a brow. "Then why do you leave so quickly... and why did you avoid me after?"

"I wanted you. I wanted to carry you to the bed and strip your clothes off and—"

He broke off and dragged a hand over the bristles on his jaw.

She waited, but he wasn't going to say more. "Forgive me for being bold, but, Nikos, that sounds really good to me."

"What if I hurt you?"

"You mean, when you make love? Do you choke your partner...hit your partner...throw her around?"

"No!"

"Then what?"

"I am carnal."

"Is that a bad thing?" She didn't have that much experience. Sex was pretty much sex. She enjoyed it but hadn't had unusual experiences or anything particularly erotic. "Is that supposed to shock me?"

"I want you, *gynaika mou*. I want to be with you. I want to take you to my bed and keep you there for hours, touching you, tasting you, making you shatter with pleasure. But if we do these things, it will complicate us, and we are already very complicated—don't you think?"

Her pulse leaped in her veins. Her mouth had gone dry. "Yes."

"And so I try to stay away from you so that I don't kiss you again and put my hands under your clothes and touch you where I want to touch you, and feel you cry against my mouth as you come."

Her eyes widened. She swallowed hard. Her heart raced

now. She felt treacherously warm and wet between her thighs. "You like sex."

"I do," he said. "But I like you even more, and so I fight myself. I try to stay away, do the right thing."

"So that's why there is all this tension between us. You're avoiding me because you want me. And I'm lonely because I want to be with you—"

"You are not lonely for me."

"Oh, I am. I like you, Nikos. Even when you're awful."

"You can't like me. You barely know me."

She reached out, tugged on his sleeve. "Then let me get to know you."

"And how will that help either of us? We know how this will end—"

"Exactly. We know how this will end. There can be no confusion about the end, either. I'm not staying here in Greece. My world and life is in Atlanta. Yours is here. Neither of us is looking for a relationship. We're just trying to stay sane. Trying to make the best of an incredibly stressful situation."

"It doesn't have to be stressful, not if we stay on different sides of the villa."

She laughed low, but there was little humor in the sound. "Am I the only realist here?"

He looked at her for a moment, his gaze fixed on her mouth. She could feel his desire. Her own body hummed with need. She slipped her hand from his sleeve to the back of his wrist. His skin was firm and warm. She stroked the back of his hand, to his fingers, lacing her fingers with his. "I can't do this for three more months, Nikos," she whispered.

His jaw flexed. "We have to."

Her eyes burned, and her pulse raced. Everything in her felt stirred up. Her emotions were all over the place. She was physically attracted to him—dangerously attracted—

and yet he was right. He was everything she couldn't want. And perhaps he did know best. But at the same time she craved him, and his touch, and the pleasure he could give her. "I'm going crazy."

He pulled away, stood up and walked across the room. "We'll just try harder to stay out of each other's way."

The lump in her throat grew. "No! I'll lose my mind, Nikos. I'm already lonely. I already feel trapped. I'm not used to being cooped up. We need a break… A little stress relief would go a long way. Can we please go somewhere tomorrow? And if not tomorrow, then later this week?"

"Have you swum today yet? You didn't swim yesterday. Get in the pool. You'll feel better."

"I don't want to swim."

He shoved a hand through inky-black hair, pushing it back from his face. "Then go for a good walk—"

"Like I did today? Climb up the mountain to get a good hike in?" she interrupted fiercely. "Or perhaps I should try running. I only jogged today, but maybe tomorrow I could try a couple hundred wind sprints like you—"

"You don't need to run."

"Running won't hurt the baby."

"Walking is better, and you know it. Tomorrow it should be mild. Good weather—"

"No!" She jumped to her feet, hands clenched. "I've walked miles on your paths and they just go in circles. I've climbed this mountain. I've done everything I can do here on Kamari, and I need a change now. Please get me off this rock. Please let me see something new."

"You will be free to explore after the delivery—"

"That's three months away."

"I thought you had to study."

"I do study. For hours and hours every day, but I'm going stir-crazy. I need to get out…go see something, or go do something."

"There is nothing good happening in the outside world. You are safe here, so I prefer you to be here."

"If I am truly your guest, treat me like a guest and not a prisoner." She drew a short, raw breath as the possibility hit her. "Or am I prisoner?"

"What a silly question."

Her chest suddenly hurt, the air bottled in her lungs. He'd brought her to this island far from everything...

He said he didn't leave Kamari... He said there was no reason to leave Kamari. Her eyes widened. Was it possible she was his hostage? "Are you afraid I'll try to escape? Run away?"

"That's ridiculous. You're getting yourself worked up over nothing."

"Then why can't we go out for part of the day? You said you had a boat. Let's head to Amorgós, or even better, Santorini."

"No."

"Because I need to see people. I need to talk to someone. You've shut me out, and I understand why now. We have this—thing—between us and you're trying to resist it, and I understand that now. But I am lonely. I'm overwhelmed." Tears began to spill.

She struggled to wipe them away.

He swore in Greek and crossed to her side. "Don't cry," he said roughly. "Do not cry." He wiped her cheeks dry with the pads of his thumbs. "Don't cry," he said more softly, his lips near her ear. "Because you make me want to comfort you, and kiss you, but when I kiss you, *agapi mou*, I want you, and I'm afraid if I claim you, I'll never let you go."

CHAPTER EIGHT

THEY TOOK A motorboat to Amorgós two days later.

On the way, Nikos told her that there was a devastating earthquake on July 9, 1956, just north of Amorgós, between Amorgós and Santorini. The earthquake registered 7.8 on the Richter scale, and a second 7.2 earthquake followed thirteen minutes later. Intense aftershocks occurred for weeks, lasting through the summer.

Fifty-three people died on Santorini alone, and villages were destroyed on many islands. Quite a few people left the islands.

"I would think the earthquakes would have created a tsunami," she said.

He nodded. "Thirty-foot waves were reported all along the coast. And as difficult as this was, it's always been part of our history. The volcanic arc stretches from Methana—" He broke off, seeing she didn't know where that was. "Methana is a town on the eastern coast of the Peloponnese, built on a volcanic peninsula. And that volcanic arc extends from Nisyros Island in the west, to the coast of Turkey in the east. The arc is filled with dormant and active volcanic islands."

"There are some still active?"

"Absolutely. Milos, Santorini, Nisyros."

She of course had heard of Santorini but wasn't familiar with the other two. "Fascinating, as well as a little bit scary."

"Santorini always breaks my heart just a little bit," he said. "The Minoan culture was beautiful and sophisticated. And it was all wiped away. One day you should go there, visit the excavation of Akrotiri on Thera. There's a museum of found objects and some of the most stunning frescoes ever created. Many people believe that Akrotiri is the basis for Plato's story of Atlantis."

"I'd love to go there."

"It'd be a shame to miss. Perhaps in June you can travel for a while before returning to the US."

"You know I have the exam, so maybe *you* should take me there. Make it our next outing."

"We're not having more outings."

"Don't say that. Please. I still have three more months here. You can't bring me all the way to Greece and keep me on your rock."

"I don't go to Santorini."

"But you just said it's amazing."

"And it is. For others. But I don't go. I won't." He looked away from her, gaze fixed on the shadowy island ahead of them. "And before you push and push and spoil the day before it's even begun, I'll tell you—it's where my wife died. So I don't go there. Ever."

Georgia swallowed hard. It was the first time he'd brought up his wife, and there had been no tenderness in his voice, just ice. And grief.

They traveled the rest of the way in silence, but Georgia didn't mind. She welcomed the sun on her face and the wind tugging at her hair and she used the silence to think about what Nikos had told her...not about Greece but about his late wife.

She wanted to know more but knew that this wasn't the time. She didn't want to upset him or spoil their outing. It felt wonderful to be off Kamari, and she was excited about having a new experience. They might be traveling only twenty-some kilometers but it felt like an adventure, and she didn't care if they did nothing on Amorgós but walk around the little town and then up through the few houses before returning to the boat.

But as it turned out, there was plenty to do in the village of Katapola, Amorgós's biggest harbor. True, there weren't many shops, but Georgia just enjoyed exploring the town. Because everything was new to her, and it was her first real taste of a Greek village; she found it endlessly fascinating.

With Nikos at her side, she explored the pretty bay, dotted with fishing boats, white windmills and the traditional blue-and-white houses. Small cafés and taverns spilled onto the sidewalk facing the water, and on a side street they popped into a bakery so Georgia could admire all the different breads and pastries.

Georgia saw the woman behind the counter give Nikos a cold look, but he seemed not to notice, ordering one of each of the cookies so Georgia could try them all. She was about to ask him about the woman's odd behavior when Nikos opened the paper bag, drew out a cookie and popped it into her mouth. "Well?" he said. "Good?"

She wiped the crumbs from her lips and smiled. "Delicious," she said around the mouthful of almonds and honey and delicate flaky pastry.

"I thought we'd save them for lunch," he said, reaching into the bag and selecting one. "But they're far too tempting." He broke the slice of baklava in half, then handed her half.

She wasn't able to get her half into her mouth without making a mess.

Nikos watched her, amused. "You have honey all over your fingers."

"Not for long," she answered, grinning and then licking the tip of her sticky finger. She saw his dark eyes spark as she sucked on her finger, and suddenly her pulse quickened and she felt suspiciously breathless.

"I'd offer you a taste," she said, "but I'm not sure if that is appropriate."

"You love to torture me."

Her lips lifted. She smiled up into his eyes, wondering why she took such pleasure in provoking him. "Yes, I do."

"Why?"

"It's fun."

He groaned and took her arm, steering her from the bakery's front steps and away from the women entering the shop, their dark gazes all so curious. "It's not fun," he said, keeping her arm as they walked up the narrow street, the road cobbled. "I can barely keep my hands off of you as it is."

She flashed another smile up into his face. "So I've noticed."

"We are here to get away from all that."

"All that is you and me."

"You know what I mean."

"I do. But all that is us, together, and it goes wherever we go. It's not Kamari." There was laughter in her voice. "But it would be funny if the energy and magic was Kamari."

"Why would that be funny?"

"Because it's not a particularly romantic island. It's an arid rock."

"It's not supposed to be romantic. It's my home."

She laughed. "You sound so grumpy right now. What's wrong with you?"

He stopped walking to face her, his hands on her shoulders. "All I want to do is tear your clothes off of you and touch every inch of you, and you're making it almost impossible to forget how much I want you—"

"So don't."

"Georgia."

"Find us a room somewhere and make love to me. Maybe once it's out of your system, you'll feel much better."

"Stop it," he growled.

"What? I'm trying to help you."

"You're not helping. Because making love to you once won't get it out of my system. It won't satisfy me. It'll just make me hungry for more." His hands pressed into her shoulders. "If you wanted to help, you'd ask me the age of the church we passed on the corner. You'd want to know why there are so many windmills on Amorgós. You'd want to know how they make the whitewash on the stucco buildings."

"But I don't want to know about whitewash or the stucco. I want to know about *you*."

"Georgia." Her name was wrung from him, a low, hoarse groan of sound, before his head descended and he was kissing her, the kiss of a man drowning, dying.

There was so much heat and need in the kiss. His mouth was hard, and it slanted over hers, forcing her lips open. His tongue found hers, probing, seducing.

She shuddered and pressed herself to him, loving the feel of him—hard, muscular, all male.

An old woman passing by muttered a rebuke, and Nikos lifted his head, ending the kiss. His expression was rueful as he stepped back.

"What did she say?" Georgia asked, touching her lips, which felt tingly and sensitive.

"That we needed to get a room."

Georgia giggled. "I told you so."

"Hmph." Nikos took her arm again. "We're here to sightsee. We're going to sightsee. And you're going to enjoy every little church and interesting view, and in an hour or two we will have lunch, and after our lunch we will return to Kamari, where I'll lock you up for your own safekeeping."

Georgia just laughed again.

He glared down at her with mock fierceness. "I'm serious."

"I know you are, which just makes me like you all the more." She patted his arm. "When you're not growling and issuing orders, you're a very nice man and very good company."

"Don't soften me up."

"Too late." She flashed him another smile. "It's already happening. You, my dear Nikos, are putty in my hands."

"A *gross* exaggeration." But he was smiling and she felt her heart turn over because when he looked at her like that, she felt as if she'd somehow won the lottery.

Georgia was right, he thought later, as they sat in the back of the small taxi that he'd hired to take them all over the island. She'd gotten under his skin and was working some kind of magic on him, and God help him, he liked it. Liked her.

She made him feel things he didn't think he'd ever feel again, and he loved her smiles and her laughter and how she seemed to radiate sunshine even on a gray, windy day.

And while he enjoyed looking at her, he enjoyed talking with her even more. She was intelligent and witty and not afraid to stand up to him. Maybe he loved that most. She wasn't scared of him and didn't run away when he was impatient or frustrated. She held her own. She even pushed back, teaching him manners.

The corner of his mouth lifted.

She noticed. "You're smiling," she said, slipping her hand into his in the back of the taxi.

He glanced down at their hands and how she'd so naturally linked them. "What are you doing?"

"Pretending you're my boyfriend."

"Why?"

"It's fun."

"We're here to get distance."

"Kind of hard when we're smashed together in a car the size of a sardine can."

He grinned ruefully. She had a point. It was refreshing. She was refreshing. She made him feel young and hopeful, as if he were but a boy with his whole life ahead of him. "You enjoyed lunch, though?"

They'd explored the north end of the island during the morning, stopping at Tholaria and then Lagada, where they'd had a light meal, and were now heading south again, approaching the monastery outside of Chora, Amorgós's principal town.

"Very much so!"

He told her they were on the way to Hozoviotissa Monastery, and he mentioned that there was a dress code, but she was fine in her long, slim skirt and lace-trimmed peasant-style blouse, which she'd topped with a cropped delicate cashmere sweater that revealed her bump.

"In summer there are crowds," he added as the taxi pulled over to the side of the parking lot to let them out. "But we are lucky that it is relatively quiet today."

It was a long, steep climb up dazzling white steps. "Is it a museum now?" she asked as they began the climb to the church.

"No. It is still a monastery, but the monks are quite welcoming. They do have rules about visitors—no short skirts, bare midriffs or shorts on men—but we're dressed appropriately and I trust you know how to behave in a church, so we shouldn't have a problem."

They ended up spending an hour in the church and adjoining rooms. Nikos could tell from Georgia's rapt expression that she very much enjoyed the visit. The interior of the church was quite austere but there was a calm inside that was profoundly sacred.

Georgia knelt at one of the rails and prayed.

Nikos stood back, wanting to give her space, and yet also determined to keep an eye on her.

Later, as they left the church, she was quiet and somber. "What's wrong?" he asked.

"Nothing. I was just thinking of my family."

They were descending the stairs, and they were taking their time as the stairs down felt even steeper than the climb up. "Did you say a prayer for them?" he asked.

"Yes. I always do. But I also said a prayer for you."

"And what did you ask for?"

"Just that God will take care of you, and the baby." She drew a breath and blinked. "He will, too. You just have to trust him."

Nikos shot her a swift glance, but her expression was serene and she was focusing on the steps.

Halfway down she paused to glance back at the tall white face of the monastery built against the cliff. "I love places like that," she said. "They always remind me of my parents."

"Because they were missionaries?"

"They loved their faith and their work. And they loved each other. They were happy."

"But when they died, they left you and your sister penniless."

She shrugged. "Money doesn't make people happy. It just pays for things."

His brow furrowed. "And what will make you happy, *agapi mou*?"

"Doing something meaningful with my life."

"Like being a doctor?"

She nodded. "And loving my family. That will make me happy."

They reached the taxi, and Nikos opened the back passenger door for her, but Georgia hesitated. "Do we have to get back in the car?" she asked. "Can we just walk for a bit?"

"Chora is not far. We were going to visit the town and then head back to the harbor. Did you want to walk there?"

"How long would it take?"

"Fifteen minutes, maybe twenty."

"Let's do it. It feels good to stretch our legs. I think I was getting a little carsick on the way from Lagada."

Nikos spoke to the taxi driver, but the driver shook his head and pointed to his watch. Nikos shrugged and pulled out his wallet, handing over a number of bills.

"He had to take his mother to the doctor," Nikos explained. "But he said there are always drivers at the tavern. It shouldn't be a problem getting a ride back to Katapola."

"You're not worried about having to find a driver?"

"No. And I agree—it's good to be out. It's a nice day. You can feel spring in the air."

They set off, and Georgia tucked her hand through his arm. "I feel like I'm finally in Greece."

"I'm glad you're happy," he said, and he meant it.

"Let's stay overnight here. Let's not go back."

"We have to."

"Why? You're the boss. You make the rules."

He'd never seen her like this, not in the nearly two weeks she'd spent on Kamari. All day she'd seemed lighter…warmer and happier. She'd been thoughtful when they'd left the church, but she'd brightened again as they talked. "But we're only an hour from home," he said. "Too close not to go home."

"But that's what makes it fun. We're having a mini-holiday…and now we can make it a bigger adventure."

"And where would we stay?"

"I'm sure there are plenty of hotels—"

"It's off-season. Most would be closed—"

"I bet we can find one that's open."

"And if we did, you'd be disappointed. They are not going to be luxurious. The rooms would be small and simple. Quite Spartan compared to anything you'd find at a resort."

"Or like your house?" she teased.

"Or like my house," he agreed.

"You just don't want to stay."

"I prefer the comfort of my bed," he agreed. "And the privacy."

"But doesn't the routine ever get to you? Don't you want a change?"

"Clearly you do." But he wasn't annoyed; he was charmed. It was impossible not to be drawn to her with the sunlight making her glow and staining her cheeks pink.

He desired her more than he'd ever wanted any woman, and yet he didn't want to hurt her, break her.

And he couldn't.

She was pregnant. He couldn't take any risks with her, not just for his son's sake but for her sake.

She mattered. She mattered a great deal.

He'd thought she was cold when she'd arrived. Cold and beautiful. But he was wrong. She wasn't cold at all. She was intelligent and complex. There were so many layers to her. She could be fierce, as well as fiercely funny. It still amused him how she'd deliberately tried to provoke him outside the bakery. It'd been impossible to resist her when she'd smiled at him, her expression so warm, the light in her eyes teasing and sexy.

How could a man resist sunshine and honey?

And yet he couldn't have her.

But that didn't mean he didn't ache for her. He craved her touch and taste, her soft skin and ripe curves calling to him...

To fight the throb of his erection, he drew her attention to the ruins on the hill ahead of them. "The Venetian castle," he said.

"A Venetian castle in Greece?"

"There are dozens and dozens of them. Venice played a role in Greece's history for a thousand years. There are still Venetian fortresses and fortified villages scattered through the mainland and islands."

"I had no idea."

"All the windmills we saw today, those can be attributed to the Venetians, as well. The Venetians introduced the windmills for milling wheat—an essential form of income for hundreds of years—but the windmills fell out of use in the middle part of the twentieth century."

They were nearing the base of the hill with the castle. Georgia stared up at it, nose wrinkling. "It doesn't look like much," she said.

"There isn't much left," he agreed.

"We don't have to climb up there, do we?"

"It's dangerous. I wouldn't let you go up there even if you wanted to."

"Does that mean we have to go back to the harbor?"

"We can get a snack in Chora and then return."

"Or, can we see if we can find a hotel…?"

"Georgia."

"I've never stayed in a Greek hotel. I've never eaten in Greek restaurants."

"You did at lunch."

"We had olives and a salad and a delicious cheese-and-spinach thingy—"

"Spanakopita. Greek spinach pie."

"And I loved it, but I want more than just that little pie. I want to try more food and see more things. This is Greece."

"I know."

"It's exciting, Nikos. You're giving me a good memory to take home with me."

He knew she didn't mean back to Kamari, but back to Atlanta in June. His gut tightened. His chest felt heavy.

He didn't want to think of June, didn't want to think of her leaving.

For a long minute he said nothing, just stared out toward town with its brilliant white buildings and bold blue accents.

"We'll get two rooms," he said.

"We don't have to get two rooms," she answered. "Not if you're worrying about money."

"*Not* worrying about money." His lips compressed. "And we need two rooms. For your safety."

"I trust you."

"That's nice, but I don't trust myself."

She laughed.

Nikos found them rooms at a small hotel in the center of the town that advertised itself as Beautiful Villa. It was neither particularly beautiful nor luxurious, but it was neat and clean, and what Nikos said was typical of hotels on the smaller islands.

There was little to do after check-in as they had no luggage, and Nikos and Georgia dutifully inspected their individual rooms. Georgia was happy to note that they were close together. Not adjoining, but just a couple of doors down the narrow hallway from each other.

They left the hotel and walked to a nearby restaurant. It was quite early still, and the restaurant was deserted.

"They will think we are American tourists," he grumbled as they were seated by the window overlooking the town square.

"Well, I am an American tourist, and you can pretend to be a Greek tourist."

"No."

She grinned. "You don't want to be a tourist?"

"No."

Georgia couldn't stop smiling.

Nikos noticed. "What's happened to you? You are all giggles and laughs today."

"I'm having a good time." She reached across the table and captured his hand. "And I hope you are, too."

He attempted a scowl. "You've become overly affectionate, as well."

"I think somewhere in your hard little heart, you like it."

His jaw shifted, expression easing, and his dark eyes glinted. "Maybe just a little bit."

She squeezed his hand. "I thought so."

Over dinner of grilled lamb and fish and flavorful salads they talked about what they'd seen that day and the austere but mystical monastery. Georgia shared that she loved all the bright blue accents—the doors, the windows, the church cupolas—that turned simple Spartan villages into charming postcards.

"We know I've had a great time," Georgia said. "But have you?"

"I have, actually. I enjoyed the day."

"And you don't resent me for forcing you to have an adventure? I know how much you cherish your time on Kamari."

"And now I think you're trying to provoke me."

"Keeping it exciting," she said.

"Mmm. A rebel, aren't you?"

She mulled this over, then nodded. "I guess I am. No, I know I am. But in the end, it's what saved my life. Leaving my family, leaving Africa. If I hadn't insisted on returning to the States, I would have died with them. Savannah, too."

"You weren't worried about going to a big university in America?"

She shook her head. "I wanted a big American school

and wanted to do all the things I'd only read about. College football games, parties, movies, dates, fun."

"And was it fun?"

She nodded. "I loved it. So much. And I pushed Savannah to do the same. I told her she could always go back to Africa, but she owed herself the chance to be just a normal American girl for four years. Take four years, experience what everyone else your age experiences, and then decide what you want to do for the rest of your life." Georgia looked away and exhaled slowly, remembering the day she'd heard about the attack that took place at the church, at the end of a Sunday service. She'd heard it on the news, not even realizing that the missionaries killed were her own family until hours later when Savannah got ahold of her.

The day everything changed.

She changed.

Her inner rebel, that wild, free spirit, died the day her family did, and she matured overnight, becoming the person Savannah needed. Someone strong and fearless. Someone confident and focused. Georgia promised Savannah that everything would be okay. She promised her sister that they'd make it through, assuring the eighteen-year-old that there was no reason to worry about anything but graduating from high school, because Georgia would take care of the rest...and Georgia had.

She'd found an apartment for both of them to live in near the high school Savannah would attend. Georgia paid bills—which often meant using her credit card for everything, putting them deeper into debt—but she wouldn't tell Savannah or deny Savannah what was left of her adolescence.

"I became a donor because I thought it was the right thing to do," she said quietly, filling the silence. "I knew it would be hard, but it seemed to be the most practical way to provide. It'd pay the bills, and there were a lot. But surrogacy…that's something else."

"Tell me."

She shook her head. "Let's talk about something else. I'm getting sad. I don't want to be sad. This is supposed to be a holiday. Let's focus on happy things, okay?"

CHAPTER NINE

NIKOS PAID THE BILL, and they left the restaurant just as it began to fill up. The night was cool but not cold, and they wandered through Chora's narrow streets, getting glimpses of families relaxing at the end of the day. Men stood outside smoking together. Boys kicked a ball despite the shadows spilling into corners. Loud voices came from one house. A dog barked in another.

As they returned to the town center, heading for their hotel, they passed a couple with a stroller. Georgia and Nikos both looked down at the toddler, who was sitting up, taking in the world with wide, dark eyes as he contentedly sucked his thumb.

"I told you why I became a donor and a surrogate," Georgia said to Nikos as they stepped back to let the couple with the baby pass. "But why did you decide that this was the right way to start a family?"

For a moment she didn't think he was going to answer her, and then he leaned over and picked up a small coin he spotted next to the curb. He rubbed it between his fingers, cleaning it. "An American penny," he said, handing it to her.

She looked down at the penny he'd placed in her palm. Smiling, she chanted the rhyme, "Find a penny, pick it up and all day you'll have good luck."

He smiled faintly. "Should we call it a night?"

Georgia nodded, hiding her disappointment. She wasn't ready to go to bed, and she wanted to hear more about his marriage and why he'd chosen a surrogate, but she knew better than to push. He'd tell her if and when he was ready to talk. And if he didn't, well, she had to respect that, too.

Upstairs on the second floor, Georgia started to unlock her door. She was aware of Nikos behind her, and she kept hoping he'd invite himself in or suggest they have an after-dinner drink, even if her drink was just the bottle of mineral water next to the side of the bed.

"It wasn't a good relationship," Nikos said abruptly. "My marriage was strained from the start. Elsa was unhappy most of our marriage, and she thought a baby would fix things. I thought a baby would only make things worse."

Georgia slowly turned around, key forgotten. "So you refused to have a baby with her?"

"No." He folded his arms over his powerful chest. "But you have to sleep together to conceive. Elsa wouldn't let me come near her."

"Why not?" And then she shook her head. "You don't have to answer. I'm sorry that I ask so many questions."

"I'm happy to talk, but I think somewhere more private would be better. We'll go to my room. It has that little balcony. We can open the doors and get fresh air."

But once inside his room there was no getting past the bed without noticing there was a bed. Georgia suddenly felt shy, which was odd considering she was pregnant with this Greek tycoon's baby.

Nikos opened his bottle of water and filled the two glasses on the dresser. "Cheers," he said.

She lightly clinked the rim of her glass to his. "To a great day with my new friend, Nikos Panos."

He flashed her a lazy smile, a smile that didn't strike her as particularly platonic. "Sit here. It looks like the more comfortable chair." He in turn sprawled on the bed.

It wasn't a huge bed, either. It reminded her of a bed in children's rooms in America. She'd read that many of the European hotels were small, and so beds were small, too, but it didn't seem like a proper size for a man Nikos's size.

"Are we really friends?" Nikos said, studying her from beneath heavy lids with long black lashes.

"I think we should be. It'd make this attraction seem more logical."

"You feel it now, then?"

"The chemistry between us?"

He nodded.

"I felt it all day," she answered honestly. "I don't even have to look at you and I can feel you. And we can be laughing about something, but I know that if you touched me, or kissed me, I'd be done for. I'd just want more kisses."

"Hmm." He dragged his nails across the plain white coverlet on the bed. "You are nothing like her."

The words were spoken so softly Georgia wasn't even sure they were meant for her. It was on the tip of her tongue to ask him to explain, but then he looked at her, dark eyes piercing, and said, "She didn't like it when I touched her. She didn't want me to touch her. Elsa was uncomfortable making love...or at least, with the way I made love."

Carnal. Aggressive.

Georgia was beginning to understand. "She was the one who made you question yourself."

"It was no longer making love, but sex, and then the sex no longer felt consensual."

"What happened then?"

"We stopped sleeping together. She moved into her own room. I had mine. We lived like that for almost a year."

"Was it that way before you married?"

"We married very fast. I was respectful. We kissed and did things, but she wanted to wait until we married to have sexual intercourse, so we did."

"And then you married and she didn't want to do it?"

"I thought she needed time. I thought it was because it was all so new. But she said no—it was me. I was always angry and yelling and scaring her."

Georgia frowned. "Were you?"

"I became frustrated as time went on. And I may have yelled once or twice, but I was never cruel. I never said mean things to her. I never treated her badly. But I wouldn't release her from the marriage vow, and this I know now was the mistake. I should have let her go. I should have divorced her. It would have been better. In hindsight, I know it would have been the right way to go. But at the time I was young. Twenty-six, twenty-seven. I had a beautiful wife. I was proud of my wife. I was not going to just give up."

"Many people would think you were being a good husband, fighting for your marriage."

He shrugged. "I fought for it too long. I should have set my pride aside and let her go."

"Or had the baby?" Georgia looked at him, troubled. "Would that have helped?"

"I don't regret that decision. It was the right decision. I wanted a family. Elsa and I discussed children before we married, and she knew I wanted them, but I could not see raising a child as we were. I wanted to wait until our relationship improved. I hated how toxic it was. Wasn't healthy and it wouldn't have been healthy for a child. And then she was gone, and I wasn't just grieving the loss of my wife but the loss of the family we'd never have."

"Wouldn't it have been easier to just marry again? Start over?"

"I didn't want to marry again. I still don't. But I did want to be a father, and I'm looking forward to being a father."

"Marriage doesn't have to be bad," she said gently. "My parents had a good relationship and a solid marriage. They were still very much in love until the end."

"How do you know they were in love?"

Georgia closed her eyes, picturing them. It had been almost six years since she'd last seen them. Four years since they died. And yet it felt like forever.

"They were affectionate and warm," she said after a moment. "They were kind towards each other. My father was protective of my mom, but also respectful. My mother wasn't shy about telling us girls that we'd be lucky to find a man as good and kind and loving as my father. She adored him. And he made her laugh, which always fascinated me since Mother was quite serious at heart. She rarely laughed with us girls, but my father could make her giggle—" Georgia broke off, lost for a moment in time, seeing her mother at the kitchen stove, making dinner, and then turning as Father entered the kitchen, her mother's face lighting up.

"They were friends," she continued after a moment. "And obviously lovers, too, but their friendship and respect for each other was at the heart of their relationship, and that's what I've always wanted. Someone who would like me and respect me and treat me as an equal."

"It sounds so very American," Nikos said.

"The desire to be treated as an equal?"

"We don't think of marriage that way in Greece. It's not about equality but about fulfilling your role. To be a good husband. To be a good wife. It's easier to do that than asking, demanding, that men and women be equal."

"And your wife knew this was your viewpoint?" Georgia asked.

His broad shoulders shrugged. "We didn't talk enough about the important things. Elsa loved fashion and shopping, and she was eager to set up our home. My job was to work and provide—"

"You know that, or you expected she would?"

"She did not want to work. She wanted to be taken care of. And she knew I had the ability to take care of her."

"Was she beautiful?"

Nikos hesitated. "Yes."

"What did she look like?"

Another hesitation. "Tall, slender, blonde."

"Greek?"

"No. Scandinavian."

Like me, Georgia thought. But she couldn't just leave it at that. She had to ask, had to get his reaction. "Is that why you wanted an egg donor who was tall, slender, blonde?"

"Yes."

Georgia had to ponder this, as it struck her as odd that he'd want an egg donor similar to his wife and yet he wouldn't have a baby with her. He must have loved her very much, and it was on the tip of her tongue to ask him, but somehow she couldn't bring herself to put the question to him.

Or maybe it was because she didn't want to hear him say the words.

Elsa was gone and not here, so why introduce her? Why make her part of their night? Because this was their night... It was an escape...an adventure. Georgia was determined to protect the adventure.

As well as the romance.

Because there was something here between them, and it felt good. Special. And for tonight that was enough.

"I think we've talked about my marriage enough," Nikos said, sitting up. "Let's talk about something far more interesting. Let's talk about you."

"I'm not that interesting."

"I disagree." He was sitting on the edge of the bed now, his muscular legs extended in front of him. He gestured to her, indicating she was to come to him.

Georgia, who'd wanted to be close to him all day, suddenly felt a spike of panic. Her heart jumped, pulse quickening. It was one thing to anticipate seduction; it was another to be seduced.

He noticed her hesitation. "Have you come to your senses? Realized what a mistake this would be?" There was a hint of mockery in his voice, and yet tension rolled from him in waves.

She could feel his intensity from where she sat. He was suddenly very big and very male, humming with a primal energy that reminded her of a great cat on the prowl.

"You're making me a little nervous," she admitted.

"Why?"

"Because the kisses are always so good, but I've learned with you there's a price for such pleasure."

"We're not doing that anymore. I'm not doing that anymore. I'm not going to hide myself from you anymore. You will see me as I am. You will see more for who I am. Good. Bad. Ugly."

"Not bad, not ugly," she said.

"You don't know that yet."

"My gut is rarely wrong."

The corner of his mouth lifted and he gestured for her again. "Come, *gynaika mou*—I want to kiss."

"Just kiss?"

"I shall leave that up to you. You control this. You are in charge. If you just want to kiss, we kiss. If you want me to put my mouth on you, and make you come, I will. If you want my body filling you, then I will do that. I am yours to command. So come. Now. I am impatient for you."

She slowly stood, finding him utterly compelling and seductive. "But I thought I was in charge. I thought you are mine to command."

He leaned forward, caught her wrist, drew her to him. "After the first kiss. Let me kiss you properly, as I've wanted to kiss you all day, and then you shall be in charge."

He pulled her down between his legs, so that she was half kneeling at his feet. His hands clasped her face. His thumbs stroked her hot, flushed cheeks.

"So beautiful, my woman, *agapi mou*," he murmured, lowering his head to hers, his lips brushing hers.

The kiss was soft, almost sweet, and she leaned into it, kissing him back, and that was all it took for her lips to burn and her tummy to flip. She shivered as he deepened the kiss, parting her mouth to drink the air from her lips.

Hot, sharp darts of sensation rushed through her, making her head spin. She reached for him, wrapping her arms around his neck. He lifted her from the floor, kissing her as he stretched her on the bed next to him.

As he kissed her, his hand went to her waist and then slid up her rib cage to cup the softness of her breast.

She arched into his hand, groaning as he circled a nipple, tugging on it to make it even harder.

"You know my body too well already," she murmured as he dropped his head to kiss her nipple through her blouse and bra. His mouth was warm. His teeth found the tip, gently biting. She gasped.

"Too much?" he asked, lifting his head.

She stared up into his eyes, which were so beautiful and dark, and she shook her head, feeling wanton and yet good. "No. Not even."

"You want more?"

"I want everything."

"Perhaps we keep it to kissing for now, make sure you don't change your mind."

"I won't."

"We'll see," he said, lifting her long skirt and pushing the knit fabric over her knees. His mouth followed, his lips and tongue cool and then hot against her heated flesh. She was wearing small white satin-and-lace bikini briefs that sat low on her hips, below the curve of her bump, and his fingers brushed her, over the panties, over her mound and down between her legs where she was wet.

He stroked again, pushing her knees farther apart until

he had her open to him. Despite the white satin-and-lace panties, she felt so very naked and exposed. His hands were at her thighs, and he ran his palms down from her hips to her knees and then up again. Every place he touched burned. Every place he looked melted.

He was examining her, a possessive light in his eyes, his dark gaze burning and intent. Hungry.

Carnal.

Her heart thudded so hard it hurt to breathe, and she couldn't look anymore, overwhelmed by his intensity and the rawness of his desire.

She closed her eyes as his mouth touched the inside of her knee, and she sighed as his lips trailed up the inner thigh, kissing higher until he'd reached the edge of the lace. He stroked over the pantie and the fullness of her mound, and then slipped beneath the elastic, lightly tracing where she was wet and then sliding the wetness over her lips and clit.

His head dropped again, and he kissed where he touched, through the satin and then peeling the panties back, where she was pink and tender and glistening.

He did things with his tongue that made it impossible to breathe. He licked and stroked, lapped and sucked, and Georgia did not want it to end. She wasn't ready to come, but he'd wound her so tightly, her nerves stretched, her body tense with pleasure that when he slipped his fingers into her and then stroked up even as he flicked his tongue over her sensitive clit, she exploded, climaxing so hard she cried out, and grabbed for Nikos's shoulder, desperate to touch him, feel him, needing his strength to anchor her and keep her from blowing away.

"Amazing," she whispered as he stretched out next to her. She pressed herself to his side, still craving his warmth and determined to keep him with her. He'd said he wasn't going to walk away, but she wasn't sure, and she wasn't ready to let him go. "You are amazing," she added.

He held her against him, and she was content to lie in the circle of his arm until her heart stopped beating so wildly, but as she relaxed, she realized he was still dressed and she was somewhat in disarray and he'd given her plea- sure but it wasn't what she'd hoped would happen.

"We need to get out of these clothes," she whispered, kissing his shoulder, lightly raking her nails over his chest.

He kissed the top of her head and then her temple and the side of her cheek, murmuring, "I think now might be a good time to get you back to your room."

"No. Can't go yet," she said, snuggling closer and lifting her face so that she could kiss him. She could taste herself on his lips and it reminded her of how giving he was, and how passionate, and how much she wanted to give him pleasure, too. "We haven't even begun."

"I don't want you to have regrets."

She wrapped her arms around his neck, welcoming the crush of her breasts to his chest and the feel of his thigh as it moved between her legs. "My only regret would be not making love to you."

"I have more scars."

"I've seen them. They're nothing."

"They're something."

"I think they're beautiful. They're part of you."

As he closed the balcony door and drew the curtains, she stripped off her clothes and then watched as he un- dressed.

Her eyes widened as his trousers fell and his shaft jutted up, long and thick and impressively erect. He turned off the lights, and she felt a little tremor of trepidation as he returned to bed, drawing the covers over them as the night was cool.

This had been her idea, but she was suddenly nervous.

Or maybe it was excited. It was hard to know when her pulse was beating double time and she felt as if she couldn't quite catch her breath.

Nikos pulled her against him, and she snuggled close, letting his powerful body warm hers, enjoying just being held. "Nervous?" he asked.

She nodded. "Just a little bit."

"We don't have to do anything."

"I know."

"Maybe you just sleep with me."

"Okay," she whispered, pressing even closer so that she could feel his hair-roughened chest scrape her breasts and his long legs intertwine with hers.

He was so warm, and he felt so big and protective. She couldn't remember when she last felt so safe.

Georgia put her hand to his chest and caressed over his rib cage, feeling the ridge of muscle beneath the firm, smooth skin. She knew his scars were higher up, on one shoulder, and along his neck. She stroked his back, savoring each hard, taut muscle, and then up higher, to the shoulder where she encountered thickened skin.

She felt him tense but didn't stop her exploration, caressing his broad shoulders and then down one thickly muscled arm.

"You have quite the hot bod," she whispered.

"The scars don't disgust you?"

"How could they? They are part of you."

"I think you will make a very good doctor."

She felt a pinch in her chest, a sharp reminder that this was all temporary, that she wasn't his for keeps, that they were just playing a game, staying busy, until June…

He must have felt the shift in her mood because he rolled her onto her back, stopping her exploration. "We don't have to do this."

He sounded somber, almost grim, and she ran her hands up and down his arms. "Oh, yes, we do."

"Why?"

"Because I want to be with you. I want to know what it's like being your woman."

For a split second Nikos couldn't breathe, the air trapped in his lungs, his chest seizing closed.

She wanted to know what it was like to be his woman.

His woman.

There was fire in his eyes. A hot, gritty sting that echoed the burn in his chest.

He didn't think he'd ever have another woman. He didn't think he deserved a woman of his own.

"It's been a long time since I've been with anyone," he said gruffly. "Years."

"Not since Elsa?"

"Yes."

"Do you like being so celibate?"

"It is better than hurting anyone."

Her hands were on his chest, stroking over the muscle that covered his heart. "You won't hurt me."

"How can you be so sure?"

"Because you're a good man. An honest man. Not perfect but definitely likable."

He dropped his head, kissed her lips and then her jaw and then lower. She lifted her chin, giving him access to her neck and sighing with pleasure as he found sensitive nerves.

Her hands were caressing him as he kissed her, stroking his stomach, his hip, his thigh before brushing light fingertips over his throbbing erection.

He gritted his teeth, holding back a groan as she wrapped a hand around his shaft, discovering his weight and heat and length.

It was all he could do not to pump into her, to hold still while she explored him, cupping him, stroking, running her thumb over the head of his shaft, rubbing the drop of moisture over the broad tip.

"You are very impressive," she whispered.

"Let's see if I remember how to do this," he said, catching her hand to lift her arms above her head even as he settled his hips between her thighs.

She gave a deep, throaty sigh as he slowly eased into her.

"Does it hurt?" he asked, holding still.

"No. You feel so, so good."

The edge of his lips lifted. "That's encouraging, but I think I can make you feel much, much better."

And he did.

Georgia woke in the night, surprised for a moment to find an arm around her, holding her, and then she remembered where she was and what they'd done and how incredibly satisfying it'd been.

She needed to use the restroom, but she didn't want to wake Nikos. She lay there for several minutes trying to persuade herself that she didn't really have to go, but she did.

"What's wrong? Do you want to go back to your room?"

She turned to look at Nikos. She could just make out his face in the dark but couldn't read his expression. "I didn't mean to wake you."

"I haven't slept."

"What time is it?"

"Probably two thirty or three."

"Why can't you sleep?"

"I have you in my bed."

"And it's a small bed."

"It is a small bed, but that's not it. I've just enjoyed lying here, holding you. You feel good." He smoothed her long hair back from her face. "Why are you awake?"

"I think the little guy kicked me, reminded me I need to use the bathroom."

"I felt him move tonight."

"Did you?"

"Yes."

"What did you think?"

"It's amazing. A miracle." His voice dropped, deepening. "That you're a miracle."

Georgia sat up and reached for the bedside lamp and turned it on. She blinked at the brightness of the light, but she wanted it on to see Nikos's face. "I'm glad you finally were able to feel him move."

"It's rather incredible, isn't it?"

"Yes." He caught her hand, carried it to his mouth, pressing a kiss to her knuckles and then her palm. "Life changing."

CHAPTER TEN

THEY RETURNED TO KATAPOLA, the main harbor, for a late breakfast after checking out of the hotel.

Nikos had wanted to stay in Chora for the meal, but Georgia pleaded to return to Katapola so they could have their last meal on Amorgós be at one of those charming restaurants on the bay.

In town, Nikos let Georgia pick the restaurant, and she took the task seriously, studying the outside of each place before examining the posted menus before finally selecting a small outdoor café close to the boats.

It was clearly a place for locals—and by locals, it appeared the local men—but Nikos entered and took a table on the shaded patio, ignoring the curious glances from the patrons already seated at tables.

They knew who he was, she thought as he held her chair for her. Just as the woman in the bakery had seemed to recognize him yesterday. Just as the woman behind the counter hadn't been friendly, these men weren't welcoming, either.

"I know you studied the menu outside, but almost everything was for lunch. Greeks don't have a big breakfast. For some it's just a coffee and cigarette, not that I'd recommend that for you," he said. "For others, it might be some yogurt with almonds and honey, or maybe a slice of cheese pie or spinach pie."

"So what would you suggest?"

"What are you hungry for?"

"Do you think they have eggs?"

"I'm sure they could cook eggs for you. I will ask." He leaned back in his chair, looking carelessly at ease.

But Georgia wasn't relaxed. She could feel the stares of the men at the table in the corner. It wasn't comfortable. She shifted in her chair, trying to block them from view. "Have you been here before?"

"To this restaurant or the island?"

"Both."

"Not to the café, but to the island, yes."

She couldn't help glancing back over her shoulder, her gaze sweeping the corner table as well as the pair at an adjacent table. Not one of the men smiled or nodded.

"Kind of an interesting energy," she said.

"Very polite of you."

She focused on him. "So you're aware of the cold shoulder?"

"Absolutely. I'm not wanted here."

"Why?"

"They are uncomfortable with me here."

"Why?"

He didn't immediately answer, and then he shrugged, wearily. "They call me *teras. Thirio.*"

Georgia silently repeated the words. "What does it mean?"

"It's not important."

"Tell me, Nikos."

He sighed. "Monster." He hesitated. "Beast."

"What?" Her jaw dropped, shocked. *"Why?"*

He gestured to his face. "This."

"That's ridiculous. Those are burns. You were injured—"

"It bothers people here that I live and she does not."

"Were you at the wheel?"

"No. I wasn't even in the car."

"Then how can they blame you?"

"It's a small island. I live close by and yet I'm a stranger to them."

"I find it hard to believe that's why they call you such horrible things."

"I'm an eccentric."

"Yes, you are. But does that warrant such cruelty?"

"I don't know. I don't really care anymore. I just try to avoid this place. It's why I didn't want to come here. It's why I stay on Kamari. It's home."

His refuge.

Georgia swallowed hard, hating what he'd told her and yet also understanding his desire to be alone. To have his own space. To be free of ignorant people's hatefulness. "How do they even know about you and Elsa? Didn't you meet her in Athens?"

"No. She was here on Amorgós on holiday with girl-friends, visiting from Oslo. They'd booked a villa for a number of weeks during the summer and while here, she met a handsome young man, a local fisherman named Ambrose, and they fell in love. He proposed. She stayed. The wedding was planned. And then she met me."

"And she abandoned Ambrose for you."

"Yes."

"People took sides."

"Yes."

"And when she died in the accident, they blamed you."

The edge of his mouth curved, but it wasn't a smile. "You know the story already."

"It's horrible."

"I am, yes."

"No." She frowned at him. "You're not horrible. The story is horrible. And they are horrible, too, if they call you such terrible names. You are not a beast or a monster—"

"I don't blame them. She's gone and look at me."

"I see you. And I think you're beautiful." And then Georgia shocked everyone in the café by leaning across the table and kissing him on the lips. "Let's go back to Kamari," she whispered. "I'm tired of playing tourist."

It rained during the return trip to Kamari. The clouds had been gathering during the morning and by the time they boarded the boat at noon the sky was gray, the clouds ominously low.

"I am wishing I'd requested the yacht," Nikos said, taking Georgia's hand to steady her as she stepped into the low, sleek speedboat. "But maybe we'll beat the storm."

She'd had such a great day and a half on Amorgós, had loved her night with Nikos, enjoying every moment of their trip until they'd sat down in that café on the harbor.

Now it was hard to get the villagers' cold stares out of her head. Nikos's explanation didn't help, as she sensed there were pieces missing from the story. She wanted to ask more questions but didn't think this was the time. "I'm not worried about getting wet," she said, flashing him a quick smile. "It's just rain."

"You might feel different when we're flying at high speed across the water."

The storm broke while they were halfway between Amorgós and Kamari, and there were a few drops and then the skies just parted and the rain came down hard, and the wind whipped at them. The rain was cold and fell in heavy wet sheets, pelting them. On the speedboat there was nowhere to go, and so the rain drenched them, water streaming from Georgia's sweater when it could hold no more.

Nikos had offered his jacket when the first raindrops fell, but she'd refused. Now he simply overrode her protest and peeled off his coat, wrapping it around her slim shoulders and buttoning it over her chest.

"Nikos, I'm fine," she laughed, pushing wet hair back from her face.

"You're not. You're chilled through," he said. He reached out to touch her cheek with the backs of his fingers. "Your skin is cold."

"I'm not that cold."

"You'll get sick."

"We'll be back soon."

"Not soon enough," he said, drawing her into his arms and holding her securely against him. "Not taking chances."

"You never do," she answered as he shifted his hold, one of his arms circling her shoulders to keep her upright, while the other moved below the hem of his coat to clasp her waist.

She had been cold, but his body was warm, penetrating her damp clothes. She loved the feel of his hand on her waist, too. The intimacy of the touch wasn't lost on her. From the beginning Nikos had been protective, and on Amorgós he'd remained close, always watchful, always there to lend a hand as she stood up or navigated a steep set of stairs, making her feel safe, desired.

It had been a long time since anyone was there for *her*. She'd grown accustomed to taking care of herself, taking care of others, and it was a novelty to have Nikos want to care for her.

Nikos's hand at her waist was sliding down to her hip, and she sucked in air, eyes half closing, trying to ignore the faint shudder of pleasure.

"I knew you were freezing," he said, his mouth near her ear, his warm breath stirring her senses.

She wanted to tell him he didn't need to worry, that she wasn't cold, just sensitive, her body still humming with emotion and sensation from their night of lovemaking.

The speedboat hit a wave and lifted. Nikos's arm tightened around her, holding her steady.

Just then the baby kicked. Nikos's head dipped. "I felt that," he said.

Georgia's heart turned over. A lump filled her throat. She put her hand over his, trying to control the panic rolling through her.

How was this going to work?

How was she going to do this?

How was she going to just get on a plane and leave Nikos and the baby?

Back on Kamari, Nikos disappeared into his room to shower and change and work, and Georgia did the same, except after her hot shower she couldn't seem to settle down enough to focus on her books.

She sat on the couch and stared off into space, her attention drawn now and then to the window, where the rain drummed against the glass.

She had to study. The exam was important. Her future was important. Her goals hadn't changed. Her priorities were still the same. Weren't they?

But as the rain pounded on the roof and the wind howled outside, tugging at the old wood shutters, she found herself unable to see herself back in Atlanta.

She couldn't imagine returning to school as if none of this had ever happened.

Uneasy with the future, unable to answer any of the questions eating away at her, Georgia forced herself to read. She would study. She had to study. Right now preparing for the test was the only thing she could control.

That evening they met for drinks in the library since the rain hadn't let up. Nikos had laid a fire and the room was toasty warm.

He'd seated Georgia in one of the oversize wing chairs flanking the fire, and he took the other. The steady drumming of the rain was almost like music. Nikos couldn't remember when he last felt so comfortable.

He was content.

It had been a good trip to Amorgós. It had been time well spent.

Georgia was studying the fire, and he used the opportunity to study her.

She was so beautiful. So uniquely Georgia Nielsen. Fierce and frustrating, provocative and strong, and ultimately breathtakingly wonderful.

He remembered tracing her face in bed, lightly running his fingertip over her stunning face, following the elegant arc of her winged brows, and then down her straight fine nose, over the generous softness of her full lips.

"You are so incredibly pretty."

He didn't even realize he'd said the words aloud until she turned and looked at him, those lovely, tempting lips curving up in a smile.

"I have a feeling blue-eyed blondes are your type," she said, her voice warm with amusement.

He frowned. "Why did you say that?"

"You were very specific in your quest for a donor. Height, weight, hair color, eye color, ethnic makeup."

"I also wanted healthy, educated, intelligent—"

"Blonde." But her lips still curved. "But I'm not shocked. Men have types. Your type just happens to be slender blondes from Scandinavia."

"No, my type just happens to be you. The world is full of blondes, but there is only one you."

They ended up eating dinner in the library and then it was just a short walk to his room.

Georgia felt Nikos's impatience as he shut the door behind him, locking it.

"I've never been in here," she said, looking around. His room was simple with a large elegant bed, low handsome nightstands and a stunning glass chandelier overhead. "It looks Venetian," she said.

"It is. I have a weakness for Venetian design."

"Maybe you have some Venetian in your blood."

He reached for her, drawing her to him. "I know I have you in my blood." He lifted her face to his, kissing her lightly, his lips brushing over hers, teasing, making her sigh and arch into him.

"Kiss me," she urged, sliding a hand into the thick, glossy hair at his nape and giving it a little tug. "Make me feel good."

That was all it took for the simmering heat to ignite.

Nikos deepened the kiss, his lips parting hers even as his hand slid down her back, to the dip in her spine. He pressed her there, urging her closer. She loved the feel of his hand in the small of her back and the way his skin warmed hers from the inside out. She could feel his palm and the press of each finger, awakening nerves, making her spark and tingle.

His tongue teased hers. His hand slipped to her hip and then to the curve of her butt, holding her securely to him, letting her feel the thickness of his erection.

She rubbed herself against him, sighing as his shaft brushed her where she was sensitive. His fingers followed, cupping her there, between her thighs, and then stroking with expert fingers, sending a bolt of white-hot sensation right through her.

"Are you wet?" he murmured at her ear.

"Yes."

"How wet?"

"You could take me now, here, and I'd come like that."

"You are too easy." His teeth nipped at her neck; he stroked and pinched her breast. "We should make this a challenge. Not let you come—"

"No, not fair."

"Force you to wait, hold back."

"That will just torture me."

"But it will make the orgasm even better."

"I don't know that I'd survive it."

He laughed softly, his hands slipping beneath her blouse, circling her waist before sliding up her rib cage to cup her breasts. "I promise you'll survive. I would never let anything happen to you or hurt you."

"You have happened to me," she said, suddenly breathless as he peeled the lace cups from her breasts to rub his palms over her taut nipples. The pleasure was intense. He made her feel wild...desperate.

Before Nikos, she didn't think she'd ever really been touched before.

She didn't think she'd ever met a man who understood a woman's body the way he did. Nikos was a master of sensuality, an expert in seduction, and she wanted it all. She wanted everything he could give her, aware that this might be all they ever had, and it would have to be enough.

Her clothes seemed to fall away, and he drew back to look at her, his dark eyes hot and bright. He examined her from head to toe, ownership in his eyes, along with pride.

It felt good to be wanted...desired...claimed.

"You are so beautiful," he murmured, brushing a hand across one of her rosy-tipped breasts, her breasts so much fuller now that she was pregnant.

"I think you've been starved for attention here on Kamari," she said.

"I am starved for you," he answered.

"You had me not even twenty-four hours ago."

"That was a taste. I want a feast."

Her cheeks flushed. She burned.

He watched her face as he stroked her nipple again, tugging on the sensitive peak. She gasped at the ache he caused between her thighs. He was making her body so hot, making her wet.

He tugged on the nipple, rolling the tip between his fingers, the sensation sharp and intense, pleasure and pain, and Georgia sucked in air, head spinning, pulse pounding.

"I don't know that I can stand much longer," she whispered.

He swung her into his arms and carried her to the bed. His hands and mouth were everywhere, touching, kissing, stroking, licking.

Her eyes closed as she felt his lips close around her nipple, making her body hotter and wetter, and then he lazily traveled between her breasts, down over the curve of her belly. He kissed the point where her thigh and hip came together, waking every little nerve, before kissing her between the thighs, fingers sliding through soft folds, parting them to expose the nub.

The cool air against her was erotic, but there was nothing like his mouth on her, his tongue and lips covering her clit, sucking hard.

She shattered immediately. She couldn't help it. He was far too good, and she felt far too much.

"That's what I mean," he teased, moving behind her to hold her against him. "There is no challenge."

"Would it be better if I didn't come?"

"I would find a way to reach you."

"So confident."

He kissed the back of her neck, her shoulder. "I blame you. You have made me so."

And then he turned her on her side, and eased into her from behind. She was wet, and he was thick and hard. She sighed as he buried himself deeply within her before pulling back, nearly withdrawing.

She protested, and he laughed softly, teasing her for a moment before thrusting deep. He reached around to stroke her as he thrust in and out.

The pleasure built, nerves tightening, sensation focus-

ing. She felt hot, and she was breathing harder, panting
as each deep, hard thrust pushed her closer to an orgasm,
but she fought it this time, not ready to give in, wanting
to prolong the pleasure as long as she could.

Making love with Nikos was powerful…electric. The
physical act somehow transformed her—them—into something beautiful and new, as if they weren't two separate
people but one.

One body.

One heart.

And then she couldn't think about anything but the
bright, intense sensation rippling through her, sweeping
her into a fierce, brilliant, shattering climax. Her body exploded, and dozens of sparkly lights danced in her eyes,
in her mind.

Heaven. It was heaven here on earth.

Georgia opened her eyes to discover Nikos was looking at
her. "How long was I asleep?" she murmured.

"A half hour, maybe an hour."

"Did you sleep?"

"I just woke up."

She smiled sleepily. It felt so good to fall asleep in his
arms and wake in his arms. She loved how beautiful and
special he made her feel, as if she were the only woman
in the world.

She could see in his eyes now that she was important to
him. She could feel it in the way he touched her.

He always put her first, too. Her pleasure. Her comfort. Her release.

She liked that. Loved it. Maybe even loved him.

There, she'd thought it. Admitted it.

She was falling in love with him, and every time they
made love, she fell that much harder.

She leaned toward him, brushed her lips across his.

"Are you just going to stare at me all night now?" she murmured.

"I was thinking about it."

She smiled slowly in response to his husky voice and lazy smile.

She loved the way he looked at her, focused on her. Loved the blistering heat in his eyes. Loved that he made her feel like she was a woman who could do anything.

"Okay," she said, nestling in and closing her eyes again. "You just do that."

Nikos watched her eyes close, and he knew by her breathing when she'd fallen back asleep.

He placed a careful kiss on the top of her head, overwhelmed by her in the best sort of way.

When he'd married Elsa he'd thought he knew what love was and how marriage would be. He'd imagined a relationship like his parents', traditional, practical.

Marriage to Elsa had instead been a constant source of conflict.

Her death had been a shock but not a total surprise. She'd threatened him so many times…threatened to hurt herself, hurt him, do something awful…

He'd been an only child. He hadn't been raised with sisters. He didn't have lots of cousins, never mind girl cousins. As he began dating, women were a bit of a mystery. Their emotions sometimes baffled him, but they also added a level of intrigue. He had girlfriends and lovers in his early twenties, but nothing in his experience had prepared him for Elsa.

He still wondered why Elsa married him. Was it his wealth? The family name? Did she think that one good-looking Greek could be interchangeable with another?

He would never know. He didn't want to know. He didn't even want to think of her anymore.

Her death, and the manner of that death, had nearly destroyed him. He was ready to put the ghosts of that past behind him, and he could with Georgia.

Georgia was strong where Elsa had been weak.

Georgia had fire and passion, courage and conviction.

Georgia's strength freed him. Her confidence and clear sense of self allowed him to be who he really was—a man, not a monster.

Her acceptance changed everything. Her acceptance made him hope for the life he didn't think he'd ever have.

A wife, children, a family.

He proposed at dinner the next night. He'd planned on making it special, wanting champagne and flowers, but it was still stormy and there weren't fresh flowers to bring in or champagne she could drink, so he just blurted the words.

"Marry me, *agapi mou*," he said, at the end of dinner, when it was just them at the table, with the flicker of candlelight.

She blinked at him, stunned.

He probably could have introduced the subject better, eased into it. He smiled at her bewildered expression. "Let's make this permanent," he said. "Stay here with me. Marry me—"

"What?"

"We are good together. We complement each other. I think we could be happy together."

She just stared at him, confusion in her eyes.

"I think this is a good solution," he added carefully, wishing he wasn't so pragmatic, wishing he was a man of romance. "We would be a family. You, me, our son."

She rose but didn't get far. Her eyes were wide. She looked almost afraid. "That wouldn't work, and you know it."

"Why wouldn't it work? You like me. I like you. We made a baby together. We should be a family."

Her eyes filled with tears. "It's not that simple."

"Of course it is."

"Nikos, I have school…exams…my residency. It will be years until I'm a doctor—"

"So wait until the baby is older and then go back to school."

"I can't do that."

"Why not?"

She shook her head and walked from the table, across the dining room floor. "I need some air," she said, heading for the terrace.

"It's raining, Georgia."

"Then I'll go to my room." She was hurrying to the hall, almost running to the stairs.

"Don't run," he commanded, cornering her in the stairwell. "Why are you so upset? You can say no. Just say no. There is no need for this. I would never force you, Georgia, to do anything."

Georgia shook her head, feeling cornered and confused.

She had been happy these past few days, happier than she could have imagined. And she didn't want to leave Nikos or the baby, but that didn't mean marriage was the answer.

"Georgia," Nikos said quietly, trying to get her to look at him.

She put a hand to his chest, torn between wanting to pull him close and push him away. "I have to finish school, Nikos. I have to finish what I started."

"But you won't have to work if you marry me. You can focus on our son. You can be a mother—"

"Nikos!" Her hand balled into a fist, and she pounded once on his chest. "I never wanted to be a mother! I wanted to be a doctor. And I still want to be a doctor. I want the life I planned."

He let her go.

In her room she curled up on her bed and grabbed a pillow, holding it tight to her chest.

That wasn't entirely true, what she'd just told him.

She did want to be a mother. She very much wanted to be part of her baby's life. But to give up her entire world back home? To give up her plans…her dreams?

To give up Savannah?

But, on the other hand, how could she give up Nikos and the baby?

There weren't tears for something like this. The questions and decisions were too huge and overwhelming.

And now Nikos thought she didn't want him, and didn't love their son…

How to fix this? What to do?

And then he was there, at the foot of her bed. She hadn't even heard him enter her room.

"Georgia."

"I'm not ready to talk."

"Okay. Don't talk. Just listen. I support you wanting to be a doctor. I think you should finish medical school."

"What?" She sat up.

"I think we can find a way to make this work. You, me, baby, medical school."

"How?"

"There are things called planes and hotels, houses and internet—"

"No internet on Kamari."

"Maybe it's worth the billion to put it in."

She laughed. "There has to be another answer. That's too much money."

"I am sure we can figure it out. If we're together."

"Yes." She left the bed, wrapped her arms around his

waist and kissed him. "Maybe we should go back to bed and talk about our options there."

"You have a most voracious appetite, *gynaika mou.*"

Her lips curved up. "Complaining about carnal activities, Nikos?"

He laughed, a deep, soft laugh that she could feel all the way through her. "Never." And then he was locking her bedroom door and taking her to bed with him.

CHAPTER ELEVEN

THE NEXT MONTH was without a doubt the happiest month Georgia had ever known. As the weeks slipped by with March turning into April, the rain disappeared and the sun shone longer, with the days warmer. It was by no means beach weather, but Georgia enjoyed changing from heavy sweaters to light wraps and sometimes no wrap at all if it was a particularly nice day.

The bougainvillea was bursting into bloom, too, and everywhere she looked there were huge clusters of hot pink and purple draped across doorways, over gates, up pristine white walls.

Georgia's heart felt lighter, and she didn't know if it was the fact that the sun always seemed to be shining and she was waking up to a blue sky over dazzling blue water, or if it just seemed brighter and sunnier because she was madly in love.

And she was madly in love.

She now also knew that she'd never been in love before. Nikos was her first true love, and after six weeks in Greece, she thought she could one day be happy here and maybe live here, but first she needed to finish school.

Nikos said they'd find a way to make it work. He said they just needed to take it a step at a time. One day at a time. It was good advice. The doctor had been there earlier in the week, and he'd said all was progressing well with the pregnancy. She was now in her thirty-second week. They discussed a birthing plan. Georgia said she'd be comfortable having the baby on Kamari as long as the doctor and the midwife were comfortable delivering there.

They discussed having a contingency plan, should there

be an emergency, and Georgia was relieved to know that a helicopter could get her to Athens quickly if needed.

All was good.

The baby was good. She gave him a little pat now.

To think he'd brought her and Nikos together. The baby had created love...a family...

Her little matchmaker.

She smiled and gave her bump another pat before leaving her couch where she'd been studying to walk across the room to put away the basket of clean clothes the housekeeper had brought up earlier.

On top of the folded clothes was a jeweled picture frame. It was a picture of her and Nikos, his arms around her, and they were smiling at the camera.

Georgia frowned, not remembering the picture. Or the clothes. Or anything about the oddly formal pose.

Maybe because that wasn't her.

It was another tall, slender blonde...

Georgia dropped the picture back onto the basket of laundry, horrified.

Elsa.

Nikos had just returned from a run and was stripping in his room to take a shower when the bedroom door crashed open. Georgia stood in the doorway, staring at him with huge eyes, her complexion ashen.

"What's wrong?" He moved quickly toward her, thinking that something must have happened to the baby. "Are you all right? What's wrong? What's happening? Do I need to alert the doctor?"

She just stared at him, looking as if she'd seen a ghost.

Nikos put his hands on her shoulders, gave her a slight shake. "I can't help you if you won't tell me what's happened!"

"Elsa," she choked.

He stiffened. His hands fell off her shoulders. "I don't understand. What are you saying?"

"She looked like me."

His jaw dropped as if he'd speak but he didn't. He couldn't. His mind was blank. "You don't want me," Georgia whispered. "You want *her*."

His brow creased. She was wrong, completely wrong. "That's not true."

"Then why does she look like me?" Georgia pulled a photo from her pocket. There were marks on the corners where it'd been worked into a frame. She thrust the photo at him, her hand trembling. "Look at her! Look. We're the same! We could be the same person."

Nikos took the photo, if only to keep her from shoving it at his face. He didn't even need to look at it again to know the one. He only had that one photo left. Elsa had destroyed the rest.

"Why didn't you just tell me?" Georgia whispered, tears shimmering in her eyes. "Why play this game with me? Why not just tell me the truth?"

"What truth?"

"That you're still in love with her, and that you miss her, and you wanted a baby that would be hers."

"But that's not how it is. That's not what this is."

"Really? Then what is it?"

But when he struggled to find the words, when he couldn't blurt out an easy answer, she shook her head and started to walk away. Nikos caught her arm, keeping her from going.

"Let me shower and dress. I just need a few minutes. And then I'll explain."

"I don't think you *can* explain, Nikos."

"You have to at least give me a chance." His dark eyes searched hers. "Meet me in the library in five minutes. Please?"

* * *

As Georgia waited for Nikos in the library, only one thought kept going through her head, over and over.

She'd been so happy.

She'd been the happiest she could remember...

This last month it had been almost impossible to study because she hadn't wanted to sit alone in her room, surrounded by books and notes. She wanted to be with Nikos. Her attention had wandered constantly, her thoughts drifting to him throughout the day. She'd wonder what he was doing, wonder if he was swimming, wonder what he was working on... It didn't matter what he was doing, either. She just wanted to be there, with him. Near him.

He'd never minded, either. He'd encouraged her to join him, be with him, sleep with him...

Now she knew why.

The library door opened and Nikos was there...tall, darkly handsome, overwhelming in every way.

He was dressed in all black, the way he usually dressed, and his expression was grim. But even then, her heart did a painful little jump and her eyes burned.

Her whole world turned inside out in just minutes. Everything she thought was true wasn't.

"Sit, Georgia, please."

His deep, commanding voice was so achingly familiar now, and yet she stiffened in protest. "I don't want to sit."

"It's a long, complicated story—"

"I prefer the shortest, simplest version possible, please."

He gave her a long look. "You've already judged me."

"It's hard to ignore certain facts."

"Maybe there is no point, if you're not even going to give me a chance."

Her chin notched up. She wasn't sure she liked his mocking tone, but at least he wasn't begging. She didn't think she could handle that. "I don't know what you can say to make it better. I don't know that there is anything that can change this. I certainly know I can't compete with her—"

"You're not supposed to compete with her!"

"But that's who I am to you. I am her twin… It's as if you've raised her from the dead." Georgia felt desperately ill. Her stomach churned with acid and her throat burned, and it was all she could do to keep from getting sick. "You don't want me. You want *her.*"

"I don't. And for your information, you're nothing like her."

"No?" Georgia glanced wildly about, looking for the photo but realizing it was in Nikos's room. But she didn't need to see the image to remember her shock as she looked at a woman who could have been her twin. "Because she looked an awful lot like me. And the resemblance cannot be by chance."

"It's not," he said flatly.

"You wanted a baby with Elsa."

"No." Nikos muttered an oath and shrugged. "Yes."

Her heart thudded hard. Her stomach heaved. "And you wanted to make love to Elsa, too."

"No."

"I don't believe you."

"You might look like her, Georgia, but you are nothing like her."

"And yet you loved her so much."

"I didn't—" He broke off, unable to deny it. "I wouldn't have married her if I didn't love her, but what I had with her is nothing like what we have."

"*Had.* What we *had.*" Her throat worked. Her eyes burned. "There isn't anything for us anymore, Nikos. There isn't an *us.* There is just you and her and all your memories of her."

"Georgia, listen to me. You are not Elsa. You are not twins. Yes, there is a strong resemblance but within minutes of you arriving here I knew you were nothing like her, and not just because your hair is lighter and your eyes have more gray in them, but because you are not her. She wasn't strong like you. She wasn't. Life was too hard for her. Love disappointed her—"

"Perhaps you disappointed her," she interrupted. *Just as you've disappointed me.*

His dark gaze hardened, shuttering. "I am sure I did." His voice had grown cold, too. "She took her life. She did it in front of me. Smashed the car into the side of the garage of our villa on Santorini. The car erupted into flames. I was able to reach in and pull her out just before the car exploded, but she was too badly injured. She died before the medics arrived."

"How do you know she meant to kill herself? How do you know it wasn't an accident?"

"She left me a note." His jaw thickened. "And every year I get a letter in the mail, from her, telling me how much she hates me and blaming me for ruining her life."

Georgia's eyes widened. "How is that possible?"

"I think it's just one letter that she wrote, but Ambrose, over on Amorgós, has made photocopies and he mails one to me every year on the anniversary of her death. The first couple years I made the mistake of opening the envelope and reading the message. Now I just throw them away."

"What does the letter say?"

"Something along the lines of, 'Nikos, you are a monster. I hate you with every fiber of my being. I hope you burn in hell.'"

"It doesn't!"

"It does."

"So why would you want this woman's baby? How could you want to be reminded of her on a daily basis?"

"I already think of her on a daily basis. I have the burns and scars from the fire. I have the letters that come without fail every August 16. But this baby isn't hers. The baby is mine. The future is mine. And she can't take that away from me…and I won't let her take you from me, either. I've lost too much to the past, Georgia. I'm not going to lose you."

This was so much to take in, so much to process. Georgia struggled to sort through her wildly tangled thoughts and emotions. "Nikos, I don't get this…I don't. And I don't want to hurt you, but it's just so…strange. It's not normal."

"Lots of people use donors. Surrogacy is quite common."

"No, I appreciate that you wanted to be a father and you found a way to do it on your own. I understand why you chose to go with a donor and surrogate, but why pick a donor that looks like *her*? Why not pick someone that makes you feel hopeful and optimistic? A donor that was the polar opposite of Elsa?"

"I did. I picked you."

"I don't understand."

"Georgia, you're nothing like her. Yes, you're blonde and have blue eyes, but that isn't the reason I selected you to be the donor. I picked you for you…your mind, your spirit, your inner strength, your desire to support your sister. In your application you wrote about growing up in Africa as a daughter of missionaries. You had goals. Ambition. Courage. And that was who I wanted to be my child's mother. I wanted a mother who had strength…who was a warrior. I wanted him to inherit your heart."

I wanted him to inherit your heart.

Her father used to say that to her mother. *I hope the girls inherit your heart.*

Georgia closed her eyes and held her breath, tears forming behind her tightly closed eyelids. It was too much, all of this. Too much emotion and too much pressure and too much shock and disappointment.

"Say something, Georgia," Nikos said quietly. "Talk to me, *agapi mou.*"

She gave her head a shake. She couldn't talk. She didn't want to cry.

"You are my light in the dark—" His deep voice cracked, and he dropped his head, his fist to his mouth. "Please," he said roughly. "Please don't shut me out."

"I need to think. I need time." She couldn't look at him. Couldn't think much less feel when so close to him.

And then she was gone, heading back to her room.

Georgia left him in the library, escaping back to her room. She locked the door and then dragged a heavy chair in front of it for good measure. She didn't want Nikos to come in. She couldn't bear the thought of Nikos coming near her, not because she hated him—she could never hate him—but she needed to sort all this out and she wouldn't be clear, wouldn't be able to focus if he was near her.

This was important, too. This wasn't just about her feelings and her life, but this was Nikos's and the baby they'd conceived…not necessarily together, but still together.

Of all of it, the child was the most important.

He was innocent in all of this. He needed to be protected. Nikos was right. Georgia was tough. She was a warrior. She'd survive whatever happened next. But the baby would be helpless and vulnerable for years. The baby needed her to think and be smart. Logic was required right now, not emotion.

And logic told her that everything about her current situation was illogical. Irrational. She didn't belong here. She needed to go.

But the idea of leaving Nikos now took her breath away because she knew that if she left, she would never be back.

She didn't belong here. And the child?

She couldn't answer that one yet. Couldn't see that far

ahead. The only thing she knew with certainty was that she had to go.

And that knowledge devastated her.

For a moment she leaned against the door, her legs weak, her body trembling. Her heart felt as if it was cracking, shattering.

She closed her eyes, fighting for control. She drew a breath, and then another, cold…chilled to the bone.

Suddenly her stomach rose, heaved. She scrambled to the bathroom, fighting nausea the entire way. She prayed she wouldn't get sick. For long minutes she clung to the toilet, but eventually her stomach settled.

And then the tears fell.

She'd always prided herself on being smart, analytical, grounded, but she'd been played…duped. Completely duped.

Her heart squeezed hard, her chest so tight that she couldn't breathe. Pain filled her, pain and confusion, and yet one thing was brutally clear: she couldn't stay.

She had to leave. And she had to leave now.

Still shaking, she changed her clothes and then packed everything into her suitcases, jamming clothing swiftly into the suitcase and her books, laptop and loose ends into the smaller bag. And then she was done.

Nikos was no longer in the library. She found him outside on the terrace, the place they always met for drinks at sunset.

She steeled herself against all feeling as he turned to look at her. She willed herself to think of nothing, to be nothing, to want nothing. She was as she'd been before she arrived here—a single woman with a single purpose. The future. Providing for Savannah. Getting through the rest of medical school and her training.

She'd survive this.

She'd survived so much worse.

"Sit, *gynaika mou*. We need to talk," he said, his deep voice a hoarse rumble.

She ground her back molars, clamping down on all emotion, steeling herself against him. Everything in her still wanted him. He had such power over her. She'd found him nearly irresistible from the start. "No, Nikos. I'm not sitting or talking. I'm leaving." Her heart beat so hard it felt wild in her chest. "Goodbye."

He looked shocked. "You haven't even given us a chance—"

"Nikos, there isn't an us."

"Of course there is, and we've invested too much to just let this be the end. We need to talk. We can work through this. You know we can—"

"But I don't want to talk, and this isn't what I thought it was, either. You aren't who I thought you were."

For a long moment he said nothing. "How will you go? Where will you go?"

"Your boat will take me to Amorgós. I will sort out the rest from there."

"It's getting late—"

"It's not late. We have hours until sunset."

"An hour maybe."

"Plenty of time to reach the island if I leave now."

"You can't go like this."

"But I can, and I am." She backed up a step as he approached her. "And don't come any nearer. And definitely don't touch me. You will never touch me again. And you will never see me again."

"Georgia!"

She swallowed hard, chin lifting, eyes stinging, hot like acid, but there were no tears. She felt too cold and sick on the inside for tears. She was in shock. She would be in shock for a while. It was all too awful, all too much to take in.

"I'm going down to the dock. Have your man meet me there. He alone will take me—"

"I won't have it. I won't let you do this—"

"You don't have a choice. I'm not staying. I will swim to Amorgós if I have to and I'm happy to start now." Her gaze met his and held. "I'm not bluffing, either, Nikos."

His narrowed gaze swept her face. "I'm not saying you are."

"So call one of your staff—Eamon or Kappo or whomever is free—and have him drive me. But if your man isn't at the boat, at the dock, in five minutes, I will strip off my clothes and start swimming."

"You are being impulsive and dramatic."

"If you say so." She shrugged carelessly. "But I don't really care what you think. Fortunately, I'm a good swimmer, a very strong swimmer, and I've spent the past month swimming a mile or more every day here."

He made a deep, rough sound, and she didn't know if it was contempt or exasperation. "Amorgós is sixteen miles from here, not one, *gynaika mou*."

"Good. It will give me time to calm down." She turned to walk away, then paused and glanced back at him. "And for your information, I am not your woman. I am merely your surrogate. Nothing more, nothing less. I will alert you when I give birth, and that is all you need to know for now."

And then she was gone, passing through the door, disappearing into the house, anxious to be gone, anxious to put distance between her and Nikos, the only man she'd ever truly loved.

CHAPTER TWELVE

GEORGIA ARRIVED ON Amorgós and found a little hotel in the harbor. It was a very small hotel, but it was open and had a room available and she was just happy to check in, put on her pajamas and go to bed.

Her plan was to just stay a night. In the morning she'd book a seat on the next ferry to Santorini. But as it turned out, in winter the ferry only traveled between Amorgós and Santorini twice a week and she'd missed it yesterday.

That meant she had two more nights until the next boat. Fortunately the owner of the hotel had no guests arriving and was happy for Georgia to stay the extra evenings.

During the day she sat in her room and studied. At night she would go to the tavern across the street and order something to go, and she'd eat her dinner in her room.

She didn't have much of an appetite, but she forced herself to eat for the baby's sake.

She tried not to let herself think of Nikos, which wasn't easy, since everything about Amorgós reminded her of him.

On her last night in town, as she paid for her dinner at the tavern, a handsome man in his late twenties approached and spoke to her in English.

"Is that his?" he asked, nodding at her belly.

Georgia stiffened. "Are you speaking to me?" she asked, voice frosty.

He ignored her chilly tone. "You look like her," he added. "Not exactly, but enough."

Georgia told herself not to engage. She was tired and hungry, and tomorrow she was leaving here for Santorini. "I'm sorry. I don't know what you're talking about."

"Somebody should have warned you when you were here last month. He is a bad man. *Teras.* Be careful."

Teras. She'd heard that word before. It was one of those derogatory terms the locals called Nikos. Monster, beast, something like that. "Who are you?"

"A friend of his late wife's." He paused a beat and then leaned forward to whisper. "He killed her, you know."

She arched a brow. "I don't know who you refer to. I think you have me confused with someone else."

"I'm not, and you know who I talk about. She was pregnant with Nikos Panos's child, too. But she'd rather kill herself, and the baby, then live with him." He gave her a dark, searching look. "You should know the truth as I'm sure he hasn't told you. Or maybe he has, and that's why you're here."

Georgia felt a wave of disgust and revulsion. "Are you the one that sends those letters every year to him? Ambierce... Ambrose?"

He straightened. "Ambrose. And so he has told you."

"Why do you do it? What is the point?"

"He was already rich. He had everything. He didn't need her. She was mine."

"If that was the case, then she shouldn't have married him." She tipped her head. "Good night."

Once back in her small room, Georgia locked her door and lay down on the bed and stared at the ceiling.

Was Elsa really pregnant at the time she died? Nikos hadn't mentioned that.

She placed her arm over her eyes to try to block out the pictures in her head, but it was difficult with Ambrose's words still ringing in her ears.

It was a good thing she was going to Santorini in the morning.

Pain woke Georgia up in the middle of the night, an ungodly cramping pain that made her fear the worst.

At thirty-three weeks the baby should be viable, but she wasn't home, and she wasn't near a major hospital.

She needed to get to a hospital. She needed help.

Struggling to get clothes on, she leaned against the wall during another sharp contraction, panting through the pain. She made it out into the hallway but couldn't take another step. The contractions were so close now. The baby was coming, and she feared the worst. She desperately needed help. She desperately needed Nikos.

Georgia opened her eyes. Bright lights shone into her eyes. There was a hum of voices and sound. A face wearing a surgical mask leaned over her, said something in Greek. Georgia had no idea what was said. She couldn't feel anything. She closed her eyes again.

The voices were just a murmur of sound, but it pulled her in. She struggled to follow. It was English. She should be able to understand. It was Nikos talking, but in English. He was talking to someone about the baby. She knew that someone, recognized the voice. A man…a lawyer, maybe? Mr. Laurent?

She tried to open her eyes to ask about the baby, but they wouldn't open. Or maybe they were open and she just couldn't see…

This time when she opened her eyes she could see. The room was dark except for a glow of light by the door. She wasn't alone, though.

Turning her head, she spotted Nikos in a chair, close to her side of the bed. He was awake, watching her intently, and his fierce expression made her heart turn over. "The baby?" she whispered.

"He's good. He's fine." Nikos's voice was rough. "You're the one we were all worried about."

"I want to see the baby."

"You will, soon. I think the doctors want to see you first."

"But he's really okay?"

"He's here a bit early, but otherwise, he's perfect."

She searched his face, trying to see what he wasn't telling her. She was certain there were things he was keeping to himself. "I heard you earlier speaking in English. I could have sworn you were talking to Mr. Laurent. Is he here?"

He hesitated for just a moment before nodding. "Yes."

"Why?"

"I wanted to make some changes to our agreement, and time was of the essence, so I flew him over. He arrived early this morning."

"What changes are you making to the contract?"

"We can discuss after the doctor has been in. He's been waiting to see you but I wouldn't let him wake you up. I can't believe how many times the nurses come in to check on you. It's impossible for you to get any rest here."

He sounded so indignant she almost smiled. "So tell me what's happening. Don't make me wait."

"I changed the documents. I gave you primary custody of our son."

She struggled to sit up. *What?*

"Shh, lie down, don't get excited." He gently pushed her back. "You are his mother, and a mother should have a voice and power and control."

"But why primary custody? Why not joint custody?"

"Mr. Laurent said the same thing." He hesitated. "But if I changed the agreement to joint custody, then I am forcing you to co-parent with me. I am forcing you to interact with me constantly, discussing everything from his holidays to his education to medical care. If we were on good terms, it would not be a problem, but if it is not good between us, it will be difficult and will create even more anger and resentment."

But she still didn't understand. "This isn't what you wanted, Nikos. This isn't what we were doing."

"He needs a mother. He needs *you*."

"And he needs a father, too. And you are his father."

"I intend to be his father. I intend to be in his life, but you will get to decide how we do this. It is my hope that you will feel empowered and secure—"

"Nikos, I never wanted to be a single mother!" she interrupted fiercely, tears filling her eyes. "This wasn't the plan!"

"I know you have school. Two more years of school. And then your residency—"

"And how am I going to do that now?"

"I will help."

"*You* will help?"

He nodded. "I am not walking away from you. I am not walking away from my son. I will provide financially, but I will also be there."

"How?"

He shrugged. "I have planes. I can fly to America, too."

"You are going to come to Atlanta?"

He shrugged. "If that is where my son is."

She opened her mouth, closed it, not at all certain what to say.

Nikos stood up. "I'm going to see if I can have them bring the baby to you. I think it's time you met your son."

Georgia was able to have a visit with her son—he was small, but, as Nikos said, he was perfect in every other way—before the nurses whisked him back to the neonatal unit, where they were keeping him warm and under close supervision.

Georgia had dozed off but was awake again, trying to sort out how she felt about everything.

So much had happened in such a short period of time

that it was difficult to separate her feelings from the facts, as well as the drama.

She'd missed Nikos when she'd been on Amorgós. And when she was in pain, and trouble, all she'd wanted was Nikos at her side.

She didn't want to raise a child on her own. She hadn't agreed to be a donor and surrogate to become a single mother. Nikos would be a good father, too. A very devoted father.

How could she take the baby to Atlanta and raise him there?

Even if Nikos agreed to go to Atlanta and share parenting responsibilities with her in America...how would that really work? And was that the right thing for any of them?

Georgia couldn't picture Nikos in Atlanta. It wasn't just because he was Greek—he was a man that needed his sea and his sky and his space. She couldn't imagine him in a city or even a suburb of Atlanta. But why was she worrying about what he needed? Why did she care?

Because she did care.

Because she loved him.

No matter how the baby had been conceived, it was their baby, and it was their responsibility to figure this out, sort it out.

She didn't know why Nikos had fallen in love with Elsa. She didn't know why Elsa wasn't happy with Nikos. She didn't know about Ambrose or any of it, and, to be honest, she didn't want to know.

She didn't want all the details. It wasn't her relationship, and she wasn't part of that bit of history. She had her own history and her own struggles and her own dreams.

She'd been happy with Nikos...blissfully happy during that month after they'd been to Amorgós, and before she'd found the photo on her laundry.

She'd wondered about the photo appearing on her folded

laundry, and she'd wondered if someone had put it there to hurt her, and then she'd dismissed the thought as irrational.

The door to her room opened, and a head appeared. "Is this Georgia Nielsen's room?"

Georgia's eyes widened, and she struggled to sit up again. "Savannah!"

Savannah grinned and closed the door behind her. "Up to having a visitor?"

"Oh, my God, yes. What are you doing here?"

Savannah rushed to her sister's side and hugged her fiercely. "I missed you!"

"I missed you, too." Georgia hugged her sister back, shocked and yet delighted. "When did you get here? How did you get here?"

Savannah sat down on the edge of the bed. "Nikos flew me over with Mr. Laurent. That Mr. Laurent is a cold fish, but Nikos is lovely." She took Georgia's hand, gave it a squeeze. "How are you feeling? Better?"

"I feel fine. A bit sore. But that will pass." She squeezed Savannah's fingers. "So you've met Nikos?"

"And the baby. He's delicious." She grinned. "Well, they're both delicious. I hope you're keeping him."

"The baby?"

"No. Nikos. I know you'll keep the baby. I didn't know how you were ever going to give him up. But Nikos. He strikes me as a little complicated, but you've always liked a good challenge."

"He's more than complicated. He's a disaster. He picked me to be the donor because I look like his dead wife."

"Yes, I've heard all that, and seen the photos. Mr. Laurent had some copies of the newspaper articles reporting her death—so tragic—but she didn't help herself any, getting pregnant with another man's baby and then trying to blackmail Nikos."

"Wait. What?" Georgia dragged herself into a more comfortable sitting position. "Slow down. Say that again."

"From what I gather, she never loved Nikos. She only married him for his money. She and her Greek boyfriend—he's a fisherman on a neighboring island—planned it from the beginning. She'd marry Nikos, accuse him of abuse or neglect and then divorce him and get a fat settlement that they could live on. But Nikos wouldn't divorce her, and then she revealed she was pregnant, and Nikos vowed to take care of her and the baby, but she didn't want to be with Nikos. She didn't want to raise a baby with Nikos. She didn't even want her Greek fisherman boyfriend. She just wanted to go home, back to Oslo." Savannah's shoulders lifted and fell. "It's crazy and sad and awful, and I can see why Nikos wanted to have a baby via a surrogate. I wouldn't want a relationship after that. Would you?"

"But I fell for him, and I thought he cared for me."

"I think he does. I am sure he does."

"What makes you think so?"

"He brought me here to see you." Savannah smiled at her. "And he gave you custody of the baby, too, which has to mean that he trusts you, and respects you…and believes in you."

Georgia exhaled slowly. "I have such a headache. I hurt. I'm not sure how I feel."

"About him?"

"I love him. I'm just not sure how this would work…or if we can even make it work."

"You don't have to know everything today, do you? Maybe you both just need to take it a day at a time until you know what you want to do. Personally I find snap decisions to be bad decisions." Savannah gave her hand another squeeze and then slid off the bed. "I'm going to go check on my nephew again, and see when they're going to be bringing him back to you. In the meantime, you've a big guy out in the hall, pacing like a caged tiger. Should I send him in, or let him keep pacing and scaring all the nurses and doctors?"

Georgia laughed. "Send him in. We don't need him frightening the hospital staff."

And then he was there in the doorway, watching her from across the room, a look in his dark eyes that she couldn't read and that made her chest squeeze tight.

"Why do you look at me like that?" she whispered, her mouth suddenly dry. She had to lick her bottom lip to keep it from sticking to her teeth.

"How am I looking at you?"

There was so much emotion in his eyes, so much worry, too. His worry made her heart ache and turn over.

"You look at me as if I'm something wonderful," she whispered.

He made a rough sound in the back of his throat. "Because you are."

He crossed the room, approached the bed. Leaning over her, he gently untangled a long golden strand of hair from her cheek, smoothing the silken strand back to lie with the others. "And I look at you with wonder because when you left me last week, I thought I'd lost you forever, and yet here you are, and here our son is, and all I know is that I cannot bear to lose either of you, but at the same time, I refuse to trap you with me. I refuse to use our son to keep you at my side."

"Is that why you gave me custody? You didn't want me to feel pressured into staying with you?"

"I want nothing more than to live together and raise him together, but it must be right for you. I want what is best for you and our child. I give you control so that you know you are not a vessel or a surrogate. You are not my captive, either." His lips twisted. "You are a beautiful, strong, intelligent woman, and I love you with all my heart."

She searched his eyes. "This could backfire on you, Nikos. You could lose everything."

"My attorney said the same thing. But I will never be happy if you aren't happy, and you have much to achieve in this world, big things ahead of you. I will not stand in your way. If anything, I'd like to support you and help you reach those dreams."

"Even if it means we live in Atlanta?"

"I am planning on living in Atlanta. I've even been looking at real estate. A big house, lots of land around us, plenty of space."

"That will be very expensive in Atlanta."

He shrugged. "I am sure I can afford it."

"You really mean this? You'd go to Atlanta…you'd help me raise the baby there while I finish school?"

"Of course. You are my woman, my love, and hopefully one day, *yineka mou*, my wife."

Her head was spinning. She couldn't quite grasp everything he was saying. "You really have looked at real estate in Atlanta?"

"Yes. I found a couple places that look interesting. I thought we could go have a look when the baby is cleared for travel. Might be a couple weeks."

He *was* serious. This was crazy but wonderful. It hadn't ever crossed her mind that he'd really be willing to go with her to Georgia. It would help things immensely if they were all together. The baby could have them both…

"I think this is a very interesting plan," she said carefully. "But it's also a lot to take in. You, me, the baby—" She broke off, frowned. "And do we even want to talk about a name for him? I think at some point he might object to just being called the baby."

Nikos laughed, a deep, rumbling laugh that filled the room and made Georgia smile. She'd never heard him laugh, not like that, and she thought it had to be the very best sound in the world.

Tears started to fill her eyes, and then she wasn't smiling but crying, and Nikos was holding her.

"What's wrong, *agapi mou*—what's happened?" He soothed her, stroking the back of her head, trying his best to comfort her.

"Everything is happening, and these hormones don't help," she choked out.

"It's okay. Cry. It might help make you feel better."

"I doubt it." She sniffed, wiping her cheeks dry, struggling to get control. "So what happens to us, Nikos, if we go to Atlanta together? How will this work?"

"What are you asking?"

"I care for you, Nikos, so very much, but there are things we don't know about each other, and things we need to discover. Can we slow things down a little? Back up a bit so that we are just dating and we can use the time in Atlanta to figure out if we are good together…happy together?"

"You're breaking off the engagement?"

"Well, I never had a ring…"

He smiled. "This is true. We couldn't possibly have been engaged then. So we're back to square one. Starting over."

"Not totally starting over. We do have a son."

He leaned over the bed, kissed her, then kissed her again. "Speaking of our son, I agree with you that it's time to consider names."

"Can you go get him, see if he can join us? I have a feeling he'd like to be present for something this significant."

EPILOGUE

GEORGIA SHOULD HAVE been stressed. She had a four-month-old baby who was still nursing around the clock and she was waiting on the results from the grueling exams she'd taken three weeks ago. She should be getting the results next Wednesday, but she wasn't worried.

If anything, she was calm, and incredibly, ridiculously happy.

She loved Alek Panos so much that it made her heart ache, but what gave her even greater joy was seeing Nikos and Alek together. No one could soothe Alek like his father. Nikos had spent many a night pacing the nursery or rocking him in the big chair in the corner of their master bedroom.

Alek had been so small, being born early, but he was quickly putting on weight and was catching up with the crucial milestones.

Tomorrow they were baptizing him and they were hosting a small dinner at their house to celebrate afterward. Savannah would be there, of course, as she was Alek's godmother, and they'd invited a few other people to join them, mostly Georgia's friends from medical school, along with Mr. Laurent and his wife.

Who would have ever imagined that Mr. Laurent would become their friend, and even a surrogate grandfather to Alek?

Life was good, Georgia thought, lightly patting Alek's back. He'd been nursing and had fallen asleep on the job. She smiled faintly, savoring the feel of him on her chest. He was so warm and sweet. She loved him to pieces…

loved him so much she wondered now why she'd thought she wouldn't be a good mother.

The door to the nursery opened, and Nikos entered.

Her heart gave a little jump as he smiled at her. She grinned back. It was impossible not to smile when she saw him. He made her so happy. He was her other half.

"Hey," she whispered.

"He's out?" Nikos asked.

She nodded. "He did pretty good. Hoping he got enough to get him through a good long nap."

"Should I put him back in his crib?"

"I'm okay holding him. It feels good just to hold him. He's getting bigger every day."

"That's good. He's healthy."

"I'm so grateful. He's a blessing." She dropped a light kiss on his tender head. "Everything okay?"

Nikos took a seat on the ottoman next to her feet. "Just a few days until you get your test results," he said.

"I know."

"Nervous?"

She thought about it. "No. I'm actually pretty Zen."

"Lots of people take them again."

"I'm not worried, either way. Whatever will be, will be." Her gaze met his and held. "I'm happy, Nikos, really happy. I love Alek. I love us. This is everything I ever wanted. Doing well on the test would just be icing on the cake."

"If you do well, you'll have many options. You'll be able to complete your training at any number of hospitals."

She nodded. "I've looked into different programs, and there are places that look good, but, Nikos, I think my first choice would be returning to Greece."

"Is there a program in Athens?"

She hesitated. "I think I'd just like to go home to Kamari… I think I'd like to just be a mother for the next couple of years and then we can talk about the rest, when we're ready. When I'm ready."

She thought he'd be excited about her decision. She thought he'd be happy for her, but Nikos wasn't smiling. He looked troubled…worried. "Can you take time off and return? Won't that set you back?"

"I can always return to school when he's older. But I'll never get these years back. And not just with him, but with you. Nikos, *agapo mou*, I adore you."

Emotion darkened his beautiful eyes. "You speak Greek now, too?"

"I've learned the most important phrases." She smiled and reached for him, drawing his face to hers. She kissed him once, and then again, whispering, *"S'agapo." I love you.*

He kissed her back, careful not to bump Alek. "My brilliant Georgia," he murmured. "You take my breath away."

He was still kissing her when the door opened and a cough sounded in the doorway. It was Savannah, and she was smiling. "Maybe you two need to get a room," she said in a stage whisper. "In fact, I know you need to get a room. Don't worry about a thing. I've got the baby."

They didn't need persuading.

Georgia carefully put Alek in his crib, and Nikos took her hand, leading her from the nursery to their master suite at the end of the hall.

It was a huge house, a Tudor-style mansion on a couple of acres in Atlanta's oldest and best neighborhood, but that wasn't why Georgia liked it. She liked it because they had the biggest bed she'd ever seen, giving her and Nikos lots of room to play and sleep.

Inside their room he slid the lock shut and drew her into his arms, kissing her with a hunger that let her know just how much he wanted her and needed her.

His hands were on her waist and then curving over her hips, pulling her close against his erection.

Georgia shivered with pleasure. "Thank goodness for sisters who love to babysit," she said. "I love her timing."

He nibbled at her neck and kissed the hollow beneath her ear. "So do I. She arrived right on schedule."

Georgia lifted her head. "What schedule?"

He smiled, kissed her. "Come see." Taking her by the hand, he led her to the table in front of the huge bow-shaped window, where there was champagne in an ornate silver bucket. Crystal flutes stood next to the bucket and there were silver trays of food, gorgeous-looking food, along with enormous vases of red roses.

Her eyes widened as she looked back at him. "Nikos... is this what I think it is?"

"Flowers and champagne? Yes. Yes, it is."

She giggled and hugged him. "Seriously. What's going on?"

"We're celebrating you. Because I love you. And you are the most beautiful and amazing woman in the world."

She swallowed hard as her eyes began to prickle and burn.

"I love you, Georgia. I will always love you." He drew a black leather ring box from his pocket and dropped to one knee.

Her heart was thudding so hard she couldn't speak. She knew what he was doing, but she hadn't seen this coming and she couldn't believe it was happening now, on a day that was already perfect.

He cracked the leather box open, and she stared at the ring in awe. It was a diamond ring with a huge center stone that sparkled blindingly bright. The center stone was surrounded with smaller diamonds, and tiny diamonds covered the sides of the narrow gleaming band. "It's stunning," she whispered.

"Savannah went shopping with me. I wanted her to tell me what she thought her beloved sister would like best. But she told me that whatever I picked for you would be the one you'd want. And this is the one I picked, because it is like you—beautiful, bright and filled with light." And then he added, his voice pitched even deeper than usual, "Marry me, *agape mou*."

She didn't even have to think about it. "Yes, yes, Nikos, absolutely."

He was on his feet, kissing her, the ring forgotten.

It was much later, after they'd made love and put the ring on her finger and then popped the champagne, that she asked him if they could marry in Greece. "I'd love to have the ceremony at the villa on Kamari, if we could."

"It'd be a very small ceremony, I fear."

"The best kind." She smiled at him and set aside her champagne. She'd had a taste but wouldn't drink more as she was nursing and hated taking chances. "What do you think about just going back...and staying? I want Alek to be raised in Greece. I want him to know his culture. He's not meant to be an American. He's your son—"

"Our son," he corrected.

"Yes, but he's a Panos, and he needs the sun and the sea and lots of space. I do, too."

"You don't have to do this for me, *agapi mou*."

"I know. And I'm doing this for selfish reasons." She struggled to smile, but it was hard with so much emotion filling her. "I want to be with you, and raise our son together, and together we will give him so much love and so much opportunity."

He drew her toward him, kissing her tenderly. "Your love takes my breath away," he said huskily. "You are the sun and the moon and the stars, and every day I thank God for you."

Tears filled her eyes. "You do?"

"I do."

He caressed her cheek, and then kissed her brow, her nose and finally her lips. "Thank you for loving me."

Blinking back tears, she tugged on a strand of his inky-black hair. "I tamed the beast."

"Yes, you did, *yineka mou*. You tamed the beast and turned me into a pussycat."

Georgia laughed. "I wouldn't go that far. You're still not that easy to manage. But it's okay. I'm up for the challenge."

"Good. I love a strong woman." He pressed another kiss to her mouth. "Or maybe it's just you. Because I do love you, and I will love you forever."

* * * * *

A ROYAL AMNESIA
SCANDAL

JULES BENNETT

I have to dedicate this book to the fabulous Andrea Laurence and Sarah M. Anderson who always come through for me when I need a plot fixed five minutes ago. Wouldn't go through this crazy journey without you guys

One

Escaping to the mountains would have been much better for his sanity than coming to his newly purchased private seaside villa off the coast of Portugal.

Kate Barton fully clothed was enough to have any man panting, but Kate running around in a bikini with some flimsy, strapless wrap that knotted right at her cleavage was damn near crippling. The woman had curves, she wasn't stick-thin like a model and damn if she didn't know how to work those dips and valleys on that killer body. Not that she ever purposely showcased herself, at least not in the professional setting, but she couldn't hide what she'd been blessed with, either. Even in a business suit, she rocked any designer's label.

Luc Silva cursed beneath his breath as he pulled his Jet Ski back to the dock and secured it. His intent in coming here was to escape from the media, escape from the woman who'd betrayed him. So why was he paying a penance with yet another woman?

To ensure privacy for both of them, he'd given Kate the guesthouse. Unfortunately, it and the main house shared the same private beach, damn it. He'd thought purchasing this fixer-upper on a private island, barely up to civilization's standards, was a brilliant idea at the time. With no internet access and little cell service, it was a perfect hideaway for a member of Ilha Beleza's royal family. He didn't want to be near people who knew of or cared about his status. Luc had only one requirement when searching for a hideout: a place to escape. Yet here he was with his sexy, mouthy, curvy assistant.

Not only that, the renovations to the property were only half-done, because he'd needed to get away from reality much sooner than he'd thought he would.

A lying fiancée would do that to a man.

"Your face is burning."

Luc fisted his hands at his sides as he approached Kate. Was she draped all over that lounge chair on purpose or did she just naturally excel at tormenting men? She'd untied that wrap and now it lay open, as if framing her luscious body covered only by triangles of bright red material and strings.

"I'm not burned," he retorted, not slowing down as he marched up the white sand.

"Did you apply sunscreen?" she asked, holding an arm over her forehead to shield her eyes from the sun.

The movement shifted her breasts, and the last thing he needed was to be staring at his assistant's chest, no matter how impressive it was. When she'd started working for him about a year ago, he'd wanted her... He still wanted her, if he was being honest with himself.

She was the absolute best assistant he'd ever had. Her parents still worked for his parents, so hiring Kate had been an easy decision.

A decision he questioned every single time his hormones shot into overdrive when she neared.

He never mingled with staff. He and his parents always kept their personal and professional relationships separate, so as not to create bad press or scandal. It was a rule they felt very strongly about after a scandal generations ago. Rumor had it the family was quite the center of gossip for a while after an assistant let out family secrets best left behind closed doors.

So once Luc had become engaged to Alana, he'd put his attraction to Kate out of his mind.

For the past three months, he'd been ready to say "I do" for two very valid reasons: his ex had claimed to be expecting his child, and he needed to marry to secure his crown to reign over Ilha Beleza.

Now Alana was gone and he was trying like hell to hang on to the title, even though he had just a few months to find a wife. And the second he was in charge, he'd be changing that archaic law. Just because a man was nearing thirty-five didn't mean he had to be tied down, and Luc wanted nothing to do with holy matrimony… especially now that he'd been played.

"You're frowning," Kate called as he passed right by her. "Being angry isn't helping your red face."

There were times he admired the fact she didn't treat him as if he was royalty, but just a regular man. This wasn't one of those times.

Before climbing the steps to the outdoor living area, Luc turned. "Did you cancel the interview with that journalist from the States?"

Kate settled back into her relaxed position, dropping her arm to her side and closing her eyes as the sun continued to kiss all that exposed skin.

"I took care of canceling all media interviews you

had scheduled regarding the upcoming wedding, or anything to do with Alana," she told him. "I rescheduled your one-on-one interviews for later in the year, after you gain the title. By then I'm positive you'll have everything sorted out and will be at the top of your game."

Luc swallowed. Not only was Kate his right-hand woman, she was his biggest supporter and advocate. She made him look good to the media, occasionally embellishing the truth to further boost his family's name.

"I simply told each of the media outlets that this was a difficult time for you, playing up the faux miscarriage, and your family's request for privacy."

Kate lifted a knee, causing a little roll of skin to ease over her bikini bottoms. Luc's eyes instantly went to that region of her body and he found himself wanting to drop to his knees and explore her with more than his eyes.

"If you're done staring at me, you need to either go inside or put on sunscreen," she added, without opening her eyes.

"If you'd cover up, I wouldn't stare."

Her soft laugh, drifting on an ocean breeze, hit him square in the gut. "If I covered up, I wouldn't get a tan. Be glad I'm at least wearing this. I do hate those tan lines."

Gritting his teeth, Luc tried but failed at keeping that mental image from his mind. Kate sunbathing in the nude would surely have any man down on his knees begging. Forcing back a groan, Luc headed up the steps and into the main house. She was purposely baiting him, and he was letting her, because he was at a weak spot in his life right now. He also couldn't hide the fact that his assistant turned him inside out in ways she shouldn't.

He'd been engaged, for pity's sake, yet before and after the engagement, he'd wanted to bed Kate.

Sleeping with an employee was beyond tacky, and he wasn't going to be so predictable as to fall into that cliché. Besides, the house rule of no fraternizing with employees was something he stood behind wholeheartedly.

He and Kate were of like minds, and they needed to remain in a professional relationship. Period. Kate stood up for him, stood by him, no matter what, and he refused to risk that by jumping into bed with her.

She had been just as shocked as he was when Alana's deception had been revealed. For once, Kate hadn't made a snarky comment, hadn't tried to be cute or funny. She'd instantly intervened, taking all calls, offering up reasons why the engagement had been called off.

In fact, it was Kate's brilliant plan that had saved his pride. She'd informed the media that Alana had miscarried, and the couple had opted to part ways as friends. At first he'd wanted to just come out with the truth, but he'd been so hurt by the personal nature of the lie, he'd gone along with the farce to save face.

So, for all the times Kate got under his skin with their verbal sparring and her torturous body, he couldn't manage this situation without her.

There were times, even before the fiancée debacle, that he'd just wished he had a place to run to and escape all the chaos of being royalty. Purchasing this home—even though it needed some updating—was like a gift to himself. The view had sold him immediately. With the infinity pool overlooking the Mediterranean Sea and the lush gardens, the previous owners obviously had to have been outdoor enthusiasts. At least Luc had a dock for his Jet Ski and his boat.

Too bad he'd had to come here before all the remodeling was complete. Kate had informed the workers they would have the next two weeks off because the house would be in use. The contractors had managed to get a few of the rooms fully renovated, and thankfully, Luc's master suite was one of them.

He stripped off his wet trunks and stepped into his glass-enclosed shower, which gave the illusion of being outside, but in fact was surrounded by lush tropical plants. The shower was an addition to the master suite and one of his favorite features in the house. He loved having the feeling of being outdoors while being ensured of the privacy he craved. That had been his top priority when he'd bought the house.

An image of sharing this spacious shower with Kate slammed into his mind, and Luc had to focus on something else. Such as the fact she was ten years younger than him, and when he'd been learning to drive, she'd been going to kindergarten and losing her first tooth. There. That should make him feel ridiculous about having such carnal thoughts toward his assistant…shouldn't it?

Water sluiced over his body as he braced his hands against the glass wall and leaned forward. Dropping his head, he contemplated all the reasons why bedding his assistant was wrong. Not only would things be awkward between them, but any bad press could threaten his ascension to the throne. Not to mention the no-fraternization rule, which had been implemented for a reason. He didn't want to be the cause for a black mark on his family's name. One major issue was all he could handle right now. Unfortunately, the one and only reason for wanting to claim her kept trumping all the mounting negatives. He had to find a way to keep her at arm's length, because if he kept seeing her parading around in that skimpy gear, he'd never make it through these next two weeks alone with her.

Scrolling through the upcoming schedule, Kate jotted down the important things she needed to follow up on once she was back at the Land of the Internet, aka the palace. Even though Luc was taking a break from life, she had no such luxury, with or without cyberspace. He might be reeling from the embarrassment of the breakup, and dodging the media's speculations, but she still had to stay one step ahead of the game in order to keep him pristine in the eyes of the people once the dust cloud of humiliation settled. Damage control had moved to the top of her priorities in her role as assistant.

Being the assistant to a member of the royal family hadn't been her childhood aspiration. Granted, he wasn't just any member of the royal family, but the next king of Ilha Beleza, but still.

At one time Kate had had notions of being a dress designer. She'd watched her mother, the royal seamstress, often enough, and admired how she could be so creative and still enjoy her work. But Kate's aspirations hit the wall of reality when she'd discovered she excelled at organizing, being in the thick of business and playing the peacemaker. The job appealed to the do-gooder in her, too, as she felt she could make a real difference in the lives of others.

Once she'd received her degree, Kate knew she wanted to work with the royal family she'd known her entire life. She loved them, loved what they stood for, and she wanted to continue to be in that inner circle.

Kate had first met Luc when she was six and he was sixteen. After that, she'd seen him at random times when she'd go to work with her parents. As Kate grew older and well into her teens, Luc had become more and more appealing to her on every level a woman starts to recognize. Of course, with the age gap, he'd paid her no mind, and she would watch as he'd parade women in and out of the palace.

She'd never thought he would settle down, but as his coronation fast approached, with his thirty-fifth birthday closing in, the timing of Alana's "pregnancy" couldn't have been better.

Too bad the spoiled debutante had had her hopes of being a queen shattered, tarnishing the tiara she would never wear. Alana had tricked Luc into believing she was expecting their child, which was absurd, because there's only so long that lie could go on. Alana hadn't planned on Luc being a hands-on type of father, so when he'd accompanied her to a doctor's appointment, he'd been stunned to realize there was no baby.

At least now Kate wouldn't have to field calls for "Lukey" when he was in meetings and unable to talk. Kate was glad Miss D Cup was out of the picture...not that there was room in the picture for Kate herself, but having that woman around had seriously kept her in a bad mood for the past several months.

As she glanced over Luc's schedule after this two-week hiatus, all she saw was meetings with dignitaries, meetings with his staff, the wedding ceremony and the ball to celebrate the nuptials of his best friend, Mikos Alexander, and a few outings that were just "spontaneous" enough for the media to snap pictures but not get close enough to question Luc. A quick wave as he entered a building, a flash of that dimpled grin to the camera, and the paparazzi would be foaming at the mouth to post the shots with whatever captions they chose.

For the past year Kate had tried to get him to take

on charity projects, not for the media hype, but because he had the power to make things happen. Good things, things that would make a difference in people's lives. What good was power and money if they weren't used to help those less fortunate?

But Luc's focus had always been on the crown, on the bigger prize, on his country and what it would take to rule. He wasn't a jerk, but his focus was not on the little guys, which occasionally made Kate's job of making him look like a knight in shining armor a little harder.

Still, working for a royal family had its perks, and she would have to be dead to ignore how sexy her boss was. Luc would make any woman smile with a fantasy-style sigh. But no matter how attractive the man was, Kate prided herself on remaining professional.

She may have daydreamed about kissing him once. Okay, fine. Once a day, but still. Acting on her attraction would be a colossal mistake. Everyone knew the royal family's rules about not fraternizing with staff. The consequences could mean not only her job, but also her parents'. A risk Kate couldn't take, no matter what she ached for.

With a sigh, Kate rose to her feet and set her day planner aside. Luc had warned her that she'd be "roughing it" at this guesthouse, but she sort of liked the basic charm of the place. The rooms were pretty much bare, the scarred hardwood floors desperately in need of refinishing and the kitchen was at least thirty years out of date, if not more. But she was in her own space and had water, electric power and a beach. She wasn't working nearly as much as she had been at the palace in the midst of wedding-planning chaos. All of those media interviews had been canceled or rescheduled, and she

was on a secluded island with her hunky boss. So roughing it wasn't so "rough" in her opinion.

Kate headed out her back door, breathing in the fresh
scent of the salty ocean breeze. Following the stone path
lined with overgrown bushes and lush plants, which led
to the main house, she was glad she'd come along even
if the circumstances made Luc only edgier, grouchier
and, well, difficult. He had every right to be furious
and hurt, though he'd never admit to the pain. Luc always put up a strong front, hiding behind that tough-
guy persona.

Kate knew better, but she still chose to refrain from
discussing the incident too much. Keeping things more
professional than personal was the only way she could
continue to work for him and not get swept away by
lustful feelings.

When Kate had first started working for Luc, they'd
had a heated discussion that led to a near kiss before
he'd pulled back. He'd informed her right then that
under no circumstances did he bed, date or get involved
with employees.

Still, long nights spent working together, trips abroad
and even the close quarters of his office had led to
heated glances and accidental brushes against each
other. The attraction most definitely wasn't one-sided.

Then he'd started dating Miss D Cup, and the obvious physical attraction between boss and employee had
faded...at least on Luc's side. Typical playboy behavior.
Kate had chided herself for even thinking they would
eventually give in to that underlying passion.

Yet here they were again, both single and utterly
alone. So now more than ever she needed to exercise
this ability to remain professional. In reality, she'd love
nothing more than to rip those designer clothes off him

and see if he had any hidden tan lines or tattoos, because that one on his back that scrolled across his taut muscles and up onto his left shoulder was enough to have her lady parts standing at attention each time he took his shirt off.

As tempted as she was to give in to her desires, too much was at stake: her job, her parents' jobs, the reputation she'd carry of seducing her boss. That wouldn't look good on a résumé.

Kate had left her phone behind and contemplated changing. But since she was comfortable and would be only a minute with Luc—five at the most—she wanted to see if he'd take her up on this venture she'd been requesting his help with for the past year. Now that his life was turned inside out, perhaps he'd be a little more giving of his time.

With her sandals slapping against the stone pathway, Kate rehearsed in her head everything she wanted to say as she made her way to the house, passing by the picturesque infinity pool.

The rear entrance faced the Mediterranean. Of course, there wasn't a bad view from any window or balcony that she'd seen, and her guest cottage was definitely on her list of places she never wanted to leave. Regardless of the updates that needed to be done, this house was gorgeous and would be even more so once Luc's plans were fully executed.

When she reached the glass double doors, she tapped her knuckles against the frame. The ocean breeze lifted her hair, sending it dancing around her shoulders, tickling her skin. The wind had kicked up in the past several minutes and dark clouds were rolling in.

Storms…she loved them. Kate smiled up at the ominous sky and welcomed the change. There was something so sexy and powerful about the recklessness of a thunderstorm.

When she knocked again and Luc still didn't answer, she held her hand to the glass and peered inside. No Luc in sight. The knob turned easily and she stepped inside the spacious living area. It led straight into the kitchen, which was only slightly more modern than hers. Basically, the main house looked the same as the cottage, only supersized, with the entire back wall made up of windows and French doors.

"Luc?" she called, hoping he'd hear her and she wouldn't startle him.

What if he'd decided to rest? Or what if he was in the shower?

A smile spread across her face. Oh, yeah. What if he *was* in the shower? Water sliding over all those glorious tanned muscles...

Down, girl.

She wasn't here to seduce her boss. She was here to plant a seed about a charity project close to her heart. If Luc thought he'd formulated the plan, then he'd be all for it, and she desperately wanted him to donate his time and efforts to an orphanage in the United States she'd been corresponding with on his behalf. For reasons he didn't need to know about, the place held a special spot in her heart. She didn't want him to go there out of pity. She wanted him to do so on his own, because he felt it was the right thing to do.

But Kate couldn't get the twins who lived there, Carly and Thomas, out of her mind, and she was driving herself crazy with worry. For now, though, things were out of her control, so she had to focus on getting Luc on board with funding and volunteering. What would that little bit hurt him, anyway? In all reality, the visit and the monetary gift wouldn't leave a dent in his time or finances, but both would mean the world to those children.

"Luc?" She headed toward the wide, curved staircase with its scrolled, wrought-iron railing. She rested her hand on the banister, only to have it wobble beneath her palm. Definitely another item for the list of renovations.

She didn't even know what room he'd opted to use as the master suite, as there was one downstairs and one upstairs. "Are you up there?" she called, more loudly this time.

Within seconds, Luc stood at the top of the stairs, wearing only a tan and a towel. Kate had seen him in swimming trunks, knew full well just how impressive his body was. Yet standing here looking up at him, knowing there was only a piece of terry cloth and a few stairs between them, sent her hormones into overdrive. And she had to keep reminding herself she was only his assistant.

Still, that wouldn't stop her from appreciating the fact her boss was one fine man. Her "office view" was hands down the best she could ever ask for.

"I'm sorry," she said, forcing her gaze to stay on his face. If she looked away she'd appear weak, as if she couldn't handle seeing a half-naked man. If her eyes lowered to the flawless chest on display, he'd know all her fantasies for sure. "I'll just wait until you're dressed."

Before she made a fool of herself by staring, babbling or drooling, Kate turned and scurried back to the living area, where she sank onto the old sofa that had been draped with a pale yellow cover until the renovations were completed and new furniture arrived. Dropping her head against the saggy cushion, she let out a groan.

Lucas Silva was one *atraente* prince. Sexy prince. After living in Ilha Beleza for a full year now, she was growing more accustomed to thinking in Portuguese as opposed to English. Even thinking of Luc in another language only proved how pathetic she was.

Get a grip.

She should've waited in the living room, or just come back later after her walk. Then she wouldn't have been tortured by seeing him wearing nothing but that towel and the water droplets that clung to those taut muscles. Had he been standing closer, the temptation to lick away all the moisture from his recent shower might have been too much to handle.

She'd held on to her self-control for a year and didn't intend to let it snap now. A man like Luc would enjoy that too much, and Kate refused to be like all the other women who fawned over the playboy prince.

Smoothing her floral, halter-style sundress, she crossed her legs, hoping for a casual look instead of the assistant-hot-for-her-boss one. The second she heard his feet crossing the floor, she sat up straighter and silently scolded herself for allowing her thoughts and hormones to control her.

"Sorry I interrupted your shower," she told him the second he stepped down into the sunken living area. "I was heading out for a walk, but I wanted to run something by you first."

He'd thrown on black board shorts and a red T-shirt. Still, the image of him wearing next to nothing was burned into her mind, and that's all she could focus on. Luc fully or even partially clothed was sexy, but Luc practically in his birthday suit was a much more dangerous thought.

"I'm not working, if that's what you want to discuss." He strode across the room and opened the patio doors, pushing them wide to allow the ocean breeze to stream in. Kate came to her feet, ready to be firm, but careful not to anger him, because this project was too important to her.

"It's just something you need to think about," she retorted as she went to stand near the open doors. "I know we've discussed charity work in the past—"

He turned, held up a hand to cut her off. "I'm not scheduling anything like that until I have the crown. I don't want to even think beyond right now. I've got a big enough mess on my hands."

Crossing her arms, Kate met his gaze…until that gaze dropped to her chest. Well, well, well. Looked as if maybe he wasn't immune to the physical attraction between them, after all.

"I was working on your schedule for the next several months and you have a gap that I could squeeze something into, but you have to be in agreement."

The muscles in his jaw clenched as Kate waited for a response. Whenever he stared at her with such intensity, she never knew what was going through his mind. If his thoughts had anything to do with the way he'd been staring at her moments ago, she was totally on board. Sign her up.

Before she realized what he was doing, Luc reached out and slid a fingertip across her bare shoulder. It took every bit of her willpower not to shiver beneath such a simple, yet intimate touch.

"Wh-what are you doing?" she asked, cursing the stammer.

When his finger trailed across her collarbone, then back to her shoulder, Kate continued to stare, unsure what he was doing. If he was trying to seduce her, he needn't try any harder. With the way he kept looking at her, she was about to throw out the window all the reasons they shouldn't be together. One jerk of the knot of fabric at her neck and that halter dress would slide to the floor.

She waited, more than ready for Luc to make her fantasy come true.

Two

Luc fisted his hands at his sides. What the hell had he been thinking, reaching out and touching Kate like that? He was nothing but a *tolo*, a fool, even to allow himself the brief pleasure.

With all Kate's creamy skin exposed, silently inviting his touch, his last thread of willpower had snapped. And as much as he hated to admit it, even to himself, he was too emotionally drained to think straight. Part of him just wanted someone as a sexual outlet, an escape, but he wouldn't use his assistant…no matter how tempted he was.

Luc hadn't tried hard enough to keep himself in check, which was the main problem. He was still reeling from the fact that Kate had stood at the base of the steps looking as if she might leap to the second floor and devour him if he even hinted he was ready. And *misericórdia*, mercy, he was ready for some no-strings affection. Still, not with his employee. How did this number-one rule keep slipping from his mind?

"You're burned," he replied, surprised when his tone came out stronger than he'd intended. "Looks like you should've taken your own advice about that sunscreen."

With a defiant tilt of her chin, a familiar gesture he'd come to find amusing, she propped her hands on her hips, which did amazing things to the pull of the fabric across her chest. The woman was slowly killing him.

The no-dating-staff rule also covered no sleeping with staff. Damn it, he was a mess after Alana. More so than he feared if he was thinking even for a second of risking his family's reputation, and his own reputation as a worthy king, by sleeping with Kate. Nothing good would come from his moment of weakness, and then he'd be out an amazing assistant, because he couldn't allow her to work for him further. And she'd have a wealth of fodder for the press if she chose to turn against him.

That was precisely the reason he needed to keep his damn hands off his assistant.

"Maybe tomorrow we can rub it on each other, then," she suggested with a mocking grin. "Anyway, back to the charity."

Charity, the lesser of two evils when compared to rubbing sunscreen over her luscious curves... But he wasn't getting into this discussion again. He sponsored several organizations financially, but his time wasn't something he'd considered giving. The main reason being he didn't like it when people in power used that type of opportunity as just another publicity stunt. Luc didn't want to be that type of king...that is, if he actually got the crown.

"We need to figure out a plan to secure my title first," he told Kate. "Everything else can wait."

Pursing her lips, she nodded. Apparently, she was backing down, which was a first. She never shied away from an argument.

"You're plotting something," he said, narrowing his gaze. "You may as well tell me now."

"I'm not plotting anything," she replied, that sweet grin still in place, confirming his suspicion. "I've been thinking about your title, but I haven't come up with a solid solution, other than a quick wedding, of course."

She turned and started through the patio doors, but Luc reached out, grabbing her arm to halt her exit. Her eyes darted down to his hand, then back up to his face, but he didn't release her.

"Why is this particular charity so important to you?" he asked. "You mention it so often. If you give me the name, I'll send as much money as you want me to."

Her eyes softened, filled with a sadness he hadn't seen there before. "Money isn't what I wanted."

Slipping from his grasp, she headed down the stairs toward the beach. Money wasn't what she wanted? Had he ever heard a woman say that before? Surely any organization could benefit from a sizable donation.

Kate was always surprising him with what came out of her mouth. She seemed to enjoy a good verbal sparring as much as he did. But something about the cause she kept bringing up was bothering him. Obviously, this was something near and dear to her, and she didn't feel like opening up about it. She'd worked for him for a year, but he'd known her longer than that, though they didn't exactly hang in the same circles. Didn't she trust him enough to disclose her wishes?

Luc shook his head as he watched her walk along the

shoreline. The woman was mesmerizing from so many different angles, and it was a damn shame she was his assistant, because having her in his bed would certainly help take the edge off this title-throne nightmare.

Glancing up at the sky, he noticed the clouds growing darker. A storm was on the horizon and he knew how much Kate loved Mother Nature's wrath. She'd always been fascinated by the sheer power, she'd told him once. And that summed Kate up in a nutshell. She was fierce, moved with efficiency and had everyone taking notice.

Part of him wanted to worry, but he knew she'd be back soon, most likely to watch the storm from her own balcony. Luc still took a seat on his patio to wait for her, because they weren't done discussing this charity business. She was hiding something and he wanted to know what it was. Why was this mysterious organization such a secret? And why did discussing it make her so sad and closed off?

He sank down onto the cushioned bench beside the infinity pool. Everything about this outdoor living space was perfect and exactly what he would've chosen for himself. From the stone kitchen for entertaining to the wide, cushioned benches and chaise lounges by the pool, Luc loved all the richness this space offered.

Glancing down the beach where Kate had set out, he found he couldn't see her any longer and wondered when she'd start heading back. Ominous clouds blanketed the sky, rumbles of thunder filling the previous silence.

When the first fat drop of rain hit his cheek, Luc continued to stare in the direction she'd gone. Since when did he give anyone such power over his mind? He didn't like this. Not one bit.

He was next in line for the throne, for pity's sake.

How could his hormones be led around so easily by one petite, curvy woman, and how the hell could he still want her after months and months of ignoring the fact?

This pull was strong, no doubt, but Luc just had to be stronger. There was no room for lust here. He wouldn't risk his family's stellar reputation, or his ascension to the throne, just because he was hot for his assistant.

The wild, furious storm had been magnificent, one of the best she'd seen in a long time. Kate had meant to get back to the house before the weather got too bad, but she'd ended up finding a cove to wait it out in and couldn't resist staying outside. She'd been shielded from the elements, but she'd gotten drenched before she could get hunkered down.

With her dress plastered to her skin, she headed back toward the guesthouse. Even being soaking wet and a bit chilly from the breeze caressing her damp skin didn't dim her mood. She had to walk up the steps to Luc's patio in order to reach the path to her place. Noticing a light on the dock and lights on either side of the patio doors, she realized she'd been gone longer than she'd intended. It was clearly very dark and not because of the storm.

"Where the hell were you?"

Startled, Kate jumped back at the sound of Luc's angry, harsh tone. He stood in the doorway to his living area, wearing the same clothes as he had before, but now his hair stood on end, as if he'd run his fingers through it multiple times.

"Excuse me?" She stepped closer to him, taking in his flared nostrils, clenched jaw and the firm line of his mouth. "I told you I was going for a walk. I wasn't sure I had to check in, Dad."

Luc's lips thinned even more. "That storm was nasty. I assumed you'd have enough sense to come back. What the hell were you thinking?"

The fact he'd waited for her warmed something in her, but the way he looked as if he was ready to throttle her had her defensive side trumping all other feelings. This had nothing to do with lust or sexual chemistry.

"I purposely left the palace, the guards and everyone to get away from my troubles," he went on, his voice laced with irritation. "You're here to help me figure this whole mess out. But if you can't be responsible, you can either go back to the palace or I'll call in one of my guards to stay here and make sure you're safe."

Kate laughed. "You're being ridiculous. I'm a big girl, you know. I was perfectly fine and I sure as hell don't need a keeper. Next thing you know you'll be calling my parents."

With her father being head of security and her mother the clothing designer and seamstress for the family, Kate had been surrounded by royalty her entire life… just without a title of her own. Oh, wait, she was an assistant. Equally as glamorous as queen, princess or duchess.

Actually, she liked being behind the scenes. She had an important role that allowed her to travel, make great money and do some good without being in the limelight. And she would continue to try to persuade Luc to visit the orphanage so close to her heart. They'd taken care of her there, had loved her and sheltered her until she was adopted. Now she was in a position to return some of their generosity.

"Your father would agree with me." Luc stepped forward, closing the gap between them as he gripped her arm. "Don't go anywhere without your phone again. Anything could've happened to you."

"You can admit you were worried without going all Neanderthal on me, Your Highness." She jerked from his grasp, but he only stepped closer when she moved back. "What is your problem? I was out, I'm back. Don't be so grouchy because you can't admit you were scared."

"Scared?" he repeated, leaning in so close she could feel his warm breath on her face, see the gold flecks in those dark eyes. "I wasn't scared. I was angry that you were being negligent."

Kate really wasn't in the mood to be yelled at by her boss. She didn't deserve to be on the receiving end of his wrath when the issue he had was clearly with himself.

Her soggy dress needed to go, and she would give anything to soak in a hot bubble bath in that sunken garden tub in her master bathroom. She only hoped it worked. She hadn't tested it yet, and the sink in her kitchen was a bit leaky...

"I'm heading home." Kate waved a hand in the air to dismiss him and this absurd conversation. "We can talk tomorrow when you've cooled off."

The instant she turned away, she found herself being jerked back around. "I'm getting real sick of you manhandling—"

His lips were on hers, his hands gripping the sides of her face, holding her firmly in place as he coaxed her lips apart. There was nothing she could do but revel in the fact that Prince Lucas Silva was one potent man and quite possibly the best kisser she'd ever experienced.

And he was most definitely an experience. Those strong hands framed her face as his tongue danced with hers. Kate brought her hands up, wrapping them around his wrists. She had no clue if she should stop this before it got out of hand or hang on for the ride, since he'd fueled her every fantasy for so long.

Arching against him, she felt his firm body do so many glorious things to hers. The chill she'd had from the rain was no longer an issue.

But just as quickly as he'd claimed her mouth, he released her and stepped back, forcing her hands to drop. Muttering a Portuguese curse, Luc rubbed the back of his neck and kept his gaze on the ground. Kate honestly had no clue what to do. Say something? Walk away without a word?

What was the logical next step after being yelled at by her boss, then kissed as if he needed her like air in his lungs for his survival? And then pushed away with a filthy term her mother would blush at…

Clearing her throat, Kate wrapped her arms around her waist. "I'm not quite sure why you did that, but let's chalk it up to the heat of the moment. We'll both laugh about it tomorrow."

And dream about it tonight.

"You just push me too far." His intense gaze swept over her, but he kept his distance. "For a year I've argued with you, but you've always had my back. I know there've been times you've intervened and stood up for me without my even knowing. As far as employees go, you're the best."

Confused, Kate ran her hands up and down her arms as the ocean breeze chilled her damp skin. "Okay. Where are you going with this?"

"Nowhere," he all but yelled, flinging his arms out. "What just happened can't happen again because you're an employee and I don't sleep with staff. Ever."

Kate couldn't help the laugh that erupted from her. "You kissed me. Nobody mentioned sex."

His gaze heated her in ways that a hot bubble bath never could have. "I don't have to mention it. When I look at you I think it, and after tasting you, I feel it."

If he thought those words would deter her, he didn't know her at all. Kate reached forward, but Luc stepped back.

"Don't," he growled. "Just go on back to your cottage and we'll forget this happened."

Smoothing wet tendrils off her forehead, Kate shook her head. "Oh, no. You can't drop that bomb, give me a proverbial pat on the head and send me off to bed. You went from arguing to kissing me to throwing sex into the conversation in the span of two minutes. You'll understand if I can't keep up with your hormonal swings tonight."

The muscle tic in his jaw, the clenched fists at his sides, were all indicators he was irritated, frustrated and angry. He had no one to blame but himself, and she wasn't going to be caught up in his inner turmoil.

"This is ridiculous," she said with a sigh. "We're both obviously not in a position to talk without saying something we don't mean."

"I always mean what I say," he retorted. "Otherwise I wouldn't say it."

Rolling her eyes, Kate again waved a hand through the air. "Fine. You meant what you said about wanting to have sex with me."

"Don't twist my words," he growled.

Kate met his leveled gaze, knowing full well she was poking the bear. "Did you or did you not say you thought of having sex with me? That you actually feel it."

He moved around her, heading for the steps leading to the beach. "This conversation is over. Go home, Kate."

She stared at his retreating back for all of five seconds before she took off after him. Just because he was royalty and she was his assistant didn't mean he could dismiss her anytime he wanted. Rude was rude no matter one's social status.

She didn't say a word as she followed him. Luc's long strides ate up the ground as he headed toward the dock. Surely the man wasn't going out on his Jet Ski now. Granted, the water was calm since the storm had passed, but it was dark and he was angry.

Just as she was about to call his name, he went down. The heavy thud had her moving faster, her thighs burning from running across the sand. She prayed the sound of him falling was much worse than any injury.

"Luc," she called as she approached. "Are you all right?"

He didn't move, didn't respond, but lay perfectly still on the wet dock. Dread consumed her. The second she stepped onto the dock, her feet slid a bit, too, and she tripped over a loose board that had warped slightly higher than the others.

The dock obviously hadn't been repaired like the rest of the outdoor spaces on this property.

Kate crouched next to him, instantly noticing the swollen knot at his temple. He'd hit his head on a post, from what she could tell.

"Luc." She brushed his hair off his forehead, afraid to move him, and hoping he'd only passed out. "Can you hear me?"

She stroked his cheek as she ran her gaze down his body to see if there were any other injuries. How could he be up one second and out cold the next? Fear threat-

ened to overtake her the instant she realized she didn't
have her phone.

Maybe she was irresponsible, but she'd have to worry
about that later. Right now she had no clue how serious
Luc's injury was, but the fact he still hadn't moved had
terror pumping through her.

Shifting so her knees weren't digging into the wood,
Kate sat on her hip and kept patting Luc's face. "Come
on, Luc. Wake up. Argue with me some more."

Torn between rushing back to the house for her
phone to call for help and waiting to see if he woke on
his own, Kate started patting down his shorts, hoping
he carried his cell in his pocket.

One pocket was empty, and before she could reach to
the other side, Luc groaned and tried to shift his body.

"Wait," she told him, pressing a hand to his shoulder
as he started to rise. "Don't move. Are you hurt anywhere?"

He blinked as he stared up at her. Thankfully, the
bright light from the lamppost was helping her assess
his injuries, since the sun had set.

Luc's brows drew together in confusion. "Why were
you feeling me up?"

Relief swept through her. "I wasn't feeling you up,"
she retorted, wrapping her arm around his shoulders
and slowly helping him to sit up. "I was checking your
pockets for a cell phone. You fell and hit your head on
the post. I was worried because you were out for a few
minutes."

Luc reached up, wincing as his fingers encountered
the bump on his head, which was already turning blue.
"Damn, that hurts."

"Let's get you back up to the house." Kate helped

him to his feet, then slid her arm around his waist to steady him. "You okay? Feeling dizzy or anything?"

He stared down at her, blinked a few times and frowned. "This is crazy," he muttered.

"What?"

With his thumb and index finger, he wiped his eyes and held the bridge of his nose. He probably had the mother of all headaches right now. All the more reason to get this big guy moving toward the house, because if he went back down, she couldn't carry him.

"I know you," he murmured. "I just… Damn it, your name isn't coming to me."

Kate froze. "You don't know my name?" This was not good. That ball of fear in her stomach grew.

Shaking his head, he wrapped an arm around her shoulders and started leading them off the dock. "I must've hit my head harder than I thought. Why isn't it coming to me?"

Kate pressed a hand to his abdomen, halting his progress. She shifted just enough to look him in the eyes. Since she wasn't a medic and never had any kind of training other than a basic CPR course, she had no idea what signs to look for with a head trauma.

"Look at me," she ordered. "You know me, Luc. You know my name."

Blowing out a breath, he hung his head. "I… It's on the tip of my tongue. Damn, why can't I remember?"

He glanced back up at her, worry filling his dark eyes. This was not good, not good at all. She was going to have to get him back to the house and call the palace doctor. Obviously, Luc's memory wasn't cooperating. But she didn't want him panicking; she could do enough of that for both of them.

"My name is Kate." She watched his eyes, hoping

to see some recognition, but there was nothing. "I'm your—"

"Fiancée." A wide smile spread across his face. "Now I remember you."

Luc leaned in to capture her lips once more, with a passion she'd never known.

Three

Fiancée? What the hell?

Mustering all her willpower, Kate pushed Luc and his intoxicating mouth away as his words slammed into her.

"Let's get you inside," she told him, trying not to focus on how hard he must've hit his head, because he was clearly not in his right mind. "I'm not comfortable with that knot you have, and you may have a concussion. I need to call your doctor. Hopefully, with the storm gone, we'll have cell service."

Luc stared at her another minute, then nodded. Slipping his arm around her shoulders again, he let her lead him up to the house. Something was definitely wrong with him. The Luc from only twenty minutes ago would be arguing that he didn't need a doctor, and he certainly wouldn't be leaning on her for support.

She couldn't even think about the fact that he believed they were engaged. Because if he thought they were sleeping together, this situation would get extremely awkward really fast.

Though she'd be lying if she didn't admit to herself just how much she liked him thinking they were a couple. How long would his mind play this trick on him? How would he treat her now that he believed they were together?

Once she had him inside and settled on the sofa, she stood up and caught her breath. Luc was one massive, thick, muscular man. She'd known he was cut, but she'd had no clue how solid and heavy he would be.

His body had leaned against hers, twisting her dress on their walk. As Kate readjusted herself, trying to refill her lungs with air and not panic, she found him staring up at her, that darkened gaze holding her in place. Shivers rippled through her at the intensity of the moment—and the man.

"What?" she asked.

"Why are you all wet?"

Plucking at the damp material that clung to her thighs, Kate shook her head. "I got caught outside in the storm earlier."

Those eyes continued to rake over her body. "You're sexy like this," he murmured as his heated stare traveled back up. "With your dress clinging to your curves and your hair messy and wavy."

Kate swallowed, because any reply she had to those intimate words would lead to a lie, and she couldn't let him keep thinking they were anything more than employee-employer, servant-royal.

"Where's your cell?" If she didn't stay on task, she'd get caught up in all those sultry looks he was giving her…and she desperately wanted to get caught up in the promise behind those sexy stares. But he wasn't himself right now. "I need to call the doctor. I hope we have service."

Luc glanced around, raking a hand through his hair. "I have no idea. I don't even remember why I was outside."

He slapped his hand on the cushion beside him and let out a string of curses. "Why can't I remember anything?"

The worry lacing his voice concerned her even more than the fact he thought they were engaged. Luc Silva never let his guard down. Even when faced with losing the crown, the man was the epitome of control and power. Sexy and strong and she wanted him. Plain and simple...or maybe not so simple considering she could never have him.

"It's okay," she assured him as she leaned down to pat his shoulder. "I'll find it. Once the doctor comes, we'll know more. Maybe this will only last a few minutes. Try not to panic."

That last bit of advice was for herself as much as him, because she was seriously in panic mode right now. She didn't know much about memory loss, but the fact that something had set his mind so off balance concerned her. She couldn't even imagine how he felt.

Kate walked around the spacious but sparsely decorated living room, into the dated kitchen and then back to the living room. Crossing to the patio doors they'd just entered, she finally spotted his cell lying on the old, worn accent table most likely left by the last tenants.

Thankfully, she knew the passcode to get into the phone. "I'm just going to step out here," she told him, trying to assure him he wouldn't be alone. "I'll be right back."

She didn't want Luc to hear any worry in her tone when she described the incident to the doctor. And for now, she wasn't going to mention the whole "fiancée" bit. She would ride this out as long as possible. Yes, that was selfish, but, well...everyone had their moments of weakness and Luc Silva was definitely her weakness.

Kate was relieved to get the doctor on the phone and even more relieved when he promised to be there within the next hour. For the next sixty minutes, Luc would most likely believe they were engaged and she would play right along until she was told otherwise.

Luc's private beach villa just off the coast of Portugal wasn't far from his own country. He was pretty much hiding in plain sight. This way he could be home quickly in an emergency—or someone could come to him.

Kate was grateful the doctor could use the private boat to get to the island. There was no airstrip and the only way in or out was via boat. Only yesterday she and Luc had been dropped off by her father, so Luc could keep his hideout a secret.

When she walked back inside, Luc had his head tipped back against the sofa cushions. Eyes closed, he held a hand to his head, massaging his temples with his fingers.

"The doctor is on his way."

Without opening his eyes, he simply gave a brief nod.

"I know you're hurting, but I don't want to give you anything before the doctor can examine you."

What if his injuries were more serious than she thought? Amnesia, temporary or not, wasn't the worst thing that could happen. People died from simple falls all the time. Even when they felt fine, they could have some underlying issue that went unnoticed.

The possibilities flooded her mind as she continued to stand across the room and stare at Luc. Should he be resting or should she keep him awake? She prayed she didn't do the wrong thing. She would never forgive herself if something happened to him because they'd been fighting and he'd stormed off. If she didn't always feel the need to challenge him, this wouldn't have happened.

The kiss wouldn't have happened, either, because that was obviously spawned from sexual frustration and anger. Luc's full-on mouth attack had been forceful, not gentle or restrained. She'd loved every delicious second of it. But now she needed to focus, not think about how good it had felt to finally have him touch her the way she'd always wanted.

As she watched him, his lids kept fluttering, and finally remained closed for a minute.

"Luc," she said softly. "Try not to fall asleep, okay?"

"I'm not," he mumbled. "The lights are too bright, so I'm just keeping my eyes closed."

Crossing to the switches, she killed the lights in the living room, leaving just the one from the kitchen on so she could still see him.

"Does that help?" she asked, taking a seat beside him on the couch, relishing in the warmth from his body.

He opened one eye, then the other, before he shifted slightly to look at her. "Yeah. Thanks."

When he reached over to take her hand, Kate tensed. This wasn't real. The comfort he was seeking from her was only because he was uncertain—and he thought they were engaged.

Oh, if they were truly engaged, Kate could hold his hand and not feel guilty. She could wrap her arms around him and give him support and love and…

But no. She wasn't his fianceé so thinking along those lines would get her nowhere.

For now, she could pretend, she could keep her fingers laced with his and feel things for him in ways she never had before. This was no longer professional… they'd crossed that threshold when he'd captured her mouth beneath his.

"I'll be fine." Luc offered a wide smile, one rarely directed at her. "Just stay right here with me."

Swallowing the truth, Kate nodded. "I'm not going anywhere."

She tried not to relish the fact that Luc's thumb kept stroking the back of her hand. She tried to fight the thrill that he was looking at her as more than just an employee.

None of this was reality. He was trapped in his own mind for now. She didn't know if she should focus on the kiss earlier or the nasty knot on his head. Both issues made her a nervous wreck.

The hour seemed to crawl by, but when Dr. Couchot finally knocked on the back door, Kate breathed a sigh of relief. Beneath her hand, Luc tensed.

"It's okay." She rose to her feet, patting his leg. "We'll figure this out and you'll be just fine."

Dr. Couchot immediately came inside, set his bag down and took a seat on the couch next to Luc.

"Tell me what happened," he said, looking at Kate. Worry was etched on the doctor's face. This man had cared for Luc since the prince had been in diapers, and held all the royals' medical secrets.

Kate recounted the events, omitting the fiancée bit, and watched as the doctor examined his patient while she spoke. He looked at Luc's pupils with his minuscule light, then lightly worked his fingertip around the blue knot. With a frown, he sat back and sighed.

"Have you remembered anything since I was called?" he asked.

Luc shook his head. "I know Kate, but she had to tell me her name. I know I'm a member of the royal family because of my name, and I believe I'm the prince. I know this house is mine and I know I wanted to fix it up, but apparently I didn't get too far, so I had to have just bought it."

All this was right. A little burst of hope spread through Kate. Maybe his injuries weren't as bad as she'd first feared.

"From what I can tell, you've got temporary amnesia," the doctor stated. "I'm not seeing signs of a concussion and your pupils are responsive." Dr. Couchot looked up at Kate. "I would like him to have a scan to be on the safe side, but knowing Luc, he'll be stubborn and refuse."

"I'm sitting right here," Luc stated, his eyes darting between Kate and the doctor. "I don't want to get a scan. I'd have to go home and face too many questions. Unless I'm at risk for something more serious, I'm staying here."

Kate shared a look with the doctor. "What about if I promise to monitor him? You said there was no concussion, so that's a good sign."

"Fine," Dr. Couchot conceded. "I won't argue. But Kate will have her eyes on you 24/7 for the next few days and I'll be in contact with her. At the first sign of anything unusual, she will get you back to the palace, where we can treat you. No exceptions."

Luc nodded. "Agreed."

After receiving her instructions and a list of things

to look for in terms of Luc's behavior, Kate showed the doctor out.

Once they reached the edge of the patio, Dr. Couchot turned to face her. "Make sure you don't force any memories on him. It's important he remembers on his own, or his mind could become even more confused and his condition could actually worsen. It's a blessing he remembers as much as he does, so I believe he's only lost a few months of his memories."

A few months. Which would explain why he didn't recall the real fiancée or the fake pregnancy.

"I'll make sure not to feed him any information," Kate promised. Smoothing her hair back, she held it to the side in a makeshift ponytail. "Can he see photos or listen to his favorite music? Maybe just subtle things that will spark his thoughts?"

"I think that would be fine. Just don't push all of that on him at once. Give this some time. He may wake tomorrow and be perfectly fine, or he may be like this for another month. Every mind is unique, so we just don't know."

Kate nodded, thanking the doctor for coming so quickly. She watched as he made his way back down to the boat, where a palace guard was waiting. Thankfully, it wasn't her father, but his right-hand man.

Kate gave a wave to the men and took in a deep breath. When the doctor mentioned unusual behavior, did that include believing you were engaged to the wrong woman?

Weary and worried, she stepped back through the doors. All her stuff was at the guesthouse, but she would need to stay here.

Luc's eyes were instantly on hers when she returned to the living room. That warmth spread through her once again as she recognized that look of need. She couldn't let him keep this up. There would be no way she could resist him. And based on his reaction after that kiss, he wouldn't be happy that he'd indulged his desire for her, no matter how good together they might be.

The warning from the doctor played over in her mind. She couldn't force memories, so for now she'd have to let him think what he wanted, until his mind started to cooperate.

"Sit with me," he whispered, holding his hand out in invitation.

Kate cringed, wanting nothing more than to take his hand and settle in beside him. "I need to go get some of my things."

Lowering his hand, he frowned. "Where are your things?"

Coming up with a quick excuse, she tried to be vague, yet as honest as possible. "I have some things next door at the guesthouse. Let me get them and I'll be all yours."

Okay, she didn't necessarily need to add that last bit, but it just slipped out. She'd have to think through every single word until Luc fully regained his memory. For now, she'd have to play along…and still try to maintain some distance, or she could find herself in a world of hurt when he snapped out of his current state. Getting wrapped up in this make-believe world, even for a short time, wasn't the wisest decision. Still, he would need her during this time and they were on this island together. How could she resist him? How could she resist more touching, more kissing?

"Why do you have anything next door?" he asked.

"I was working there earlier." Still not a lie. "Give me five minutes. I'll be right back."

She escaped out the back door, unable to look at the confusion on his face any longer. If she got too far into the truth as to why she had things at the cottage, she'd have to come clean and produce the information his mind wasn't ready for.

As quickly as she could, she threw a change of clothes into her bag, adding a few essential toiletries. Everything else she'd have to smuggle over a little at a time, provided she stayed at the main house for longer than a few days.

Her biggest concern now was the fact she hadn't packed pajamas, assuming she'd be living alone. She stared at her pile of silky chemises in various colors. There was no getting around this. She didn't even have an old T-shirt to throw on for a sleep shirt.

With no other choice, she grabbed the pink one and shoved it in her bag before heading back to the main house. There was no way she could let Luc see her in this chemise, but how could she dodge a man who thought they were engaged? Most likely he assumed they slept together, too.

Kate froze on the path back to the main house. There was no way she could sleep with Luc. None. If they shared the same bed, she'd be tempted to give in to his advances.

As the moonlight lit her way back, Kate was resigned to the fact that things were about to skyrocket to a whole new level of awkward.

Four

Kate glanced over her shoulder, making sure she was alone as she slipped back out onto the patio to call her mother. There were times in a woman's life she just needed some motherly advice, and for Kate, that time was now.

"Darling!" Her mother answered on the second ring. "I was just thinking of you."

"Hey, Mama." Kate leaned against the rail on the edge of the patio, facing the doorway to make sure Luc didn't come up behind her and overhear things he shouldn't. "Are you busy?"

"Never for you. You sound funny. Everything all right?"

Not even close. Kate sighed, shoving her hair behind her ear. "I'm in a bit of a bind and I need your advice."

"What's wrong, Katelyn?"

Her mother's worried tone slid through the line. Kate swallowed back her emotions, because tears wouldn't fix this problem and they would only get her a snotty nose and red eyes. Not a good look when one was shacking up with one's sexy boss.

"Luc fell earlier."

"Oh, honey. Is he okay?"

"Well…he has a good-sized goose egg on his head. And he has temporary amnesia."

"Amnesia?" her mother repeated, her voice rising an octave. "Katelyn, are you guys coming back to the palace? Do his parents know?"

"I actually called them before I called you. Dr. Couchot was just here and he's assured us that Luc is okay, no concussion or anything. He isn't sure when Luc will regain his memory, but he's confident it's a short-term condition."

"I can't even imagine how scary this must be," her mother commented. "What can I do to help?"

"Right now Luc and I are staying here as planned," Kate stated, her eyes darting to the patio doors on the far side of the house. Luc stood there for a moment, looking out at the ocean, before he turned and disappeared. "The doctor said keeping him relaxed and calm is best for now. Luc had wanted to get away, so staying here is still our best option."

"I agree. So what else has you upset? If the doctor has assured you this is temporary, and you're staying there as planned, what's wrong?"

Pulling in a deep breath, Kate blurted out, "He thinks we're engaged."

Silence settled over the line. Kate pulled her cell away from her ear to make sure the connection hadn't been cut.

"Mom?"

"I'm here. I just need to process this," her mother stated. "Why does he think you're engaged?"

"He's only lost the past few months. He knew I was familiar, but at first he couldn't place me. When I told him my name, he assumed we were engaged. I was worried and didn't say anything, because I wanted the doctor to look him over. Dr. Couchot said not to feed Luc any information, because giving him pieces of his recent past could mess up his memory even further."

Kate rambled on. She knew she was talking fast, but she needed to get all this out, needed to get advice with Luc out of earshot.

"The doctor and Luc's parents have no clue that Luc believes we're engaged," Kate went on. "That's what I need your opinion on. What do I do, Mom? I don't want to go against the doctor's orders, but at the same time, I can't have him thinking we're a couple, but he doesn't even recall I work for him. You know how this family feels about dating or having such personal relationships with their staff."

"Oh, Katelyn." Her mother sighed. "I would wait and see how tonight goes. If this is temporary, maybe Luc will wake up tomorrow and everything will be fine. You can't go against the doctor's wishes, but I wouldn't let this lie go on too long. Luc may cross boundaries that you two shouldn't cross if he thinks you're his fiancée."

Cross boundaries? Too late. The kiss they'd shared moments before his fall flashed through her mind.

"Thanks, Mom. Please don't say anything. You're the only one who knows Luc thinks we're getting married. I don't want to humiliate him any further or have anyone else worry. I just needed your advice."

"I'm not sure I helped, but I'm definitely here for you. Please, keep me posted. I worry about you."

Kate smiled, pushing herself off the railing and heading back toward the doors. "I know. I'll call you tomorrow if the cell service is good. It's pretty sketchy here."

"Love you, sweetheart."

"I love you, Mama."

Kate disconnected the call as she grasped the doorknob. Closing her eyes, she pulled in a deep breath and blew it out slowly. She needed strength, wisdom and more self-control than ever.

And she needed to remember that Luc was healing. That he was confused. Whatever emotions she'd held on to after that kiss had no place here. Being this close to grasp onto her fantasy, yet not being allowed to take all she wanted was a level of agony she hadn't even known existed.

Luc stood in the spacious bedroom. Apparently, his master suite and luxurious attached bath, with a most impressive shower that gave the illusion of being outdoors, had been at the top of his list for renovations. Fine with him, because this room was fit for romance, and his Kate had looked all sorts of sexy the way she'd worried over him, assuring him he would be okay.

When she'd said it, her sweet, yet confident words had sliced through the fear he'd accumulated. He'd seen the worry in her eyes, but she'd put up a strong front for him. Was it any wonder she was the one for him? Dread over the unknown kept creeping up, threatening to consume him, but Luc wasn't giving up. Being unable to recall bits of his life was beyond weird and frustrating. He actually didn't have the words to describe the emotions flooding him. All he knew was that his beautiful fiancée was here, and she was staying by his side, offering support and comfort.

His eyes drifted from his reflection in the glass patio doors back to the king-size bed dominating the middle of the room. Sheers draping down from the ceiling enclosed the bed, giving an impression of romance and seduction. There was a reason this bed was the focal point of the room, and he had to assume it all centered around Kate. He could already picture her laid out on those satin navy sheets, her black hair fanned out as they made love.

Damn it. Why couldn't he remember making love to her? Why couldn't he recall how she felt against him? How she tasted when he kissed her? Maybe their intimacy would help awaken some of those memories.

Luc cringed inwardly. No, he wasn't using sex or Kate in that way. He wanted to remember their love on his own, but he definitely wanted her by his side tonight while he slept. He wanted to hold her next to him, to curl around her and lose himself to dreams. Maybe tomorrow he'd wake and all this would be a nightmare. His memory would be back and he and Kate could move forward.

There had to be something lying around, some clue that would spark his memory. Granted, he hadn't really brought anything personal to the place, judging by the hideously dated furniture in the majority of the rooms, but surely there was something. Even if he looked through the clothes he'd brought, or maybe there was something in his wallet that would kick his mind back into the proper gear. Perhaps he'd packed something personal, like a picture, or maybe he should go through the contacts on his cell. Seeing a list of names might be just the trigger he needed.

Luc searched through his drawers, finding nothing of interest. It wasn't as if his underwear drawer would reveal any hidden clues other than the fact that he liked black boxer briefs.

Slamming one drawer shut, he searched another. By the time he was done looking through the chest and hunting through his bathroom, he was alternating between being terrified and being furious. Nothing new popped up except a healthy dose of rage.

There had to be something in his cell phone. He started out the bedroom door, only to collide chest to chest with Kate. Her eyes widened as she gripped his biceps in an attempt to steady herself.

"Sorry," she said, stepping back. "I just got back with my things. I called your parents and gave them the rundown. They're worried, but I assured them you would be fine and you'd call them yourself tomorrow. I also called my mother. I didn't mean to be gone so long. Are you heading to bed?"

Was she shaking? Her eyes darted over his shoulder toward the bed, then back to meet his gaze. The fact she had been rambling and now kept chewing on her lip was proof she was nervous. About the amnesia?

"Are you all right?" he asked, reaching out to smooth her hair away from her forehead. He tipped her chin up, focusing on those luscious, unpainted lips. "You seem scared, more than you were just a few minutes ago."

Kate reached up to take his hand in hers. "I guess all the events finally caught up with me. I'm tired and worried. Nothing more."

"That's more than you need to handle," he told her, stroking his thumb over her bottom lip. "Let's go to bed."

That instant, holding Kate completely trumped finding his phone and seeking answers. There was a need inside him, an ache he had for this woman that was so primal he couldn't even wrap his mind around it. His phone would be there when he woke up, and right now all he wanted was to lose himself in Kate. She looked dead on her feet, and she still hadn't changed from her wet dress, which had now mostly dried. There was no way she was comfortable.

"Why don't you grab a shower and meet me in bed?" he asked.

Her eyes widened. "Um…I'm not sure we should…"

Luc waited for her to elaborate, but she closed her eyes and let out a soft sigh. When her head drooped a little, Luc dropped his hand from her chin and squeezed her shoulder.

"Are you afraid to be with me because of the memory loss?"

Her lids lifted, her dark eyes searching his. "I'm not afraid of you, Luc. I think it would be best if we didn't… you know…"

"Make love?"

A pink tinge crept across her tan cheeks. "Yes. You're injured. You need to rest and relax. Per the doctor's orders."

Luc snaked his arms around her waist as he pulled her flush against his body. "I plan on relaxing, but I want you lying beside me. It's obvious we came here to get away, and I don't want to ruin this trip for you."

Delicate hands slid up his chest, fingers curling up over his shoulders. Just her simple touch was enough to have his body quivering, aching. Everything about her was so familiar, yet new at the same time.

"You're not ruining anything for me." She offered a tired, yet beautiful smile. "Let's just concentrate on getting you better, and everything else will fall into place."

"So no sex, but you'll lie down with me?"

Her eyes held his as she nodded. "I'll lie with you."

He hadn't recalled her name at first, but he'd instantly felt a pull toward her. No wonder they were engaged. Obviously, they shared a special, deeply rooted bond. Their chemistry pushed through the damage to his mind, and that alone would help him pull through this.

"I'll just go shower in the guest bath, real quick," she told him, easing away from his embrace. "Give me ten minutes."

Confused at her need to retreat, Luc crossed his arms over his chest. "Why not just use the shower in here? The other bathroom hasn't been renovated and this one is much more luxurious."

She looked as if she wanted to argue, but finally nodded. "You're right. A quick shower in here would be better. I just didn't know if I would disturb you trying to rest."

"You won't bother me. You can take advantage of the sunken garden tub, you know." He took her hands, leading her farther into their bedroom. "No need to rush through a shower. Just go soak in a tubful of warm water and relax."

"I'll be quick in the shower. Why don't you lie down?"

He leaned forward, gently touching his lips to hers. "Don't take too long or I'll come in after you."

She shivered beneath his touch, and it was all Luc could do to keep from hauling her off to the bed and taking what he wanted, throwing every reason he shouldn't straight out the window.

Retreating into the bathroom, she closed the door. Luc frowned. Was she always so private? Why did some things seem so familiar, while other, mundane things had disappeared from his mind?

As he stripped down to his boxer briefs, he heard the

shower running. An image of a wet, soapy Kate flooded his mind. He couldn't wait to get beyond this memory lapse, beyond the annoyance of the headache, and make full use of that spacious shower with her.

He would make this up to her, somehow. His Kate was exhausted, and still worried about him. She was sacrificing, when this was supposed to be a romantic trip away.

As of right now he only remembered they were engaged. He recalled some buzz about wedding invitations and upcoming showers. He'd let his assistant handle all of that…but he couldn't recall who his assistant was at the moment.

Raking a hand down his face, Luc sighed. Now wasn't the time to think of staff, not when he was about to crawl into bed with his fianceé. Right now he wanted to focus on Kate, on their trip and somehow making this up to her.

Kate showered quickly, constantly watching the door she'd closed. She should've known he'd want her in his room, that he wouldn't even question the fact.

But sleeping with him under false pretenses was an absolute no.

No matter how Luc made her body tingle and the nerves in her belly dance…she couldn't let her thoughts go there.

She was still Luc's assistant, which meant looking out for his best interest. And it was in the interest of both of them to keep their clothes on. Easier said than done.

Kate dried off, wrapped her hair up in a towel and slid into her chemise. She truly had no other option unless she asked Luc for a T-shirt, but she didn't know if he was one of those guys who would be even more turned on by seeing a woman in his clothes, so she opted for her own gown.

Rubbing the towel through her wet hair, she got all the moisture out and took her time brushing it. Perhaps if she stayed away a few extra minutes, Luc would get tired and fall asleep before she went back out there.

Their argument before his fall had taken on a life of its own, and she still couldn't get that kiss from her mind. Of course, if her lips weren't still tingling, maybe she could focus on something else. Such as the fact that the man was suffering from memory loss and was scared and angry over this sudden lack of control with his own mind.

Still, between the toe-curling kiss and the fact she was about to slide between the sheets with her boss, Kate didn't know how to act at this point. What was the proper protocol?

After applying some lotion on her legs and shoulders, Kate hung up her towel and faced the inevitable: she was going to have to go out into the bedroom and get in that bed. The sooner she moved beyond the awkward, uncomfortable stage, the sooner she could breathe easily. All she needed to do was go in there, lie beside Luc and wait for him to fall asleep. Then she could get up and go to the sofa or something. No way could she lie nestled next to him all night. The temptation to pick up where their kiss had left off would be too strong.

But the doctor had been adamant about not saying too much, to allow the memories to return on their own. Kate didn't want to do anything that would cause Luc more damage.

Somehow she had to abide by his no-fraternization

rule and still manage to play the doting fiancée. Was that combination even possible?

Taking a deep breath, she opened the bathroom door. The darkened room was a welcome sight. At least this way she wouldn't have to look him in the eye and lie. Now the only light spilled from the bathroom, slashing directly across the bed in the center of the room as if putting all the focus on Luc and his bare chest. The covers were up to his waist; his arms were crossed and resting on his forehead.

"Turn off the light and get in bed."

The memory loss didn't affect his commanding ways. The man demanded, he never asked, and he expected people to obey. Still, the low, powerful tone he used was enough to have her toes curling on the hardwood. This was her fantasy come to life, though when she'd envisioned Luc ordering her into bed, she never imagined quite this scenario.

What a way for fate to really stick it to her and mock her every dream with this false one.

"Is your head still hurting?" she asked, remaining in the bathroom doorway.

"It's a dull pain, but better than it was."

Kate tapped the switch, sending the room into darkness, save for the soft moonlight sweeping through the balcony doors. The pale tile floor combined with the moon was enough to light her path to the bed.

Pulling the covers back, she eased down as gently as possible and lay on her back. On the edge. As stiff as a board. And the ache for him only grew as his masculine scent surrounded her and his body heat warmed the minuscule space between them.

The bed dipped as Luc rolled toward her. "Are you okay?"

His body fitted perfectly against hers. Just the brush of the coarse hair on his legs against her smooth ones had her senses on alert…as if they needed to be heightened.

Was she okay? Not really. On one hand she was terrified. On the other she was completely intrigued…and spiraling headfirst into arousal. And arousal was taking the lead over so many emotions. With his breath tickling her skin, she was fully consumed by the one man she'd wanted for so long. It would be so easy, yet so wrong, to roll over and take what she wanted.

"I'm fine," she assured him.

With the darkness surrounding them, the intimacy level seemed to soar. She should've insisted on a small light or something. But then she would see his face. Honestly, she had no clue what was more torturous.

"You're tense."

Understatement of the year.

Luc's hand trailed up her arm, moving to rest on her stomach. If he thought she was tense before, he should just keep touching her. She was about to turn to stone.

She needed to regain control of her body, her hormones. Unfortunately, her mind and her girlie parts were not corresponding very well right now, because she was getting hot, restless, as if she needed to shift toward him for more of that delicate touching he was offering.

No. This was wrong. Her even thinking of wanting more was wrong. Just because he'd kissed her earlier didn't mean a thing. He'd done so to shut her up, to prove a point and to take charge as he always did.

Yet given the way he'd masterfully taken over and kissed her with such force and passion, there was no way he'd been unmoved. And she would've called him on it, but now she was dealing with a new set of issues surrounding her desires.

"If you're worried about me, I'm fine," he assured her. "I just want to lie here and hold you. Scoot over against me. I feel like you're about ready to fall out of the bed."

Just as she started to shift, her knee brushed against him. His unmistakable arousal had her stopping short.

"Ignore it," he said with a laugh. "I'm trying like hell."

Squeezing her eyes shut, Kate sighed. "I can't do this."

Five

Luc grabbed Kate around the waist just as she started to get up. Pulling her flush against him, her back against his chest, he held on tight. Her silky gown slid over his bare chest, adding fuel to the already out-of-control fire.

"Don't," he whispered in her ear, clutching the silk material around her stomach, keeping her body taut against his own. "Just relax."

"You need to be sleeping."

Her body was still so stiff, so rigid beneath him. Something had seriously freaked her out and she wasn't telling him what it was. Damn it, was it something he already knew but couldn't recall? Or was this not about her at all, but something to do with his fall?

A sliver of fear slid through him.

"Did the doctor say something you're not telling me?" he asked.

"What? No."

She shifted, relaxing just a touch as she laid her hand over his on her stomach. The first contact she'd initiated since climbing into bed.

"He didn't say much when I walked him out," she went on. "Just that he felt it necessary for you to remember on your own."

"The only thing I want to do right now is to get you to relax."

Luc slid his hand out from beneath hers, to the lacy edge of her silk gown. Her body stiffened briefly, then arched as if she was fighting her own arousal. When she sucked in a breath, Luc knew he had her.

"Luc, you need to rest."

Her shaky voice betrayed her, indicating she was just as achy and excited as he was. He pushed one of her legs back, easing his fingers beneath the silk until he found the delicate elastic edge on her panties.

"What I need to do is pleasure my woman," he whispered in her ear, pleased when she trembled.

Kate's back arched again and her head fell against his shoulder. "Luc, you don't have to—"

He nipped at the tender flesh of her earlobe as he eased his hand inside her panties to stroke her. "I want to."

Her soft moans, her cry when he found just the right spot, left his mouth dry. It didn't take long for her body to give in and shudder beneath his touch. She gasped, trembled all the while Luc trailed kisses along her shoulder, her neck when she'd turn just so and the soft spot below her ear.

Yet nothing triggered any memories.

All the same, he didn't regret giving her pleasure. Everything about this private moment only made him want her, yearn for her more.

"Are you always this responsive?" he whispered.

Slowly, she rolled toward him, rested a palm on his chest. With the pale glow from the moon, he didn't miss the shimmer in Kate's eyes.

"Baby, don't cry."

She blinked, causing more tears to slide down her flushed cheeks. "You didn't remember, though, did you?"

He smoothed her damp hair away from her face. "No."

When her hand started down his abdomen, toward the top of his boxer briefs, he gripped her wrist.

Kate had been through a rough time, and even though he was the one suffering the medical concern, he wasn't about to let her think he'd given her pleasure only to get his own. This moment was all about her, reassuring her that he—no, that they—would be okay.

"We both need to rest right now," he told her, dropping a kiss to her forehead. "You're exhausted, I'm recovering. We'll make love tomorrow and I'll make this up to you, Kate. Our trip won't be ruined. I promise."

So stupid. Foolish, careless and flat-out irresponsible.

First she'd let him touch her, then she'd cried. The tears came instantly after she'd crashed back into reality after the most amazing climax she'd ever had.

The moment had been so consuming, so mind-blowing. That's when she knew Luc hadn't remembered anything, or he would've been angry to be in that position with her.

So when the tears fell, she'd had no way to stop them.

What should've been a beautiful moment was tarnished by the situation. She hadn't expected Luc to be so powerful in bed. She truly had no idea how she'd hold him off from becoming intimate now that they'd shared such passion.

Kate had eased from the bed early this morning. Her vow to leave and sleep on the couch as soon as he fell asleep had gone out the window. After his mission to relax her had been a success, she'd been dead to the world.

How had this bizarre scenario spiraled so far out of control? She'd just spent the night in her boss's arms, a boss who was a prince, a boss who thought she was his fiancée. He was a man who prided himself on control and keeping his professional and personal lives separate. The rule was very clear at the palace.

Everything that had happened in the past eighteen hours was a colossal mess.

Kate had hurried back to her cottage early this morning while Luc slept. She'd managed to smuggle a couple sundresses and her swimsuit over. That should get her through the next few days, though she prayed she wouldn't be here that long.

Her cell phone vibrated in the pocket of her short dress. Pulling it out, she was thankful the service seemed to be holding up. The doctor's name lit up her screen.

"Good morning, Dr. Couchot," she said, as if she hadn't had the most life-altering night she'd ever experienced.

"Kate, how is Luc this morning?"

Glancing over her shoulder toward the open patio doors, she saw him still sprawled out on the bed, asleep. She kept checking on him, but he'd grumble and roll back over. She had to assume he was fine, since he was resting so well.

"He's sleeping in today," she told the doctor, turning back to watch the gentle waves ebb and flow against the shoreline. "He was exhausted last night."

"I imagine so. Still nothing new to report? No change in the memory or new symptoms?"

Kate leaned against the wrought-iron railing and wondered if the toe-curling intimacy was worth reporting. Probably best to leave that out of the conversation.

"No. He's the same."

The same sexy, determined, controlling man he always was, just with a sweeter side he was willing to share. And he was oh so giving between the sheets…

Dr. Couchot reiterated how Kate was to just let Luc think on his own, let the memories return as slowly or as fast as his mind needed them to. As if she needed reminding. Nearly all she could focus on was keeping this colossal secret.

Once she hung up, she turned, leaning her back against the rail. Watching him sleep was probably wrong, too, but why stop now? She hadn't done anything right since she'd gotten here. In the span of three days she'd fought with him, kissed him, come undone in his bed and played the part of the doting fiancée. How could she make things any worse?

Kate just prayed he'd get his memory back so they could move on. The lies were eating at her and she didn't know how she could keep up this charade.

Luc was a fighter in every way. He wouldn't let this memory loss keep him down. He'd claw his way back up from the abyss and then…

Yeah, that was the ultimate question. And then… what? Would he hate her? Would he fire her? Would he look at her with disdain?

A sick pit formed in the depths of her stomach. Would her parents lose their jobs? Surely her mom and dad would be disappointed in her for breaking the royal protocol.

This couldn't go on. Luc had to remember. So far she hadn't given Luc any extra information regarding his past, and she didn't intend to because she didn't want to make his issue worse. But there was only so long she could go on not telling him things. The man wanted to sleep with her.

How did she keep dodging that fact when she wanted it, too?

The way he'd looked at her, with affection, was so new and so tempting. And all built on lies.

Luc called out in his sleep. Kate straightened as she slowly moved closer. When he cried out again, she still couldn't make out what he was saying. She set her phone on the nightstand and eased down on the edge of the bed. His bronze chest stared back at her and Kate had a hard time not touching him, not running her fingertips over the tip of the tattoo that slid perfectly over one shoulder.

The sheet had dipped low, low enough to show one hip and just the edge of his black boxer briefs. She'd felt those briefs against her skin last night. More impressively, she'd felt what was beneath them.

"Tell me," he muttered, shifting once again. His eyes were squeezed tight, as if he was trying to fight whatever image had him twisting in the sheets.

Kate froze. Was he remembering something? Would his memory come back and play through his mind like a movie?

When his face scrunched even more and his chin started quivering, she knew he was fighting some demon, and she couldn't just sit here and watch him suffer. She might not be able to fully disclose the truth, but she didn't have to witness the man's complete downfall, either.

"Luc." She placed her hand on his shoulder and shook him gently. "Luc."

Jerking awake, he stared up at her, blinking a few times as if to get his bearings. Kate pulled her hand back, needing to keep her touching at a minimum.

Raking a hand down his face, his day-old stubble rustling beneath his palm, he let out a sigh. "That was insane. I was dreaming about a baby," he murmured, his gaze dipping to her midsection. "Are we having a baby, Kate?"

On this she could be absolutely honest. For once.

"No, we're not."

"Damn it." He fell back against the pillows and stared up at the sheers gathered together at the ceiling. "I thought for sure I was having a breakthrough."

Kate swallowed. He was remembering, but the memory was just a bit skewed. With the pregnancy lie from his ex still fresh, Kate figured it was only a matter of time before he had full recollection of the situation.

She didn't know whether to be terrified or relieved. They still hadn't slept together, so she prayed their relationship could be redeemed once the old Luc returned.

"It just seemed so real," he went on. "My hand was on your stomach, and I was so excited to be a father. I had no clue what to do, but the idea thrilled me."

Her heart swelled to near bursting at his reaction. The thought of having a baby with him made her giddy all over. But they were treading in dangerous territory. This was going to go downhill fast if she didn't do something. She might not be able to feed him his memories, but that didn't mean she couldn't find other ways to trigger him.

"How about we take the Jet Skis out for a bit?" she suggested.

His eyes drifted from the ceiling to her. "I don't want to go out right now."

Wow. She'd never known him to turn down anything on the water. Especially his Jet Ski or his boat. She needed to get him out of the house, away from the temptation of the bed, the shower…anyplace that might set the scene for seduction.

"Do you want to just go relax on the beach and do absolutely nothing?"

Though the thought of them lying next to each other wearing only swimsuits didn't seem like a great idea, now that she'd said it aloud. Granted, they'd seen each other that way before, but not with him thinking they were in love and planning holy matrimony…not to mention his promise to make love to her today.

A wide smile spread across his face. "I have an even better idea."

That naughty look was something she definitely recognized. He had a plan, and she didn't know if she should worry or just go along for the ride.

Six

Sweat poured off his head, his muscles burned and he was finally getting that rush he needed.

Kate grunted, sweat rolling off her, and he didn't recall ever seeing her look more beautiful. Of course, he didn't recall much, but right at this moment, she was positively stunning.

"I can't do this anymore," she panted, falling back against the wall.

Luc eased the sledgehammer down to rest, the wood handle falling against his leg. "We can take a break."

"I kind of meant I can't do this anymore…ever."

Luc laughed. They'd just torn out the old vanity in the main bathroom off the hallway, and the scene was a disaster. The construction workers had left the majority of their smaller tools here, so he figured he'd do something useful while he waited for his memory to return. No, he'd never done any home projects before.

He was a prince, for crying out loud. But he knew this bathroom would be gutted and replaced, so he was just blowing off some steam while helping the workers along at the same time.

"What are we going to do with all of this mess?" Kate asked as she glanced around the room.

They stood amid a pile of broken ceramic material, some huge hunks and some shards.

"Leave it," he told her. "When the guys come back to finish this, they can haul it out."

She dropped her hammer on top of the disaster and turned to stare at him. "So we're just causing destruction and closing the door on our way out?"

Luc shrugged. "I'm not really known for my renovating skills. Am I?"

Kate laughed, swiping a hand across her forehead. "No. You're royalty. I don't know of too many blue bloods who go around remodeling."

Stepping over the debris, he made his way to the door. Kate was right behind him. Extending his hand, he helped her over the rubble and out into the hallway.

"How about we take our tools to the kitchen?" he said, smiling when she rolled her eyes. "That room is hideous."

"I'd rather go to the kitchen and make some lunch, because you only had coffee for breakfast and my toast wore off about my fifth swing into that vanity countertop."

Her glistening forehead, the smudge of dirt streaked across one cheek, instantly had Luc recalling a little girl with a lopsided ponytail chasing a dog through a yard.

"You used to play with Booker," he muttered, speaking before he fully finished assessing the image. "At my family's vacation house in the US."

Kate's eyes widened. "That's right. I did. Did you have a memory?"

Rubbing his forehead, Luc cursed beneath his breath when the flash was gone. "Yeah. I've known you a long time, then."

Kate nodded, studying him. "I've known you since I was six."

"I'm a lot older than you."

A smile spread across her face. "Ten years."

"How long have we been together?"

Kate glanced away, biting her lip and focusing on anything but him.

"I know the doctor said to let me remember on my own. But I want to know."

Those doe eyes came back up to meet his gaze. "I started working for you a year ago."

Shock registered first. "You work for me?"

He tried to remember, tried to think of her in a professional atmosphere. Nothing. He'd actually rather remember her in an intimate setting, because that was what crushed him the most. They were engaged, they were obviously in love and he couldn't recall anything about the deep bond of their relationship.

"What do you do for me?" he asked. "Besides get me hot and make me want you. And how did we manage to get around the family rule about not mixing business with pleasure?"

Pink tinged her tanned face as she reached out, cupping her hand over his cheek. "I'm your assistant. I'm not telling you anything else. All right?"

Sliding his hand over hers, he squeezed it, then brought her palm to his mouth. "All right," he said, kissing her. "But I can't believe I let my fiancée work."

Her lips quirked. "Let me? Oh, honey. You've never let me do anything."

Laughing, he tugged her against him. "I have a feeling we do a lot of verbal sparring."

A lopsided grin greeted him. "You have no idea."

When he started to nuzzle the side of her neck, she eased back. "I'm sweaty and smelly, Luc. I don't think you want to bury your nose anywhere near my skin right now."

He slid his tongue along that delicate spot just below her ear. "I plan on having you sweaty later anyway, Kate."

Her body trembled. He didn't need to spell out how their day would end. Sleeping next to her last night had been sweet torture, but seeing her come apart at his touch had been so erotic, so sexy.

He couldn't wait to have her. Couldn't wait to explore her, get to know her body all over again.

"Has it always been this intense between us?" he asked, still gripping her hand and staring into those eyes any man could get lost in.

"Everything about our relationship is intense," she murmured, staring at his mouth. "I never know if I want to kiss you or strangle you."

"Kissing," he whispered against her mouth. "Always choose kissing, my *doce anjo*."

Sweet angel. Had he always called her that? When her lips parted beneath his, he knew the term was accurate. She tasted so sweet each time he kissed her. Wrapping one arm around her waist, he slid his palm over her backside. She still wore that short little sundress she'd had on all morning. She hadn't changed when they'd done the bathroom demolition, and seeing her bent over, catching a glimpse of her creamy thighs, had nearly driven him crazy.

Gathering the material beneath his hand, he cupped her bottom. "I've wanted you since last night," he muttered against her mouth. "The need for you hasn't lessened, and I may not remember our intimacy before, but something tells me I've been infatuated with you for a long time. This ache inside me isn't new."

A shaky sigh escaped her. "That's something I can't attest to. I don't know how long you've wanted me."

Luc eased back, still holding on to her backside. "Forever, Kate. I refuse to believe anything else."

Moisture gathered in her eyes. "You might end up remembering differently."

Then she stepped away, leaving him cold and confused. What did that mean? Did they not have a solid relationship, a deep love, as he'd thought?

Luc let her go. Apparently, they both had emotional demons to work through. Regardless of his temporary amnesia, he wouldn't let her go through this alone. They both needed each other, that was obvious, and even if she tried to push him away, she'd soon find out he wasn't going anywhere.

They were in this together no matter how he'd been before. She was his and he would be strong for her. He would not let this memory loss rob him of his life or his woman.

Kate threw on her suit and headed down to the beach. Luc might have been content with busting things up as a stress reliever, but she needed a good workout. There was nothing like a swim to really get the muscles burning and endorphins kicking in.

She hadn't lied when she'd told him their relationship had always been intense. And she hadn't lied when she'd said she had no clue how long he'd been infatuated with her.

But he was right about one thing. The emotions he was feeling, his actions toward her, weren't new. All that desire, that passion, had been lying dormant for some time now, and she'd wondered if it would ever break the surface. Never in her wildest dreams had she imagined it would take a major injury to further exacerbate this chemistry.

The question now was were these feelings truly directed toward her, or were they left over from his ex? A year ago he'd admitted to an attraction, but had put the brakes on it because of their professional relationship and her parents working so closely with his family. And it was then that he'd explained in great detail why members of his family never dated or got involved with an employee. The list of reasons was lengthy: reputations on the line, the employee could turn and go to the media with a fabricated story... There was too much at stake—even Luc's crown in this case—to let staff in on their personal lives. Kate didn't have a clue how Luc and his ex had been in private. She actually tried to never think of that. But now she couldn't stop herself.

Did Luc really have such strong emotions for her? If so, how had he kept it bottled up all this time?

Kate loosened the knot on her wrap, letting the sheer material fall onto the sand. Running straight into the ocean, the world at her back, she wished she could run from this whole ordeal and stop lying to Luc. She wished she could kiss him and sleep in his bed and have him know it was her and not the fake fiancée he'd conjured up.

He'd said they would be sleeping together later. Dodging that was going to be nearly impossible.

She was in desperate need of advice. She'd wanted to phone her mother earlier, but the call hadn't been able to go through. She would try again later. More than anything Kate needed her mother's guidance. Holding back from Luc was pure torture. How could she say no to the one thing she'd fantasized about for so long?

The warm water slid over her body as she sliced her arms through the gentle waves. The hot sun beat down on her back and her muscles were already screaming from the quick workout.

Kate pushed herself further, breaking the surface to take another deep breath and catch her bearings. Panting heavily, she dived back in for more. She'd not fully worked through her angst just yet.

Before she knew it, she'd gone so far up the coastline she couldn't see Luc's home anymore. She swam to the shore, trudged through the sand and sank down onto dry land. Pulling her legs up against her chest, Kate wrapped her arms around her knees and caught her breath, willing the answers to come.

One thing was clear. She and Luc needed to stay away from the house as much as possible. With just the two of them alone, there was no chaperone, nobody else to offer a buffer. At least back at the palace there was a full staff of butlers, maids, drivers, assistants to the assistants, guards, his parents, her parents, the cooks… the list was almost endless.

Perhaps an outing to the small village was in order. Anything to hold off the inevitable. The hungry look in Luc's eyes, the way he constantly kept touching her, were all indications that the moment was fast approaching. And yes, she wanted that moment to happen more than she wanted her next breath, but she didn't want it to be built on desperation and lies.

Pushing herself up off the sand, Kate stretched out her muscles. She'd never been a fan of running, but she wasn't done exorcising those demons. She headed back toward Luc's home, passing other pristine beach houses. Some were larger, some smaller, but they all had the same Mediterranean charm, and their own docks, with boats bobbing against the wood planks.

The island was a perfect getaway for a prince. Under normal circumstances, he could hide away here without the media hounding him, without the distractions of the internet and the outside world.

This place would be heaven on earth for any couple wanting a romantic escape.

Too bad she was only a figment of Luc's imagination.

As Kate ran, she kept to the packed sand that the waves had flattened. Her thigh muscles burned and sweat poured off her as the sun beat against her back. This felt good, liberating. She would go back to the house and go over Luc's schedule for when they returned to Ilha Beleza. Looking at all his duties and responsibilities would surely help jog something in his mind.

And the memories were returning. Apparently, her dirty state earlier had shot him back to the moments when she'd been a little girl and had gone to work with her parents. She'd loved the Silvas' old sheepdog, Booker. She used to play with him, roll around in the yard with him and be completely filthy by the time she left.

Luc's parents would just laugh, saying how they missed having a little one around. They'd gotten Booker when Luc was eight, so by the time he was a teen, he wasn't so much into running through yards and spending hours playing with a dog.

Kate was all about it. When Booker had passed away, she had taken the news harder than Luc had. Of course, he'd had his women "friends" to occupy his time and keep his thoughts focused elsewhere.

Finding her discarded wrap in the sand where she'd dropped it, Kate scooped it up and quickly adjusted it around her torso. At the base of the steps leading up to Luc's home, she rested her hands on her knees and pulled in a deep gulp of air. She was going in as professional Kate. Keeping her hands and mind off Luc was the only way to proceed. Flirty, dreamy Kate had no place here. They hadn't made love yet, so she could still turn this around, and pray Luc wasn't totally furious once he remembered what her role in his life actually was.

Seven

Luc's phone bounced on the couch cushion when he tossed it aside. Useless. He recognized his parents' names, his best friend, Mikos, and Kate. Other than that, nothing.

Raking a hand down his face, Luc got to his feet and crossed to the patio doors. Kate had been gone awhile and he knew her frustrations had driven her out the door. He'd like to run from his problems, too; unfortunately, they lived inside his head. Still, he couldn't fault her for needing some time alone.

He stepped out onto the patio, his gaze immediately darting down to the dock. As he stared at the Jet Ski on one side and his boat on the other, he wondered what he'd been doing before he fell. Was he about to go out on the water so late in the evening? Was Kate coming with him? Everything before the fall was a complete blank to him. He had no idea what they'd been doing prior to his accident.

Hell, he couldn't even recall how he and Kate had started working together. And some family rule about not getting personal with staff members kept ringing in his head. He reached into his mind, knowing this was a real memory. The Silva family didn't get intimate with employees. So had Kate come to work for him after they'd become a couple? Had she been so invaluable in his life that he'd wanted her to be his right-hand woman in his professional world, as well?

The questions weren't slowing down; they were slamming into his head faster than he could comprehend them. He'd go mad if he didn't get his memory back soon, or if he kept dwelling on something that was out of his control.

Damn it. Of one thing he was certain. Losing control of anything was pure hell, and right now he'd spiraled so far he hoped and prayed he could pull back the reins on his life before this amnesia drove a wedge between him and Kate.

Luc straightened as the idea slammed into him, pushing through the uncertainty he'd been battling. All that mattered was him and Kate. This was their time away, so all he had to do was enjoy being with her. How hard could that be? A private getaway with one sexy fiancée would surely be just what he needed.

A shrill ring came from the living room. Luc ran in and found Kate's cell phone on one of the end tables. His mother's name was on the screen. Odd that she would be calling Kate.

Without giving it another thought, he answered. "Hello."

"Lucas? Darling, how are you feeling?"

His mother's worried tone came over the line. Her

familiar voice had him relieved that his mind hadn't robbed him of that connection.

"Frustrated," he admitted, sinking onto the worn accent chair. "I have a hell of a headache, but other than that I feel fine. Why did you call Kate's phone?"

"I didn't want to bother you if you weren't feeling good, or if you were resting. I spoke with Kate last night, but I needed to check on you today."

"There's no need to worry, Mom. Kate is taking good care of me and the doctor was thorough. I just need to relax, and this is the best place for me to do that."

His mother made a noise, something akin to disapproval. "Well, you call the doctor first thing if you start having other symptoms. I'm still not happy you're not home. I worry, but you're stubborn like your father, so I'm used to it."

Luc smiled, just as Kate stepped through the door. A sheen of sweat covered her. Or maybe that was water from the ocean. Regardless, she looked sexy, all wet and winded. Would his need for her ever lessen? Each time he saw her he instantly went into primal mode and wanted to carry her back to bed.

"Nothing to worry about," he said, keeping his eyes locked on Kate's. "I'm in good hands. I'll phone you later."

He ended the call and rose to his feet. Kate's eyes widened as he moved closer to where she'd stopped in the doorway.

"Were you on my phone?" she asked, tipping her head back to hold his gaze.

"My mom called to check on me. She tried your cell in case I was resting."

Kate's eyes darted around. "Um…is that all she said?"

Reaching out to stroke a fingertip along her collarbone, Luc watched the moisture disappear beneath his touch. "Yes. Why?"

"Just curious." She trembled beneath his touch as her eyes locked back onto his. "I need to go shower. Then we need to discuss your schedule and upcoming events."

Heat surged through him as he slid his mouth over hers. "Go use my shower. We can work later."

She leaned into him just slightly, then quickly pulled back. Something passed through her eyes before she glanced away. As she started to move around him, he grabbed her elbow.

"You okay?"

She offered a tight, fake smile. "Fine. Just tired from my swim and run."

The shadows beneath her eyes silently told him she hadn't slept as well as she'd claimed. He nodded, releasing her arm, and listened as she padded through the hall and into the master suite.

Waiting until he was sure she was in the shower, Luc jerked his shirt over his head and tossed it, not caring where it landed. By the time he reached his bedroom, his clothes were gone, left in a trail leading to the bedroom door.

The steady hum of the water had Luc imagining all kinds of possibilities. And all of them involved a wet, naked Kate.

When he reached the spacious, open shower, surrounded by lush plants for added privacy, he took in the entire scene. Kate with water sluicing down her curves, her wet hair clinging to her back as she tipped her face up to the rainfall showerhead. She was a vision…and she was his.

Luc crossed the room and stepped onto the wet, gritty

tile. In an instant he had his arms wrapped around her, molding her back against him.

Kate's audible gasp filled the room, and her body tensed beneath his. "Luc—"

He spun her around, cutting off anything she was about to say. He needed her, needed to get back to something normal in his life. Kate was his rock, his foundation, and he wanted to connect with her again in the most primal, natural way possible.

"Luc," she muttered against his mouth. "We shouldn't."

Her words died as he kissed his way down her neck. "We should."

That silky skin of hers was driving him insane. Kate arched into him, gripping his shoulders as if holding on.

"You're injured," she panted.

He jerked his head up to meet her gaze. "The day I can't make love to my fiancée is the day I die."

Luc hauled her up against him, an arm banded around her lower back to pull her in nice and snug, as his mouth claimed hers once again. There was a hesitancy to her response. Luc slowed his actions, not wanting her to feel she needed to protect him.

But this all-consuming need to claim her, to have her right now, had his control slipping.

"I want you, Kate," he whispered against her mouth. "Now."

Nipping at her lips, he slid his palms over her round hips, to the dip in her waist and up to her chest, which was made for a man's hands…his hands. She was perfect for him in every way. How had he gotten so lucky to have her in his life?

As he massaged her, she dropped her head back, exposing that creamy skin on her neck. Luc smoothed his tongue over her, pulling a soft moan from her lips.

After backing her up, he lifted her. "Wrap your legs around me."

Her eyes went wide. "I… Luc…"

"Now, Kate."

Just as her legs encircled his waist, he grabbed her hands and held them above her head. Sliding into her, he stilled when she gasped.

"You okay?"

Eyes closed, biting down on her lip, she nodded. Luc gripped her wrists in one hand and used his other to skim his thumb across the lip she'd been worrying with her teeth.

"Look at me," he demanded. "I want to see those eyes."

Droplets sprinkled her lashes as she blinked up at him. He moved against her, watching her reaction, wanting to see every bit of her arousal, her excitement. He might not remember their past encounters, but he damn well was going to make new memories with her, starting right now.

Kate's hips rocked with his; her body arched as he increased his speed.

"Luc," she panted. "Please…"

Gripping her waist, he trailed his mouth up her neck to her ear. "Anything," he whispered. "I'll give you anything. Just let go."

Her body tensed, shuddering all around him. As she cried out in release, Luc followed her.

Wrapping her in his arms, he couldn't help but wonder if each time they were together felt like the first time, or if this particular moment was just so powerfully intense and all-consuming. This woman had the ability to bring him to his knees in all the right ways.

So why was his beautiful fiancée—who'd just come apart in his arms—sobbing against his shoulder?

* * *

Oh, no. No, no, no.

Kate couldn't stop the tears from coming, just as she couldn't stop Luc from making love to her.

No. Not making love. They'd had sex. He didn't love her, and once his memory returned, he wouldn't even like her anymore. She'd been worried about tonight, about going to sleep. She'd truly never thought he would join her in the shower. The sex just now with Luc was unlike any encounter she'd ever had. Nothing could have prepared her for the intensity of his passion.

How had this entire situation gotten even more out of control? The reality of being with Luc had far exceeded the fantasy. And now that she had a taste of what it could be like, she wanted more.

"Kate?"

She gripped his biceps, keeping her face turned into his chest. She couldn't face him, couldn't look him in the eyes. Not after what she'd done. He would never understand.

Was this how he'd treat her if he loved her? Would he surprise her in the shower and demand so much of her body? Part of her wanted to bask in the glorious aftermath of everything intimacy should be. But she knew it couldn't last.

Luc shut off the water behind her, and in one swift move, he shifted, lifting her in his arms.

"Talk to me, baby." He stepped out of the shower and eased her down onto the cushioned bench. Grabbing a towel from the heated bar, he wrapped it around her before securing one around his waist.

Kate stared down at her unpainted nails. Focusing on her lack of manicure would not help her out of this situation. Luc gripped her hands as he crouched before her.

"Look at me."

Those words, said only moments ago under extremely different circumstances, pulled her gaze away from their joined hands and up into his dark eyes. Worry stared back at her. Didn't he know she was lying? Didn't he know he should be worried about himself?

She could come clean. She could tell him right now that she wasn't his fiancée, that she'd been dying for him to make a move on her for years. But all that sounded even more pathetic than the truth, which was that she'd gotten caught up in this spiral of lies. In an attempt to protect him, she'd deceived him. There was no turning back, and if she was honest with herself, she couldn't deny how right they'd felt together.

"Did I hurt you?" he asked.

Swiping the moisture from her cheeks, Kate shook her head. "No. You could never hurt me."

"What is it? Did you not want to make love with me?"

A vise around her heart squeezed.

She shook her head. Eventually she was going to strangle herself with this string of lies.

"I'm just overwhelmed," she admitted. "We hadn't been together before."

Luc studied her a moment before his brows rose. "You mean to tell me we hadn't made love before?"

Shame filled her. She couldn't speak, so simply nodded.

Luc muttered a slang Portuguese term that no member of the royal family should be heard saying.

"How is that possible?" he asked. "You said we've been working together for nearly a year."

"Your family has a rule about staff and royal members not being intimate. We've been professional for so long, we both just waited. Then we ended up here on this getaway and…"

She couldn't finish. She couldn't lie anymore. The emotions were too overwhelming and her body was still reeling from their passion.

Luc came to his feet, cursing enough to have her cringing. He was beating himself up over something that was 100 percent her fault.

Unable to stand the tension, the heavy weight of the guilt, she jumped to her feet. "Luc, I need to tell you—"

"No." He turned, facing her with his hands on his narrow hips. "I took advantage of you. Kate, I am so, so sorry. I had no clue. I got caught up in the moment and wanted to forget this memory loss and just be with you."

"No. This is not your fault in any way." Holding on to the knot on her towel, Kate shivered. "Let's get dressed. We need to talk."

Eight

Luc grabbed his clothes from the bedroom and went to the spare room to get dressed. Of all the plans he'd had for Kate, taking her when she wasn't mentally prepared for it sure as hell wasn't one of them.

Their history explained why she'd tensed when he'd come up behind her in the shower, explained the onslaught of tears afterward. Not to mention the way she'd stiffened against him in bed last night.

Luc cursed himself once again for losing control. He'd thought he was doing the right thing, thought he was getting them both back to where they'd been just before his ridiculous accident.

Heading back down the hallway, he spotted his clothes. Looking at them now he felt only disgust, as opposed to the excitement and anticipation he'd felt when he'd left them behind without a care.

He grabbed each article of clothing and flung them

and his towel into the laundry area. He'd worry about that mess later. Right now he had another, more important mess to clean up, and he only hoped Kate would forgive him.

Guilt literally ate at him, killing the hope he'd had of making this day less about his amnesia and more about them.

By the time she came out, she'd piled her hair atop her head and sported another one of those little sundresses that showcased her tanned shoulders and sexy legs. The legs he'd demanded she wrap around him.

Kate took a seat on the sofa and patted the cushion beside her. "Just relax. Okay?"

Relax? How could he when this entire mess had started with him forgetting every single damn thing about the woman he supposedly loved?

Wait, he *did* love her. When he looked at her and saw how amazing and patient she was with him, and damn it, how she'd let him take her in the shower, and didn't stop him, how could he not love her? When he looked at her, his heart beat a bit faster. When he touched her, his world seemed to be a better place.

He just wished he could remember actually falling in love with her, because all he could recall was this all-consuming, aching need that was only stronger now that he'd had her.

"Luc." Kate held out her hand. "Come on."

He crossed to her, took her hand and sank onto the couch beside her.

"Tell me you're okay," he started, holding her gaze. "Tell me I didn't hurt you physically or emotionally."

A soft smile spread across her face. "I already told you, I'm fine. You were perfect, Luc."

She held on to him, her eyes darting down to where their hands joined.

"Before you fell, we were fighting," she told him. "I take full responsibility for everything that's happened to you, so don't beat yourself up over the shower."

Luc squeezed her hand. "The shower was all on me. If we were fighting before my fall, then that took two, so don't place all of that blame on yourself."

Kate smiled. Her eyes lifted to his. "We could play this game all day," she told him, her smile dimming a bit. "But I need to talk to you."

"What's wrong?"

Her tone, the worry in her eyes, told him something major was keeping her on edge.

"There are so many things that you need to know, but I've been holding back because I don't want to affect your healing process."

Luc edged closer, wrapping an arm around her shoulders and pulling her to his side. Easing back against the cushions, he kept her tucked against him. "If something is worrying you, tell me. I want to be here for you. I want to be strong for you."

Kate's delicate hand rested on his thigh. She took a deep breath in, then let it out with a shudder.

"I was adopted."

Her voice was so soft, he wondered if she actually meant to say it out loud.

"Did I already know this about you?" he asked.

"No. The only people who know are my parents."

His mind started turning. Her parents worked for his parents. Memories of them in his house flashed for an instant.

"Scott and Maria, right?"

"Yes." Kate tilted her head up to meet his gaze. "You're remembering."

"Not fast enough," he muttered. "Go on."

Settling her head back against his chest, Luc wondered if it was easier for her to talk if she wasn't looking right at him.

"I was born in the States," she went on. "Georgia, to be exact. My parents adopted me when I was six. I only have vague memories of being there, but it's always held a special place in my heart."

Luc listened, wondering where she was going with this and how it all tied back into what was happening between them now.

"My parents ended up moving to Ilha Beleza to work full-time at the palace. They used to just work at the vacation home back in Georgia. Your family has one off the coast."

Closing his eyes, he saw a white house with thick pillars extended to the second story. A wraparound porch on the ground floor had hanging swings that swayed in the breeze. Booker and a young Kate running in the yard…

Yes, he remembered that house fondly.

"Since I've been your assistant, I've wanted you to visit that orphanage, the one I came from, but we've butted heads over it."

Luc jerked, forcing Kate to shift and look up at him.

"Why were we fighting over an orphanage?" he asked.

She shrugged. "I have no idea why you won't go. To be honest, I just think you don't want to, or you didn't want to take the time. You've offered to write a check, but I never can get you to go there. I just felt a visit from a real member of royalty would be something cool for those kids. They don't have much and some of them have been there awhile, because most people only want to adopt babies."

Luc glanced around the sparsely furnished room, hoping for another flash of something to enter his mind. Hoping for some minuscule image that would help him piece it all together.

"Is this why we were arguing before I fell?" he asked, focusing back on her.

"Not really. I tried bringing it up again, but you blew it off." She let go of his hand and got to her feet, pacing to the open patio doors. "We were arguing because we're both stubborn, and sometimes we do and say things before we can fully think them through."

He could see that. Without a doubt he knew he was quite a hardhead, and Kate had a stubborn streak he couldn't help but find intriguing and attractive.

"When your memory comes back, I want you to know that everything I've ever done or said has been to protect you." Her shoulders straightened as she kept her back to him and stared out the doors. "I care about you, Luc. I need you to know that above all else."

The heartfelt words, the plea in her tone, had Luc rising to his feet and crossing to her. Placing his hands on her shoulders, he kissed the top of her head.

"I know how you feel about me, Kate. You proved it to me when you let me make love to you, when you put my needs ahead of any doubts you had."

She eased back against him. "I hope you always feel that way."

The intensity of the moment had him worried they were getting swept into something so consuming, they'd never get back to the couple they used to be. Even though he didn't remember that couple, he had to assume they weren't always this intense.

"What do you say we take the boat and go into town?" he asked. "Surely there's a market or shops or restaurants to occupy our time. We need to have some fun."

She turned in his arms, a genuine smile spreading across her face. "I was going to suggest that myself. I haven't shopped in forever. I'm always working."

She cringed, as if she just realized what had come out of her mouth.

"It's okay," he told her, kissing the tip of her nose. "I'll make sure your boss gives you the rest of the day off. You deserve it."

That talk didn't go nearly the way she'd rehearsed it in her head. Coming off the euphoria of having mind-blowing sex with Luc in the shower had seriously clouded her judgment, and obviously sucked out all her common sense.

So now here she was, wearing her favorite blue halter dress, letting the wind blow her hair around her shoulders and face while Luc steered his boat to the main dock of the island's small town. Most people traveled by boat to the village, where scooters were the preferred mode of transportation. The marina was lined with crafts of various sizes and colors. As they'd made their way toward the waterfront, they'd passed by other boaters and waved. Kate really liked this area. Too bad she'd probably never be back after the mess she'd created came crashing down on her.

Through her research she knew the locals would line up along the narrow streets, set up makeshift booths and sell their goods. From what she'd seen online, she might find anything from handmade jewelry and pottery to flowers and vegetables. She was excited to see what caught her fancy, perhaps taking her mind off the fact her body was still tingling from Luc's touch.

She'd never be able to shower again—especially in that master bath—without feeling his body against hers, his breath on her shoulders. Without hearing his demanding words in her ear as he fully claimed her.

Then he'd let his guard down and opened up to her about his feelings. Slowly, she was falling in love with the man she'd been lying to, the man who was off-limits in reality. She'd opened up about her past, wanting to be as honest as she could in an area that had nothing to do with what was happening right now.

Luc secured the boat to the dock, then extended his hand to help her out. With a glance or simple touch, the man had the ability to make her stomach quiver, her heart quicken and her mind wander off into a fantasy world. Still, that was no excuse to have let the charade go this far.

There was no going back now, though. The charade may be all a farce, but her emotions were all too real.

Kate knew she should've told Luc about the false engagement when he'd hinted that he wanted to make love to her. She should've told him right that moment, but she hadn't, and now here she was on the other side of a monumental milestone they would both have to live with.

She was falling for him; there was no denying the truth to herself. What had started as physical attraction long ago had morphed into more because of his untimely incident.

How did she keep her heart protected, make sure Luc stayed safe until he remembered the truth on his own and keep hold of the man she'd come to feel a deeper bond for? There was no good way this scenario would play out. Someone was going to get hurt.

"You okay?" Luc asked, hauling her onto the dock beside him.

Pasting on a smile, Kate squeezed his hand. "Fine. Let's see what this island has to offer."

Other boats bobbed up and down in the water on ei-ther side of the long dock. Luc led her up the steps to the street. Once they reached the top, Kate gasped. It was like a mini festival, but from all she'd heard about this quaint place, the streets were always this lively.

Brightly colored umbrellas shaded each vendor. A small band played live music in an alcove of one of the ancient buildings. People were laughing, dancing, and nearly every stand had a child behind the table, working alongside an adult. Obviously, this was a family affair.

Kate tamped down that inner voice that mocked her. Her dream was to raise a family, to have a husband who loved her, to watch their babies grow. Maybe someday she'd have that opportunity. Unfortunately, with the way her life was going now, she'd be looking for a new job as opposed to a spouse.

Suddenly, one of the stands caught her eye. "Oh, Luc." She tugged on his hand. "I have to get a closer look."

She practically dragged him down the brick street to the jewelry booth. The bright colors were striking with the sun beating down on them just so. It was as if the rays were sliding beneath the umbrella shading the area. The purple amethyst, the green jade, the yellow citrine—they were all so gorgeous. Kate didn't know which piece she wanted to touch first.

"Good afternoon."

The vendor greeted her in Portuguese. Kate easily

slid into the language as she asked about the wares. Apparently, the woman was a widow and the little girl sidling up against her was her only child. They made the jewelry together and the girl was homeschooled, oftentimes doing lessons right there at the booth.

Kate opened her small clutch to pull out her money. There was no way she could walk away and not buy something from this family.

Before she could count her cash, Luc placed a hand over hers and shook his head. He asked the lady how much Kate owed for the necklace and earrings she'd chosen. Once he paid and the items were carefully wrapped in red tissue paper, they went on their way to another booth.

"You didn't have to pay," she told him. "I don't expect you to get all of the things I want, Luc."

He shrugged, taking her hand and looping it through his elbow as they strolled down the street. "I want to buy you things, Kate."

"Well, I picked these out for my mother," she said with a laugh.

Luc smiled. "I don't mind buying things for my future mother-in-law, either. Really, think nothing of it."

What had been a beautiful, relaxing moment instantly turned and smacked Kate in the face with a dose of reality. A heavy ball of dread settled in her belly. This was getting all too real. Kate's parents had been inadvertently pulled into this lie. They would never be Luc's in-laws, and once he discovered the truth, they might not even be employees of his family.

They moved to another stand, where the pottery was unique, yet simple. Kate eyed a tall, slender vase, running her hand over the smooth edge. Before she knew it, Luc had paid for it and the vendor was bagging it and wrapping it in several layers of tissue for protection.

"You don't have to buy everything I look at," she informed Luc.

"Did you like the piece?" he asked.

"I love it, but I was wondering what it would look like in your new house."

Luc kissed her softly on the lips before picking up the bag and moving away. "Our house, Kate. If you like it, then it's fine with me. I'm not much of a decorator."

"No, you prefer to demolish things."

Luc laughed. "Actually, our little project was my first experiment in destruction, but I did rather enjoy myself. I really think I'll tackle that kitchen before we leave, and give the contractors a head start."

They moved from place to place, eyeing various trinkets. Kate ended up buying a wind chime and fresh flowers while Luc was busy talking to another merchant. She wanted to liven up the dining area in the house, especially since the room was in desperate need of paint. The lavender flowers would look perfect in that new yellow vase.

Once they had all their bags, they loaded up the boat and headed home.

Home. As if this was a normal evening and they were settled in some married-couple routine. Kate shouldn't think of Luc's house as her home. She'd started getting too settled in, too comfortable with this whole lifestyle, and in the end, when her lie was exposed and his inevitable rejection sliced her in two, she would have nobody to blame but herself.

These past few hours with Luc had been amazing, but her fantasy life wouldn't last forever.

Nine

Sometime during the past hour, Kate had fully detached herself. She'd been quiet on the boat, quiet when they came into the house. She'd arranged fresh flowers in that beautiful yellow vase and placed them on the hideous dining room table without saying a word.

She'd made dinner, and the only sound he'd heard was her soft humming as she stirred the rice. Now they'd finished eating, and Luc couldn't handle the silence anymore.

He had something to say.

"Kate."

She stepped from the kitchen, wiping her hands down her dress. Luc remained standing, waited for her to cross to him.

"I know you've got a lot on your mind right now," he started. "But there's something I need to tell you."

"Wait." She held up a palm. "I need to go first. I've

been trying to figure out a way to talk to you about your amnesia."

She sighed, shaking her head. "I don't even know how to start," she muttered. "I've racked my brain, but nothing sounds right."

"The doctor said not to prompt me." Luc reached into his pocket and pulled out a small, velvet pouch. "While you're thinking about the right words, why don't you take this?"

She jerked her gaze up to his, then stared down at the present in his hand. "What is it?"

"Open it."

Her fingers shook as she took the pouch and tugged on the gathered opening. With a soft gasp, she reached in and pulled out an emerald-cut amethyst ring.

"Luc." She held the ring up, stared at it, then looked to him. "What's this for?"

"Because you don't have a ring on your finger. It hit me today, and I don't know why you don't, but I didn't want to wait and find out. I saw this and I knew you'd love it."

When she didn't say anything or put the ring on, his nerves spiked. Strange, since he'd obviously already popped the question. Unless she just didn't like it.

"If you'd rather have something else, I can take it back to the lady and exchange it. When I saw that stone, I remembered something else about you."

Her eyes widened. "You did?"

A tear slipped down her cheek as she blinked. Luc swiped it away, resting his hand on the side of her face. "I remembered your birthday is in February and that's your birthstone. I remembered you have this amethyst pendant you've worn with gowns to parties at the palace. That pendant would nestle right above your breasts. I used to be jealous of that stone."

Kate sucked in a breath as another tear fell down her face. "You say things like that to me and I feel like you've had feelings for me for longer than I ever imagined."

Taking the ring from her hand, he slid it onto her left ring finger. "There are many things I don't remember, but I know this—I've wanted you forever, Kate."

He didn't give her a chance to respond. Luc enveloped her in his arms, pulled her against him and claimed her mouth. He loved kissing her, loved feeling her lush body against his. Nothing had ever felt this perfect, as far as he could recall. And he was pretty sure if anything had ever felt this good, he'd remember.

Kate's hands pushed against his shoulders as she broke the kiss. "Wait."

She turned, coming free from his hold. With her rigid back to him, Luc's nerves ramped up a level. "Kate, what's wrong?"

"I want to tell you," she whispered. "I need to tell you, but I don't know how much I can safely say without affecting your memory."

Taking a step toward her, he cupped his hands over her shoulders. "Then don't say anything. Can't we just enjoy this moment?"

She turned in his arms, stared up at him and smiled. "I've never been happier than I am right now. I just worry what will happen once you remember everything."

His lips slid across hers. "I'm not thinking of my memory. I only want to make up for what we did this morning."

A catch in her breath had him pausing. Her eyes locked onto his.

"I want to make love to you properly, Kate."

Her body shuddered beneath his hands. "I've wanted you for so long, Luc."

Something primal ripped through him at the same time he saw a flash of Kate wearing a fitted skirt suit, bending over her desk to reach papers. He shook off the image. She'd already said she was his assistant, so that flash wasn't adding anything new to the mix.

Right now he had more pressing matters involving his beautiful fiancée.

"I want you wearing my ring, the weight of my body and nothing else."

Luc gave the halter tie on her neck a tug, stepping back just enough to have the material floating down over her bare breasts. With a quick yank, he pulled the dress and sent it swishing to the floor around her feet. Next he rid her of her silky pink panties.

With her hair tossed around her shoulders, her mouth swollen from his kisses, Luc simply stared at her, as if taking all this in for the first time.

"Perfect," he muttered, gliding his hands over her hips and around her waist. "Absolutely perfect and totally mine."

The breeze from the open patio doors enveloped them. The sunset just on the horizon created an ambience even he couldn't have bought. And everything about this moment overshadowed all that was wrong in his mind with the amnesia.

Guiding Kate backward, he led her to a chaise. When her legs bumped against the edge, Luc pressed on her shoulders, silently easing her down. Once she lay all spread out for his appreciation, he started tugging off his own clothes. The way her eyes traveled over his body, studying him, did something to his ego he couldn't explain. He found himself wanting to know what she thought when she looked at him, what she felt. All this was still new to him and he wanted to savor every single moment of their lovemaking.

"I've dreamed of this," he murmured.

Her brows quirked. "Seriously? You don't think it was a memory of something?"

Luc rested one hand on the back of the chaise, another on the cushion at her hip. As he loomed over her, his body barely brushed the tips of her breasts.

"I'm sure," he whispered. "You were on my balcony, naked, smiling. Ready for me."

A cloud of passion filled her eyes as she continued to stare up at him.

"Maybe I had that fantasy when I first looked at this place, or maybe I had that vision since we've been here." He nipped at her collarbone, gliding up her exposed throat. "Either way, you were meant to be here. With me. Only me."

Kate's body arched into his as her fingertips trailed up his biceps and rested at his shoulders. "Only you," she muttered.

Luc eased down, settling between her legs. The moment his lips touched hers, he joined them, slowly taking everything she was willing to give. This all-consuming need he had for her only grew with each passing moment. Kate was in his blood, in his heart. Was it any wonder he wanted to marry her and spend his life with her?

Kate's fingertips dug into his skin as she rested her forehead against his shoulder. Luc knew from the little pants, the soft moans, that she was on the brink of release.

He kissed her neck, working his way up to that spot

behind her ear he already knew was a trigger. Her body clenched around him as she cried out his name. Before she stopped trembling, he was falling over the edge, too, wrapped in the arms of the woman he loved, surrounded by a haze of euphoria that kept away all the ugly worries and doubts.

All that mattered was Kate and their beautiful life together.

His hand slid over her flat stomach. There was a baby, his baby, growing inside her. He hadn't thought much about being a father, but the idea warmed something within him.

Dropping to his knees, he kissed her bare stomach. "I love you already," he whispered.

Luc jerked awake, staring into the darkness. What the hell was that? A memory? Just a random dream? His heart beat so fast, so hard against the wall of his chest. That had been real. The emotions, the feel of her abdomen beneath his palm, had all been real.

Luc wasn't one to believe in coincidences. That was a memory, but how could it be? Kate wasn't pregnant. She'd said they hadn't made love before the shower, so what the hell was that dream about?

Glancing at the woman beside him, Luc rubbed a hand over his face. The sheet was twisted around her bare body, and her hair was spread over the pillow. Luc placed a hand on her midsection and closed his eyes. That dream was so real he'd actually felt it.

Surely it wasn't just a fantasy of the day he and Kate would be expecting in real life.

He fell back against his pillow, laced his hands behind his head and blinked to adjust his eyesight to the darkened room. No way could he go back to sleep now.

There was too much on his mind, too many unanswered questions.

Something involving a baby had happened to cause such a strong flashback, for the second time now. It just didn't make sense. His mind was obviously the enemy at the moment.

"Luc…"

He turned toward her, only to find her eyes were still closed. She was dreaming, too. Her hand shifted over the sheets as if seeking him out. Instantly, he took hold of her hand and clasped it against his chest. Tomorrow he would have to seek some answers. This waiting around was killing him, because tidbits of his life weren't enough. He wanted the whole damn picture and he wanted it now.

Maybe if Kate talked about herself, her personal life, that would trigger more memories for him. He was done waiting, done putting his life in this mental prison.

How could he move on with Kate when he couldn't even remember their lives before a few days ago?

Ten

She should've told him. No matter what the doctor said, she should have just told Luc that they weren't engaged. Everything else he could remember on his own, but the biggest lie of all needed to be brought out into the open.

Of course, now they'd slept together twice, and she still hadn't said a word.

The heaviness of the ring on her hand wasn't helping the guilt weighing on her heart, either. Instead of trying to make this right, she'd let every single aspect spin even more out of control.

Stepping from the bathroom, Kate tied the short, silky robe around her waist. As soon as she glanced up, she spotted Luc sitting up in bed, the stark white sheet settled low around his hips. All those tanned, toned muscles, the dark ink scrolling over one shoulder, the dark hair splattering over his pecs. The man exuded sex appeal and authority.

"You needn't have bothered with that robe if you're going to keep looking at me like that," he told her, his voice husky from sleep.

Kate leaned against the door frame to the bathroom. "Did you know you never wanted to marry?" she asked, crossing her arms over her chest.

Luc laughed, leaning back against the quilted headboard. "That's a bit off topic, but no. I didn't know that."

Swallowing, Kate pushed forward. "You had no intention of taking a wife, but Ilha Beleza has some ridiculously archaic law that states you must be married by your thirty-fifth birthday in order to succeed to the throne."

"My birthday is coming up," he muttered, as if that tidbit just hit him. Luc's brows drew together as he laced his fingers over his abdomen. "Are you saying I'm not entitled to the throne if we aren't married by then?"

This was the tricky part. "You aren't crowned until you're married."

"That's ridiculous." He laughed. "I'll change that law, first thing. What if my son doesn't want to marry? Who says you have to be married by thirty-five?"

Kate smiled. "That's exactly what you said before you fell. You were dead set on having that law rewritten."

His eyes held hers another moment, but before she could go on, he said, "I had a dream last night. It was real. I know it was a memory, but I can't figure it out."

Kate's heart beat faster in her chest. Was their time over? Was the beautiful fantasy they'd been living about to come to a crashing halt?

"What was the dream?" she asked, gripping her arms with anticipation.

"I had a dream you were pregnant. That image in my

head has hit more than once." His eyes drilled into her. "Why would I keep dreaming that, Kate?"

"Did you see me in the dream?" she asked, knowing she was treading on very shaky ground.

He shook his head. "No. I had my hands on your bare stomach and I was so happy. Nervous, but excited."

"I've never been pregnant," she told him softly. "Do you think maybe you're just thinking ahead?"

Kate glanced away, unable to look him in the eyes and see him struggle with this entire situation. Why couldn't this be real? He'd told her more than once that he loved her, but that was just what he thought he was supposed to say...wasn't it? Still, what if he was speaking from his heart? What if that fall had actually pulled out his true feelings? But even if she stood a chance with the man she'd fallen in love with, Kate had lied and deceived him. He would never forgive her.

She just wanted today, just one more night with him. She was being selfish, yes, but she couldn't let go just yet. Not when everything right at this moment was beautiful and perfect.

"Do you want children?" he asked. "I assume we've discussed this."

Kate pushed herself off the door frame and smoothed her hair back from her face. "I do want kids. It's always been my dream to have a husband who loves me and a houseful of children."

He offered her a wide, sexy smile. "We will have the most beautiful children."

Oh, when he said things like that she wanted to get swept away and believe every word. Yet again, Luc had been weaved so tightly into this web of lies she'd inadvertently created. Her heart had been in the right place. She only hoped Luc saw that once all was said and done.

"I think any child with the Silva genes would be beautiful," she countered. "Even though you're an only child, your father has a long line of exotic beauties on his side. Your mother is a natural beauty, as well."

Luc tossed his sheet aside and came to his feet. Padding across the floor wearing only a tattoo and a grin, he kept his gaze on hers.

"As much as I'd love to work on those babies, I think I'd like to do something that will help get my memory back sooner rather than later."

Kate forced her gaze up… Well, she made it to his chest and figured that was a good compromise. "What's that?"

"Maybe we should tackle that work schedule you'd mentioned." His smile kicked up higher on one side of that kissable mouth. "You know, before we got sidetracked with being naked."

Kate laughed. "Yes. Work. That's where we need to focus."

Finally. Something they could do that actually needed to be done. She could breathe a bit now.

"I'll go get my laptop," she told him. "I've got a spreadsheet there of your tentative schedule, and I have a speech written out for you that you need to look over."

As she started to walk by, he reached out, snaking an arm around her waist. "You write my speeches?"

"For the past year I have."

His eyes roamed over her face, settled on her lips, then came back up to meet her gaze. "You really are perfect for me."

Kate swallowed. "Better put some clothes on. You can't work in your birthday suit."

His laughter followed her from the room, mocking her. She wasn't perfect for him. She wanted to be. Oh, mercy, how she wanted to be. She'd give him every-thing, but this dream romance was about to come to an end. His memories were coming back a little each day. Time was not on her side.

Maybe by focusing on work, he'd start to piece more things together. Perhaps then she wouldn't have to worry about saying anything. Honestly, she didn't know what scenario would be worse, her telling him the truth or him figuring it out on his own.

Was she a coward for not wanting to tell him? Ab-solutely. Not only did she not want to see that hurt—and quite possibly hatred—in his eyes, she didn't want that confrontation. There were no right words to say, no good way to come out and tell him he'd been living a complete lie for these past few days.

The end result would be the same, though, no mat-ter how he found out. He would be disgusted with her. Suddenly, losing her job, or even her parents' positions, wasn't the main problem. After this time away from their ordinary lives, she couldn't imagine life without Luc.

And every bit of this scenario made her seem fool-ish, selfish and desperate.

When had she become that woman? When had she become the woman Luc had actually been engaged to? Because Kate was no better than his lying, scheming ex.

Luc glanced over Kate's shoulder as she sat in a patio chair with her laptop on the mosaic-tiled table. They'd opted to work outside to enjoy the bright sunshine and soft ocean breeze.

Resting his hands on the back of the chair, Luc leaned in to read over the tentative spreadsheet, but he was finding it impossible to focus. Kate's floral scent kept hitting him with each passing drift of wind.

"I can move these engagements around," Kate told him, pointing to the two green lines on the screen. "Both appointments are flexible. I scheduled them like this because I thought it would save time."

"Fine. You know more about this than I do," he told her.

She shifted, peeking at him over her shoulder. "I know about scheduling, but this is your life, Luc. Give me some input here. I can add or take away time. Usually, when you don't want to stay at an event too long, I make an excuse and cut the time back."

His brows quirked. "Seriously?"

"Well, yeah. How else would you escape and still look like the charming prince?" She laughed.

"Wow, you really do everything for me." With a sigh, he straightened. "What you have works for me. You've done this for a year, so you obviously know what you're talking about."

Kate turned fully in her chair and narrowed her eyes. "That's the Luc I used to work with. You never wanted to help with the schedule. You always trusted me to make it work."

Another flash of Kate in a snug suit, black this time, filled his mind. A dark-haired woman stood next to her. Luc closed his eyes, wanting to hold on to the image, needing to see who it was. Who was this woman?

Alana.

The image was gone as fast as it entered his mind, but he had a name.

"Luc?"

He opened his eyes, meeting Kate's worried gaze. She'd come to her feet and stood directly in front of him.

"Who's Alana?" he asked.

Kate jerked as if he'd slapped her. "Do you remember her?"

"I had a flash of you and her talking, but I couldn't tell what you guys were saying. It's like a damn movie that plays in my head with no sound."

He raked a hand down his face, meeting her eyes once more. "Who is she?" he repeated.

"She was a woman you used to date."

Luc tried to remember more, but nothing came to mind. Only that the woman's name stirred emotions of anger and hurt within him.

"Were we serious?" he asked.

Kate crossed her arms and nodded. "You were."

She was really sticking to the doctor's orders and not feeding him anything more than he was asking. Damn it, he wished she'd just tell him.

Pacing across the patio, Luc came to a stop at the edge by the infinity pool and stared out at the ocean. With the world at his back, he wished he could turn away from his problems so easily.

Alana Ferella. The name slid easily into his mind as he watched the waves roll onto the shore. His heart hardened, though. What kind of relationship had they had together? Obviously, not a compatible one or he'd still be with her. Something akin to rage settled in him. She hadn't been a nice woman, that much he knew.

He didn't want to keep asking Kate about an ex-girlfriend, and most likely Alana didn't matter, anyway. He just wished he could remember more about Kate, more about the plans they'd made.

"Are we getting married soon?" he asked, turning back to face her.

She blinked a few times, as if his question had thrown

her off. Hell, it probably had. He'd just gone from quizzing her on his ex to discussing their own nuptials.

"There's no set date," she told him.

That was weird. Once they'd announced their engagement, wouldn't the proper protocol have been to set a date? "Why not?" he asked. "With my birthday approaching, the throne in question and being a member of a royal family, I'm shocked we don't have something set."

Biting on her lip, Kate shrugged. "We can discuss the details in a bit. Can we finalize this schedule first? I'd like to make some calls later, if the cell service is working, to confirm your visit. I also need to let my dad know, so security can be arranged."

She was dodging his question for a reason. Did she simply not want to discuss things because of his memory loss, or was there something more to it? She'd admitted they'd argued before his fall. Had they been arguing over the wedding? Had they been arguing over…what? Damn it.

Smacking his palm on the table hard enough to make it rattle, Luc cursed, then balled his hands into fists. Kate jumped, taking a step back.

Kate started to step forward, but he held up a hand.

"No," he ordered. "Don't say anything. There's nothing you can do unless you want to tell me everything, which goes against the doctor's orders."

The hurt look on her face had him cursing. She was just as much a victim in this as he was.

"Kate, I didn't mean to lash out at you."

She shook her head, waving a hand. "It's okay."

"No, it's not." Closing the gap between them, he pulled her into his arms. "You've been here for me, you've done so much and I'm taking out my anger and frustrations on you when you're only trying to protect me."

Kate wrapped her arms around his waist. "I can handle it, Luc. It's partially my fault you're in this position, anyway. If we hadn't been arguing, if I hadn't made you so angry you went down to that wet dock, none of this would be happening."

Luc eased back. "None of this is your fault. At least pieces of my life are finally revealing themselves, and I'm sure it won't be long before the rest of the puzzle is filled in."

Kate had sacrificed so much for him. Yet he hadn't heard her tell him once that she loved him. Luc eased back, looking her in the eyes.

"Why are you marrying me?" he asked, stroking her jawline with his thumbs.

Her body tensed against his as her eyes widened. "What do you mean?"

"Do you love me?" he asked, tipping his head down a touch to hold her gaze.

Instantly, her eyes filled. Kate's hands came up, framed his face. "More than you'll ever know," she whispered.

Relief coursed through him. He didn't know why, but it was imperative to know her true feelings.

"I want to do something for you." She placed a light, simple kiss on his lips. "Tonight I'm going to make your favorite dinner. We're going to have a romantic evening and there will be no talk of the amnesia, the wedding, the work. Tonight will just be about Kate and Luc."

Wasn't that the whole point of this getaway? She cleverly circled them back around to the purpose of this trip. One of the many reasons he assumed he'd fallen in love with her. She kept him grounded, kept him on track.

Tugging her closer to him, he nuzzled her neck. "Then I expect one hell of a dessert," he growled into her ear.

Eleven

She had to tell him. There was no more stalling. The anguish, the rage that was brewing deep within Luc was more than she could bear. No matter what the doctor said, she had to come clean, because Luc getting so torn up had to be more damaging than just learning the truth.

And the truth beyond this whole messed-up situation was that she loved him. She hadn't lied when he'd asked. Kate had fallen completely in love with Luc and to keep this secret another day just wasn't acceptable.

She put on her favorite strapless green dress and her gold sandals. With her hair piled atop her head, she added a pair of gold-and-amethyst earrings.

A glance down at her hand had her heart clenching. He'd given her a ring. She wore a ring from a man she loved, yet he truly had no idea who she was.

At this point, she didn't recognize herself. She'd never been a liar or a manipulator. Yet here she was, doing a bang-up job of both.

Even with the patio doors open, the house smelled amazing with their dinner of fish and veggies baking in the oven. No matter how the evening ended, Kate wanted one last perfect moment with Luc.

Her mother would be relieved that Kate was finally telling the truth. What would Luc's parents say? Would they insist she be fired? Would they dismiss her parents from their duties as well, as she'd feared all along?

No matter the ramifications, Kate had to do the right thing here.

She headed to the kitchen to check the progress of dinner. When she glanced out toward the ocean, she noticed the darkening skies. Another storm rolling in. How apropos. Hadn't this entire nightmare started with a storm? For once in her life she wasn't looking forward to the added turmoil from Mother Nature.

Luc stood on the patio with his phone. Kate had no idea who he was talking to, but whoever it was, their call would be cut off soon due to this crazy weather.

Nerves settled deep in Kate's stomach. She wanted nothing more than to go back in time and have a redo of the night Luc fell. First of all, she never would've argued with him. If he didn't want to do the orphanage visit, fine. She'd been beating her head against that proverbial wall for nearly a year and he'd never given in. Why had she assumed he'd grow a heart all of a sudden and go?

Of course, now that he was drawing a blank on certain aspects of his life, he seemed to have forgotten how cold he used to be. Kate truly wished this Luc, the one she'd spent the past few days with, the one who had made love to her as if he truly loved her, was the Luc who would emerge after all the dust settled.

The worry eating at her would not help her be strong when she most needed to be. Everything that Luc threw at her would be justified, and right now she just needed to figure out the best way to come clean, because she truly didn't want to harm him any more than she had to.

After checking the dinner, she pulled the pan from the oven. Once she had their plates made, she started to call him, but realized he was still on the phone. The electricity flickered as rumbles of thunder resounded outside. Kate quickly searched for candles, because inevitably the lights were going to go. Perfect. It seemed Mother Nature was on her side. With the lights off, Kate wouldn't have to see the hatred on Luc's face when she told him that everything he knew about her, about them, was a lie.

"Darling, did you hear what I said?"

Luc concentrated on his mother's voice, the words she was saying, but something still didn't fit.

"You said Alana contacted you because she wants to see me," he repeated slowly, still trying to process all this.

Kate had told him Alana was an ex, but why would she be contacting him if he was engaged to Kate?

"Yes," his mother confirmed. "She's called me twice and she's very adamant that she wants to see you. I'm not going to stick my nose in this—you can respond however you want—but I don't think it's a good idea."

Luc's eyes locked onto the orange horizon. This view alone was reason enough to buy this property, no matter how many upgrades he wished to have inside. But right now, his head was pounding as if memories were rushing to the surface, waiting to get out all at once.

"Why would she contact you at all?" he asked. Resting one hand on the rail, he clutched the phone with his other, struggling to hear through the static. "Alana is in my past."

"So you remember her? Good. Then you don't need me to say how ridiculous this notion is that she can just come back into our lives after the entire baby scandal..."

His mother's voice cut out, but in the midst of her talking Luc did catch the word *baby.*

He rubbed his forehead. A flash of a diamond ring, a snippet of Alana in tears saying something about a pregnancy...

"To think she could trick you into marriage simply by saying she's pregnant was absurd," his mother went on, oblivious to his inner turmoil. "The timing of you purchasing this getaway house was perfect. Alana has no idea where you are."

The timing?

Luc spun around, glancing in through the open doors. Beyond the living area was the kitchen, where Kate stood preparing dinner. Instantly, he saw it all. His mother's single, damning word *timing* had triggered an avalanche of memories.

Kate was his assistant. No doubt about that, but they weren't engaged. They were strictly employee-employer, and that had been the extent of their relationship...until just a few days ago.

He felt sick to his stomach as he reached out, seeking the edge of a wrought-iron chair. He needed support, and right now all he could call upon was an inanimate object.

"Alana has no place in this family, Lucas."

Luc swallowed, his eyes remaining locked on Kate. Obviously, he'd been played by two women in his life—two women he'd trusted and let in intimately—on so many levels.

No wonder she was always so hesitant to let him in on his past. Kate's silence probably had little to do with the doctor's warnings and everything to do with her own agenda.

How could he have been so blind? How the hell could Kate have taken advantage of his vulnerability like that? Being manipulative wasn't like her, or at least not like the Kate he'd known. What had changed? Why had she felt it necessary to lie to his face, to go along with this charade that they were engaged?

Luc closed his eyes, gritting his teeth. "Mom, I'll call you back later. The connection is bad with the weather."

The call was cut off before he could finish. This storm was going to be a big one and he didn't just mean the one brewing outside.

Luc held the phone down at his side, dropped his head and tried like hell to forget the images, the emotions that went along with the fact he'd slept with Kate. He'd had sex with his assistant. He'd thought himself in love with her, believed that he'd be marrying her, making her the next queen.

She knew full well he didn't step over the line of professional boundaries. He'd outlined that fact for her a year ago when their attraction had crept to the surface, and he'd wanted to nip it in the bud. Kate knew every single thing about him and she'd used that to her advantage. She knew of the real fiancée, the fake pregnancy, and even after he'd brought up having visions of a baby, she'd said nothing.

How far would she have let this farce go? How long was she intending to lie straight to his face? Earlier she'd claimed she loved him.

Luc's heart clenched. Love had no place in the midst of lies and deceit.

Bringing his eyes back up, he caught her gaze across the open space. She smiled, a smile that he'd once trusted, and Luc felt absolutely nothing but disgust.

He knew exactly what he had to do.

When he hadn't returned her smile, Kate worried. Again she wondered who he'd been talking to on the phone. Something or someone had upset him.

Well, whatever it was, she couldn't let that hold her back. She couldn't keep finding excuses to put this discussion off.

"Dinner is ready," she called, setting the plates on the old, scarred table.

She glanced at the bouquet she'd purchased just the other day at the street market. She and Luc had shared so many amazing memories in such a short time, but she couldn't even relish them because they were built upon the lies she'd created using the feeble excuse that it was for his benefit. No, it would be to his benefit to know exactly what was going on in his life.

Nervousness spiked through her, settling deep. Kate smoothed a hand down her knee-length halter dress and took a deep breath as she stood beside her chair and waited for him to come in. Luc entered through the patio doors, closed them, set his phone on the coffee table and crossed to her.

"Smells great," he told her, offering a wide smile.

When he leaned down to kiss her cheek, Kate closed her eyes for the briefest of moments. Getting wrapped up in this entire scenario of playing house would only hurt her more. She wished more than anything that every bit of this scene playing out were true. Wished Luc would always look at her as if he loved her, as if he wanted to spend his life with her.

"My mother called," he told her after a long moment of silence. "She asked how everything was."

Kate moved the fish around on her plate, too nervous to actually eat. "I'm sure she's worried about you."

"She cares about me. I assume anyone who cares for me would be worried."

Kate's eyes slid up to his, a knot in her throat forming when she saw him staring back at her. "Yes. You have a great many people who love you."

"And what about you, Kate?" He held her gaze another moment before looking back to his plate. "Do you love me?"

Kate set her fork down, reached over to take his hand and squeezed. "I have so much in my heart for you, Luc."

When he said nothing, they finished eating, picked up the dishes and set them on the counter.

"Leave them," Luc told her, taking her hand. "Come with me."

When he led her toward the bedroom, Kate's heart started beating harder in her chest. She couldn't let him start kissing her, undressing her or even touching more than just her hand, because she'd melt instantly and not be able to follow through with her plan to spill her guts.

She trailed into the room after him. The bed in the center of the floor mocked her. Never again would they lie there in a tangle of arms and legs.

They never should have.

"Luc." She pulled her hand from his. "We can't."

He turned, quirking a brow. "Can't what?"

Kate shook her head, glancing away. She couldn't look him in the eyes. She didn't want to see his face when she revealed the truth.

"You can't make love to me?" He stepped closer, rest-

ing his hands on her shoulders. "Or you can't continue
to play the role of doting fiancée? Because I have to
tell you, you did a remarkable job of lying to my face."

Kate jerked her head up, meeting his cold, hard stare.
All breath whooshed out of her lungs as fear gripped
her heart like a vise.

"Apparently my real fiancée has been trying to get
in touch with me," he went on, dropping his hands and
stepping back as if he couldn't stand to touch Kate anymore. "After I heard my mother say that, the pieces
started clicking into place."

Kate wrapped her arms around her waist. "You remember everything?"

"I know you're my assistant and you lied, manipu-
lated and schemed to get into my bed." Luc laughed,
the sound mocking. "Now I know why we never slept
together before."

The pain in his voice sliced her heart open. Words
died in her throat. Any defense she had was moot at
this point.

"How far would you have gone, Kate? Would you
have walked down the aisle and pretended to love me
forever?"

She did love him. She'd chosen the absolute worst
way to show him, but she truly did love the man. Kate
pressed her lips together and remained still, waiting for
the continuation of her punishment.

"Would you have gone so far as to have my kids?"

He took a step forward, but Kate squared her shoulders. She wasn't afraid of him and she wasn't going
to turn and run, no matter how much she wanted to.
Right now, he was entitled to lash out at her, and she
had to take it.

"How could you do this to me?" His voice was low,

calm, cold. "Now I know why you cried after we had sex in the shower. Apparently, the guilt got to you, but only for a short time, because you were quick to get back in my bed."

Kate squeezed her arms tighter, as if to keep his hurtful words from seeping in. She glanced away, out the glass doors toward the sun, which had all but set.

"Look at me," he demanded. "You don't get to drift away. You started this and you're damn well going to face reality and give me the answers I want. Are you even going to say anything?"

Kate shook her head. "Anything I say won't change the fact that I lied to you, and you won't believe any defense I have."

Luc threw his arms out. "What was your motivation, Kate? Did you think I'd fall in love with you? Did you think you'd play with my mind for a bit?"

"No," she whispered through the tears clogging her throat. "Hurting you was the last thing I wanted to do."

"Oh, you didn't hurt me," he retorted, his face reddening. "I can't be hurt by someone I don't love. Didn't you know that? I'm furious I ever trusted you."

Kate nodded. "When we made love—"

"We didn't make love," he spat. Luc took a step closer, so close she could see the whiskey-colored flecks in his eyes. "We had sex. Meaningless sex that never should've happened."

Kate looked into his eyes, hoping to see a flicker of that emotion she'd seen during their days together, or when they'd been intimate. But all that stared back at her was hatred. Anything he thought he'd felt days ago, even hours ago, was false. The old Luc was back and harsher than ever.

"I'll call for someone to come pick me up," she told

him. "I'll be at the cottage until then. Anything I have here I can send for later."

Kate walked out of the room, surprised he didn't call her back so he could finish her off.

Mercifully, he let her go. She couldn't cry in front of him, didn't want him to think she was using tears as a defense. Her tears were a product of her own selfishness. She'd lived it up for a few days, had had the man she loved in her arms and had even worn his ring.

Kate stepped out onto the patio and glanced down at the gem on her finger. Thunder rolled, lightning streaked in the not so distant sky as fat drops of rain pelted her.

"Kate," Luc called from behind her.

She froze.

"What the hell are you doing, just standing in the storm?"

Kate turned, blinking the rain out of her eyes. At this point she couldn't honestly tell what was rain and what were tears.

"Do you care?" she asked.

"I'm angry, but I don't want to see anyone struck by lightning."

Luc stood in the doorway, his broad frame filling the open space. The lights behind him flickered and then everything went black, save for the candles she'd lit on the dining room table and the fat pillar on the coffee table.

Cursing under his breath, Luc stepped back. "Get in here."

Slowly, Kate crossed the wet patio, hugging her midsection against the cool drops. She brushed by him, shivering from the brief contact and cringing the second he stepped back and broke the touch.

"I just—"

"I'll be in my room." He cut her off with a wave of his hand as if she was nothing more than a nuisance. "Don't take this as a sign that I care. You can stay in here until the storm passes, and that's all."

Luc went to the dining room table, picked up a candle and walked away, leaving her shivering in the darkened living room. The pillar on the coffee table flickered, but she couldn't see much beyond the sofa. Kate sank down, pulling her feet up onto the cushion, hugging her knees to her chest.

Closing her eyes, she dropped her head forward and sighed. For the first time in her life she prayed the storm would stop. She had to get to her cottage, pack her things and call for someone to come and get her.

The hurt that had settled into this house was more than she could handle, and she didn't want to be here when Luc came out of his room. She didn't want to see that anger, that wounded look in his eyes again, knowing she'd put it there.

Whatever they'd had, be it their professional relationship or this fake engagement, she'd ruined any chance of ever having Luc in her life again. She'd taken what didn't belong to her, and she had no choice now but to live with the consequences.

Twelve

Luc must be insane. That was the only explanation for why he found himself crossing the path between the main house and the cottage so early in the morning. He hadn't slept all night. Every moment since his fall kept playing out in his mind like a movie, only he couldn't stop this one.

Kate's rigidity when he would initially touch her, her hesitancy to make love to him, why she was so adamant about him not buying her things at the market. The signs were there, but he'd assumed she was his fiancée, and she'd never said any differently. She'd had time, plenty of time, to tell him the truth. Even if the doctor hadn't given the order to not feed him any information, Luc was pretty sure she still would've kept up the charade.

Now that he'd had time to think, he'd fully processed how deeply her betrayal had sliced him. How could someone get so far into his life, work with him every single day, and manage to take advantage of him like that? Had he been that easy to manipulate? More important, how far would she have been willing to take that twisted game she'd played?

He wanted answers and he wanted them five minutes ago. He wasn't waiting another second to find out what the hell she'd been thinking to even contemplate getting away with such a potentially life-altering, monumental lie.

The anger raging inside him didn't stem just from her deception, but from the fact he'd fallen for her; making her betrayal even worse, Kate knew the emotional state he was in, just coming off a major breakup. Not only that, she knew he didn't date, much less sleep, with staff. How could she claim to care about him and then betray him in the next breath?

Even now that he knew everything, he still cared. He still ached for her, because with his old memories, he also had fresh ones. Memories he'd made with Kate, now tarnished by lies.

As Luc stepped into a clearing of lush plants, he glanced down to the dock. He froze when he spotted Kate standing by the water, two suitcases at her feet. She was not leaving without telling him why the hell she'd done this to him. She didn't get to escape that easily.

Marching toward the steps leading down to the beach, Luc had no clue what he'd say to her. She had plenty of explaining to do, but there was so much inside his mind, so much he wanted to say, he didn't even know where to start. He figured once he opened his mouth, things would start pouring out, most likely hurtful things. He couldn't care about her feelings just yet... if ever.

Kate jerked around as he approached. The dark circles beneath her eyes, the red rims, indicated she'd slept about as well as he had. The storm had lasted most of the night and he truly had no clue when she'd ended up leaving the main house. He'd closed the bedroom door, wanting to shut her out. Unfortunately, his bedroom was filled with visions of Kate.

The shower, the bed, her pair of flip-flops by the closet door, her robe draped across the foot of the bed. She was everywhere, and she'd wedged herself so intimately into his life, as no other woman had.

She'd had so much control over the situation and she'd used that power to consume him. Now he had to figure out how the hell to get out from under her spell, because even seeing her right now, with all his bubbling rage, he found his body still responded to her.

Damn it. How could he still want her? Anything that had happened between them was dead to him. He couldn't think back on those times, because just like this "engagement," they meant nothing.

Her eyes widened as he came to stand within inches of her. "I'm waiting for a boat. My father is sending one of the guards to pick me up."

"Why?" Luc asked, clenching his fists at his sides. "Before you leave, tell me why you lied to me."

Her head tipped slightly as she studied him. "Would it matter?"

Strands of her long, dark hair had slipped loose from her knot and were dancing about her shoulders. She had on another of those little strapless sundresses, this one black. Appropriately matching the color of his mood.

"Maybe not, but I deserve to know why you would betray my trust and think it was okay."

Dark eyes held his. Part of him wanted to admire her

for not backing away, not playing the victim or defending herself. The other part wished she'd defend herself and say something, so they could argue about it and get everything out in the open. He needed a good outlet, someone to yell at, and the perfect target stood directly in front of him.

"I was shocked at first that you thought I was your fiancée," she told him, her pink tongue darting out to lick her lips. She shoved a wayward strand of hair behind her ear and shrugged. "Then I wanted to see what the doctor would say before I told you otherwise. He said not to give you any information, so I didn't. I didn't want to lie to you, Luc. I was in a tough spot and everything blew out of my control before I knew what was happening. I tried to keep my distance, but once we had sex, I wanted more. I took what I shouldn't have. Nothing I can say can change that fact, but I am sorry I hurt you."

Luc propped his hands on his hips, waiting to hear more, but she remained silent and continued to hold his gaze. "There has to be another reason, a deeper motivation than you simply being afraid to tell me."

Kate's eyes darted away as she turned her back to him and focused on the water again. Not a boat in sight. He still had time to get answers from her before she left.

"My reasons are irrelevant."

He almost didn't hear her whispered answer over the ocean breeze. With her back to him, Luc wasn't sure what was worse, looking her in the eyes or looking at that exposed, creamy neck he could practically taste. He would never taste that skin again.

He cursed beneath his breath, raked a hand down his face and sighed. "What were you trying to gain?" he demanded. "I'm giving you the opportunity to say something here, Kate. Tell me why I shouldn't fire you, why I shouldn't remove you from every aspect of my life."

The low hum of a motor jerked his attention in the direction of the royal yacht moving toward them. Kate said nothing as she turned, picking up her suitcases.

Here he was gearing up for a good fight, and she couldn't even afford him that? Did she feel nothing at all? How had he misread her all these years?

If she wasn't going to talk now, then fine. He wasn't done with her, but if she needed to go, he'd let her. She could stew and worry back in Ilha Beleza. Luc actually wanted her uncomfortable, contemplating his next move. She deserved to be miserable, and he had to steel himself against any remorse.

His mother had always taught him to respect women, which he did, but right now that didn't mean he had to make her life all rainbows and sunshine, either.

"Go back to the palace," he told her, hating how she refused to look at him. "I'll be home in a few days and we'll add on to that schedule we finalized the other night."

Kate threw him a glance over her shoulder. "What?"

Luc stepped around her, blocking her view of the incoming boat. He waited until her eyes locked onto his. "You're not quitting. You're going to be with me until I know what game you're playing. And don't try to get sneaky once you're back. I have eyes and ears everywhere."

Her chin tipped up in defiance…a quality he'd once admired when she was speaking with the media or other pushy individuals. "I think it's best if I resign."

Luc gripped her shoulders, cursing himself for having a weakness where she was concerned, considering all she'd done. "I don't care what you think is best.

You're mine until I say otherwise. You started this game, Kate. You're going to see it through to the end."

Pushing away from her, he stalked toward the main house. Not once did he consider glancing back. He was finished looking over his shoulder to see if anyone was stabbing him in the back or betraying him. From here on out, he was regaining control, and he was damn well going to come out on top.

Luc stared at the area he used to call his kitchen. If this royalty thing didn't work out, he was seriously getting a job with a contractor. Demolishing things was an excellent outlet for his anger.

Wiping his forearm across his forehead, he sank down onto a dining room chair and surveyed his destruction. The cabinets were torn out; the countertop lay beneath the rubble. He'd pulled the fridge out enough that he could get to the food, but other than that, he'd completely torn up the space.

Kate had been gone a week. Two weeks had passed since he'd arrived here, and he was heading home tomorrow. In these past seven days alone, he'd had more than enough time to reflect on everything, and he still had no clue what he was going to do once he saw her again.

He'd had to sleep in the guest room on a lumpy old mattress because he couldn't lie in his master suite without smelling her, seeing her…feeling her at his side. The shower he'd so loved when the renovations started was now tainted, because all he could see was Kate's wet body as he claimed her with the false knowledge they were a real couple. They'd been damn good together, but he would never, ever admit that to her or anybody else.

Luc's cell chimed. He thought about ignoring it, but figured he'd at least see who wanted to talk to him.

Crossing the open room, he glanced at his phone on the coffee table. Mikos, his best friend.

Considering he had called Mikos three days ago and spilled his guts like some whiny high school girl with sad love songs playing in the background, Luc assumed his friend was calling to check on him.

"Hey, man," he answered with a sigh.

"You still sound like hell."

Luc laughed, sinking onto the sofa, resting his elbow on the arm. "Yeah, well, I feel like it. What's up?"

"Just checking in."

"Shouldn't you be planning the wedding of the century?" Luc asked, feeling a slight pang of envy.

Envy? Why the hell would he be envious? Sure, he needed to be married because of the throne, but he didn't want to be tied to one woman. No, Mikos had found the perfect woman for him, and Luc was happy for both of them.

There was no perfect woman for Luc. Hadn't he proved that by getting too close to two very convincing liars?

"The wedding is planned down to the last petal and place card," Mikos stated. "Are you still in?"

Luc was supposed to stand up with Mikos, right next to Mikos's brother, Stefan. An honor Luc wasn't letting Kate's untimely backstabbing steal from him.

"I'm in. I'm not letting my disaster ruin your day."

"Have you talked to Kate?"

Luc closed his eyes. Even hearing her name elicited a mixture of feelings, a myriad of emotions. Beyond the hurt, the anger and the bitterness there was still that underlying fact that he wanted the hell out of her. How twisted was that?

"No. I'm heading back tomorrow," Luc answered.

"What are you going to do?"

"I have no clue, man."

Mikos sighed. "Want my advice?"

"You're going to give it anyway, so why ask?"

"I am," Mikos agreed with a laugh. "Figure out why she lied. You told me once you had a thing for her. Maybe she was acting on her own feelings and taking a cue from yours before the accident."

"Are you defending her actions?" The last thing Luc wanted to hear was a justifiable cause. Damn it, he wanted to be angry, wanted to place all the blame on her.

"Hell, no. I'm saying love is a strong emotion."

"You're too blinded by this wedding," Luc replied. "Kate doesn't love me. You don't lie and scheme with those you love, no matter the circumstances."

"I did to Darcy," Mikos reminded him. "She had no idea who I was, and I was totally in love with her. I nearly lost her, but she forgave me. You know how things can get mixed up, Luc."

Luc recalled that time when Mikos's nanny had first been hired. She'd had no clue Mikos was a widowed prince. The two had fallen in love before Mikos could fully explain the truth.

"Our situations are completely different," Luc muttered. "I'm not forgiving her. No matter what."

"Just make sure you really think this through before you go off on her once you get home," Mikos warned. "What she did was wrong, no doubt about it. But she's not like Alana. I know that's something you'll never forget or get over, but Alana had an ulterior motive from the start. You've known Kate for years and she's never once done you wrong."

Luc finished the call, unable to think of anything else but the truth Mikos had laid out before him. No, Kate had never deceived him in any way before. She'd been the best assistant he'd ever had. To be honest, the only reason he hadn't pursued her before was because of their working relationship and possible repercussions to his ascension to the throne. With the mess he'd gotten himself into lately, it would be a miracle if the press didn't rip his family's reputation to shreds if the truth came out.

Once he returned to Ilha Beleza, he and Kate would have a one-on-one chat, now that they'd both had time to absorb all that had happened. They needed to talk. He couldn't keep her around if he didn't trust her. And that was the problem. When it came to his professional life, he trusted no one else.

Unfortunately, when it came to his personal life, he didn't trust her one bit…but that didn't stop him from wanting her. Even this week apart hadn't dimmed his attraction toward her. Which begged the question: What the hell was going to happen once he got home? And would he be able to control himself?

Thirteen

His desk was exactly how he always kept it—neat, tidy and organized, with his schedule in hard copies just as he wanted it. He knew there would also be emails on his computer with the same information.

Kate had kept up her end of the bargain and continued working just as if she hadn't torn their entire lives to shreds. He didn't know whether to be relieved or angry that she was still here, still within reaching distance... not that he was going to reach out to her. He had more pride than that.

Luc flipped through the papers, even though he'd looked through his email earlier and knew what he had coming up. Mikos's wedding was only two weeks away, and other than that, there were a handful of meetings and social events at which he was expected to make an appearance. He'd been knocked down so many times in the past few months he didn't know if he had the energy to put forth for anyone outside his immediate family and staff. He was so exhausted, spent and depleted from trying to perform damage control on his personal life, there was no way he could keep up with his royal obligations, too.

Thankfully, from the looks of his schedule, Kate had helped him dodge any media interviews over the next few months. For that he was grateful, but not enough to seek her out and thank her. He wasn't ready to thank her for anything…and he might never be.

"Oh, sweetheart. You're back."

Luc glanced toward the high, arched doorway as his mother breezed in. The woman possessed more elegance and grace than anyone he'd ever known. With her polished style and loving grin, she made the perfect queen, but her reign was soon coming to an end. Well, it would be if he managed to find a way to secure his title before his birthday, and without a wife.

Luc crossed the room and relished her embrace. Even though he'd always been close with his parents, he didn't have it in him to discuss all the ways he was struggling right now.

"How are you?" she asked, pulling back to assess him. Clutching his arms, she studied his face. "No more symptoms? You remember everything now?"

Luc nodded. "I'm perfectly fine."

She held on to him another moment, then broke the contact. "We need to talk."

He crossed his arms as his mother shut the double doors, giving them complete privacy.

"Have you seen Kate since you've been back?" she asked.

Luc shook his head. "No."

"Darling, she told me what happened." His mother

reached out, took one of his hands in hers and squeezed. "I'm sure she left out some details, but I know you believed she was your fiancée, and she went along with it."

Luc gritted his teeth. Seriously? Kate went to his mom?

"I wished I'd learned this from you," she went on. "I can't imagine how angry you must be, and I know you're feeling betrayed—"

"Don't defend her," Luc growled. "I'm not near that point."

"I'm not defending her actions." His mother smiled, tipping her head. "I just want you to really think about how you're going to handle this. Kate is a wonderful woman and I've always been so fond of her. I know we have a rule about remaining distant from employees, but she and her parents have been around so long, they're like family."

His feelings for Kate were far from family-like, and he sure as hell hadn't been feeling brotherly in that shower.

"I will admit I'm surprised you didn't fire her," his mother added. "She's good for you, Luc. She's the best assistant you've ever had. I'm proud of you for not blowing up."

"It was tempting."

Temptation. The word seemed to go hand in hand with Kate's name.

"I still don't know what to do, but for now, she's going to be working for me like always. I don't have time to find a new assistant, and I sure as hell don't want to have to get to know someone new. I've got enough of a mess to deal with."

"We do need to figure out what's going to happen on your birthday." His mother pursed her lips, as if in deep thought. "Your father would change the law if he could, but the truth is, we never dreamed…"

Luc laughed, the sound void of all humor. "I know. You never thought a child of yours would still be single at thirty-five. It's okay to say it."

She squeezed his arm. "We'll figure something out. We have to."

Luc nodded, unable to speak past the lump of worry in his throat. Failure was not an option. Ever. He was the next leader, for crying out loud. Why couldn't he figure out a way around this ridiculous issue?

"I'll let you get settled back in, then." His mother reached up, kissed him on the cheek. "Glad you're back home and safe. And I'm glad you didn't fire Kate. She means more to this family than you may realize."

What did that mean? Did his mother actually think he and Kate…

No. That was ridiculous. As torn as he was, he couldn't entertain the idea that Kate could remain in his life as anything other than his assistant…and even that role was still up in the air. He'd have to worry about that later. At this point, time was against him, and finding another assistant before finding a wife—or before the coronation—was impossible.

Once he was alone again, Luc turned and went to his desk. Bracing his palms on its glossy top, he leaned forward and closed his eyes. He would do a great job ruling this country, as his father had before him. Luc just needed a chance to prove he could do so without a wife.

The echo of soft footsteps hit him and he knew instantly who would be behind him. He didn't turn, though. He wasn't quite ready to take in the sight of Kate with all her beauty and sexiness.

The click of the heels stopped, Luc's heart beat faster

than he liked. Damn it, he hadn't even turned to look at her, hadn't said a word, yet she had already sent his body into overdrive.

"I'll come back."

Her soft words washed over him as he turned to face her.

"No." He spoke to her retreating back, and she froze in the doorway. "Come in and close the door."

She stood still so long, he thought for sure she wasn't going to stay. After a moment, she stepped back, closed the door and whipped around to face him.

Luc hadn't thought it possible, but he still found her breathtakingly gorgeous and arousing. Seeing Kate in a dark blue suit, with a fitted jacket that hugged her waist and accentuated her breasts, and her snug skirt made it hard for him to form words right now. As her heels clicked across the floor, his eyes were drawn to her open-toed, animal-print pumps. Damn, she looked like a woman who was ready to be stripped and laid out on his desk.

What was worse, now that he'd had her wrapped all around him, he knew exactly how amazing they were together. Why was he paying a penance in all this? He was the victim.

She stopped well out of his reach, clasped her hands in front of her and met his gaze. "I didn't know you were back," she said. "I was just coming in to make sure your computer was ready to go when you needed it."

Luc tore his gaze from her painted red lips and glanced at his desk. He hadn't even noticed the new computer. Hell, he hadn't even asked for one. Once again, she stayed on top of things and kept his life running smoothly.

"Where's my old one?" he asked.

"All of the palace computers have been upgraded, and they put yours in while you were gone. I made sure the security on yours was set up the same as your old one, and I also made sure your old files were transferred. Everything is on there under the same names, just how they always were."

When he glanced back at her, there wasn't a hint of any emotion on her face. Not a twinge of a smile, no dark circles under her eyes to indicate she'd been losing sleep. Absolutely nothing.

Which pissed him off even more.

"Is this how it's going to be?" he asked, gritting his teeth. "With you pretending you didn't change the dynamics between us?"

Kate blinked, pulled in a deep breath and shook her head. "I don't know what you want from me. I can't erase what happened, yet you still want me to work for you, so I'm doing what I can under the circumstances. I can't tell you what you want to know, because—"

She spun around. Luc waited for her to finish, but she kept her back to him as silence settled heavily between them. There was no easy way, no secret formula for them to get beyond this. He wasn't all that convinced they could move on, despite what his mother and Mikos had said during their pep talks.

"Because why?" he pressed, when she remained quiet. "Why can't you tell me your reasons? I'm ready to hear it. I *need* to hear it, Kate."

Still nothing. Luc stepped forward, closing the space between them. "Damn it, I deserve more than your silence. You can't hide like this. You don't get that right. Tell me what prompted you to not only lie, but keep up the charade and play me so perfectly that you ended up in my bed."

"Don't," she whispered. "Don't make me say it."

Luc grabbed her arm, spun her around and forced himself to hold her watery gaze. "I refuse to let you out of this scot-free."

Squaring her shoulders, tipping her chin up and swiping a hand beneath her eye as one lone tear streaked out, Kate nodded. "Fine. You want to know why I did it? Why I lied to you so easily? Besides the doctor's orders of not saying anything more, besides the fact that the deception just got out of control, I knew it was the only time in my life you'd ever look at me like you cared for me. Like you actually wanted me. I knew it was wrong. I never justified my actions, and I won't defend them, because there's no way to make any of it okay. But don't make me tell you more. I can't, Luc."

Her voice cracked on his name. Luc kept his hand on her arm as he took a half step closer, nearly towering over her. "You can," he murmured. "Tell me the rest. Now."

He was so torn between arousal and anger. He'd always heard there was a fine line between hatred and passion. No truer words were ever spoken.

"I fell in love with you," she whispered, her eyes locking onto his. "Is that what you wanted to hear? Do you hate me so much that humiliating me is the only way to make yourself get past the anger? Well, now you know. I've bared my soul to you, Luc. You know about my adoption, which few people do. You know my secret fantasies—you're the only one in that category—and that I'm in love with a man who'd rather belittle me than ever forgive me, let alone love me back. My fault, I know, but that doesn't stop the hurt."

A viselike grip squeezed his heart at her declaration. Why did he feel anything akin to sympathy toward her? She'd done every bit of this to herself, pulling him along for the ride.

"You don't love me." He dropped his hand and stepped back. "You don't lie to someone and manipulate them, taking advantage of their weaknesses, when you love them."

"I never lied to you before this and I won't lie to you again," she vowed, crossing her arms over her chest. "So when I tell you I love you, I'm being honest. I know my word means nothing to you, and I know I went about everything the wrong way. There is no excuse for my behavior, so I'm not going to stand here and try to make one."

Luc watched as she pulled herself together, patting her damp cheeks, smoothing her hair behind her shoulders and standing tall.

Even through all this, she remained strong. He wanted to hate her, because that would be so much easier than to stand here and be torn in two. She'd betrayed the trust they had built, yet at the same time she had tried to keep her distance. He'd been the one to pursue the intimacy. He could look at this situation from so many angles, but none of them gave him the answer or made things any easier.

"You have every right to fire me—I deserve it. But if you insist on keeping me, I think it's best if we keep our relationship professional and try to move on. That means no rehashing the mistakes I made. I can't have you throwing them in my face."

The longer she spoke, the stronger her voice got. The woman who'd emotionally professed her love for him just moments earlier had transformed back into the businesslike assistant he'd always known. Who was the real Kate?

Was she the loving, passionate woman back at the beach house? Was she the take-charge assistant, or was she the conniving woman who'd ruthlessly insinuated herself into his life when he'd been weak?

"I agree that from here on out, we'll keep our relationship strictly professional."

Luc prayed like hell he was telling the truth. He needed to keep his head on straight, focus on securing the title and not think about how much he'd fallen for his assistant.

Well, that plan to keep things professional was about to get blown apart.

Kate closed her eyes, gripped the stick and willed the results to be different.

Peeking through one eyelid, she still saw the two pink lines glaring back at her. If they had been on a billboard or neon sign they couldn't have been any more eye-catching… She couldn't look anywhere else.

And no matter how long she stared at it, the results were still going to be the same. Positive.

Something between a moan and a cry escaped her as she came to her feet. Staring at herself in the vanity mirror, Kate didn't know what she expected to see. She didn't look any different, but in the past three minutes the course of her entire life had been altered.

Now what should she do? She was pregnant with Luc's baby and the man practically loathed her, unless she was writing a speech for him or running interference for some engagement he didn't want to attend.

There was no getting around this. She'd been on the pill since she was a teen, to keep her cycle regular, but they hadn't used a condom the times they'd been intimate, and birth control wasn't fail-safe…obviously.

There was only one answer. She'd promised Luc she'd never lie to him again, and she certainly wasn't going to start off by keeping this baby a secret.

Laying the test stick on the back of the vanity, Kate washed her hands and stepped out of the restroom. She wanted to find Luc now. This couldn't wait, because the nerves in her stomach were threatening to overtake her. She had to find him.

At this point in the day, she honestly had no idea what he was doing, but she did know he was working from home. If she stopped to think, she could figure out his schedule—she had created it. But her mind wasn't in work mode right now and she couldn't process anything other than the fact she was having a baby with a man she loved…a man who could hardly look at her. She was on the verge of freaking out.

Her lies had not only killed the trust Luc had for her, now the whirlwind of secrets had formed a new life…literally.

Kate's hand slid over her stomach as she made her way out of her office and into the wide hallway. She smiled as she passed one of the maids, but her smile faded the second she reached Luc's office door. In just moments, both their lives and the future of this country would be changed forever.

She was carrying an heir.

Kate rested her forehead against the smooth wood and closed her eyes. The sooner she told Luc, the sooner they could start figuring out what to do. Summoning all the strength she possessed, she tapped on his office door, cursing her shaking hands. She heard familiar voices on the other side. Apparently, he was having a private meeting with his parents. Still, this couldn't wait.

Yes, they were the king and queen. Yes, Kate was being rude by interrupting. But she didn't care.

Fisting her hand, she knocked louder and longer, until the door jerked open to an angry-looking Luc. His jaw clenched, his lips thinned, and once he saw her, his eyes narrowed.

"Kate? We're in the middle of something."

Pushing by him, she offered a shaky smile to his parents, who sat with their eyes locked on her. "I'm sorry, but this can't wait."

Ana Silva rose to her feet and crossed the room. Kate swallowed as her heart started beating faster. She was going to be sick. The overwhelming urge to pass out or throw up all over the Persian rug had nothing to do with the pregnancy.

"Darling, you're trembling," Ana said. "Come, sit down."

"We're in the middle of something," Luc repeated.

Luc's father stood, gesturing toward the chair he'd just vacated. "Here, Kate."

Luc muttered a string of Portuguese slang.

"I'm sorry," Kate muttered. "I didn't mean to cause a scene. I just need a few minutes with Luc."

His parents exchanged a look and Kate noticed Luc standing off to the side, arms crossed, jaw still clenched. He wasn't happy. Too bad she was about to drop another bomb on his life. Would he be even angrier at her? Most likely, but hiding the pregnancy wasn't an option.

Kate closed her eyes as she rested her elbows on her knees and dropped her head into her hands. Luc's parents muttered something to him and moments later Kate heard the office door click shut.

"What the hell is this all about?" Luc demanded.

Kate pushed her hair away from her face as she looked up. He was leaning against the edge of his desk, ankles crossed, palms resting on either side of his slim hips. Wearing dark designer jeans and a fitted black T-shirt, he didn't look like a member of the royal family, but he still exuded power. It was the stare, the unyielding body language, that told her she needed to get on with her speech…one she hadn't rehearsed at all.

"I…" Kate shook her head, came to her feet. No way could she remain still; her body was too shaky, too wound up to stay seated.

"Just say it."

Luc's harsh words cut through her. Kate stopped pacing, turned and gazed at him. "I'm pregnant."

He stared at her for several moments without saying a word. Then suddenly, he burst out laughing, and straightened.

"Nice try, Kate." His expression sobered. "That's already been used on me."

"What?"

His words took a moment to sink in. He didn't believe her. Of course he wouldn't. Why should he? He'd been played for a fool by his ex-fiancée, who tried the pregnancy trap, and Kate had also lied to him.

"Luc, I'm not lying," she reiterated. "I have the test in my office bathroom. I need to call Dr. Couchot to confirm with a blood test, though."

Something dark clouded Luc's eyes. "You did this on purpose."

Fury rose to the surface, pushing through the nerves. No matter how much she loved him, no matter how much she wished he would see her as a woman worthy of his love and trust, Kate refused to stand here and be degraded and blamed for something they'd both taken part in.

"I think it was you who came to me," she retorted,

crossing her arms over her chest. "You think I wanted a child with a man who doesn't love me? I made a mistake by lying to you, but I'm not pathetic and I'm not trying to trap you. I promised I would always be honest with you, and I just found out about this myself ten minutes ago. So lose the ego. I don't want to snag you that much."

Kate turned to go and managed to get across the room with her hand on the doorknob before Luc grabbed her arm and spun her back around. Leaning flat against the door, trapped between the wood and Luc's hard body, she stared up into those eyes that could make a woman forget all her problems…almost. Even the great Prince Lucas Silva wasn't that powerful.

"You think you can drop that bomb and then just walk out?" he demanded. "We're not done here."

"We both need to process this before we say anything we might regret." Though they'd already said plenty to cause damaging scars. "I just need… I need to think this through, Luc."

His eyes widened. "What's there to think through? You're having my child. I will be part of his or her life."

A sliver of relief coursed through her. "I would never deny you the chance to be with your child."

Tears welled up, the familiar burn in her throat formed and Kate cursed herself. She absolutely hated crying, hated the predicament she was in, but hated even more that she was pulling in an innocent child.

"I'm scared," she whispered, closing her eyes.

She jerked when Luc's hand slid over her cheek. Focusing back on him, she saw something in his eyes she hadn't expected…fear. Obviously, she wasn't the only one with insecurities.

"No matter what happened prior to this moment,

I won't leave you alone with a baby." He dropped his hand, but didn't step back. "Our baby."

When he stood so close, smelling so amazingly familiar and feeling so sexy against her, Kate couldn't think straight. She wished she didn't still want him, wished she'd never lied to him to begin with. And she truly wished something as beautiful as creating a life with the man she loved hadn't been tainted because of her lies.

"I don't want our baby to suffer from my actions," she told him. "I want to be able to work with you on this, and I know the timing—"

She cut herself off with a sad laugh. "Sorry. There would be no good timing," she corrected. "I just meant with the throne, your birthday and all of that on your mind, I didn't mean to add to your stress, but you needed to know."

When he said nothing, Kate carefully turned. There was no way to avoid rubbing up against him, because he'd barely moved since he'd trapped her against the door.

Luc's hands came up to cup her shoulders as he moved in behind her.

"Who are you, Kate?" he whispered.

Her head dropped against the wood as she tried to ignore all of the ways her body responded to his. Tried and failed miserably.

"Are you the efficient assistant? The woman who stands up for me to the public? Are you the woman who lied to me for selfish reasons? Or are you the woman who claims to love me and who's now carrying my child?"

Drawing in a shaky breath, Kate glanced over her shoulder just enough to catch his gaze. "I'm all of them."

"Part of me hates you for what you did." Luc's eyes darted down to her lips. "I wish I still didn't want you so damn much."

Breath caught in Kate's throat as Luc pushed away and stalked back to his desk. He kept his back to her, as if that revelation had cost him dearly. She had no doubt he hadn't meant to let that slip, and as much as she wanted to revel in his obvious discomfort over the fact that he wanted her, Kate had to put this baby first, above all else.

Even the fact that her own heart was still beating for only one man.

Fourteen

He hadn't planned on taking Kate to Greece for his best friend's wedding, but once she had opened her heart to him and bared her soul, Luc wasn't able to deny the fact that he still wanted her.

Plans were taking root in his mind and he was going to have to take action. Perhaps he could have Kate, the crown and his child without ever putting his heart on the line where she was concerned. Surely she'd stay for the sake of their child. Why not make it official, so he could keep the title that was rightfully his?

But if he wanted to sway her into marriage, he needed to start convincing her, or she'd never say yes.

No, he hadn't forgiven her for lying, but she was pregnant, confirmed by Dr. Couchot, and Luc knew the child was his. The plan forming in his mind was anything but nice, but he couldn't back down. Too much was at stake.

Luc glanced across the aisle to where Kate had re-clined her seat and was curled onto her side, with her hand beneath her cheek. She'd been exhausted when they'd left that morning, and he'd nearly told her to stay behind, but he knew she was just as stubborn as him and wouldn't listen. Either the baby was making her more tired than usual or she wasn't sleeping because of the stress. Knowing her, it was probably both.

He'd cursed himself every which way after she'd left his office a few days ago. He'd hated how his heart had flipped when she'd whispered her fears. Damn it, he didn't want his heart to be affected by this woman. There was no space in his life for such things. He had a title to secure, and now he had an heir to think about. Kate couldn't fall under the category of things he cared about, because if he allowed that, then she would have the upper hand. Wanting her physically was difficult enough to have to deal with each time she was near.

His mind kept wandering back to how right it had felt when they'd been playing house. He'd gladly dis-missed his family's rule about fraternizing with staff. He would have done anything for her. He'd never felt so connected to a woman in all his life.

Kate embodied sex appeal, that was a given. It had been what had drawn him to her when she'd first come to work for him. He vaguely recalled the little girl, and later on the teen, who used to hang around the palace with her parents.

Then when the time came that he'd needed an assis-tant and Kate had been recommended, he'd jumped at the chance, because her family knew his so well and he knew she'd be a trustworthy candidate. Plus her refer-ences and academics had been superb.

Yet somehow, over the course of a professional relationship that had started out with an attraction, and involved his messy engagement to another woman, Luc's life had spiraled spectacularly out of control.

The irony that he'd gone from a fiancée with a fake pregnancy to a poser fiancée with a real pregnancy was not lost on him. He was a walking tabloid and fodder for the press. Thankfully, Kate was in charge of press releases, and no doubt she'd come up with something amazingly brilliant once they were ready to go public.

Kate stirred in her sleep, letting out a soft moan. The simple sound hit his gut with a swift punch of lust he couldn't ignore. He'd heard those moans in his ear as she'd wrapped her body around his. He'd felt the whisper of breath on his skin that accompanied her sighs.

But no matter how compatible they were in the bedroom, no matter how much he still ached for her on a level he'd never admit aloud, Luc wouldn't, couldn't, allow himself to be pulled into whatever spell Kate had over him.

Even if he would let his guard down and shove the royal rule aside and see a staff member personally, Kate had killed any chance of him ever trusting her fully. So she could sit across from him and make all the noises she wanted; he was ignoring them.

Too bad his body hadn't received that memo, because certain parts of him couldn't forget the intimacy they'd shared.

Luc needed to focus on the brilliant plot he'd started forming. Would she be angry when he approached her with the solution? Yes. Did he care? No. He was plenty angry still, but he wanted her, wanted the crown and refused to allow his heart to become vulnerable again.

The phone near Luc's seat rang and the pilot informed him they'd be landing within a half hour. Once

Luc hung up, he crossed the space and sank down in the plush white leather chair next to Kate. He hated waking her up. Not that he was worried about disturbing her sleep; he was more concerned with the fact he'd have to touch her, have to see her blinking back to reality as she sat there, looking all rumpled and sexy.

As if she was ever *not* appealing. But he couldn't be blinded by lust and sexual chemistry. He didn't need a bed partner, no matter what his body told him. Making love with her was how he'd gotten entangled in this web to begin with.

"Kate."

He purposely said her name loudly, so she'd wake without him having to lay a hand on her. She let out a soft snore and Luc gritted his teeth and called her name again.

Still nothing.

Who was he kidding? It didn't matter if he touched her or not. He wanted her, his body responded to her as it had to no other woman and she was carrying his child. As if he needed another reason to be physically pulled toward her. Knowing she was carrying his child was beyond sexy. There was something so primal about knowing Kate sat there with their baby safely inside her body.

Even when Alana had said she was expecting, Luc hadn't felt this much of a tug on his heart. He'd had an instant protective instinct toward the child, but he'd never felt a bond with Alana.

Damn it, he couldn't afford a tug on his heart or some invisible bond. Kate wasn't trustworthy. Regardless, he didn't need her trust for his plan to work. He didn't need anything from her, because he wouldn't take no for an answer.

Marrying Kate was the only solution. As much as he hated to give in to his country's archaic rule, it was the only way to come out of this situation on top. Some marriages were based on far less than sexual chemistry and they worked just fine.

The fact remained that he still wanted her something fierce. He wanted her with an intensity that scared him, but he had to risk his heart, his sanity, in order to get what he wanted.

Luc reached around, pulled on her seat belt and fastened it with a click. Just as he was about to move away and fasten his own, Kate jerked awake. Sleepy eyes locked onto his and he realized his mistake. He'd leaned in too close, so close he was only inches from her face, and his hand hovered over her abdomen.

"What are you doing?" she asked, her voice husky from sleep.

"Preparing you for landing."

Why hadn't he eased back, and why was he staring at her lips?

"You can't look at me like that, Luc," she whispered. "You don't even like me."

Something clenched in his gut. Something harsher, more intense than lust.

He was a damn *tolo*. Fool. That was the only explanation for having these reactions after what she'd done to him. He needed to focus on the plan, the throne, the baby. Everything else—including his lustful feelings—would have to be put aside.

"I don't trust you," he countered. "There's a difference."

Those heavy lids shielded her dark eyes for a moment as she stared down to where his hands lay on her stomach.

"I didn't trap you," she whispered as her eyes drifted back up to his. "No matter what you think of me, I'd never do that to you or an innocent child."

Luc swallowed as her hand settled over his. There was so much emotion in her eyes, so much he was too afraid to identify, because if he did, he'd start feeling more for her, and he refused to be played like a *fantouche*, a puppet, for a third time.

Pride and ego fueled his decisions. Power and control ran a close second. And all those things combined would get him everything he'd ever wanted…everything he was entitled to.

Luc shifted to sit up, but didn't remove his hand, and for some asinine reason he didn't break eye contact, either. Obviously, he was a glutton for punishment.

"I want you to move into the palace."

Of course, he had bigger plans, but he had to ease her into this. She wasn't the only one skilled at manipulation.

"I'm not sure that's a good idea."

She removed her hand from his, a silent plea for him to move, so he pulled back. The first slight dip in the plane's decent reminded Luc he hadn't fastened his seat belt because he'd been worried for her. He quickly buckled it, then turned his attention back to Kate.

"Why not?" he asked. "Moving into the palace is the ideal solution. We'll be sharing responsibilities. I know we'll hire a nanny, but I plan on being a hands-on dad."

Kate shoved her hair away from her face. A thin sleep mark ran down her cheek. It made her seem so vulnerable, and it was all he could do not to touch her again. "What will happen when you want to actually marry someone? Are you going to explain to your bride that your baby mama is living there, too?"

Luc laughed. "That's a pretty crass way to put it."

Kate shrugged, lacing her fingers together as she glanced out the window. "I'm not sugarcoating this situation and neither should you."

Luc didn't say anything else. He would sway her with his actions, not his words. She would come to see that living with him, ultimately marrying him, would be the best way to approach their predicament. And when they married, she would be sleeping in his bed again. He'd make sure of it.

Now he just needed to get his hormones under control, because he was physically aching for her. Being near her now that he'd had her was pure hell. The woman was made for him. Nobody had ever matched him in the bedroom—or shower—the way she did.

Yet Kate was so much more than a sex partner. He'd discovered an emptiness in him now that they were back to keeping things professional. No matter the circumstances surrounding the false engagement, Luc couldn't help but think back and realize those days spent on the island were some of the happiest of his life.

Kate had been to many royal events over the past year as an official employee of the Silva family. Before that, she'd seen enough to know that royalty never did anything halfway, especially when it came to weddings.

The ceremony uniting Darcy and Mikos Alexander had taken place earlier in the day, and now only the couple's closest family and guests, of which there appeared to be several hundred, remained for the reception.

No expense had been spared for the event taking place both in the ballroom and out in the courtyard at the palace on Galini Isle, off the coast of Greece. Every stationary item was draped with something crystal, shimmering or sheer.

As she watched the bride and groom dance, Kate couldn't help but smile. Mikos had lost his first wife suddenly, leaving him to care for their infant daughter alone. Needing a break, he'd gone to Los Angeles to get away and think. He'd hired Darcy to be his daughter's nanny, and before long the two had fallen in love…even though Mikos had slightly deceived Darcy, because she'd had no idea he was royalty. Of course, none of that had made it to the press, but Kate knew the whole story from Luc.

Luc and Mikos had been best friends forever. Kate was quite familiar with Mikos and his brother, Stefan, who was also in attendance, with his stunning wife, Victoria.

Even if the crystal chandeliers, flawless ice sculptures, millions of clear twinkling lights and yards upon yards of sheer draping hadn't screamed elegance and beauty, the gorgeous people milling about certainly would have.

This was definitely one of those times she was thankful her mother was the royal seamstress. By the time Luc had sprung the trip on her, Kate hadn't had time to go shopping. So her mom had taken an old gown and made enough modifications to transform it into something lovely and totally unique. What had once been a simple, fitted silver dress was now unrecognizable. The sleeves had been removed and the top had been cut into a sweetheart neckline to give the allure of sexiness with a slight show of cleavage. Her mother had then had the brilliant idea of taking strands of clear beads and sewing them so they would drape across Kate's arms, as if her straps had fallen and settled just above her biceps.

Kate actually felt beautiful in this dress, and judging from the way Luc had stared at her without saying a word when he'd come to get her for the wedding, she had to assume he thought she looked nice, as well.

She still couldn't get the image out of her mind of him waking her for the landing. He'd been so close, staring at her as if he wanted to touch her, kiss her. Their chemistry wasn't in question, that was obvious, but he clearly battled whether or not to act on it.

Maybe their time apart would have him coming around, to see that she truly wasn't aiming for the crown. She sure as hell wasn't Alana.

Nervously glancing around the room, Kate toyed with the amethyst pendant that hung just above her breasts. She hadn't worn the ring Luc had bought her; that would've just felt wrong. She'd actually placed it in his desk drawer days ago, though she had no clue if he'd found it.

Since Luc had started his best-man duties, she'd pretty much been on her own. That was fine, actually. The more she was around Luc, the harder she was finding it to face the reality that while she was having his baby, he'd never see her as more than a speech writer who happened to be giving him an heir.

Once the evening wound down, perhaps they could talk. She held out hope that he would remember the woman she was before his accident, not the liar she'd turned into for a few short days.

"Champagne, ma'am?"

The waiter, balancing a tray full of flutes of the bubbly drink, smiled at her. Kate shook her head.

"No, thank you."

As soon as he moved on another man approached her. He'd been only a few feet away and she'd seen him a few times during the evening. The tall stranger with tanned skin and black hair was hard to miss, especially when she'd caught him eyeing her more than once. He'd been smiling her way for a while, and now he was closing the gap between them.

"You turned down champagne and you're not dancing," he said in lieu of hello. "One would think you're not having a good time."

Kate smiled, trying to place his accent. Not Greek. Mikos had friends and acquaintances all over the world, so who knew where he was from?

"I'm having a great time," she told him. "It's so beautiful, I'm just taking in all the scenery."

"I've been taking in the scenery, too."

His eyes held hers, and the implication was not lost on her. At one time that line may have worked on her, but she felt absolutely no tingling or giddiness in her stomach when this man approached, blatantly hitting on her. Good thing, because she was certain she didn't have the strength to be tied up with more than one man.

"Would you care to dance?"

Kate glanced around. She hadn't seen Luc for a while, and more than likely he was schmoozing with people he rarely got to see. Besides, it wasn't as if he had a claim on her. He'd pretty much brought her here for one of two reasons: as a lame plan B or to keep an eye on her. Either way, he'd ignored her most of the evening, and she was entitled to some fun, too.

"I'd love to."

Kate slid her hand through the stranger's arm and held on to the crook of his elbow as he led her to the dance floor. When he found an opening, he spun her around until she was in his arms. Kate purposely kept her body from lining up against his as she placed her hand on his shoulder and curled her fingers around his outstretched hand.

"I'm Kate, by the way."

A smile kicked up at the corner of his mouth. "I'm Lars."

"Pleasure to meet you," she said as he turned her in a wide circle. "You're a great dancer."

"I'm actually a professional ballroom dancer." He laughed as he led her into a slower dance when the song changed. "Stick with me tonight and we'll be the envy of all the other couples."

Kate couldn't help but laugh at his blatant ego. "I should tell you, I'm taken."

Well, she wasn't exactly taken, but she was having another man's child, and she was in love with said man, even though he didn't return the feelings. So she felt it necessary to let Lars know he stood no chance with her.

He leaned in closer to whisper into her ear. "Yet he's not here and I am." When he leaned back, his smile remained in place. "Don't worry. I just wanted to dance with the most stunning woman in the room."

"I think that honor goes to the bride," Kate corrected.

Darcy had looked magnificent in a fitted ivory dress with an elegant lace overlay, complete with a lace train that would make any princess envious. Darcy had looked like a character from a fairy-tale romance, and her Prince Charming at the end of the aisle had had nothing but love on his face for his bride.

Would Kate ever find that? Would she ever find a man who looked at her as though there was nothing greater in the world than the fact she lived in it?

"Uh-oh. I'm going to start questioning my skills if you keep frowning."

Kate shook the thoughts away. "Your dance skills

are perfect, though I'm sure you already knew that. I think the jet lag is getting to me."

Not to mention the pregnancy…which she and Luc still hadn't discussed announcing. So for now, she was keeping it to herself. Granted, not many people knew who she was, but the same could not be said for Luc.

Lars opened his mouth to say something, but his eyes darted over Kate's shoulder as he came to a stop.

"It's time to go, Kate."

Turning, she saw Luc standing less than a foot away.

"I'm dancing right now," she commented, not letting go of her partner's hand. "I can find my way back. You go on."

Luc pasted on a deadly smile and glanced at Lars. "I'm sure he will understand. Won't you, Lars?"

The other man merely nodded and stepped back, but not before kissing Kate's hand. "It was truly my pleasure."

Then he disappeared in the crowd of dancers, most likely heading to find another partner. Kate jerked around, clenching her teeth.

"Watch what you say," Luc warned as he took her arm and led her away. "I've got plenty to tell you, too, so save it until we're alone."

"What makes you think I'm going anywhere with you?" she said through gritted teeth. "You can't tell me who to spend time with."

Luc's fingers tightened around her arm as he leaned in closer to her side. "Oh, we're going to be alone, and I'm going to explain to you exactly why that little scene will never happen again."

Fifteen

Luc was seething. He hated like hell that his emotions had overridden common sense, but the second he'd seen Kate dancing with Lars, all rational thoughts had vanished.

The palace was big enough to house the special guests of the bride and groom, so Luc was glad he didn't have to drag Kate too far before he lit into her.

He'd purposely avoided her as much as he could because of her body-hugging dress. That damn gown nearly had him babbling like some horny teen, but he'd somehow managed to keep his tongue in his mouth when he first saw her. Luc knew if he'd stayed too close to Kate this evening, there would be no way to hide his obvious attraction.

And he couldn't let the attraction show, because Kate might try to use that...for what? Wasn't he set on using her?

Only now that he'd seen her in the arms of another man, the game had just changed. Luc wanted her. Right now.

He reached the second floor and headed down the hall to his suite. He had no clue if Kate was deliberately toying with him, but she had him tied in knots he'd never be able to untangle thanks to that little stunt with Lars…a man Luc despised.

"I want to go to my room," she demanded, yanking from his hold as soon as he stopped in front of a set of double doors. "I'm not going in there with you."

Resting his hand on the knob, Luc threw a smirk over his shoulder. "You are."

Kate's eyes narrowed. "No, my room is down the hall."

Before he realized his intentions, he'd pulled her around, wedging her body between his and the door. "Your room is right here until I'm done with you."

"Well, I'm already done talking. You were completely rude down there. You can't just—"

His mouth covered hers. If she was done talking, then he'd find better use for that mouth and ignore all the damn red flags waving around in his mind. He didn't care about all the reasons this was wrong, didn't care that moments ago she'd been in another man's arms. Right now she was in *his* arms, and he was taking full advantage of that lush, curvy body.

Kate's hands came up to his shoulders to push at him, but Luc settled his palms on her hips and pressed against her. Suddenly, her fingertips were curling into his tuxedo jacket.

The feel of her rounded hips beneath her killer dress was just as potent as this steamy kiss. Kate tipped her head slightly, but the silent invitation was all he needed to trace a path with his tongue down the column of her throat.

"Luc," she panted in a whisper. "We're in the hallway."

Gripping her hips, Luc rested his forehead against her collarbone. "You make me crazy, Kate. Out of my mind crazy."

Reaching around her, he opened the door. As soon as they were inside, he closed it, flicked the lock and leaned back against it.

"Did you bring me to your suite to talk or to have sex?" she asked, her arms folded across her beautifully displayed chest. "Because I know what you said, but that episode in the hall has me confused."

Luc remained where he was as he raked a hand down his face. "Lars isn't a good idea." He ignored her narrowed gaze. "Seeing you in his arms… He's a player, Kate."

She held Luc's eyes for a moment before she burst out laughing. "You're kidding me. You interrupt my dance, you manhandle me out of the ballroom and up the steps, and then you attempt to make out with me in the hallway because you're jealous? And you're calling someone else a player?"

"First of all, I'm not jealous." Wow, that almost sounded convincing. "Second, I never manhandled you, and third, you were completely on board with what was going on in the hallway. You moaned."

Kate rolled her eyes and turned to stalk across the open suite. "I did not moan."

Luc didn't know which view was better, the front of Kate's gown with the glimpse of her breasts or the back, where he could fully focus on the perfection of her shape. She stood at the desk, her hands resting on it, her head dropped forward.

"I don't know what you want from me." Her voice was so low he had to move closer to hear. "I won't allow you to pull me all these directions because of your out-of-control emotions, Luc. You know how strongly I feel for you, and yet you continue to torture me."

He was counting on those feelings to get him what he wanted. As much as he hated to admit it, he needed Kate in every way.

Before Luc realized it, he'd completely closed the distance between them. Sliding his hands around her waist, he pressed his palms against her still-flat stomach and jerked her body against his.

"You think you don't torture me?" he asked, his lips brushing the side of her ear. She shivered against him. "You think seeing you dressed like this, moving your body against another man's, isn't pure hell?"

"Why do you care?"

"Because just the thought of you turns me inside out. Because knowing how sexy you are wearing only a smile that I put on your lips turns me on faster than anything."

Luc eased her around and framed her face with his hands. "Because I'm so torn up over what to do about you, all I can think of is getting you out of this damn dress and seeing if this chemistry is real or if it only existed when I thought we were engaged."

Kate's breath caught in her throat as she stared back at him. "I can't sleep with you as an experiment, Luc. I love you." Her voice cracked and her eyes filled with tears. "I'm not hiding how I feel. I can't. But I also can't be used on a whim, whenever you get an itch you need to scratch."

"You're more than an itch."

"What am I?" she whispered.

Luc couldn't put a label to this madness that had become his life. He'd planned on seduction, but he hadn't planned on the jealousy that had speared through him moments ago. Kate was his.

"You're the woman I'm about to put on this desk and strip until she's wearing nothing but that pendant. You're the woman who is going to forget everything else but what's happening right here, right now."

"Sex won't solve anything."

"No, but it will take the edge off for both of us."

Luc leaned closer, rubbing his lips across hers, so slowly. He reached around, found the zipper and eased it down. When the material parted in the back, he splayed his hand across her bare skin, relishing the way she trembled against him.

"Tell me you don't want this," he murmured against her mouth. "Tell me you don't want to see what happens right now between us, and you can walk out that door before we get too far to turn back."

Luc started to peel her dress away from her body. He stepped back just enough for the gown to ease down and puddle at her feet, leaving her standing in a strapless bra and matching panties, and that purple stone that rested against her flawless skin. Trailing his fingertips over the swell of her breasts, Luc smiled when she arched against his touch.

"Say the word, Kate, and I'll stop."

Her eyes closed as she dipped her head back. "You don't play fair."

"Oh, baby, I haven't even begun to play."

She was going to put a stop to this...then Luc had to go and say those words dripping in seduction while he tempted her with just the tips of his fingers. The man was potent. He knew exactly what to do to get her aroused, to get her wanting more.

Why was she letting this happen? He had no intention of professing his love. He wouldn't even give her a straight answer earlier when she'd asked who she was to him.

Yet here she stood, in her heels, her underwear and goose bumps from his touch.

How could she deny him? How could she deny herself? All she wanted was this man, and here he was. If she had even a glimmer of a chance to get him to see how good they were together, she'd take it. Her heart couldn't break any more...could it?

Luc's mouth followed the trail of his fingertips along the tops of her breasts, just over the lacy bra cups. "I'll take your silence as a go-ahead."

Kate slid her fingers into his inky-black hair as she looked down at him. "I can't say no to you."

"I didn't intend to let you."

He crushed her body to his as his mouth claimed hers. Kate shoved his tux jacket off and to the floor. Without breaking contact, she started unbuttoning his shirt. The need to feel his skin next to hers was all-consuming.

Luc wrapped his hands around her waist and lifted her onto the desk. He jerked his shirt off, sending the rest of the buttons popping and scattering across the hardwood floor. The sight of that bare chest, the familiar tattoo and a smattering of chest hair had her heart beating in double time and her body aching.

He stepped between her thighs, encircled her torso with his arms and jerked her to the edge.

"Wrap your legs around me."

His husky demand had her obeying in an instant.

What was it about this man that could have her throwing all common sense aside and practically bowing to his every wish?

Love. That's all it boiled down to. If she didn't love him, if she hadn't been in love with him for some time, she never would've allowed herself to be put in this vulnerable position.

Luc managed to work off her bra and panties with a quick, clever snap and torn material. The fact he was so eager sent warmth spreading through her. She'd made him this reckless, this out of control.

And that right there told her she had the upper hand.

Squeezing her legs tighter against his narrow hips, Kate gripped his head and pulled him down to her mouth. Instantly, he opened, groaning against her. His hands seemed to be everywhere at once. How else could she explain all the shivers, the rippling, the tingling?

"Lean back," he muttered against her lips.

Kate leaned back on the smooth desk, resting her weight on her elbows. When his eyes locked onto hers, the moment he joined them, Kate couldn't help the burn in her throat, the instant tears pricking her eyes. Even though their bond may have started off with a lie, it didn't diminish the fact she loved him. He cared for her more than he let on, too, or they wouldn't be here right now.

Kate shoved aside all worry, all thoughts, and reveled in the moment. Luc was here, with her. He was making love to her in a slow, passionate way that was polar opposite to the frantic way he'd stripped them both moments ago. Did she dare hope he wanted more from her?

Luc leaned over her, kissed her softly and rested his forehead against hers. With Luc's hands gripping her waist, she held on to his shoulders and kept her gaze on him.

Within moments, her body climbed, tightened. Luc muttered something she didn't quite understand. Between the Portuguese and the low whisper, his words were lost. But then his own body stiffened against hers as he squeezed his eyes shut.

Once the tremors ceased, Luc picked her up and carried her to his bed, draped in gold-and-white sheers. He laid her down and slid in beside her, pulling her body against his.

"Sleep." His hands immediately went to her stomach. "Rest for our baby."

Kate closed her eyes, wondering if this blossom of hope in her chest would still be there come morning. Wondering if the man she'd fallen in love with was actually starting to love her back.

Sixteen

Nausea hit her hard. Kate prayed that if she just lay
still the queasiness would pass. Until now, she'd had no
symptoms of pregnancy, save for the missed period and
being tired. Those things she could handle.

As for the man who had put her in this situation in
the first place, well, that was another story.

Kate tried to focus on the fact she'd spent the night
in Luc's bed, this time with him fully aware of who she
was and why she was there. Surely that meant something. Surely they'd crossed some major barrier and
things would only get better from here.

Kate wasn't naive, but she was hopeful. She had to be.

But the bed next to her was empty, cool. She sat up,
clutching the sheet to her chest. That abrupt movement
had her stomach roiling. Bad idea. She closed her eyes
and waited for the dizziness to pass before she risked
scanning the oversize bedroom for Luc.

He stood near the floor-to-ceiling window, sipping a cup of coffee. His bare back, with bronze skin and dark ink, stared back at her. She didn't want this to be awkward, but she had no idea what to say, how to act. She'd selfishly given in to her desires last night, not thinking of consequences. Well, she had thought of them, but she'd chosen to weigh heavily on the side of optimism.

Her legs shifted beneath the warm satin sheets. Luc glanced over his shoulder at the sound, then focused his attention back on the sunrise. She had to admit the orange sky glowing with radiant beauty was a sight to behold, but was he not going to say anything?

Please, please don't let this be awkward.

Kate eased back against the headboard and tucked the sheet beneath her arms to stay fully covered. Not that he hadn't seen all of her multiple times, but she was getting a vibe that this wasn't going to be a good morning, and the last thing she wanted to do was go into battle fully naked.

"I've been trying to figure out what the hell to do here."

His words sliced right through the beauty of the morning, killing any hope she'd built. His tone wasn't promising. If anything, it was angry, confused.

"I watched you sleep," he went on, still not looking at her. Damn it, why wouldn't he turn around? "I even tried to rest, but there are so many thoughts going around in my mind that I don't even know where to start or what's real."

"Everything that happened in this room last night was real." If nothing else, she wanted, needed, him to realize that. "Did you only bring me here for sex, Luc?"

Speaking her fear aloud had her heart cracking. She

wanted to be strong, she truly did, but there was only so much a woman could take.

"I wanted you." Luc turned to face her, but made no move to cross the room. "I've fought this urge since you came to work for me. I got engaged to another woman knowing full well I wanted you physically. Even after that engagement ended, I still had this ache for you, even though I knew I couldn't act on it."

Kate clutched the sheet as he went on.

"I wasn't in a good spot when we were at the beach house," he continued. "I was an emotional wreck, and I never should've had you come with me, not when I knew just how much I wanted you."

Her eyes darted back to his. "You were angry with me," she reminded him. "Before the accident, you kissed me—"

"I kissed you because I couldn't keep fighting the attraction. I kissed you out of anger toward myself, and then I was even angrier. I was rough with you, so I stomped off like a child."

And then he'd been injured and forgotten everything.

Kate licked her dry lips. "I don't know what to say."

"Honestly, I don't, either." Luc slowly walked toward the bed, coming to stand at the end of it and holding her gaze. "There's part of me that wants to be able to trust you again, but you hurt me, Kate. I never thought that was possible. And that's what had me up all night."

Kate cringed at his harsh words. What could she say? He was right.

"I thought we were going to move past that," she stated, praying the possibility even existed. "You said we'd move on, that we'd have a professional relationship."

Luc's arms stretched wide as he eyed the bed. "Is

this professional? I sure as hell don't feel like your boss right now, Kate. You're having my child, the next heir to the throne after me."

"And is that all I am, then? The mother to the next heir?" She needed more. Even after her lies, she deserved to know. "Are you using my feelings against me? You know how I feel, and you got so jealous last night. Was that all to stroke your ego or to puff your chest out because you're in control?"

Luc propped his hands on his narrow hips as he stared down at her. He'd put on his black tuxedo pants, but hadn't buttoned them. It was hard to sit here and discuss all of this with him half-dressed and her wearing a sheet, but Kate had her pride, and she refused to give in to her body's needs. She didn't need Luc; she wanted him. Yes, it hurt to know he didn't feel the same, but she wasn't going to beg…ever.

His silence was deafening. Kate shook her hair away from her face. The nausea hadn't lessened; if anything, she felt worse. She placed a hand beside her hip on the bed, closed her eyes and took a deep breath.

"Kate?"

The mattress dipped beside her. When Luc grabbed her hand, she pulled back. "No." She met his worried gaze. "I'm not playing the pregnancy card for your sympathy and attention. You don't get to pick and choose when it's convenient to show affection."

"You're pale. Are you all right?"

If only he would have cared first thing this morning instead of starting this day with voicing his doubts and crushing her hopes.

"I'm dizzy. It's to be expected." She shifted, scooting a bit farther away from him. "I'm not going to be pulled in different directions depending on your moods, either. You either want me, on a personal level and not just for sex, or you don't. If my dancing with some guy bothers you, then maybe you need to reevaluate your feelings. But don't come to me again unless you're sure I'm more than just a warm body to you."

Slowly, Luc came to his feet and nodded. "I plan on having you, Kate. I plan on marrying you, actually. You'll become my wife before my birthday. I'll secure the title and you'll get to live out whatever fantasy you had when you wanted to play the engaged couple."

"What?" Shock replaced her nausea instantly. "I'm not marrying you just so you can get a title. I want to marry for love."

Luc's eyes narrowed. "You say you love me, so why not marry me?"

"Because you don't love me. I won't be used as a pawn in your royal quest."

Air whooshed from her lungs. She'd never thought herself naive, but that's exactly what she was. She should've gone into this with eyes wide-open and seen his motivations for what they were…lust and greed. Any love between them was absolutely one-sided, and she had no one to blame but herself…yet again.

She should've seen this coming, should've known nothing would ever get in the way of the great Luc Silva and his crown. The man she'd grown to love from the island was just as fake as their engagement. Then, he'd been warm, open. Now he was all business.

"I'm going back to the palace as soon as I get my stuff together," she told him. "I'll have the pilot come back whenever you want to leave, but I won't be flying with you. I also won't be working for you. I'll finish out my duties for the next couple of weeks, but after that, I'm done."

"As my wife, I wouldn't expect you to work for me."

Kate clenched her teeth, praying she didn't burst into angry tears. "I won't be your wife."

Luc shoved his hands in his pockets, hesitated, then made his way to the door. "Don't make any hasty decisions. I'll leave you to get your dress back on."

Then he was gone, leaving only the deafening sound of the door clicking shut as she sat there in the rumpled sheets.

That was it? Luc may have walked out of this conversation, but he wasn't going to back down on this ridiculous notion of them getting married. Kate needed to prepare herself, because this fight was just getting started.

She tossed back the sheet and was thankful she wasn't dizzy when she got to her feet. At least she had one thing going for her this morning.

Of course, now she had to put on her dress from last night and do the walk of shame down the wide, long hallway to her own suite, to change and pack. Which was fine, because she wasn't staying any longer. If he planned on using her, using her feelings against her in some ploy to get ahead, then maybe he wasn't the man she loved at all. Maybe she'd been living a lie this entire time...

There was no way she could continue working for Luc indefinitely. No way she could look at him every single day and know she was good enough for sex, but not good enough to build a life with if the throne wasn't at stake. They'd made a baby and he still was only looking out for his title. Well, she sure as hell wasn't sticking around to see him parade his possible future wives in and out of his life.

Kate had been a fool to think their intimacy had

changed Luc's mind. The struggle of seeing him every day, knowing he didn't return her love, would be just too hurtful.

When she returned to the palace, she would call her parents and make plans. She would finish up the projects she and Luc had begun, and then she needed to get away. She needed to focus on what was truly important in her life.

Luc brought the sledgehammer up and swung it through the partial non-load-bearing wall. Busting this drywall to expand the living space with the kitchen wasn't even remotely helping to quell his frustration and anger. All he was doing was working up a good sweat and a bit of nostalgia from when he and Kate had torn into the bathroom.

When Luc had gotten back to the palace, he'd taken his boat—sans guards, much to Kate's father's disapproval—and headed to his beach house. Luc knew the workers would be done for the day, and since the house was only an hour from the palace, he needed time to think, to reflect on what an insufferable jerk he'd been in that bedroom three days ago.

His intention had been to get Kate to agree to marry him. He hadn't cared about her feelings. But the way she'd sat there, all rumpled in a mess of satin sheets, as she'd stared up at him with hurt in her eyes, had seriously gotten to him. He hadn't expected to feel anything beyond want and need for her. Yet it was hard to ignore the constant lump of guilt that kept creeping up when he thought of how he'd broken her so fast, with so few words.

Luc eased the sledgehammer down on the rubble and wiped his arm across his forehead. His mother would probably die if she saw he had blisters on his hands from manual labor, but he needed the outlet. Unfortunately, it wasn't doing the job.

And it didn't help that Kate was everywhere in this house. The empty yellow vase on the scarred dining table mocked him. He couldn't even look at the damn shower in his master suite. The balcony, the chaise in the living room, the bed, the beach… The memories flooded his mind. She'd touched literally every surface here.

Just as she'd touched every part of him.

Luc reached behind his neck and yanked his T-shirt over his head. His cell vibrated in his pocket and he thought about ignoring it, but with Kate being pregnant, he had to be on full alert.

Pulling the cell out, he glanced at the screen. Swallowing a curse, he let out a sigh and answered.

"Yes?"

"You rushed out of here and didn't take a guard?"

His mother's question didn't require an answer, because she already knew. "I needed to be alone."

"That's not smart. You can't be taking off like this, Lucas. You know your birthday is less than two months away. You need to be home so we can figure out what we're going to do."

Luc raked a hand over his damp face and stared out at the sun, which was starting to dip toward the horizon.

"I just needed a few days to myself."

"Is this about Kate? Darling, I know she hurt you, but that poor girl is miserable. I didn't want to say anything, but since the wedding she's been looking pale and drained."

Luc straightened. "Is she sick?"

"I'd guess she's pregnant."

Silence filled the line and Luc's heart sank. They hadn't said a word to anybody, and the pain in his mother's tone came through loud and clear.

"We haven't told anyone," Luc stated in a low voice, suddenly feeling like a kid again for lying to his mother. "She just found out before the wedding, and we had a bit of a fight. Is she okay?"

"A fight?" Of course his mom honed in on that and not his question. "Lucas, the woman is carrying your child and you argue with her? No wonder she looks exhausted. She's been working like a dog since she got back. That's why I wanted to know why you left the palace so suddenly."

Luc gripped the phone. "It's best if I'm not there right now."

"I think you two need to talk. If you're worried about the no-fraternizing rule, I think we can make an exception for Kate. Maybe she's the answer to—"

"I've already thought of that," he interrupted, cutting her off. "Kate doesn't want to marry me."

"Why don't you come home," his mother stated. "We can't solve any problems with you brooding alone."

He glanced at the mess he'd made. It wasn't as if he knew what to do next, but the contractors had done an amazing job of renovating the bathroom he and Kate had torn into. They'd come to finish the kitchen once Luc gave the go-ahead after this wall was gone.

"I'm leaving now," he told his mother. "Tell Kate I want to see her."

"I'll see what I can do, but she may have left for the day."

If she'd left, he'd go to her place. She didn't live too far from the palace, and if he had any say, she'd be inside that palace by the time their baby came.

Anything else was unacceptable.

Having her that last time had changed something in him, and nearly changed his marriage plan. That's why he'd been up all night, second-guessing his motives. He'd thought he could check out emotionally, but he felt too much—guilt, desire…more.

He'd hurt her in ways he'd never, ever imagined he could. Yet she still did her job. She'd still come with him to the wedding. She still supported him.

And he loved her. His feelings were as simple and as complicated as that. He loved Kate with everything he had and he'd messed up—man, had he messed up.

Luc needed to tell her how he felt. More important, he needed to show her. Saying the words was easy; proving to Kate how much she meant to him would be the hurdle. But he hadn't gone through all of this to give up now. Kate was his and he damn well wasn't going to let her go.

Seventeen

It had been nearly a week since he'd last talked to Kate, and he was going out of his mind.

He'd come back to his office and found a letter of resignation on his desk. She'd left a message through her mother that she was fine and the baby was fine, but she wanted to be on her own for a bit.

A bit was longer than he could stand.

He'd lived without this woman for too long and refused to live that way another second.

His birthday was fast approaching, but even the looming date hadn't entered his mind. For the past few days all that had played over and over was how stupid he'd been, how heartless and crass he'd been with his words, his actions. No wonder Kate wanted to leave, to steer clear of him. She loved him and he'd proposed to her with the pretense that he was doing so only to climb higher on the royal ladder.

He hadn't needed much time after their last night together to realize walking away had been a mistake. Letting her believe he wanted her only for the crown was wrong.

Luc wanted Kate because she made him whole.

It had taken him some time to get the information on her whereabouts from her parents, and to have the construction crew finish some of the renovations on his beach home. He'd pulled some strings to get her here, but he wanted this to be perfect when he finally revealed the house and his true feelings. Nothing but the best for Kate from here on out.

He'd taken that extra time to find out more about the woman he loved. And he hoped the surprise he'd planned would help her understand just how much he wanted her in his life.

Luc stood in the living room watching the water, waiting for that familiar boat to dock. He'd recruited the help of Kate's parents. Of course, in order to do that, he'd had to pull out all the stops and really grovel to them. If everything worked out the way he'd hoped, every ego-bursting, pride-crushing moment would be worth it.

When the boat finally came into view, Luc's nerves really kicked into gear. He might have planned every bit of this evening, but Kate ultimately held all the power and control.

Her father helped her up onto the dock, leaned forward for a hug and watched as Kate mounted the steps. Luc moved to the doorway and waved as the man began to pull the boat away from the berth.

By the time Kate got to the top of the steps, Luc's heart was beating faster than ever. She lifted her head, pushing her windblown hair away from her face. The second her eyes locked onto his, Luc felt that familiar punch to his gut. The punch that said if she turned him down he would be absolutely crushed and broken.

"I was hoping you wouldn't put up a fight," he told her, remaining in the doorway.

"I was tempted to jump overboard a couple of times, but I knew my dad would only go in after me." She clasped her hands together and remained still. "What am I doing here, Luc, and why am I being held hostage?"

"You're not a hostage," he countered.

She glanced over her shoulder before looking back. "My father left with the boat and the only other one here is yours. By my accounts, I'm here with no way out except with your permission."

"Come inside."

Her brow quirked as she crossed her arms over her chest…a chest that was more voluptuous than when he'd seen her last.

"Please," he added, when she didn't move. "Please come inside so we can talk."

Finally, she moved forward, and Luc let her pass him and enter first. The familiar, floral scent teased his senses and mocked him. He'd lain awake at night imagining that scent, pretending she was by his side.

"Oh, Luc."

Her gasp was enough to have him smiling. "Looks a little different, doesn't it?"

He watched her survey the newly designed, open floor plan. Thick columns stood as support beams, but they didn't take away from the romantic ambience, they merely added to it. He'd left the back wall of patio doors open, to put the Mediterranean on full display.

"It's gorgeous," she exclaimed, running her hand along the marble-topped table behind the sofa. "This was all done so fast."

"I wanted it done before I invited you back." He remained in the doorway, but kept his eyes on her as she walked through the living area and kitchen. "I even helped the contractors and learned how to do more than tear things down."

She stopped by the old dining table and her eyes landed on the yellow vase, then darted across the room to him.

"I couldn't get rid of either of those," he told her. "We shared too many meals at that table, and even though it's not new, it reminds me of you. Every time I see that vase I think of how excited you were that day at the market."

She picked up the vase, running her hands around it. For a moment Luc worried she might launch it at his head, but she finally set it down and turned back to face him. With her arms crossed over her midsection, she let out a sigh.

"What do you want, Luc?"

Her eyes held his. Now that they were face-to-face, he couldn't deny the force that hovered between them.

"Are you feeling okay?" he asked, taking slow, cautious steps toward her. "Everything all right with our baby?"

"We're both doing great," she informed him. "And you could've texted or called or replied to the emails I sent."

"You sent final work emails through your father."

She nodded. "That's because I quit, remember? I've outlined your next year of engagements. I'm assuming you came up with a way to secure your title? Is that why you can bother with me now?"

"No. I didn't secure the title."

Kate gasped. "Your birthday is only weeks away."

"I'm aware of that." He stood directly in front of her, so close she had to tip her head up to look him in the eyes. "That's why you're here."

Her lips thinned as she narrowed her gaze at him. "You've got to be kidding me. You brought me here to use me? You still think I'm going to swoon, fall at your feet and marry you so you can get a shiny new crown?"

Just as she started to push past him, Luc grabbed her arm and halted her escape. "No. I think you're going to listen to me and look in my eyes when I tell you how much I love you."

Those dark eyes held his, but he saw no emotion there. "Did you hear me?"

"I hear you just fine," she said through clenched teeth. "How convenient that you love me right before you're set to lose it all if you don't have a wife."

He turned to face her fully as he gripped both her bare shoulders. "You and these damn sexy strapless dresses," he muttered, stroking her skin with his thumbs. "Cause me to forget the powerful speech I was about to make. I'm pretty proud, considering it's the first one I've had to write for myself."

"I don't want to hear your speech and I don't want you touching me."

Luc smiled. "Then why is the pulse at the base of your neck pounding as fast as my heart? You may lie to yourself, Kate, but your body is telling me the truth."

Her eyes widened. "Oh, no. You brought me here for sex? You think I'll fall back into bed with you and then, in the throes of passion, agree to a marriage?"

Luc laughed, then kissed her full on the mouth before easing back. "Your imagination is running away with you and I'm royally screwing this up."

"That's the only thing that's getting screwed tonight."

His heart was so full, he couldn't help but keep smiling. "I've missed that smart mouth."

Kate didn't say a word, didn't move and didn't make any attempt to touch him.

"Tell me I didn't mess things up so badly that I've lost you forever."

"You never fully had me," she told him. "I wanted everything with you, but went about it the wrong way. Then you decided to use my love and try to force me into marriage. That's no foundation to build a relationship on."

"We both messed up," he agreed. "I never meant to hurt you, but I was so confused. I wanted to trust my feelings, but how could I when I couldn't even trust you? I thought if you wanted me so badly, you'd marry me and I'd get the title. I didn't realize you truly had no ulterior motive."

"I understand why you couldn't trust me." She reached up, wrapped her hands around his wrists and pulled his hands off her shoulders. "What I can't understand is why you used my feelings against me, why you made love to me at Mikos's wedding and then acted like you had no clue where to slot me in your life."

Luc shoved his hands in his pockets. She didn't want to be touched, and right now he was dying to have her in his arms. This was going to be trickier than he'd thought, but he wasn't giving up. She'd come, she was talking to him and that had to mean a lot.

"I have something to show you."

He walked to the desk tucked in the corner of the room and grabbed the email he'd printed out. When he handed it to her, she didn't take it.

"Please?"

Kate slid the paper from his grasp. Luc watched her face as she read. When her eyes filled with tears, her hand came up to cover her quivering chin and her lips, Luc knew she wasn't completely lost to him.

She clutched the letter to her chest. "You went to the orphanage?"

"I did." And he'd loved every minute of it. "I met Carly and Thomas. I was told they were friends of yours."

Kate nodded, the jerky movement causing a tear to spill. "I love those two so much. They are such sweet kids, but most people want to adopt new babies. The twins are nine, but they have such big hearts and they say they want the babies to go to new homes. Still, I know they long for a set of parents to love them."

"I was told it's hard, too, because most people are only looking to adopt one," he added.

"I try to get there to visit them as often as I can," she said, swiping at her eyes. "I call them if I get too busy working and can't make it."

"They're at the orphanage you were living in as a baby." Luc cupped her damp face. "And that's why they are so important to you. I can completely see why you wanted me to go visit. Those little kids thought talking to a real prince was so neat. I didn't talk much about the royalty side of my life with Carly and Thomas, but we did discuss Portuguese culture, and they were so fascinated."

"I can't believe you went and didn't tell me," she exclaimed.

"Actually, we just missed each other. When I arrived, I was told you had left the day before."

Kate's eyes widened. "I wish I'd known."

"Why, Kate? Would you have stayed there? Would you have waited for me?"

She shook her head. "I—I don't know."

"I want to start over with you." That sounded so

lame he laughed. "I've been miserable without you and I went to that orphanage not because you kept asking me to, but because I wanted to know more about you. I wanted to know more about the woman I had fallen in love with. I love you, Kate. I want a life with you, a life just like the one we had when we were all alone here."

Kate closed her eyes as her body fell into his. Her forehead rested against his chest. "You don't mean all of that," she whispered. "Because if you even think I can just try this out, or be with you because of some tradition, you're wrong."

When she lifted her head, Luc smoothed her hair away from her damp cheeks. "I don't want to try it, Kate. I want to do it. My calling you here has nothing to do with the throne, my birthday or the baby. I mean, I want to build a family with you, but I'm not using the baby to do so. I want you for you. The days we spent here were some of the best of my life. I want more days like that, and nobody else will do. You're it for me, Kate."

When her mouth parted in another gasp, he kissed her. Luc nipped at her lips and nearly cried when she responded and opened for him.

The gentle, tender kiss had that sliver of hope in his chest practically exploding now.

"I missed you," he murmured against her lips. "I missed holding you, I missed watching you cook, I missed seeing you smile, and even arguing with you over stupid things like my schedule. I missed seeing you wearing my ring."

Her brows drew in as Luc pulled the amethyst ring from his pocket.

"Você vai casar comigo?" he asked.

Will you marry me?

"Not because of the throne, not because of anything else but us," he quickly said, before she got the wrong idea of his intentions. "I can feel utter fullness and love only with you, Kate. You're the only one who can make me complete."

Without waiting for her reply, he slid the ring onto her finger and gripped her hand in his. "This is where the ring belongs, until I can get you a diamond or whatever you want."

Kate stared down at her hand and said nothing. She studied the ring, even toyed with it before she smiled up at him. "I don't want another ring. I want this one. It's exactly what I would have chosen, and I don't need anything more."

"Does this mean you'll marry me?" he asked.

Kate threw her arms around his neck, buried her face against his skin and squeezed him tight. "I'll marry you, Luc. I'll raise babies with you and grow old with you."

Luc crushed her body to his and let out the first good breath he'd had since she stepped into his house. No, their house.

Kate jerked back. "Wait. We need to marry soon. Your birthday—"

"It will be fine. My father may have rigged the law a tad to buy us a few extra weeks. I want to give you the wedding you deserve."

"I don't want a huge, highly publicized wedding. Is that okay?"

Luc framed her face, sliding his thumb across her full bottom lip. "Perfectly fine with me. But right now I'd rather have you in my shower, where I can properly show you how much I've missed you."

"I do love that shower of yours."

He kissed her smile. "After I make love to you, we

can discuss the wedding. Oh, and the fact I'd like to adopt Carly and Thomas. I wanted to talk to you first. With the new baby and all I wasn't sure—"

Kate's mouth cut him off as she rained kisses all over his lips, his chin, his cheeks. "Yes, yes, yes. I'd love to have them with me. I love those two so much. I just felt such a connection the first time I saw them."

"I did, too, honey." Luc picked her up and headed toward the master suite. "We'll discuss that later, too."

"You can't carry me," she cried. "I've gained weight."

His eyes dipped to her chest. "I've noticed, and I'm certainly not complaining."

She slapped his shoulder. "That's so typical of a man, to say that when bigger boobs are involved."

"There better never be another man eyeing your boobs," he scolded. "That's my job."

Kate's head fell against his shoulder as she laced her fingers together behind his neck. "Always, Luc. You're the only man for me."

* * * * *

LET'S TALK
Romance

For exclusive extracts, competitions
and special offers, find us online:

 facebook.com/millsandboon

@MillsandBoon

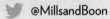 @MillsandBoonUK

Get in touch on 01413 063232

For all the latest titles coming soon, visit
millsandboon.co.uk/nextmonth